Praise for
Axe of Iron Series

"The student of history and the reader who loves historical romances and accounts of explorations of new lands will love this book."

Lucille Robinson, Alternative-Read Reviews

"Author J. A. Hunsinger is an expert in the mores and customs of the Northmen, the Vikings, and the Norse in general. His research is beyond reproach and he provides an educational, yet attention-getting plot. The characters are believable, filled with faults and foibles, most realistic. The descriptions of ancient North American shores are vivid, and in depth. Readers can picture the landscape, the animals, and the settlement of the settlers."

Shirley Roe, Allbooks Review

"Hunsinger creates a scintillating, adventurous tale that happened over one thousand years ago when the Vikings (or Norsemen) settled Greenland and then settled parts of Canada and the upper Midwest of the United States."

Michelle Davis, Armchair Interviews

"This great historical chronicles the Norse culture of 1008 AD. Six ships of Norse families, including their livestock, horses, and dogs, sail to the American continent. The details of how they lived and supported themselves are both practical and believable. The author's writing reminds me of the great Mika Waltari, who produced so many detailed historical novels and clearly defined the genre. I found this to be a fascinating read and rated it five hearts."

Bob Spear, Heartland Reviews

"It's the details that grab the reader's attention in J. A. Hunsinger's historical novel, *Axe of Iron: The Settlers.* The book is the first installment in a planned series of stories about the migration of Norsemen Greenlanders to North America. From the introduction, which provides background information, to the brutal ending, Hunsinger uses his extensive knowledge of the history and culture of Norsemen to craft a story that exposes the lives of an ancient people with an admirable sense of adventure and value for community.

Axe of Iron: The Settlers is a hearty, adventure-packed history lesson. I highly recommend it."

Melissa Levine, IP Book Reviewers

"Though raised in a violent and combative culture, Halfdan and his lieutenant Gudbjartur realize that if this new society is going to thrive, they must be as friendly as possible to the native people. In addition to worrying about these indigenous Skraelings, the settlers must contend with an unfamiliar land, wildlife attacks, their own brutal temperaments and the typical jealousies that arise in any community."

Kirkus Discoveries Review

"For fans of historical fiction, this book is a wonderful read on early Viking life in North America. It is exciting, lively and descriptive at every turn. Hunsinger's research is extremely thorough on this topic. He does not miss any detail in the description of Viking religious customs (Pagan and early Christian rites), Viking traditions like the "einvigi" (a duel to the death), hunting, burial practices, daily camp duties, the use of thralls (slaves who provided unskilled labor in the Viking communities), and women and their place in Viking society."

Sandra Alvarez, Medievalists Review

"Author Hunsinger weaves his story line into a magnificently researched and crafted literary work that takes us into the lives of these Medieval Norse, whose culture has brought them to the leading edge of Iron Age Technology. His writing paints the details of their skills as sailors and watermen, farmers and trades people. It is obvious that the volume of detailed onsite research Mr. Hunsinger has invested in this project far outweighs that of this volume and of those to follow."

J. R. Hauptman, Author—The Target

"We become well-acquainted with the main characters and minor characters swell the scenes including credible and fierce villains. I confess to re-reading pages to recall the characters, but then became more involved in their lives, interactions and thoughts. I wanted to know how their stories would play out. And play out they did in a carefully-crafted, somewhat involved but always engrossing plot. I recall the English master E. M. Forster's definition of the novel: "Yes—oh dear yes—the novel tells a story." And *Axe of Iron* tells a story, an enthralling, believable story."

Donald Hansen, Viking Trader Review

"As historical fiction, the author successfully captures a glimpse of the life of the Norsemen. It becomes quite clear that a great deal of research went into creating the story. The attention to detail is quite remarkable. That is, the author's descriptions of Norse ships, Norse customs, dress, the day to day struggles to survive that include hunting techniques, food preparation, weapons, and tools. As well, Hunsinger provides a detailed historical perspective of the time period, a glossary, and a map to assist readers in following the journey. The author clearly shows his knowledge and expertise on the subject."

Tracy Roberts, Write Field Services

"This novel is extremely well researched and provides great historical detail about the daily life of the Vikings, their sources of food and methods of cooking, tool making, hunting, and sailing. I enjoyed the story and the character development; the author did a good job of portraying the social tapestry of this hearty group of people. Packed with fascinating information about this little known time period, readers of historical fiction, nautical fiction and adventure novels would all enjoy this book."

Tome Travelers Web Log

"*Axe of Iron: The Settlers* is an accurate glimpse into the lives of the Northmen. You get to see how brutal and savage and how ordinary and gentle the Northmen were. It is about a time period that one does not normally read about. Overall, I found this book to be a fantastic read. I look forward to the other books in this continuing saga. I can't wait to see what happens to this group of first settlers in North America. I give it 4.5 Stars."

Shawn Oehlberg, Reading Mama Blog

Confrontation

An Axe Iron Novel

by

J. A. Hunsinger

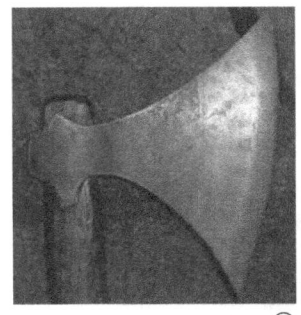

®

DISCLAIMER

This is a work of fiction. The characters, incidents, and dialogue, while possibly having parallels in history, are products of the author's imagination and are not to be construed as real. Any resemblance to actual persons, except those who are mentioned in an historical context, living or dead, is entirely coincidental.

Published by
Vinland Publishing
661 Tamarron Drive
Grand Junction, CO 81506

Printed in the United States of America

Dedication

As always, this novel is for them, the four thousand Greenland Norse people who disappeared from the Greenland settlements and history so long ago. I also wish to dedicate a place on the stage for the pre-historical ancestors of the Cree (Naskapi), Ojibwa (Anishinabeg), and Iroquois (Haudenosaunee) Indians who play a pivotal role in this novel.

Special thanks go to my brother, Tom Hunsinger, CO, for his encyclopedic knowledge of the Indians of North America and his tireless research in spite of the dearth of information extant on their pre-historical ancestors. His efforts begin to play a part here and will finally manifest themselves as this story continues.

My editor, Cheryl C. Malandrinos, of MA, USA, held me to a very high standard. I appreciate her expertise and professionalism. My appreciation and gratitude also go to cover artist Debi DeSantis of Wild Orchid Book Cover Design, for the 2nd Edition cover jacket scene.

And most especially, thanks go to my wife, Phyllis, for put- ting up with me: she is my mentor, my best friend, and the person who motivates me to continue my tale.

J. A. Hunsinger
2009

Foreword

Previously in *The Settlers*, the **Historical Perspective** furnished the reader with a sense of time and place. This historical content is essential for an understanding of the premise behind the *Axe of Iron* series of character-driven, historical fiction novels.

Those readers who had trouble with the names of characters/ places in the first book will have even more difficulty with those issues in this book. I suggest you do what I do when confronted with an unpronounceable name: pronounce it phonetically as best you can. Nobody will fault you for this approach, as nobody today knows how these names sounded. In all cases the names have been researched and they are authentic as far as is known. *Confrontation* contains many prehistorical native names, male and female. Nobody knows how the words of the various languages were spelled because the spelling of these words that we use today were interpreted by somebody over the past centuries from their sound—the native speakers had no written language. In most cases, I use a diminutive form of a particular name or term in the interest of brevity because their common names usually were a phrase, e.g., 'Woman of Bright Water'. They are representative of names given to the people of a particular tribe. The Norse names are somewhat simpler by comparison. The linguist will find pronunciation keys for the various Norse letters, e.g., 'Hákon or Haakon,' the 'á' or 'aa' is pronounced 'ow,' thus literally 'Howkon'.

In *The Settlers*, the first book of the *Axe of Iron* series, the story begins with a six-ship expedition under the leadership of Halfdan Ingolfsson and his lieutenant, Gudbjartur Einarsson. These two leaders set out from Greenland as soon as the harbor ice breaks up in the early spring of 1008, and with 315 men, women, and children, they set sail for the unexplored continent to the west, to the land that history would later refer to as Vinland.

I, too, make many references to Vinland for want of a better name; however, we do not know what the Greenland Norse themselves called North America.

The expedition makes its way into present-day Hudson Bay—the Canadian province of Quebec—and then south along the east coast to a river fjord on the southeastern shore of James Bay, where they find everything that they are seeking. Soon the longhouses and palisades of a permanent settlement mark their new home.

Standing in their way are uncounted numbers of indigenous peoples, the pre-historical ancestors of the contemporary Cree (Naskapi), Ojibwa (Anishinabeg), and Iroquois (Haudenosaunee) Indians. From the outset, the warriors of these various tribes violently resisted the incursion of the tall, pale-skinned invaders.

The overwhelming number of the native peoples in Vinland holds the fate of the Northmen in their hands. The success or failure of the settlement at Halfdansfjord hangs in the balance.

In this book, *Confrontation,* two calamitous events occur that pave the way for the hostile beginnings of an assimilation process to occur between these disparate peoples. The first mixing of cultures occurs when Thora and Deskaheh the Haudeno marry. This union, accepted enthusiastically by the Northmen, opens a window into the native mind. For all the people of this land the way is rocky and fraught with danger at every turn, but the acceptance and friendship that develops between the Northmen and the Naskapi over an affair of honor, the eventual acceptance of a young boy of the Northmen by his Haudenosaunee captors, and a scenario that seems ordained by the will of the gods, makes it all begin to fall into place, as it must for the Northmen to survive. Will this developing relationship allow the Northmen to remain in the homeland of the Naskapi, or are they doomed to failure? The settlers must deal with that question on a daily basis.

A glossary of Norse and Native terminology is included to define the many words and terms unfamiliar to the reader.

Confrontation begins where *Settlers* ended, Halfdansfjord, Vinland. It is late summer in the year of 1008. A moose hunt is unfolding.

I hope that you find this story as pleasurable in the reading as it was in the writing.

JAH

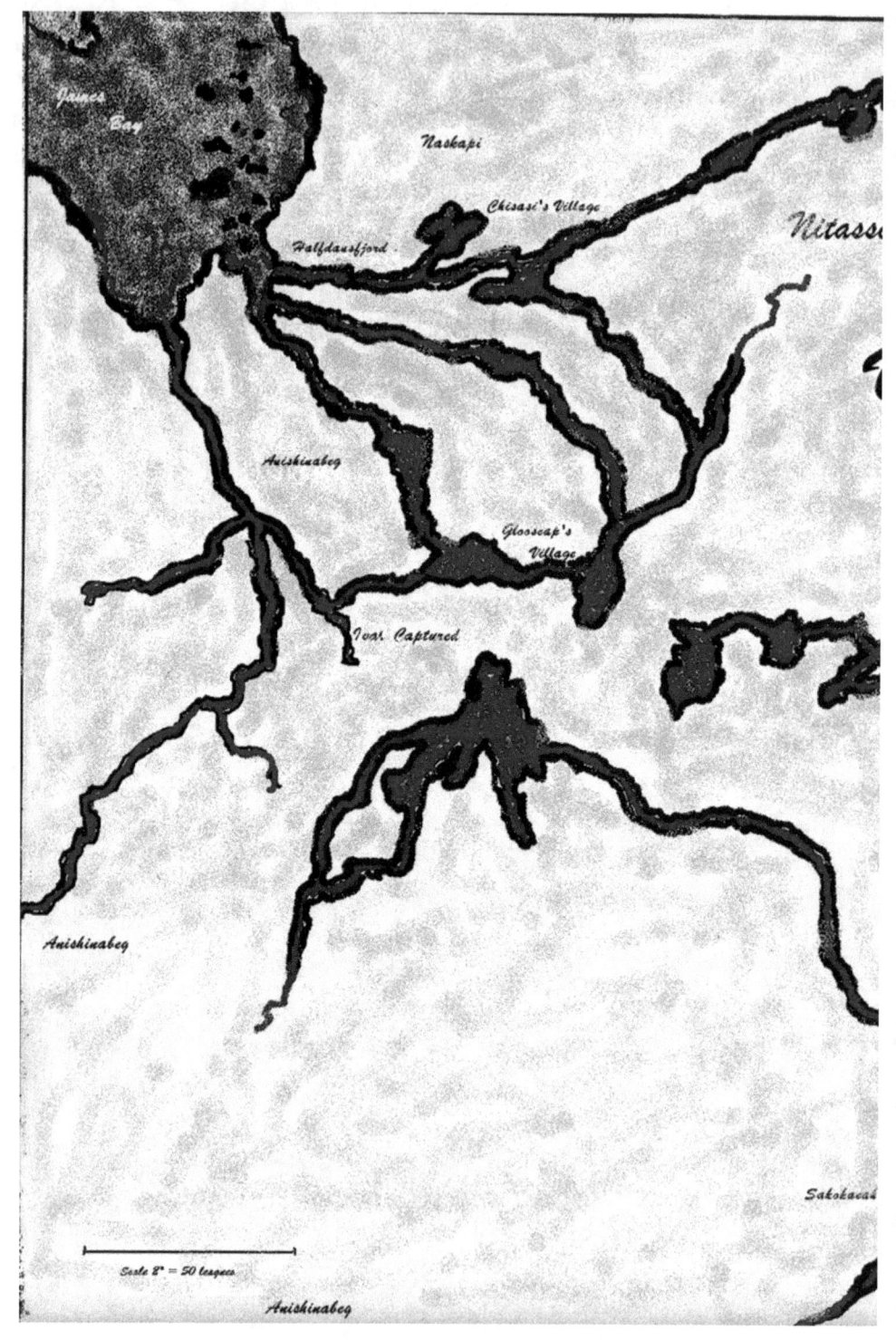

James
Bay

Naskapi

Chisasi's Village

Halfdausfjord

Nitasse

Anishinabeg

Glooscap's
Village

Ivar Captured

Anishinabeg

Sakokavah

Scale 8" = 50 leagues

Anishinabeg

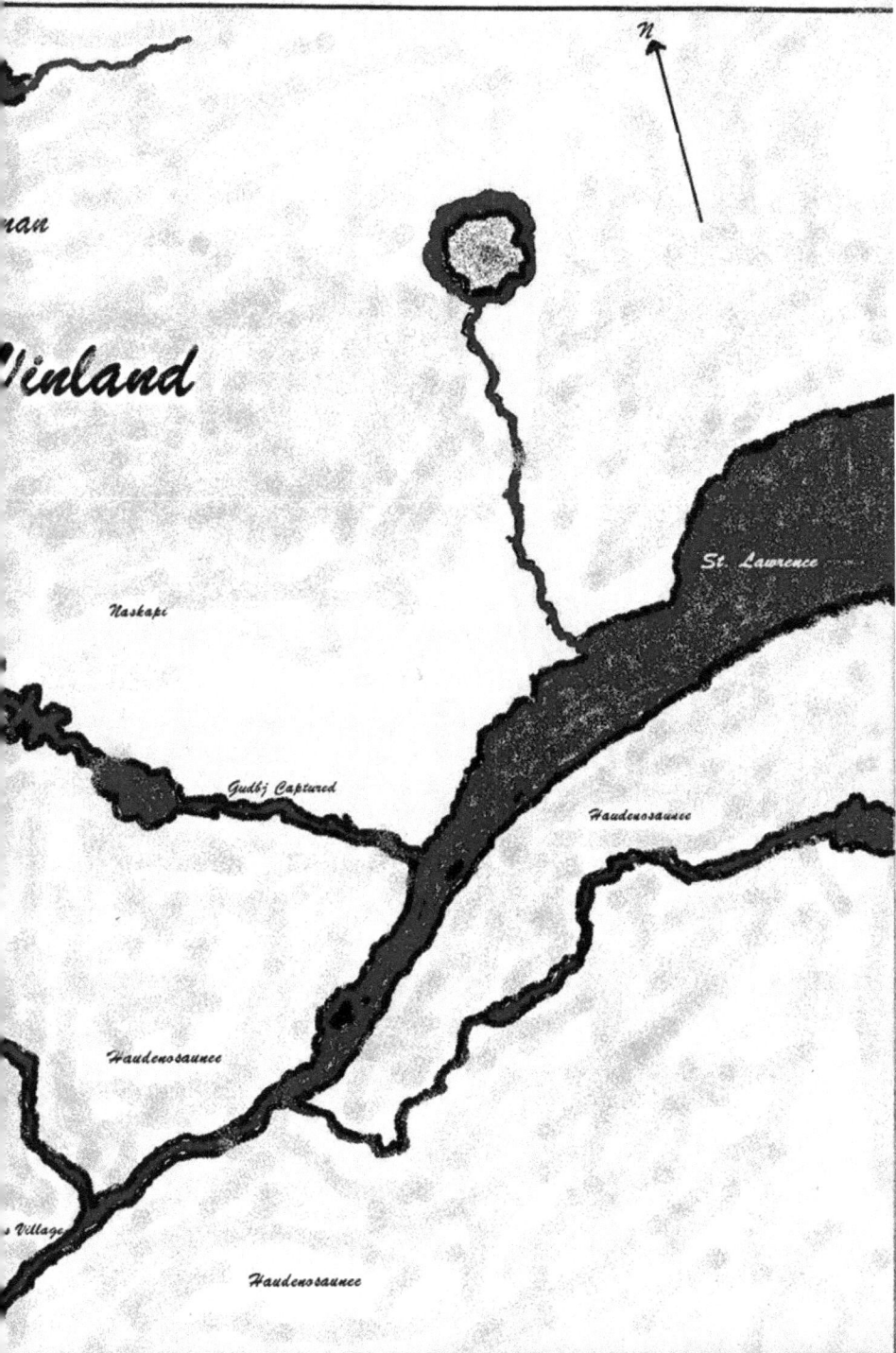

N

man

Vinland

Naskapi

St. Lawrence

Gudbj Captured

Haudenosaunee

Haudenosaunee

s Village

Haudenosaunee

Contents

Chapter One

Halfdansfjord, Vinland
Late summer, AD 1008

Out of long habit, the Northman, Gudbjartur Einarsson, carefully examined his surroundings every morning. He climbed a ladder to the palisade parapet and circled the settlement looking out over the bay, the fen, and surrounding countryside. Alert for the slightest danger or anything that did not belong in his world, the daily ritual, and a wave from the two tower guards assured him that all was well. He turned back toward his longhouse, his immediate thoughts being the coming adventure for his sons, Ivar and Lothar, and their small friend Yola.

He entered the house to find his sons almost finished with their morning meal. "When you are done, go and get Yola. Yesterday, I spoke to his mother about the hunt. He will be ready to go," Gudbjartur said.

Watching his sons run excitedly from the house, Gudbjartur shook his head at such exuberance on a full stomach. He rubbed his stomach at the thought of food, and smiled a greeting to his wife as she moved the kettle from the hearth tripod to the stone warming ledge.

She ladled the steaming fish chowder into a bowl and handed it to him. "They are really looking forward to this, Gudbj," Ingerd said.

Gudbjartur sat down in his high seat and began to eat. "It is time. This is their rite of passage to manhood." He noisily slurped the thick liquid from the bowl, leaving a few chunks of cod in the bottom, which he ate with gusto. Suddenly he stopped chewing, pulled a long rib bone from his mouth, and examined it ruefully. "I could have choked on this, Ingerd."

She chuckled at him. "That is why we should *chew* our food instead of bolting it down in chunks. Honestly, you are as bad as the boys."

Grinning at her, he got to his feet and placed his empty bowl and spoon with the other dirty utensils. "Thank you. The chowder was delicious."

"It should be. We made it with butter and milk. You ate so fast I am surprised you could taste it."

"I tasted it, all right. I am in a hurry. The boys are eager to get going." He watched her for a moment. "They will be men soon, Ingerd, whether we want them to or not," he said gently, mindful of her feelings on the subject.

She leaned against the wide shoulders of this man she loved so much, warm and content as he put an arm around her. She gazed up into his pale blue eyes. "I know. I know. But they seem so young."

"They are young. Soon they will be men. You were only two years older than Ivar is now when you birthed him."

"And well I know it. The birthing was very hard for me and that is why we have had no more children. Something came loose in me."

"I know, Ingerd. I think that is why the gods sent us Lothar. He is our son, too, as if you birthed him."

The boys rushed in with Yola in tow, effectively shattering the moment, much to Gudbjartur's relief.

He gave Ingerd a final squeeze, released her, and gave his attention to the three boys. "I have told you what you can take with you, and I see you have your packs and weapons in order. The only food we will have is dried meat. We will use it if the hunt is unsuccessful." His glance played over the three boys. A slight smile pulled at the corners of his mouth. Their barely checked exuberance, as they listened intently to him, caused a flush of pleasure through his chest. "Say goodbye to your mother, and we will be off."

The best the boys could manage was a perfunctory peck on her cheek before they ran from the longhouse. Gudbjartur hugged and kissed Ingerd, examined her appreciatively at arm's length, and then hugged and kissed her again. Then he picked up his gear and walked from the longhouse to begin the much-anticipated hunting expedition.

Ingerd watched him go. A heat rose in her. She smiled and hugged herself with pleasure. She began to clean up the mess from the morning meal, whistling softly as she worked.

* * *

As Gudbjartur walked into the settlement commons, he saw his chieftain, Halfdan Ingolfsson, talking to the two men tending the charcoal kiln. He joined them, not interrupting the conversation beyond a nodded greeting.

"It takes all day for the charcoal in the kiln to cool enough to shovel it out when we open it up in the morning," Grimr said, glancing from Halfdan to Gudbjartur. "After we empty the kiln it takes a short time to fill it back up with wood and light the fire. We throw the wood in through the vent hole on top until the kiln is full. Then we light it at the bottom opening." He gestured as he spoke. "After it catches fire we place the flat rock over the vent and roll another rock in front of the bottom opening. By dawn the next day we have a kiln full of charcoal." The man grinned through the grime that covered his face.

"The woodcutters haul the dry wood in for us," Barthur, his companion, said. "We would rather do this than cut wood, but I know we will be swapping jobs soon. As you told us, Gudbj, it keeps us from getting bored."

Gudbjartur acknowledged him with a nod and spoke to Halfdan. "The boys are waiting for us."

They took their leave of the kiln tenders, shouldered their packs and weapons, and headed for the landing beach to meet the boys.

"They gave me a report on the winter charcoal supply," Halfdan said, as he and Gudbjartur strolled slowly along the log walkway toward the main gate. "The bins in each longhouse are almost full. Then they will pile the excess charcoal under the shed roof next to the kiln until they judge there is plenty for winter. I left that up to them. They know more about it than I do."

"I spoke to them several days ago. Since they started using the new kiln their job is much easier. The charcoal is all made of dry birch wood. Birch will give us better heat than the pine we normally use," Gudbjartur said as they walked through the gate and down the hill toward the landing beach.

* * *

Further conversation about the charcoal supply ended when the three boys saw the men and ran to meet them.

"Which boat are we taking?" Ivar asked breathlessly.

"This one." Gudbjartur swung his pack aboard. "Your mother has already put a pack of dried meat aboard in case you boys do not kill us fresh meat."

"We will not fail, Father," Lothar said, a determined look on his thin face.

Gudbjartur could not remember the boy ever calling him father before. Taken aback, the big man gripped the boy's shoulder in a rare display of affection. "I never thought you would, Lothar." Gudbjartur glanced at the smiling Halfdan and turned away, unaccustomed to the feeling one word had brought to him. He carefully laid his bow, quiver of hunting arrows, and axe across the boat's thwarts. "Load your gear, boys. We will launch the boat and get under way."

The boys gathered their scattered gear and loaded it aboard. The two men, eagerly assisted by the chattering boys, pushed the boat's bow off the beach and all clambered aboard.

* * *

They sailed up a wide river until the wind off the bay became too variable from the dampening effect of the forest to be of any further use. The three boys had taken turns at the steering oar as the hunting party progressed inland. Now, Ivar had the helm.

Gudbjartur pointed ahead to the mouth of a tributary stream that issued from a small lake partially hidden back in the forest. "Steer for that stream, Ivar. Beach the boat anywhere along the left bank. Lothar, you and Yola lower the sail just before the boat reaches the shore."

The two boys craned forward to watch the shoreline, the tag end of the halyard clenched in their hands, ready to jerk it loose from the cleat and lower the sail. Lothar glanced anxiously at Halfdan, who watched them from his seat on the bow thwart. He smiled and nodded at him, but said nothing.

Ivar put the helm over and the boat headed into the shore.

"Now Yola," Lothar hollered, as he jerked the halyard loose. The small sail plummeted down the mast as the boys lost their grip on the halyard, covering them as they lost their footing and fell in a heap when the boat ground to a halt on the stones of the stream bank.

"See, there is nothing to it," Halfdan said, as he and Gudbjartur pulled the sail off the two struggling boys. "You dropped the sail at just the right time."

Ivar, hands on hips and a smile on his face, stood at his place in the stern as he watched his brother and Yola regain their feet.

"What are you grinning at?" Lothar asked.

"I saw the whole thing," Ivar said, his superior attitude coming to the fore. "That was a pretty funny way to lower the sail. You are supposed to lower it hand-over-hand, not just turn loose of the halyard."

"We know that. It was heavier than we thought and the halyard slipped through our hands."

The grinning Gudbjartur caught a wink from Halfdan as the two men, barely able to keep from laughing aloud, enjoyed the moment with their young charges.

"All right, boys. You all did well. Roll the sail up on the boom as we showed you, and secure the boat to a tree. Then we will go find a good place to hunt around yon lake," Gudbjartur ordered, gesturing inland.

* * *

They walked in single file, with Halfdan and Gudbjartur in the lead, around the shoreline to the north shore of the closest of the several small lakes in the area. Moose tracks seemed to be everywhere. Well-used game trails naturally funneled animals to the shoreline of the lake the men selected for the hunt.

Gudbjartur briefed the boys on his plan. "There is no wind so the moose will not smell you. You all saw the deep game trails winding down here from the forest. The moose use these trails every evening when they leave their bed grounds to water and feed on bulrushes on the lake bottom. Halfdan and I will find hiding places for you that will allow us to drive the animals to you. If we spring the trap at the right moment the moose will come right by your positions when they run away from Halfdan and me."

"How will we know when to shoot?" Lothar asked.

Ivar snorted at the question.

"That is a good question, Lothar." Halfdan entered the conversation to show Ivar that questions were a part of learning. "Each of you knows your range limit for accurate shots. Your quarry is a big moose. Even the calves are big, as you all know. The target you are shooting at is an area in the chest that is as big around as your mother's stew pot. About like so." He held both hands out in a circle to demonstrate a diameter equal to the length of a man's forearm. "The arrow must hit that target to kill him. If you hit him anywhere else, he may die, but he will run away and be lost to us because we probably will never find his carcass."

"Try to wait until your target is quartering and heading away from where you are." Gudbjartur demonstrated the proper angle with his hands. "If you get that angle, aim for the paunch, just back of the short ribs. There is no heavy bone there and all his vital organs are lying low in his chest cavity when he is on his feet. Your arrow will slice forward into his chest cavity, hitting a tub full of guts, the liver, at least one lung, and maybe the heart. It will be a killing shot."

"Aye, that is the best shooting angle on any game we kill with an arrow. Another important thing to remember when you get an arrow into him and he runs away—let him go. Wait for Gudbj and me." Halfdan looked at each of the boys. "Yola, why should you wait?"

Yola looked at his two friends and then back to Halfdan. "Because we should give him time to bleed to death."

"That is right!" Halfdan exclaimed enthusiastically. "If the animal has not seen you he will not know what happened. Maybe the wound will only burn. He will feel secure because you have not scared him. As he weakens, he will lie down. Why do we want him to lie down, Ivar?"

"So he will bleed to death quietly rather than run away in a panic until he finally drops dead. We would probably lose him then. And the meat would not be as good if he was all heated up when he died."

Halfdan smiled and nodded. He winked at Gudbjartur and stepped aside.

"Good, Ivar," Gudbjartur said, looking from boy to boy. "Remember, we will all be focused only on animals coming to the lake from this game trail. There may be others but ignore them unless they are about to step on you." The boys laughed. "You will see the moose before they get to the lake. They will be nervous. Their senses will be on full alert. Stay still and do not take a shot, no matter how tempting it is. Wait until they relax and Halfdan and I decide the time is right to drive them to you. You may get only one shot so take your time. Make your shots count. All it takes is one well-placed arrow and the moose is meat on the board." He grinned at them. "All right, I think you all know what to do. Now, check your arrows and knives. Make certain they are sharp. You will have need of them. Are there any questions before we lay our trap?"

The boys shook their heads. They busied themselves giving each arrowhead a final swipe or two with their whetstones. All were understandably nervous.

* * *

A short time later, all three boys lay concealed in the underbrush well back from the game trail. The trap lay ready for the quarry.

The men separated and each walked to a position across the lake from each other and with the targeted game trail roughly centered. When they sprang the trap, each man would cover half the shoreline as they converged on the quarry, thereby

ensuring the flushed animals would have to make their bid
to escape right by the three hidden boys.

While he waited in concealment Gudbjartur cut a short
piece of green willow shoot, chewed the end until it frayed
and softened, and used it to scrub his teeth. For him it was
a daily ritual. He watched the scene unfold much as he and
Halfdan had told the boys it would.

* * *

As the shadows lengthened toward day's end, a trio of moose
stepped from the dense forest surrounding the lake. The lead
animal, an old cow, paused and carefully surveyed the lake environs. Her sensitive nose tested the still air while the huge ears
turned this way and that, listening to the cries of birds and the
buzz of insects. Her senses told her that all was well. She continued down into the willow scrub along the lake shoreline.
She and her calves nibbled at the tender tips of willow before
stepping into the shallow waters of the lake. Their kind did
this same thing, just before sundown every day, when hunger
and thirst drove them from their bedding grounds to begin
another night of foraging.

* * *

Gudbjartur watched the cow moose and two large calves
walk with caution from the cover of the forest. The quarry
grazed slowly through the thick willows along the shoreline
before wading into the lake. The animals began to relax as
they grazed along the lake bottom on an abundance of bulrushes and other underwater forage plants, oblivious to the
threat lurking nearby.

Gudbjartur waved to Halfdan and the two men began closing in from both sides of the boys' position. They walked
along the shoreline making no attempt at stealth. Gudbjartur figured that he and Halfdan would be almost up to the
animals before they became alarmed. If everything worked as
planned, the three moose should pass the boys' hiding place
as they ran from the lake.

* * *

Greenland Sea, east of the Helluland coast

Five hundred sea leagues to the northeast of Halfdansfjord, the four ships of the settlement's trading flotilla to Greenland rolled and plunged in the heavy swells of the strait separating Helluland and Greenland. The flotilla had sailed from the strait between Markland and Helluland, through the southerly current flowing along the Helluland coast the preceding morning, and into the open ocean area of relatively slack currents between Helluland and Greenland.

Seabirds had recently joined the ships, diving and swooping in their constant quest for food, indicating land was not far off. Estimating there were some fifty leagues remaining in the voyage for the ships bound for Eiriksfjord, Greenland, Bjorn Kjetilsson, flotilla commander, signaled the ships to heave to into the wind as they approached a bank of thin fog and sea mist.

Fog banks of varying thickness and the pervading sea mist had been their constant companion during the twelve days of the voyage. Although it had not been necessary to heave to, the Fog Giant and reduced visibility preyed on Bjorn's mind. Command of more than his own ship weighed heavily on him. He thought the cargoes of green timber would be most welcome in both Greenland settlements and should induce the local farmers to part with all manner of trade goods from both Iceland and Vestfoldland. The ships had managed to stay in contact while running in the thin fog by sailing in close company and frequently sounding their bullhorns. The sound of the horns reverberating from ship to ship lent a surreal quality to the damp blanket as the ships alternately appeared and disappeared within its shroud.

After turning into the wind to heave to, the heavily laden ships remained close together. As they paid-off slowly downwind, their unfettered sails flapped loosely, and the crews shouted back and forth.

"If the visibility was not so poor the masthead would have the clouds of Greenland in sight to leeward. We will part company when the coast is sighted. As agreed, Athils and Sweyn will steer for Lysufjord, and Brodir and I will make for Eiriksfjord," Bjorn shouted across the narrow expanse of water separating the ships. "Good luck trading with the Tornit on your return voyages. I hope you kill many walrus with them. We will see you at Halfdansfjord before winter."

"Brodir," Sweyn shouted through cupped hands, "I hope you fill your ship with the trade goods we need in Halfdansfjord. Good luck trading with the Thalmiut on your return voyage, Bjorn. Trade them out of another pair of those big dogs." He waved and turned back to his waiting crew to get his ship underway.

Shouted farewells drifted across the water as crews bid their opposite numbers farewell and sheeted their sails home. A freshening wind out of the northwest began to blow the tatters of fog away and the flotilla rapidly gathered way as each ship answered her helm and steadied on course.

The ships would shortly come under the influence of the current sweeping into the north along the coast of western Greenland, speeding them toward their individual destinations. This fast-moving current would be especially useful to the two ships bound for Lysufjord, more than one hundred and fifty leagues north of Eiriksfjord.

* * *

The moose hunt

Unseen by the five moose hunters, a large bull moose ambled from his bed grounds toward the same lake. He stopped briefly to graze on the tender tips of ferns that had drawn his attention. The muffled snap of a breaking twig caused him to jerk his head erect. His senses went to full alert. The last mouthful of ferns dangled forgotten from slack lips as his small eyes stared in the direction of the sound. He detected a slight movement and his heightened attention fastened on the object. The animal's brain registered a warning, possible danger. Long, brown guard hairs along the top of his neck and back slowly came erect as his agitation increased.

The object of the bull's attention happened to be Yola. The boy stirred ever so slightly in his place of concealment. A small, dry twig snapped under him as he shifted position.

The bull knew not what the creature was, but it had no place in his ordered world. His rigid stance went from interest to alarm to rage in a moment, as he became aware that the creature was between him and the cow and calves. He began to move very slowly, almost noiseless for an animal of his bulk. The only sound of his passage was a slight whispering of the grass and ferns as they parted before him. His little eyes fixed unblinkingly on the creature he stalked.

"Yola, look out!" Lothar shrieked in alarm. The bull broke into a trot. He covered the short distance to the prone boy before Yola was aware of the mortal danger descending upon him.

Yola had but a heartbeat to turn toward the sound before the full force of the bull's charge descended upon him. The great spread of palmated antler pinned the struggling boy to the ground. The beast struck the center of Yola's chest with a flailing front hoof, breaking the breastbone in two. A violent whoosh of breath blew from the boy's mouth as the bull's head crushed his chest and cut off his screams.

In another heartbeat, the bull scooped Yola from the ground in his antlers and slammed his body against the trunk of a tree. Repeatedly, he smashed the now lifeless body against the tree trunk until it was a bloody pulp.

Ivar and Lothar stood immobilized by the suddenness and ferocity of the attack, but only for a moment. Ivar screamed in fear and rage. Tears streamed down his cheeks. He nocked an arrow on his bowstring as he ran to the bull's side. Without hesitation he drew the hunting arrow to its razor-sharp head and loosed it into the bull's heaving ribcage from pointblank range as the beast worried the bundle of bloody rags that had been his friend.

* * *

Gudbjartur and Halfdan ran as fast as conditions permitted toward the mayhem. Branches and saplings whipped and tore at their faces.

The cow and calves they had intended to drive toward the boys' hiding place froze in position in the chest deep water as the yelling apparitions swept past. Disturbed water and bulrushes flew in all directions as the cow ran into the security of the forest, closely followed by her calves.

* * *

As Ivar loosed his third arrow, realization slowly dawned on the bull that an enemy was nearby and he wheeled to confront him. The remnants of little Yola hung in tatters from his antlers as he charged, mowing down saplings and standing dead trees he crashed toward the new target.

"Shoot him, Lothar!" Ivar shrieked at his brother. He darted around a tree and loosed his fourth arrow into the center of the bull's chest. Gasping in fright, he wheeled and ran for his life. Unconsciously he used the trees and undergrowth to slow the animal's charge, darting in a tight circle to give Lothar a clear shot. A big tree saved his life when he swerved around the trunk a heartbeat before the bull crashed into it. Ivar jumped back and forth around the tree trunk while the enraged bull, an arm's length away, blew snot over him in his effort to hook the boy with his bloody antlers.

Lothar, who had stood rooted in place while Yola died and his brother shot arrow after arrow into the great beast that towered over him, suddenly regained his senses. Ivar's screams galvanized him to action and he ran to the side far enough to get a clear shot through the trees. "Yahhh!" He screamed to distract the bull from Ivar, pulled his bowstring to the head of the nocked arrow, and loosed it into the animal's ribcage. The shaft penetrated all the way to the feathers without visible effect.

The bull wheeled toward him and charged. Lothar darted behind a small evergreen. The tree bent over and snapped off at the ground like a twig as the bull crashed against the trunk. The boughs of the falling tree ensnared Lothar. The bull straddled the tree's trunk and swung his head back and forth, as he tried to crush the crawling boy with his antlers. Lothar's whimpering terror seemed to enrage the animal further. His flailing front hooves stripped limbs from the evergreen's trunk like dry leaves, missing the boy's body by a hand's breadth.

A yelling Ivar ran to the animal's side and shot his last arrow low into the ribcage behind the bull's shoulder.

Lothar scrambled from under the entanglement of boughs. His bow snagged on something and he let it lie, running for his life.

The bull charged after the running boy.

"Run, Lothar! He is coming after you!" A shrieking Ivar went in pursuit.

* * *

The men burst through the undergrowth with Halfdan in the lead. Yelling to distract and confuse the bull, Halfdan swept his arm back and threw the heavy hunting spear with all his strength at the bull's shoulder. The razor-sharp head sliced through the animal's shoulder muscles and lodged in the massive shoulder joint. The bull staggered from the force of the impact, dropping his head to regain his balance.

Gudbjartur leaped toward the bull with his axe held high for the stroke.

"Odin!" The battle cry rang through the forest as he closed the distance.

Without checking his forward momentum, Gudbjartur chopped the axe blade down across the juncture of the beast's neck and shoulders. The bull's straining neck muscles popped apart like overripe fruit as the keen blade sliced down through them.

The bull's head dropped. The corded neck muscle no longer supported the weight of his head and neck. He crashed to the ground, all but beheaded by the axe stroke.

A shudder shook the beast. He tried to rise. Slowly he rolled onto his side. Muscles twitched in confusion. His brain no longer sent usable signals to his body. With a great sigh, he died; accusing dark eyes gazed unseeing on his slayers.

Gudbjartur left the axe stuck in the bull's body and bolted toward Ivar. Dropping to his knees, his arms encircled the boy, crushing him to his chest as emotion swept over both of them. The young boy trembled in his father's arms. Gudbjartur was speechless in his relief at finding his son unharmed.

Halfdan attended to Lothar. He turned the boy round and round, inspecting for injuries. Lothar unashamedly wept with relief and sorrow. Halfdan hugged him and patted his back.

"It is over, boy. You are all right." He turned to Gudbjartur. "Lothar is all right, Gudbj, just scratched up some."

"Come here, son." Gudbjartur held an arm out to the boy.

Lothar walked to his father, his eyes downcast and wet with tears. Gudbjartur wrapped his arms around both his sons. Kneeling before them on the ground, he rested his head on their shoulders. A shudder shook his body as pent-up emotion receded. "Thank the gods you are safe."

"I can hardly breathe, Father. You are crushing me." Ivar's words served to calm the three of them.

Gudbjartur released the boys and searched their faces for a heartbeat. "You did well," he said, his voice husky with feeling.

Halfdan let Gudbjartur have his moment with his sons by examining the dead bull. When finished, he pulled the buried axe blade from the animal's neck and stepped over to join them. "They shot six arrows into him, Gudbj. Any one of them would have killed him. But not before he got both of them." He handed the bloody axe to Gudbjartur.

"I only shot him once. Ivar shot him the most," Lothar's voice caught in misery. "I could not move I was so afraid. But not Ivar. He shrieked at the bull while he shot arrows into him."

The two men made brief eye contact. They keenly appraised Ivar while the boy relived the events with his brother.

"Your arrow *saved* me, Lothar. He almost got to me before you shot him. My last arrow may have saved you. I think it hurt him because he blinked. If you had not scampered from under the tree right then and tried to run away, he might have turned on me."

Ivar grinned at his brother. "I was just as scared as you were. Anger and fear made me act. I was trying to save Yola. I did not know he was already dead." Ivar spoke in a strong voice, his emotions controlled.

"You both did well, as your father has told you. I know grown men who could not stand their ground under such a threat." Halfdan gestured toward the bull's corpse. "You did better than well, both of you. I am proud to have you as my young warriors. The people will tell tales of this hunt for some time to come."

Both boys were silent; the tragedy that had befallen them filled their thoughts. They basked in their chieftain's praise, but stole furtive glances at the remains of Yola.

Halfdan had taken the small broken body from the bull's antlers and laid it on the damp ground beside the corpse of the animal that had killed him.

"It is best if you go look upon Yola. Remember your friendship with him, for it will be the last time you see him. His spirit is still here with us. He is watching," Gudbjartur said gently.

The boys looked at each of the men. Halfdan nodded and gestured with a lift of his chin, and the boys walked slowly toward the corpse. The men let them go alone, following closely. Life could be cruel, but the young must know how to accept it. Violent death would follow them all the days of their lives, to swoop down without warning; they must learn to confront the specter of death without shirking.

The boys bravely looked down at the remains of their friend. Ivar's inner strength held him rigid, while tears coursed in rivulets down Lothar's cheeks. Yola's head had been crushed like an egg, his body torn to pieces. The smooth, young features were distorted and misshapen. "His face is gone," Ivar said. Broken ribs, white as teeth, stuck out of the squashed chest. Splintered bones protruded from one leg. The bones of the other leg were intact except that the upper leg muscle hung asunder. One arm hung from the exposed socket. Ivar glanced at his brother. "He does not look like Yola anymore."

Lothar's shoulders shook with silent sobs. He nodded abjectly at Ivar's assessment and turned toward the men. "Will we bury him here?"

Halfdan answered. "Yes, we will do it now. We cannot take him back with us. He should rest here where he died. No useful purpose would be served by his mother seeing what remains of her son." He took a breath. "We will camp here for the night. It will be dark soon, so let us be about it." He finished gruffly, feeling an unfamiliar surge of emotion. *I must be getting old. On the other hand, maybe it is because of Frida. I feel things more intensely now. She has changed me in many ways.*

Gudbjartur put a hand on the shoulder of each of his sons. "Come, boys, we will all bury Yola together. You must help us prepare Yola for the afterlife. He was your friend and you must do him this final honor. Afterwards, Halfdan and I will show you how to butcher the bull you killed and prepare the meat for the boat trip back to Halfdansfjord."

The four of them grouped around Yola, each with his own thoughts.

Gudbjartur tried to soothe his sons. "Yola did not suffer. I heard him scream once as the bull attacked, but then he died. He was so afraid that he would not be able to feel pain. That is the way of things when we fight; our fear dulls the pain of our wounds."

"He did not have time to fight before he died," Lothar said. "I was right next to him and the bull had hold of him before he could move."

"He fought nonetheless, Lothar. Even the least of us will fight to survive." Halfdan put a hand on the boy's shoulder. "Now, let us put your friend in the earth, to rest."

They cleaned up the small, torn body as best they could, washing away the blood and gore and putting the torn flesh back in place. Both boys had to overcome their initial revulsion at touching the grisly remains.

"I cannot do this," Lothar said, stepping away to retch as the gorge rose in his throat.

"Come, boy, you must steel yourself." Gudbjartur held an arm out for his son. "It is the way of things and the reason you both were included in these preparations. In this way, you will know what you must do for a burial. Playing an active part fosters acceptance of your friend's death."

Lothar reluctantly returned to the task. His face was tight, his lips bloodless and pressed into a severe line as he fought down nausea.

Finally, they finished the work with the body. They straightened the shattered limbs and wrapped the corpse in a wool sleeping robe. Then with Gudbjartur at one end and both boys at the other end, they lifted the pitiful bundle and carried it to the grave. Tenderly they laid their burden in the dark, shallow hole.

"We want to bury him with his weapons." Ivar looked at his father, his chin thrust out, his eyes defiant.

Gudbjartur regarded his sons in silence. He looked from one to the other. Then he nodded. "I think that is proper. The gods will make the young warrior welcome. He will have need of his weapons in the afterlife."

The boys sat at the graveside and snapped the arrows and bow in two as they had seen the men do, to kill and release the spirits within. Ivar forced the blade of Yola's knife into a crack in a handy boulder and leaned into it to bend the blade over. They arranged the weapons on either side of the body. Then their final act for their friend was to push the cold earth over his body, refill the grave, and mound it over with earth and rocks.

* * *

Later that evening, after the men gorged on chunks of spitted moose liver, the four sat around the campfire staring into the flames.

"Eat some more of this liver." Gudbjartur urged the boys.

"I cannot eat, Father." Ivar glanced at his brother.

"Nor I. The liver makes me sick," Lothar said.

"How about a steak then?" Gudbjartur asked.

Both boys shook their heads.

Conversation ebbed back and forth for a time before silence reigned.

Halfdan told us that our arrows would have killed the bull. Glancing in the direction of his father and Halfdan, Ivar's mind sifted through the events of the day. Catching his brother's eye, he winked and smiled slightly at him. Lothar returned a weak smile, bobbed his head slightly, and sighed, telling Ivar without words that he knew what he was thinking. Ivar looked at his brother for another moment, and then laid back full length on the ground, hands clasped behind his head. He stared at the countless stars winking in the clear night sky. A meteorite scribed a bright trail across the blackness overhead. *A spark from Thor's hammer.* His eyes followed its path until the light winked out. *Yes, we did kill that bull. Father cut off his head, but Halfdan said he would have died from our arrows. And all but one of them came from my bow.*

* * *

Halfdansfjord

Two days after returning from the fateful hunting trip with his sons and Halfdan, Gudbjartur sat at the edge of the cliff from which he had thrown Gizur's body into the sea, lost in contemplation. He came here often. The place offered solitude, a commanding view of the bay and much of the hinterland. Here he sorted his thoughts and assigned them their proper position in his mind's queue of things to be done.

Thoughts of Gizur and Ulfar intruded into his mind occasionally when he came here. He had killed both men: Ulfar for dishonoring Halfdan and the duel, the Einvigi; and Gizur for plotting against Frida, blaming her for his crippling wounds from the duel with Ulfar. He had warned Gizur. However, the man's mind was poisoned and he became irrational. After watching Gizur's actions carefully over time he had perceived a threat to his chieftain. He had followed the troubled man here to his hiding place. He observed him watching Frida, killed him, and threw his body from this very cliff into the sea. *I did not kill Gizur. He killed himself by not heeding my warning.*

He looked out over the bay. His conscious mind registered what he saw and heard: a small pod of white Beluga Whales to the west; a flock of birds squabbling over baitfish in the shallows below his lofty vantage point; the cry of a loon from the fen behind him; the quacking of fussing ducks; the ever-present buzz and mutter of wildlife.

But he dwelt on none of it. Instead he reflected on the heartache and sense of loss suffered by his people over the death of one little boy. He carried a feeling of guilt because he had been responsible for the boy's safety on the hunt. Yola's death was not anyone's fault. Hunting dangerous game was a dangerous business. But that did not make it any easier to bear nor did it make him feel better to think of it in those terms. If he had been with them, beside them, as they waited for the game to appear, Yola would still be alive.

Halfdan chided him for his feeling of guilt and pointed out that the gods had claimed the boy and that no mortal man could have intervened. In his heart, he knew this to be true. However, the young mother's anguish over the loss of her only son cast the entire populace into a funk; a state most still struggled to rise above.

He shook himself back to the present. The cries of gulls alerted him to a ship rounding the point with a large whale roped along either side. It was Gudrod's ship, followed by four catcher boats. The system he had devised of the mother ship and catcher boats had been so successful in hunting the big whales, thanks in part to the toggle-headed harpoon design copied from the Tornit, that the larders bulged with a full winter's supply of whale oil and cured meat. The whales also provided a steady supply of fresh meat near at hand before the onset of winter drove them from the bay.

* * *

As the ship coasted in toward the landing beach, the lookout saw him atop the cliff and waved. Gudbjartur stood; stretched muscles cramped by inactivity, and raised his arm in greeting. He sighed at the interruption, turned, and began making his way down the escarpment toward the landing beach. The ship and boat crews, assisted by those waiting on the beach for their arrival, would not need his help or guidance to butcher the catch. Mindful of his footing on the treacherous path, he paused one last time to survey the bay. Because his elevation afforded a panoramic view, he chanced to see a large shark with a snow-white underbelly, visible in the clear water, following the blood trail of the dead whales. He picked up his pace so he could warn Gudrod and his crew.

* * *

Life in the bustling village of Halfdansfjord settled into a normalcy like any Norse settlement. The artisans, who produced the wares, whether they were hard goods, clothing, or food products, carried out daily commerce of every type. Everyone shared the bounty of the land and sea while everything they manufactured they bartered for other goods.

After warning Gudrod about the shark, Gudbjartur walked back toward the settlement. He stopped by a crowd gathered around two boys who had just come from the woods with a recent discovery. In spite of numerous bee stings, the two had managed to pilfer two buckets of honeycombs from the first beehive found in Vinland. Honey was the only sweetener known to the Northmen, and was the prime ingredient of mead, a staple.

Gudbjartur pushed his way to the front of the crowd. He arrived in time to hear the older of the two boys, Haki, son of Thorvard the Tanner, relating their adventure.

"Atli and I watched the bees gathering nectar from the flowers in the fen," Haki explained while both boys put mud on their bee stings. "They always flew in the same direction. Every day we lost sight of them in the shadows of the forest. Today we finally found their hive. It is well hidden at the base of a big tree."

"It is just over there, on the other side of the barley field." Atli gestured vaguely toward the forest verge. "The bees live under the roots of a tree, not in a hollow trunk like they usually do."

The bystanders were appreciative of the important discovery.

"I hope you find more honey, Atli," Thorvard, his father said. "Before the bees are holed up in their hives for winter."

"We will, Father. Every day we will try to follow other bees that are on a beeline for their hive."

"You boys did well," Gudbjartur said. "I am sure someone here will show you how to smoke the bees so they will not sting you the next time. We need the honey and beeswax. Find it and you will have all the help you need to harvest it."

A group of men and women with buckets soon formed and the boys led them out of the north gate. They would harvest all the extra honey, leaving only enough to sustain the bees through the long winter.

* * *

Ingerd and Thora were in a bad mood. Both were unhappy about the upcoming scouting expedition. Gudbjartur planned to take Deskaheh, leaving both women without their men for at least a moon. Neither had mentioned it to their men, knowing it to be pointless. Both of them had unnatural periods of silence that was out of character for them, especially the talkative Thora.

* * *

Gudbjartur and Deskaheh knew their women did not want them to go, but the dilemma was without solution. The expedition was too important to delay departure any longer.

Gudbjartur busied himself putting a pack of basic supplies together for the long-delayed scouting trip into the hinterland toward Deskaheh's homeland. Halfdan wanted him to scout an inland route to the sea and make contact with the Naskapi and Haudeno tribes. His work here was finished for the time being and Halfdan could spare him for a while. The time had come to depart.

Late in the afternoon Gudbjartur walked from his longhouse, his preparations complete. He headed toward the sweat lodge where he had arranged to meet Halfdan for a sweat before the final meal of the day. Gudrod had mentioned earlier that he and most of his crew would join them there when they had finished butchering the whales. Gudbjartur paused at the doorway to strip before entering the low building. Two thrall women were tending the fire under the new steam boiler. The boiler was his idea and he had only recently broached the idea to the smithies. Understandably curious to see it in operation, he stepped over to watch them. "How is the boiler working?"

"Very well, Gudbj," Genevra answered. "Yesterday was the first time we fired it up. It gets so hot in there we had to rig this counterweighted leather flapper to the top of the boiler to let the steam out." The dark-haired Celtic beauty pointed out the flapper covering a hole in the boiler's top. "Sigmund cut the hole in the boiler yesterday and helped us get the flapper working."

Gudbjartur bent over to examine the flapper assembly. His eyes followed the leather thong attached to the flapper to the point where it disappeared into the sweathouse wall.

Halla, Genevra's helper, responded to his questioning look. "The thong has a loop on the other end. We drove a peg in the inside wall to hook the loop. When the loop is hooked on the peg this flapper is open, letting most of the steam out into the air. You take the loop off the peg and let the thong go to close the flapper. It gets hotter right away. It works very well, almost too well." She chuckled. "We cooked them in there yesterday. Everyone ran outside because it was too hot. But we have it figured out now. We are glad you thought of the boiler." She smiled up at him. "It is easier to tend the fire and refill the boiler than it is to pack hot rocks in and cold rocks out. We do not need to stay here all the time. We just add wood and water occasionally."

"Good! As soon as the others get here, we will give it a try." Gudbjartur crouched down to inspect the boiler itself, housed within a mud-daubed stone fireplace. The smithies had found two old pots to rivet together for the boiler and they used a section of rolled copper sheet for a pipe to carry the steam into the sweat lodge. They attached the copper pipe near the top of the boiler, and then mudded it in along its entire length through the wall of the sweat lodge to preserve the steam temperature. "A clever design. They did well."

"Yes," Genevra answered proudly, "Sigmund did that work, too. He is very good with his hands."

A slight smile played about Gudbjartur's lips. "I have heard that you would be the one to know about that, Genevra."

Halla laughed.

Genevra blushed to her hair roots. She glanced at the two smiling people; her face reflected an inner turmoil. "I did not mean any disrespect, Gudbj." She twisted a fold of her apron in confusion. "It is just. . . It is just. . ." Her voice trailed off and she dissolved in tears.

Gudbjartur, taken aback, started to speak, but a look from Halla stopped him.

"She does this often, Gudbj. Do not concern yourself." Halla put her arm around her friend's shoulders.

Not knowing how to respond, he mumbled something unintelligible and seized the opportunity to walk away. As he walked toward the sweat lodge entrance, a great sigh escaped his lips. *Women!* He snorted and shook his head.

Halfdan and the others arrived at the same time. "What is the matter, Gudbj?" Halfdan asked, stopping in front of him.

"Nothing important. Women and their reactions to simple things will always be a mystery to me." He glanced back at the two women sitting on a bench, their heads together in conversation.

Halfdan watched Gudbjartur, a question in his eyes as the man turned toward him.

"Genevra started crying when I jested about her and Sigmund. She must get over the problem she has with being pregnant with his baby. She is a thrall and he is a freeman. They cannot marry. There is no solution to it unless Brodir frees her after his return from Greenland, and I doubt he will. Or you decide to free all the thralls, as we spoke of earlier." Gudbjartur looked at Halfdan and the others. None had anything to say. He shook his head. "Let us go into the sweat lodge before something else happens."

The men stripped off their sweaty tunics, hung them on one of several wooden pegs adjacent to the entrance, and filed through the low doorway into the circular room. The steam-laden interior beckoned as they scattered to take seats on the wooden benches positioned around the interior wall of the low building. Two flickering oil lamps dimly lit the interior.

"Now, this is more like it. It is *hot* in here," Gudrod said as he sat down.

Grunts and groans of pleasure came from around the room.

Halfdan spoke into the opaqueness. "Your steam boiler idea works well, Gudbj. It is hotter in here now than it ever was with the heated rocks." Halfdan flicked sweat from his face.

"Aye, it does work better. Halla told me the boiler made it much easier for them to provide steam. Hauling hot rocks in and out was hard work. Finding a better method was the reason I proposed the change." He told them what he had learned about temperature control with the new system. "If anybody gets too hot, there is a loop on the end of a thong over there on the inside wall opposite the boiler." He pointed. "Just hook the thong loop on the peg and you will open a weighted leather flapper atop the boiler to allow most of the steam to go into the air instead of in here." He got to his feet and demonstrated. "I am told it will get hot in here quickly, so whoever is closest to the flapper control can regulate the temperature for all of us." He took a seat on the bench beside Halfdan.

Silence followed for a time while the men relaxed in the heavy heat. Occasionally someone whipped himself with a leafy willow branch to promote circulation.

Gudbjartur finally broke the silence. "I am departing at first light on the scouting trip, Halfdan. The nine men I have picked are ready to go. Our settlement is ready for winter. I am running out of projects, so it is time."

Halfdan looked at his lieutenant. "Who is going with you?"

Gudbjartur gestured toward the silent men watching the interchange between their leaders. "They are here. It is time to change the boat crews and most of the old crew wanted to go with me. Today I assigned new crews to the catcher boats." He turned to Gudrod. "The new men will meet at your ship tomorrow morning for orders."

"I will miss these men." Gudrod acknowledged his old crew. "They know their work well. We have forged a good team."

"The new crews will do just as well," Gudbjartur said. He knew his statement would get a rise from the old crew. And it did.

Halfdan smiled and nodded as he waited for the humorous remarks and laughter to subside. He used the time to study his friend, detecting a disquieting undercurrent from this man he knew so well. In spite of his cheerful demeanor, something troubled the man. "Are you taking Deskaheh?"

"Aye. I doubt I could leave here without him. He has told me we would not be successful without his help. After seeing the way he moves through the forest, he may be correct."

"Where is he? Why is he not here with us for this last sweat together?" Halfdan asked.

"He is showing Ingerd, Thora, and the other cooks, how to prepare the pemmican his people depend on. The women have harvested so many berries that they are going to make berry wine and use the leftover pulp in the pemmican rather than whole berries like Deskaheh's people do. They will use a combination of dried fish and dried meat to make our pemmican. Deskaheh's people do not use fish, just meat. I have tried some. They pour it hot into bark molds. After the pemmican mixture cools, they cut it from the mold and it is ready to store or eat. It keeps almost indefinitely."

"What does it taste like?" Gudrod had a dubious expression on his face.

"It is good, sweet, and filling. The bars are tough, but limber like dried fish. They are ready to eat and are not difficult to chew. Pemmican will make a good trail ration. Deskaheh told me that he will bring enough for all of us."

"It does not sound good to me. I would rather have meat or fish," Snorri said from across the room.

Several agreed.

Gudbjartur dismissed their concerns with a wave of his hand. "We all prefer fresh fish and meat, but we will be traveling fast and we cannot take time to hunt. You all know that. Pemmican is better than anything else we could carry. We will grow accustomed to it."

Halfdan directed a question to Gudrod. "How did you handle the big shark that I heard came after the whales you were butchering?"

"Snorri killed it before it had the first mouthful. His killing lance chanced to go in one of the shark's eyes. It thrashed around for a time before dying." Gudrod chuckled at the recollection. "It was tense for a time. The shark is longer than three men are. It could have stove in the side of my ship if its tail had hit it solidly. It conveniently died before that happened. Thralls are butchering it now. They tailed it up on the beach with one of the windlasses we use to haul out the ships. The meat is tough and stringy, but the dogs and pigs will not mind. We saved the liver to render out its oil. The rough hide is good for sanding wood, shoe soles, plates for armored war vests, hinges, and many other things. Even with all our needs, this sharkskin is so big we will not need another for some time. We used a team of horses to pull the hide from the carcass as the thralls cut it loose. They staked it upside down on the beach and salted it to keep the flies away. The ravens will peck a few holes in it before it dries, but there will be plenty left for us." Gudrod stood, stretched, and rubbed his stomach. "I am hungry. It must be about time to eat, so I am going down to the beach to cool off before the cooks call us."

His men followed him out through the hide-draped doorway, leaving Gudbjartur and Halfdan alone.

The two men made eye contact; Halfdan sighed and looked away. "I will miss having you here, Gudbj. But your mission is of vital importance. You are the only man here who can do it justice. For some reason I feel a sense of disquiet. I do not know why."

"I feel the same. I feel that the gods ordain this mission. We must have answers to our questions concerning this land. With the help of the gods, I will accomplish this mission for you, and our people."

The two men locked eyes.

Halfdan nodded, slapped Gudbjartur on the knee, and got to his feet. "I know you will. Come; let us join the other men at the beach to wash off this sweat."

* * *

Chapter Two

Halfdansfjord, Vinland

Predawn light began to soften the deep shadows of the settlement. Gudbjartur made his customary rounds of the palisade and returned to the longhouse. He left the double entry doors open and propped open the long shutter on the east window to admit the morning sunlight and fresh air into the gloom of the interior. Other residents of the longhouse began to stir as another day began. Ingerd tended the morning soup on the communal hearth. Stopping near her, he looked around for his sons. "Where are the boys?"

Ingerd had watched Gudbjartur's every movement as he tried to look busy. "They left right after you did to empty and rebait their crab traps."

He grunted unintelligibly, picked up his pack, upended it on their part of the platform bench, and sat down to examine the meager contents, again. He avoided eye contact with her, seemingly intent on his task.

Annoyed at his attitude, she pursed her lips. Standing with both hands fisted on her hips her body language bespoke a troubled woman.

He looked up, knowing he must address the issue. "What?"

"What do you mean, 'what' Gudbj? We must talk about this. I do not want you to go."

"I know that, Ingerd, but I must."

"Why? Send someone else."

"No! Halfdan wants me to go."

"Tell him you do not want to go. Tell him that *I* do not want you to go."

He got to his feet and stepped over to her. Gently, his eyes on her eyes, he took hold of her hands. "I would never do that, Ingerd, not even for you. Halfdan is my friend, my chieftain. He depends on me and I have his trust. I am honor bound to do his bidding."

"I know." Her forehead made contact with his broad chest. "I have bad feelings about this scouting trip," she said in a small voice.

He held her at arm's length. "Hear me, my love. I will come back to you. As long as I have life I will return."

She searched his face, a single tear coursed down her cheek. "And as long as I have life I will be waiting for you."

* * *

Seven days after Gudbjartur and his men departed on the scouting trip into the hinterland, a chilly dawn greeted the residents of Halfdansfjord. However, cloudless skies brought the promise of another hot day. As the rising sun chased the chill from the settlement, a gentle breeze stirred the heavy, humid air to life, bearing with it a strong smell of the sea as it wafted across the fjord from the southwest. As women stoked the morning hearth fires smoke rose from the longhouses and settled out over the fen.

* * *

Toward midday, Halfdan strolled across the open ground just outside the north gate of the settlement palisade. The dog, Fang, walked beside him. From time to time, the dog ranged out ahead when something caught his attention. Halfdan's eyes swept the countryside ahead as he walked. To his right, the edge of the large fen became indistinct in the distance where it joined with the forest verge. He was not aware of any particular destination; he just strolled slowly along kicking at dirt clods in the freshly turned soil of next year's barley field. Thoughts of Gudbjartur's departure, the importance of the mission, and the fact that he and the nine men accompanying him would be gone for at least one full moon occupied his mind. He did not expect them back until the end of the Haymaking Time Moon or perhaps the beginning of the Harvest Moon. They did not know how far it was across the peninsula to the long bay from the sea or how long they would stay once they reached their destination. Even Deskaheh had not been able to answer the vexing questions. Not knowing troubled him.

He paused in his stroll and crouched down to examine the rich earth recently turned up by one of several iron-tipped ard plows the workmen had used to till wood ash, manure, and rotted seaweed into the soil. It was common practice to prepare the soil in this way, one season ahead of time—normally following harvest—thereby increasing the soil's yield potential for planting their precious barley seed the following spring during the Sowing Time Moon. Workers guided a single horse hitched to their ard plows and drove it back and forth in the field until they deemed the soil tilled sufficiently to turn over the surface. Soil tilth would improve as the added material rotted in the earth. He crumbled the dark soil in his hands. Rising to his feet, he dusted off his hands and looked out over the plowed ground. The stones he saw piled along the field edges already formed the outline of a fence. As more stones worked their way to the surface from the annual plowing, and the erosion of wind and water, they, too, would become a part of the fence. He resumed his stroll. Thoughts of the bountiful crops they could expect next year came into his mind. At the same time, he thanked the gods for leading his people to this land of plenty.

He stopped and looked out over the land and the edge of the forest. A pair of ravens cawed from the top of a dead birch. The snapping sound of flying grasshoppers came to his ears. He stooped to pick up a stick. "It will be hot today after this breeze stops."

Fang sat close by. His ears pricked up and he turned his head from side-to-side at the sound of Halfdan's voice. The long tongue lolled from the side of his mouth while he watched his master.

Halfdan clucked low in his throat. The animal obediently came to his outstretched hand. Absent-mindedly, he scratched the dog's erect ears. Without another word, he continued his stroll.

Fang's slanted eyes followed him for a moment. Then he, too, examined the countryside ahead, an ingrained habit of his kind, before he followed his master.

Halfdan threw the stick off to the side without thought. Fang went to retrieve it. By nature, the dog was too sedate to run after the stick so Halfdan did not notice he had retrieved it until he chanced to glance at him a short time later. There was the stick clenched in the dog's mouth. The bushy tail wagged slightly as Fang watched his master come to a stop and turn toward him.

"So, you think I want that stick?" Halfdan laughed and took the stick from the dog. He threw it once and, as before, the dog sedately retrieved it. He scratched the dog's ears again and they resumed their stroll. He came to the edge of the field in a place where the virgin forest began, where the workers had not clear-cut the trees to supply the settlement's needs. The ground underfoot changed from the tilled surface of the field to the firmness of the undisturbed lichen of the forest floor. Suddenly, he realized Yggdrasil was before him.

A chill coursed through his body as the superstition associated with Yggdrasil and the World Tree possessed him once again. Since Yggdrasil's chance discovery, his duties had kept him from a return visit—truth be known he had forgotten about it—but others had not, as evidenced by the offerings that festooned the branches of the great ash tree. Everything from dead animals to personal items hung from the branches. For within the branches was the realm of Asgard, abode of the gods, the highest level of the World Tree, Yggdrasil.

Gazing at the tree, the chill endured, bringing forth wild thoughts from his subconscious mind. *The gods are trying to tell me something, of that I am certain. That is why they led me to Yggdrasil. But what is it?*

Unbeknownst to him initially, the feeling of unease concerned Gudbjartur. He attributed the chills to a visitation from the gods as he stood before Yggdrasil.

However, it was not that at all. Rather he felt the same degree of angst Gudbjartur felt only for a different reason. Gudbjartur was in mortal danger. He was not.

At that moment, having reached their destination, Naskapi warriors were pursuing Gudbjartur and his men. When Halfdan felt the chill of impending doom, Gudbjartur's pursuers were pressing him hard, and his mind emitted a jumble of thoughts, all focused on survival.

It was this intense anxiety that caused Gudbjartur's predicament to intrude into Halfdan's conscious mind like a lightning bolt. In an instant Gudbjartur's angst crossed the leagues separating him from the two people he loved above all others, his wife, Ingerd, and his chieftain, Halfdan.

* * *

Halfdan shook himself, turned away, and strode purposefully back toward the settlement, vowing this religious furor possessing him was most likely nonsense. Nevertheless, there was no denying that thoughts of Gudbjartur had suddenly filled his mind.

A group of women returning from berry picking in the fen drew his attention as he approached the palisade gate. His eyes fastened on his wife, Frida, and Gudbjartur's wife, Ingerd. He altered course to intercept them. His attention focused on Ingerd.

The two women stopped when they saw him coming. Ingerd saw his expression; her smile slipped, worry clouded her face.

"Come with me, both of you," he ordered, as he swept past.

"But Halfdan, what. . ." Ingerd's voice rose.

"Just come!"

He heard their footsteps as they followed. When he was out of earshot of the rest of the group, he wheeled to face them.

"What is the matter?" Frida's state of confusion began to turn to one of anger.

"Something just happened to me that concerns Ingerd, probably all of us. As soon as I saw you two I knew I had to talk to her about it."

"What happened?" Ingerd grabbed his arm, a look of concern on her face. "It is about Gudbj. I knew something was not right. I felt a chill before you came to us. Now what is it, Halfdan?"

"I do not know, Ingerd, nothing that I know of. But the gods tried to tell me something about Gudbj. Something is not right or they would not have come to me."

"When did this happen?" Frida asked.

"Just now. At Yggdrasil." He gestured toward the Sacred Grove of Odin. "I was walking in the barley field, not really conscious of what I was doing, my mind a jumble of thoughts. You know how it is. I was not thinking about anything in particular. I suddenly became aware that I was standing at the base of the World Tree. The strangest feeling came to me. Like someone was trying to tell me something about Gudbj. Something is wrong. I feel that it will turn out all right, but not before there is trouble with the Naskapi. All of this came to me as clearly as I am talking to you."

"I knew before he left that something would happen." Ingerd twisted her apron as she became steadily more agitated. "What can we do, Halfdan? I cannot stand this separation if I think something has happened to him."

Frida took hold of her friend's hand as Ingerd began to lose control.

"Settle down, Ingerd," Halfdan said, taking hold of both her shoulders. "I do not know what, if anything, is the matter. We have no choice but to wait. For some reason, that makes no more sense than the feelings that came to me from Yggdrasil about impending doom. I feel that everything will come out all right in the end. That fact is as clear as my thoughts that something has happened to Gudbj. Just because something has happened to him does not mean it is bad. I tell you these things only because the gods bade me to tell you. They are in control of everything. As in all things, we must wait to see what it is they are trying to tell us. It will become clear with time. Gudbj has only been gone seven days. As the time approaches for his expected return, we can become concerned. Until then, we wait. Go about your business as if nothing is wrong, because we do not know that anything is wrong. You are the wife of one of our leaders; you must be strong, as he would expect you to be, as I expect you to be. People are watching us," he gestured with a lift of his chin. "Act happy. Smile. Everything will be all right in the end."

Ingerd smiled miserably, the three of them turned and strolled toward the settlement gate behind the gossiping berry pickers.

"If you say so, Halfdan," Ingerd said. "I wish I felt certain, but I do not."

"Give it a chance, Ingerd," Frida said. "There is little we can do but hope for the best."

Ingerd continued with her friends, the normal bounce gone from her step.

* * *

Later that afternoon Ingerd stared into the coals of the fire pit, a long-handled fork clutched in the fist she rested on her hip. Her life continued as before. The demands of the daily work saw to that. Each morning and evening, she did her share of the milking and cooking. In between, she kept busy sewing, mending, churning butter, making cheese, or helping with the many other daily tasks. She felt best when the work was so hard she could think of nothing else. At other times, especially at day's end, she could not shut off her thoughts of Gudbjartur. Inner turmoil wore a hole in her heart. She clipped her responses to direct questions or comments. She had little to do with everyday gossip. Her friends attributed this change in demeanor to Gudbjartur's absence.

Frida, of course, knew better.

Thora guessed that her friend's moodiness was a little more than loneliness for her man. Ingerd did not share her thoughts, much to Thora's private displeasure. Try as she might, no inkling of the problem came her way. Over time, she shifted her attention to other things. She, too, missed her man, but she knew that was not Ingerd's problem. It was something else, something much deeper.

* * *

At dawn, the wail of a guard tower warning horn jerked Halfdan from his morning languor.

He lurched from the comfort of the sleeping platform, threw on his clothes, and ran from the longhouse.

"I am coming too," Frida called after him, vaulting from their bed.

The palisade parapet that faced inland was filling with men as Halfdan nimbly mounted one of the ladders. "What is it?" Halfdan joined those staring out over the sharpened tops of the palisade logs.

"We have visitors. They look like Naskapi." Gudrod pointed to the northwest where a large group of people stood along the bluff above the river.

"Aye, I think you are right." Halfdan turned and shouted to a man near the north gate. "Tostig, open the gate!" He turned back to Gudrod. "I do not want them to think we are afraid."

"Unlike our first meeting with them I do not see women with this group." Gudrod studied the Naskapi carefully.

"They may be in the back. All I see are warriors and they are armed." Halfdan looked both ways at the men grouped along the parapets. "Come with me, all of you. Arm yourselves," he called back over his shoulder as Gudrod and the eight men near him hurried to follow.

Frida arrived in time to witness the men scatter to Halfdan's orders. She looked over the tops of the palisade logs and saw the Naskapi.

"Find Thora, Frida. I will want both of you with us. Meet us at the north gate," Halfdan ordered as he swept by her.

Frida scampered down the parapet ladder and ran to fetch Thora. She knew that Halfdan wanted Thora at the meeting with the Naskapi because of Thora's association with, and recent marriage to, Deskaheh the Haudeno, their former prisoner. Thoughts cascaded through her mind as she ran toward Thora's longhouse. *Thora speaks the Haudeno language. It is different from the dialect spoken by the Naskapi, but they understand each other well enough to communicate. Halfdan wants me along because of my natural facility with languages.* She smiled to herself. *Why, I can communicate with the natives almost as well as Thora.*

Frida found Thora near the animal pens, carrying a bucket of fresh milk from the morning milking. "Come, the Naskapi are back. Halfdan wants us to meet him at the north gate."

"I heard. Wait until I get rid of this milk."

"There is no time. Bring it," Frida said. "The men will be waiting."

* * *

Halfdan smiled when he saw the bucket of milk.

Thora shrugged. "I had to bring it. There was no time."

Gudrod lifted his chin toward the Naskapi. "Maybe the Naskapi will be thirsty."

The others laughed.

"The milk is a good idea. Bring a dipper, too, Thora," Halfdan said.

"There is one in the bucket."

"All right, let us go see what they want." Halfdan hitched up his sword belt, his men shouldered their spears and other arms, and they headed across the barley field toward their visitors.

Halfdan tried to count the warriors as he walked toward them, but finally gave up because they kept moving as men toward the back of the group craned this way and that trying to watch the Northmen.

"More Naskapi came this time. I make it fifteen or twenty. If I am not mistaken that tall man in the center is the leader we talked to before," Gudrod said.

Halfdan nodded. "It looks like him. There are women with them, too. See the one that just came out of the willows carrying a basket?"

"Aye, I see her."

"There are more in the willows," Tostig said from behind Halfdan and Gudrod.

"There are several baskets stacked behind those warriors," Frida said.

"Sling your bows men," Halfdan called over his shoulder. "I think they have come to trade."

"Thank the gods," Thora said.

"Gods, Thora? I thought you were a Christian." Frida's lips twitched slightly in a small smile.

"Not all the time," Thora quipped.

The others laughed. The Naskapi saw the smiles and heard the laughter.

"Keep it up. They like it," Halfdan said over his shoulder.

Halfdan came to a halt in front of the tall Naskapi warrior. He raised his hand toward the man, palm out. "I welcome you to Halfdansfjord in the name of my people."

A silence followed his greeting while each group took the other's measure.

The tall Naskapi's expressionless eyes regarded Halfdan. He said nothing. He nodded slightly. His black eyes shifted to Thora.

"Where is your man, woman?" He spoke to Thora in a deep clear voice. His eyes flicked to the bucket of milk.

Thora gestured into the hinterland. "My man hunts," she said simply. She sat the bucket down.

He inclined his head slightly in assent. His eyes played over the group of Northmen. They missed nothing, taking note of the bows slung over the men's shoulders and the grounded spear butts. He spoke over his shoulder to his men. They slung their bows and grounded their spears.

Halfdan looked at Thora.

"He asked me where Deskaheh was. I told him he was hunting," Thora said.

At mention of the name, Deskaheh, the tall Naskapi was all ears.

"He heard you, Thora." Halfdan held out a hand. "Give me a dipper of milk."

Thora handed him the dipper.

Halfdan raised the dipper to his lips, his eyes fixed on the Naskapi leader's face. He took a long drink of the still-warm milk, refilled the dipper, and passed it to the Naskapi. "Drink, it is fresh, warm milk."

Thora translated.

The man reached for the dipper and took a tentative sip. A look of surprise crossed his face; a smile transformed the grim, hard visage. He spoke a single word and drained the dipper.

Thora picked up the bucket. "Here, have some more." The other Naskapi responded to her radiant smile and crowded around their leader for a taste of milk.

Frida stepped up beside Halfdan. "Did you see the other women in the willows down by the river?"

"Aye, I did. He will decide when to have them come out." Halfdan saw the Naskapi leader watching him. He answered Frida without turning his head toward her.

"Why not ask him to come into the village to trade?"

"I will Frida. Be patient." He glanced at her in exasperation. "Thora, invite their leader to trade in the village." He looked toward Frida in time to see her arched eyebrow and smile. He sighed and stepped over to Thora and the leader.

"He has accepted, Halfdan."

"Good. I want to know his name."

Thora turned back to the Naskapi. She pointed at Halfdan.

He heard his name repeated as Thora spoke and signed.

The Naskapi spoke. "Halfdan, I am called Chisasi."

His pronunciation of Halfdan's name was close enough the group of Northmen understood.

Halfdan laughed. "I understood him," he said, grinning at Thora. "Chisasi." He rolled the word off his tongue, feeling it. "Chisasi, I, Halfdan, make you welcome here."

The two leaders shook hands.

"Is Chisasi the chief of the Naskapi?" Halfdan asked.

The Naskapi made eye contact with Halfdan as Thora asked the question. He shook his head. "I am not, Halfdan. I am a war chief of my Naskapi band."

"I thought he might be a war leader," Halfdan said, after Thora translated. "Tell him that Gudbj is our war leader."

Chisasi nodded thoughtfully, then turned and spoke to his men. One of the men wheeled away and trotted down to the riverbank.

"They have more women with them, Halfdan. He just told that man to go get them."

"Frida and I saw them. Their leader has decided to trust us."

Within moments, a single column of seven Naskapi women filed up out of the thick riverside willows. All carried packs and baskets of trade goods.

Gudrod looked back toward the village when he noticed movement out of the corner of his eye. People atop the palisade thinned and soon began flooding from the gate. Dogs circled the crowd yipping and barking. "Halfdan." Gudrod lifted his chin toward the village.

Halfdan looked at the crowd of his people walking toward them, and then back at the milling Naskapi. "Let them come. I think these people want to be friends."

The crowd of men, women, and children from the settlement merged with the two groups on the river's bluff. Barking dogs circled the milling people, caught up in the excitement.

With Halfdan and Chisasi surrounded by their people, the crowd walked toward the palisades of Halfdansfjord.

* * *

While he watched the bustle of trading between the Naskapi and his people, Halfdan reflected on the new village and all that had happened since they completed construction early this past spring during the Lambing Time Moon.

With the shorter days between the Haymaking and Harvest Time Moons, peaceful progress with the Naskapi finally came. *We built our settlement in Nitassinan, their Homeland, without their permission. Until today, I did not know if they would allow us to remain in this place. Now, I believe there is hope.* His eyes sought the tall figure of Chisasi. Thora stayed with Chisasi to interpret while the man watched his people trade and did some trading himself.

Halfdan's thoughts flashed back to their first meeting. An enraged Chisasi and twelve warriors appeared on the same river's bluff one morning. The man had come to confront the Northmen because two of them had raped two of his women. Upon hearing of the foul deed, Halfdan sent Gudbjartur to single the culprits out and bring them forward. He turned one rapist over to the Naskapi for their justice. The other, the instigator of the rape, suffered a horrible death at his chieftain's own hand. The Naskapi bore witness that justice was swift and terrible. Had he not acted decisively, Halfdan had no doubt the result would have been war. The man he now knew as Chisasi spoke not a word to him after the death of the two rapists. He just looked into his eyes a moment, nodded, and he and his men turned back the way they had come. There had been no further contact with the Naskapi until they made their appearance today.

* * *

Ingerd and Helga reclined against Thalmiut backrests on a bearskin rug with seven Naskapi women. They, too, had the same backrests, but the Naskapi women all leaned forward in postures of rapt attention. Several warriors stood idly by watching the expertise of the two Norse women as they plied one of their many skills.

"While Helga strings those pretty glass beads, I will cut two thin pieces off this copper sheet with my scissors and make a bracelet." Ingerd deftly sheared two long strips from the soft copper sheet. "I will twist each strip around and around until they are twisted along their entire length." She demonstrated by handing one end to the nearest woman, miming her instructions, and twisting her end while the woman held the other end still. She repeated her action with the second strip. Her audience, so far, was attentive. That was to change.

Ingerd held the two lengths of twisted copper up for all to see. "Helga and I are going to twist these two pieces of copper together now." They carefully joined the two twisted copper strips. Ingerd laid one end of the joined pieces on a small steel mandrel; with a few hammer blows, she forced the soft copper end into one of several different sized depressions in the mandrel's face. She repeated the process on the other end, swaging each end into a half-flattened ball. "Now comes the magic part." She grinned at her audience. "I will turn this round mandrel on edge and form the bracelet with my hammer." She hammer-formed the copper around the edge of the mandrel slowly and painstakingly, so as not to damage her creation.

Her audience still did not know what they were seeing.

Ingerd carefully worked the bracelet from the mandrel and used the edge of her knife to burnish the sharp edges. "Now I will polish this bracelet with a piece of soft leather and wood ashes." She looked at each of the women as she vigorously polished the finished bracelet. With a flourish, she revealed the shiny bauble.

Her audience gasped.

"Here, you helped, so I will give it to you." She placed it over the wrist of the young woman who had helped with the twisting.

Pandemonium broke out among the Naskapi women when they realized what Ingerd had created right before their eyes. Each of them had to try it on before it made its way back to its proud new owner.

Ingerd and Helga laughed happily at the display of genuine gratitude from the young woman. "Here," Helga said, "You should have this necklace. I made it for you." She draped the bead necklace over the head of another woman.

Squeals of delight went around the group as the necklace changed hands. Within a short time, every Naskapi woman had a bauble that the two artisans created for her. A pile of Naskapi trade goods—baskets, furs, leather clothing, and bark containers—accumulated between Ingerd and Helga as they produced copper bangles, baubles, and glass bead necklaces.

* * *

Halfdan watched the show from a distance. He had seen it all before, in the town of the Thalmiut. He shook his head at the skill and resourcefulness of the two Norse women. His eyes searched the crowd for the tall figure of Chisasi. Normally his height made him easy to see, but he was not standing erect, rather he stood next to the animal pens with several of his warriors and Thora. Halfdan got to his feet and strolled down to the pens to see what was happening. As he approached, he chuckled to see Chisasi and some of his men stooped over next to the fence, their elbows resting over the top rail. They looked as if they had watched animals thusly all of their lives. *I doubt that they have ever before seen an animal pen or a domestic animal larger than a dog,* he thought with amusement as he stepped up beside them. "What are you talking about?" he asked.

Chisasi and Thora turned toward him. "They are very curious to know what kind of animals we keep and what we do with them. I have shown them our cows, sheep, and goats, and explained that we make our cloth from wool and get the milk that they drank from them. I think it is too much all at once," Thora said.

"I cannot imagine how strange we are to them. We have much to learn from each other."

At that moment, a pig squealed, and one of the warriors pointed to a sow as she ran from inside her shelter and out into the large pen. The men had obviously never before seen a pig. Soon all of the Naskapi laughed at the spectacle of the muddy sow followed by her nine little piglets, their ears bouncing with every step, as she led them away from whatever had alarmed her. One of the men said something to the man next to him, and he laughed and slapped the fence rail.

Halfdan laughed with them. "Pigs are funny. Tell him that a sow with piglets is also dangerous."

Thora explained to Chisasi. "Pig," he said in a perfect imitation of the Norse word. "Women, too, can be dangerous when they have young." He laughed with his men. Thora smiled, giving Halfdan a sharp look.

"What did he say?" Halfdan asked.

"He said that women can be dangerous when they have young," Thora said.

Halfdan laughed with the Naskapi. "I can agree with that."

Thora changed the subject as they turned away from the animal pens. "He is pleased with the trading," she said. "Our people have been more than fair with every trade and I believe the Naskapi and our people are happy with the outcome."

Halfdan smiled upon hearing her report. "That is good. You have been a great help to me Thora, and I appreciate it."

She started to answer, but a question intruded.

"Where is your war leader?" Chisasi asked.

"I think he wants to know why Gudbj is not here," Thora said.

"My war leader, Gudbj, is away exploring the hinterland to the southeast. He will return during the next moon."

Thora spoke and signed to Chisasi at length. "He understands, but he still wonders why Gudbj is exploring rather than being here." Thora eyed her chieftain. "Chisasi was impressed when Gudbj threw his axe and brought down Ketill when he tried to run away, but did not kill him. He told me that his people have befriended us because you gave the rapist, Eyvindr, to him for their justice. Moreover, the other rapist, Ketill, died by your hand. Because of these things he stands here before you."

Halfdan made eye contact with Chisasi. "Those men deserved to die in a manner befitting their crime. Their attack on those young girls could not be forgiven." Halfdan gestured with his chin. "Tell him my words."

"He knows, but I will tell him anyway." Thora spoke to the Naskapi.

Chisasi held Halfdan's eyes. "You are a hard man, Halfdan. That is good. You have honor, too. That is better."

Thora translated.

The two leaders appraised each other. Their understanding and respect increased with the passage of each moment.

Halfdan came to a decision. He unbuckled his belt and removed his knife and its ornately carved scabbard. He draped the belt over his shoulder and examined the knife and scabbard. "I want to give him my knife." He took Thora by surprise.

"I thought you would not trade our weapons," Thora said.

"I am making an exception with this man. That is how important our friendship is with them. Tell him exactly what I am saying, Thora."

"I will do my best."

Halfdan handed the knife and scabbard to Chisasi. "I want you to have this gift, Chisasi, as a token of our friendship and the high personal regard I have for you. It is my hope that the trades we have made this day will be the first of many for our people, mine and yours."

Chisasi seemed taken aback by the generous personal gift. He examined the knife and scabbard. Easing the knife out of the scabbard, he admired the heat-blued blade and tested the honed edge with his thumb. A trickle of blood oozed from the cut. His face split in a grin. He raised the knife above his head and called to his men. They clustered around him as he showed them the knife and his cut thumb.

"You did the right thing. Your gift has impressed them." Thora watched the Naskapi. Chisasi sent one of his men away. "He told his man to fetch one of their baskets. I think he will want to give you a gift in return."

"That is not necessary," Halfdan said.

"It is to him, Halfdan. Deskaheh has told me of this custom. You must receive his gift as an equal to the gift you gave him or he will be insulted. It is their way," Thora said, as Chisasi walked toward them.

"I understand."

Chisasi presented Halfdan with a fur bundle tied at each end with a leather thong. "This is a life talisman of my people, Halfdan. It will protect you wherever you travel in Nitassinan."

Thora translated his words and signs.

"This fur is beautiful. Ask him what animal it comes from," Halfdan said as he untied the bundle.

"It is the fur of the skunk bear," Chisasi said before Thora could ask the question.

"It is from a skunk bear," Thora repeated.

"I do not know what that is, but the fur is thick and luxurious like a wolverine." Having untied both thongs, he unrolled the fur bundle.

Frida joined the group in time to see the expression on her husband's face when he caught sight of the contents of the bundle.

Halfdan straightened out the object and just stared, at a loss for words. He held it out so Frida and Thora could see.

The talisman consisted of a circlet of almost white leather, a hand's length wide, scraped thin, and worked until it felt like fine cloth. Radiating from a small, polished seashell in the center were closely spaced concentric rows of thin, highly polished bone splints with a tiny hole in each end. Each row of splints, stitched in place, radiated out to the outer edge of the leather on which they were mounted. The outer edge of the leather circlet was finished with closely spaced stitches. Braided sinew whippings within the circlet secured it to a polished withe of uniform thickness, the ends so cleverly mated that the joint was indiscernible.

"That is beautiful!" Frida exclaimed. "Whoever made this is a skilled seamstress and artisan. What is it for?"

"Chisasi told me that it is a life talisman that will protect me wherever I travel in Nitassinan," Halfdan said.

Chisasi picked up the talisman from the skunk bear skin. "You wear it around your neck." He tied it loosely at the back of Halfdan's neck and stepped back.

The talisman hung in the center of Halfdan's chest, suspended on a braided white leather cord. Halfdan held the talisman out and continued to examine it. He made eye contact with Chisasi. "I will treasure your gift of life."

The Naskapi nodded and thrust his new knife into the waist belt of his leggings.

"We have prepared food for everyone," Frida said. She turned to Chisasi and signed while she added her invitation. "We want you and your people to eat with us."

He nodded his understanding and spoke to one of his men, who left to gather the others. The Naskapi seemed fascinated by Frida's mass of red, curly hair and Chisasi was no exception. He reached out slowly and fingered her hair. She smiled and maintained eye contact with him.

"What is your name, woman?" Chisasi asked.

"I am called Frida." She pointed to Halfdan. "I am his woman."

"Frida," he repeated, looking from her to Halfdan. "Frida and Halfdan, I understand." He held his fists out and bumped the extended index fingers together.

Halfdan laughed. They all joined in as they walked to the community meeting hall. The hall comprised over half of Halfdan's longhouse, and the cooks had prepared the food on its large central hearth.

* * *

The size and construction of the longhouse fascinated the Naskapi. Halfdan took them on a tour, including the living area where he and Frida lived with their thralls.

Chisasi gestured around the living quarters. "Naskapi houses are similar but smaller." He pointed to the central hearth. "Our hearths are this high." He indicated his waist. Walking to a clear area of the inner wall, he bent forward to inspect the horizontal rows of saplings interlaced on the vertical roof support posts. He turned to Halfdan. "This is well-built and strong. Our walls are saplings covered with rolls of birch bark. Our houses last only a few seasons before the women must build new ones."

Thora translated as Chisasi spoke.

"We built our village to last many seasons, Chisasi, because we hope to live here in Nitassinan with the Naskapi." Halfdan watched the man's expression as Thora translated.

Chisasi's face conveyed not a hint of his feelings. "Whether or not you stay in this land is not my decision. Sachem will decide after a council of all the bands of the Naskapi. Only he will make the final decision."

"Where is Sachem? When will this council meet?"

"Sachem lives many days from here. I do not know when he will call the council together. It is late in the summer. Most of my people do not know you are in Nitassinan. I do not think the council will meet until next summer after all the bands of my people know you are here. It will take much time for this." Chisasi's eyes shifted between Halfdan and Thora as she translated.

"You have given me much to think about, Chisasi. I hope all the bands of the Naskapi will come here to meet us and that we can be friends."

Chisasi listened intently as Thora translated. His expression did not alter. He made no comment.

Halfdan's mood became circumspect as his conversation with Chisasi remained in the forefront of his thoughts. He did not expect the Naskapi to welcome his people warmly but he refused to succumb to thoughts of failure. *The gods led us here. They will show us the way to remain.*

* * *

To the cooks' credit, they fed the large crowd quickly, all eating their fill. Whale steak and codfish stew was the fare. It was obvious that the Naskapi were unfamiliar with both.

Nevertheless, they took to the food with gusto, following the lead of the helpful Northmen. Most of the people filled their individual trenchers and bowls, and then went outside to eat and bask in the warm sun.

A mixed crowd of Naskapi and Northmen remained in the hall, taking their meal at the trestle tables. Halfdan could see that the Naskapi had never before seen a table and benches. However, they quickly caught on.

After gorging on three half-raw whale steaks Chisasi discovered the codfish chowder. He washed down the steaks with two bowls of chowder, then sat up straight on the bench and gave vent to a tremendous belch. People laughed appreciatively. Freed of the filling gas bubble, his stomach could accommodate another bowl of chowder.

"The Naskapi eat like the Thalmiut we traded with on the voyage down here." Frida chuckled at the memory. "They gorge on food."

"Aye, they have known much hunger, I think. It is good to see them enjoying our food." Halfdan turned and looked out over the crowd in the hall. He was gratified to see his people mingled with their Naskapi guests. "Thora, tell Chisasi that they are welcome to stay the night if they wish. They can get an early start tomorrow." He watched the man while Thora translated.

"He will stay next time, Halfdan. They are eager to tell their band what they have learned here."

Halfdan nodded at the Naskapi. "I would do the same."

* * *

A large mixed group of Northmen walked to the river with Chisasi and his Naskapi. People scattered along the riverbank to help load and launch the six canoes.

Halfdan and Chisasi watched the easy mingling of their people from the bluff above the river.

Halfdan unconsciously fingered the life talisman. He shook hands with Chisasi, the two men made eye contact. "We have forged a friendship. I will see you again."

The Naskapi nodded and smiled. "You will see me again." He turned away and walked down the bluff to the canoes.

The flotilla made rapid progress against the slow-moving current with all the occupants wielding paddles. Chisasi looked back just before he went out of sight around the first bend. Halfdan lifted his arm in farewell. The Naskapi held his paddle aloft in reply.

Frida and Thora joined Halfdan. He had a distant look on his face.

"I know what you are thinking, my man. There is hope for our people here in Vinland," Frida said, looking into his eyes.

"Aye, there is. They will come back, and there will be others. If all are treated honestly and fairly the friendships forged here today will ensure the success of our two peoples." He looked at Thora. "You are responsible for much of our success, Thora. You did well."

Thora averted her eyes a moment, embarrassed. "I thank the gods for Deskaheh, for without him I could not have spoken with the Naskapi."

Halfdan smiled at her.

"Pishekat told me their village is on the shoreline of a lake a long day's paddle from here," Frida said, as the trio walked with the others back toward the village gate. "She said they will camp at dark today and resume their journey at dawn tomorrow. They will be home before midday."

"Pishekat, is she the young woman you spent so much time with?" Halfdan asked.

"Yes. She is pregnant with Ketill's child. Because of the child, her people will shun her. It is taboo among the Naskapi to have sex before a woman is mated according to custom."

"She was taken by force. It is not her fault, she was raped, Frida." Halfdan stopped walking and looked at his wife.

"I know that, but it does not matter. It is their way."

Halfdan accepted her explanation without comment as they continued toward the village gate.

"I saw Grimr watching you two talk. He was never far from Pishekat," Thora said.

"I noticed him, too," Frida said. "Although he had nothing to do with the rape, nor did he see what Ketill and Eyvindr did, he apparently feels sorry for her. However, I think it is more than that. He is attracted to her and she is aware that he is."

"This might be a good thing. I will speak to Grimr," Halfdan said. "I did not see the other young girl who was raped; she was not with them this time."

"No, she stayed in their village for some reason. Pishekat told me that the other girl is not with child. That is a blessing," Frida said.

"Aye, it is. Chisasi invited me to his village. I will think on it. In the meantime, I will talk to both Grimr and Thorkell about those two young Naskapi women. Perhaps, if they are interested in having a Naskapi mate I will take them with me to visit the band of Chisasi. If all are agreed, putting the four of them together might prove to be a good thing for our two peoples. And it also might serve to right some more of the wrong two of our men did to them." He paused in thought as they walked through the palisade gate. "Aye, I will think on these things."

* * *

Greenland Sea, west of Eiriksfjord

Late in the afternoon of the fifteenth day of the voyage from Halfdansfjord, Bjorn stood amidships; one hand rested on the rail and the other gripped a shroud to steady himself to the ship's motion as he strained to see through the opaque wetness that enveloped him and his ship. A dense fog bank and the calm wind that spawned it had forced the two ships bound for Eiriksfjord to drift with the current just offshore and almost within sight of their destination.

Crying seabirds, invisible overhead, told him that land was near. *But how near?* He felt like his head was in a bucket. Sound came to him hollowly, fooling his sense of direction, compressing time, and distance. In spite of his clothing being soaked, he did not feel chilled. The heavy wool of his tunic and cloak served to trap his body heat within its damp embrace. *In spite of delays because of fog or adverse wind, we have made a swift passage.* He wiped his streaming face with an equally wet hand. *Njord has smiled on us. I do not wish to anger him by complaining at this inconvenience.*

Accumulated moisture ran down every vertical surface of the ship, falling like rain from the standing rigging. Steed of the Sea rolled uneasily in the swells; the abrupt surge and snubbing action served to shake even more accumulated water from aloft. Normally taut rigging and blocks creaked and banged against unseen obstacles. The noise set his teeth on edge. *This god-cursed fog. I would not see Brodir's ship if she was right beside us.* That fact and his general sodden discomfort served to increase his angst at finding himself off a lee shore in command of Halfdan's ship. *I would not want to try to explain to my chieftain how Brodir and I tangled our ships together in the fog and piled up on the rocks at the entrance to Eiriksfjord.* He snorted to himself. *By Hel, I would rather drown in the surf than face him.* He gritted his teeth as the lookout's horn bellowed into the fog, followed a moment later by a similar blast from Brodir's ship. The sound reverberated back at him. He glanced at the sail, dimly visible as it hung limply from the yard, swinging back and forth it snubbed abruptly against the sheets after each roll of the ship. *Not a breath of wind. Great Thor, great Njord, chase the Fog Giant back into his lair and send the wind.*

"Deck there, I have sight of the Greenland icecap above the fog," Gauk shouted from his lookout post atop the sail's yard. "I think the Fog Giant will soon flee to his lair." He saw the deck dimly through the fog. The fog had thinned enough during the past hour that the icecap swam out the surrounding whiteness, just now becoming visible to him.

"How close are we to the shoreline?" Bjorn shouted back.

"I do not know. All I can see is the top of the icecap. There are many birds about so I think we are close. I might hear the surf soon." The disembodied answer came from aloft.

"By the gods," Bjorn cursed. *I will wait a little longer. Then we will have to row offshore until I can see where we are.* He chewed on his lower lip. He knew that the ship was in the grip of the Greenland current. It sped them north along the coast. *But to where?* Coming suddenly to the inevitable decision, he cupped his hands around his mouth.

"Thorgill, man the sweeps," he shouted aft to his second-in-command, knowing the big redhead expected the order and stood at the ready with his men. He made his way quickly aft along the catwalk around the load of timber and the bustle of his men as they deployed the long sweeps. "Gorm," he said, stepping up beside the helmsman a moment later, "steer us directly into the swells. I want to get offshore until I see where we are."

"Good idea." Gorm pushed the tiller away to adjust the big steering oar. He could not see the swells through the fog but instinctively made good the desired course by the motion of the ship as the speed slowly increased to steerageway. They all knew that swells came out of the northwest along this part of the Greenland coast under normal conditions. Rowing into them would ensure that the ship would gain the sea room necessary to remain a safe distance from the hazards of the rock-strewn coast.

The boom of the stroke drum echoed hollowly into the whiteness as the crewmembers rowed to its beat. *Brodir will hear the drum and follow*. His eyes searched the fog along the port side where he expected Brodir's ship to be.

Later, Bjorn estimated that they had rowed Steed of the Sea far enough so that he could relax until the fog cleared. "Hold the stroke," he called to his crew. The men rested at their sweeps, the drum ceased its measured booming, and he cupped a hand at his ear. Faintly he heard a drum beat through the fog. "Brodir," he said, grinning at Gorm. He called aft. "Stow the sweeps, men. That is enough for now. Gauk, give Brodir three blasts of your horn," he called aloft to the lookout.

The triple horn signal would tell Brodir of danger ahead so that he did not inadvertently row his ship into Steed of the Sea as she drifted north in the current. A moment later, a single long answering horn blast came through the fog.

"Deck there," Gauk shouted from the masthead. "I see the top of Brodir's mast above the fog, about five ship's lengths off the port beam. I cannot hear his drum so he has stopped rowing."

"Good!" Bjorn answered. "Can you see the coast yet?"

"No! Just the top of the icecap is visible. A light breeze just started. The fog begins to swirl," the lookout shouted.

Bjorn nodded in satisfaction. "It should not last much longer, then. I am ready for a drink of water and some fish. Do you want something Gorm?" he asked the helmsman.

Gorm shook his head. "No, I am going to wait until we get to Eiriksfjord. Some hot food will taste good after this dried meat and fish that we have eaten since we sailed from Halfdansfjord."

"Aye, it will," Bjorn said as he turned to make his way toward the food bags secured near the mast step.

* * *

Several days later, the two ships from Halfdansfjord bobbed at anchor far enough off the beach at Brattahlid in Eiriksfjord, to protect them from grounding damage during the huge daily tidal fluctuations. The cargoes of timber previously unloaded, or that which remained after the lively trading it occasioned, lay stacked on the rocky beach. Bags of barley, rolls of flax cloth, bars of smelted iron, clothing, leather bags of dried meat and fish, a sack or two of amber, large iron pots, kettles, assorted weapons, and cooking implements of every description accumulated in place of the priceless timber.

Bjorn shook his head as his eyes played over the bounty. People came in from farms as far away as Einarsfjord and Hrafnsfjord, a day's sail to the southwest, to trade as the word spread. A boat from Gardar, on the south shore of Eiriksfjord, had just traded a bale of arctic fox for a single log. The men carefully stowed the heavy green log, which barely fit along the keel, and gingerly pushed the overloaded boat off the beach as Bjorn watched with amusement. *A single puff of wind and they will swamp.* He chuckled as the boat rocked back and forth.

The small crew muttered oaths to the god Thor and at one another as they tried to turn the unstable craft around so that they could begin the long row home. Finally, in the true fashion of men born to the sea, the boat got safely underway.

Brodir stepped up at that moment, accompanied by a stranger.

Bjorn turned to them and laughed out loud. "This is crazy. People are not using good sense. Those men selected a log too heavy for that boat. They would not cut it in two so they could make two trips out of it, and look at them," he gestured.

Brodir and the stranger watched the spectacle for a time. "They do not have much freeboard to spare," the stranger observed with a chuckle. "Your log may float back in with the flood tide tonight after they swamp their boat."

Bjorn made eye contact with the man. "Perhaps," he said, glancing back toward the boat. "They should have brought a bigger boat or made two trips."

Brodir gestured at the stranger. "Bjorn, this is Thorgeirr. That is his ship that came in from Iceland yesterday," he said, pointing toward the ship anchored across the fjord.

The two men shook hands.

"You are an Icelander?" Bjorn said.

"Nay, I am from Hortafjorden."

"A Hortalander!" Bjorn exclaimed. "It is a long voyage you have sailed."

"Aye, and we are not finished yet," he said, a twinkle in his eye. In response to a questioning look from Bjorn he continued. He gestured toward his ship. "We had a meeting of the minds yesterday," he said, referring to the members of his ship's company. "With the exception of a man and woman who have kin on Greenland, my shipmates wanted me to ask you if we can sail with you to Halfdansfjord."

Bjorn glanced at Brodir.

"I told them all about our settlement. They agreed to a man," Brodir said.

Bjorn said nothing for a moment as he digested this news. "You do not need to ask me, Thorgeirr. You are a freeman. You may come if you wish, and welcome."

"Good, so be it then," Thorgeirr said with obvious enthusiasm. "Come, I would like you to tell my people the good news."

Bjorn glanced doubtfully toward their trade goods and the ricks of logs.

"Go ahead, Bjorn, I will stay here to handle our trading," Brodir rumbled in his deep voice.

Bjorn absentmindedly twisted the end of one of his sideburn braids as he paused in thought. "All right, I will go with you to your ship, Thorgeirr. I want to get something from my ship first. You might have need of it on the voyage to Halfdansfjord," he said over a shoulder as he pushed a boat from the shore and began to row to his ship.

Thorgeirr looked quizzically at Brodir who shrugged. The two sat back down on the logs to wait.

Brodir reclined back into the natural depression between two logs, clasped his hands behind his head, and watched several dark brown, great skua gulls wheeling overhead in their eternal quest for prey. "How long would it take those skuas to fly to Halfdansfjord?"

Thorgeirr shielded his eyes as he glanced aloft. "Not as long as will take us, judging from what you have told me."

"They could fly high and in a straight line. The Fog Giant could not reach them," Brodir mused. Reverie broken by the rattle of oars coming aboard as the bow of the ship's boat crunched ashore, he lurched to his feet to see what Bjorn had brought. He instantly recognized the tightly rolled leather cylinder. "Gudbjartur's map," he said. "That is a good idea. We might become separated on the return voyage."

Bjorn spread the map out atop a log. "Halfdan's lieutenant, Gudbjartur Einarsson drew this map of our voyage to Halfdansfjord. This is a copy that he made."

Brodir pointed out prominent landmarks and course bearings with a stick as the three pored over the details of the map. "Every time we changed course, Gudbj took a bearing. As you can see, the result is a good outline of the coast."

"I have never before seen anything like this," Thorgeirr said, his tone conveying his impression of the map's usefulness.

"The map begins here at Snorrisfjord." Bjorn pointed out the fjord and other landmarks at the top edge. "We sailed almost due west until rounding this headland. These islands are a good ways further west, but we sailed between the big island and the headland. There are skerries close to shore, as Gudbj has drawn here, so do not cut the corner too closely. Following the coastline will bring you around to a southerly course once you clear the headland. Except for avoiding the islands and skerries he has drawn, your course will be mostly southerly all the way to here." He pointed to Halfdansfjord at the bottom.

Thorgeirr shook his head as he continued his examination of the map's details. "I am not good with the runes. Fortunately, there are two runesmiths onboard. What are these numbers with some of the courses?"

A deep rumbling laugh came from Brodir. "I cannot read them either, but they are soundings for when you get close inshore."

Thorgeirr grinned at the two men. "I will look forward to meeting Gudbj. With his map I can find my way to Halfdansfjord." He stabbed a finger down on a good drawing of a large whale. "He is a man of many talents to be able to draw these animals so that I can know what kind they are."

"Deskaheh is the artist. Gudbj told us that he drew all the animals and fish on the map," Bjorn said.

"Who is Deskaheh?" Thorgeirr stumbled over the unfamiliar name.

"Brodir and I captured him after a battle with his men. He is a Haudeno war chief and the only survivor. We killed all his fellows," Bjorn said.

"It is a long story. He is one of us now and all our people have accepted him." Brodir chuckled at the look of confusion that crossed Thorgeirr's face. "He is a good man; you will grow to accept him, as we all did. You will find that there will be much for you to get accustomed to at Halfdansfjord."

"I suppose so," Thorgeirr answered dubiously. He rolled up the map and thrust it into his belt.

"Good. Brodir will tell you the sailing directions from here to Snorrisfjord before you make sail. Now, let us go to talk to your people," Bjorn said.

Brodir resumed his comfortable position among the logs. Without further comment, the other two men launched a boat for the row across the fjord to Thorgeirr's ship.

* * *

Several days later, Bjorn and Brodir sat on their diminished supply of trade logs. The small pile represented all that remained of the two ships' loads that they had brought to Greenland. They had been watching a small boat row from the other side of the fjord while they chewed on cold meat joints.

"Eirik comes," Brodir said. Eirik, his unmistakable red hair blowing in the wind, and his companion, stepped from their boat and made their way up the beach toward them.

"Aye, and the man with him is his son, Leif, I think. I have only seen him once, but I think that is he," Bjorn said, as they got to their feet.

"I do not know him," Brodir said, "but if he is Eirik's son that is good enough for me."

"Aye, that may have been his ship that sailed into the fjord this morning." Bjorn said.

Eirik came to a halt. He nodded a greeting to the two men and gestured at his companion. "This is my oldest son, Leif." He lifted his chin toward Bjorn and Brodir. "These men are Bjorn Kjetilsson and Brodir Thorfisson. They are Halfdan Ingolfsson's men."

The four men shook hands all around.

"Leif returned this morning from Vestfold by way of Herjolfsnes and Ketilsfjord," Eirik said. "He has seen the king." Eirik regarded his son, a twinkle in his eye. "The king does not hold me against Leif. He told me that the king did not even mention me." His great booming laugh echoed out over the fjord. "How soon they forget, eh?"

"He remembered you all right. Otherwise I could not have gotten an audience with him." Leif glanced toward the mountain of trade goods. "You men have done well. A ship comes here from Ketilsfjord tomorrow. I think they will take the remaining logs."

"First come, first served as they say. There may not be any left when they arrive," Brodir rumbled.

Bjorn revealed their plans in response to the looks directed at Brodir for his rather direct statement. Brodir did not know the meaning of diplomacy, nor did he seem aware of how Eirik and Leif regarded his statement.

"We are anxious to return to Halfdansfjord. Brodir sails on the ebb tide tomorrow with our trade goods. I will sail on the ebb tide the following day. That is provided the remaining logs are gone." Bjorn had no wish to antagonize these two powerful men.

Eirik nodded. "It is good to return soon. The Fog Giant remains in his lair for the present. This morning the chill of weather change crept into my bones. This time of year, Njord can bring a storm any day on the bosom of the north wind. Then you might not sail at all."

Leif glanced at Brodir. "We heard that Thorgeirr sails with you."

"Aye, he sails with me. Bjorn will trade with the Thalmiut on his way back to Halfdansfjord. I am not stopping."

"Thalmiut?" Eirik said.

Bjorn laughed. "They are natives of the tundra. Twelve men came to our encampment one day. We called them Skraelings before we met them. They are good people. Halfdan has traded with them and he values their friendship. He wants to cement our relationship with more trading. They will recognize his ship."

"That will be a novelty, being on friendly terms with the natives. We certainly do not have that on Greenland. The Skraelings stay away from us and we seldom try to trade with them," Eirik said.

"Perhaps we should try to trade with them," Leif observed.

"When you are the chieftain you can do that, Leif. While I am chieftain we will not change our dealings with the Skraelings." Eirik's infamous temper simmered just below the surface. He held it loosely in check, ready to burst forth at the slightest provocation, real or perceived.

Leif abruptly changed the subject. "Thorgeirr has forty-eight people in his expedition. We hoped they would remain on Greenland, but after he talked to you, Bjorn, he told us that they had a meeting among themselves, deciding Vinland was best for them."

"Aye, two people have kinfolk at Lysufjord," Bjorn said. He glanced across the fjord. "They will stay here to wait for the next ship to sail up north. At first, we thought we could drop them off on the way by. I changed my mind because too much time would be lost working the ship into and out of Lysufjord. They do not mind waiting. Everyone else goes to Vinland. Thorgeirr's ship is crowded. He wants to spread his people out into our ships. Even with all our trade goods we have small crews so there is plenty of room for them."

His companions nodded without comment. Brodir had been watching his friend keenly.

"What do you keep looking at over there, Bjorn?" Brodir asked, his eyes sweeping the opposite shoreline.

"Nothing, really," he said.

"He is watching that tall, blonde woman," Eirik said, a big grin on his face.

Bjorn grinned at his companions. "Aye, I am. I did not see her in the ship's company when I was there the other day." His eyes followed her as she worked at various tasks. "She looks good from here."

The men laughed at him.

"She looks even better from over there," Leif said. "She is as tall as you. I think you two would be eye to eye. Fine sons would be made by the two of you."

Bjorn grinned at him. "I wonder why I did not see her the other day. She is hard to miss."

"She and some other women from Thorgeirr's ship were visiting with my wife, Thjodhildr," Eirik said. "They must have been at our hall when you and Thorgeirr talked to his people."

Bjorn paused in thought, his eyes still followed the woman's movements. "Does anyone know her name?"

The men shook their heads.

"Go ask her, Bjorn. I will be here until your return," Brodir said. "I did not know that you were interested in women." He watched his friend closely.

"I have never been interested." Bjorn glanced at each of the men. "Now I might be."

Eirik and Leif seemed amused. "Go ahead, Bjorn. We are going to trade Brodir out of the remaining logs while you are gone," Leif said.

"Good, you do that. I will sail with Brodir and Thorgeirr with the ebb tide if you can make your trade," he said with enthusiasm. He turned and strode purposefully down to one of several boats drawn up on shore.

"We may not see you before you sail. Have a good voyage, Bjorn," Eirik called after him.

He waved a hand in response. The laughter of his companions faded as he rowed away. A pleasant smile curved his lips. *Yes, it is time I thought of a mate. Another long winter comes and company in my bed would be welcome. Perhaps this is the one.*

* * *

Later, Bjorn rowed slowly back to his ship. He had arranged with Thorgeirr for the transfer of eight volunteers to his ship. A similar number would transfer to Brodir's ship.

He felt warm all over. A strange feeling had come over him, one in which he was unaccustomed. He and Ingunn had an instant bonding. Each saw in the other what they had searched for through the years. Their first time together was necessarily brief for much work remained before the ships sailed from Eiriksfjord. The promise of things left unsaid occupied their minds as each went to their work.

Her name rolled off his tongue, enchanted him, "Ingunn," he said aloud. "Ingunn Hákonsdattur." He smiled happily. *She will come aboard Steed of the Sea with the others by nightfall. We sail before dawn tomorrow, together.* Firmly in the grip of his daydream and unaware of his position relative to the shoreline, sudden awareness returned as the boat's bow collided with the stony beach.

* * *

Chapter Three

Halfdansfjord

Chisasi and his people had departed for their village two days hence when Halfdan happened to notice Grimr and Thorkell returning from a successful hunt late in the afternoon. Seeing the two jogged his memory. *I intended to talk to them about the Naskapi girl. Now, I have forgotten her name,* he thought, as he walked toward the two men.

Grimr and Thorkell stopped when they saw Halfdan turn in their direction. They exchanged uneasy glances. They had done their best to avoid his attention, hoping the incident to which they had borne witness in the recent past would fade from the collective memory, especially Halfdan's memory. Their chieftain was a fearsome man, brutal if need be, and well they knew it.

Halfdan stopped, nodding a greeting to them. "I want to talk to you about those two Naskapi girls," he said, getting right to the point. His eyes squinted in the bright sunlight as he looked from man to man, making it hard to read his expression.

"Halfdan, we. . .," Grimr began, his discomfort obvious.

Halfdan's lips curved in a smile. His low chuckle interrupted Grimr in mid-sentence. "The rape of those girls continues to plague you both." The matter-of-fact statement did nothing to hearten the two. His hard eyes belied the warmth the slight smile would indicate. "Good! It is well to remember the fate of Ketill and Eyvindr. Had you not distanced yourselves from their act your spirit would roam the Underworld with them; your bones would lie scattered by the beasts of the darkness, as theirs do."

Grimr shuddered and darted a glance at his companion. "Well we know that, Halfdan. It is something that we will never forget."

Halfdan looked at Thorkell. The man had not spoken. He returned the look of his chieftain without flinching, bobbing his head slowly in agreement.

"The matter is over. You men have no reason for concern. I bear you no malice," he said. He turned his attention to Grimr. "If you are willing, I have a suggestion. I am aware that you have an interest in one of the young Naskapi women. I have forgotten her name."

"She is called Pishekat," Grimr said.

"Pishekat. Aye, that is it," Halfdan said. "She seems to approve of your interest. You are aware that she is with child?"

Grimr nodded.

"Chisasi invited me to his village. He, too, is aware that you have this interest." He looked at Grimr. "Do you want to go?"

Grimr held Halfdan's eyes. "Aye, I would," he answered without hesitation.

"Her people will shun Pishekat. No Naskapi will take her to his lodge." Halfdan took a seat on a handy bench. Grimr and Thorkell followed his lead.

"Why will she be shunned?" Grimr asked. Sudden awareness came before Halfdan answered. He frowned. "The Naskapi will blame her even though none of it was her fault."

Halfdan nodded. "Thora has told me that this is their way. Both girls will be shunned because they have lain with a man and are not married."

Silence reigned for a time.

Halfdan looked at Thorkell. "Are you interested in a mate?"

"I have not thought about it. Why?" He shifted on the hard bench and watched Halfdan expectantly.

Halfdan leaned forward, looking from one to the other. He paused a moment for emphasis before answering. "Think about it now, Thorkell. Both of you are young men. You should raise families. I have no doubt that you would, were it possible." He grinned at them. "I can tell you from my own experience that a mate will change your life."

Grimr returned the grin. Thorkell seemed dubious. He pulled his fingers through his beard. "I am uncertain that I want the change, Halfdan. Women can weigh a man down with their demands." He took out his knife, shaved a splinter from the edge of the bench, and picked his teeth in contemplation.

"Gudbj and I have spoken several times about the women problem that we have always had. Gudbj told me once that the solution might rest with the native people. I view this situation as an opportunity for my people. You two men might provide the beginnings of a solution. In so doing we can forge a bond founded in mutual trust between our two peoples. Think about it, both of you. Give me your answer as soon as possible." Halfdan stood and stretched.

"I have thought of little else, Halfdan. I look forward to the journey," Grimr said, getting to his feet.

Halfdan glanced at Thorkell, who stood up as well. "I will think about it. That other girl is too young to want a mate. She might not be interested in me anyway, Halfdan. We have never spoken. I do not even know her name," Thorkell said, his lame excuses doing nothing to dissuade either of his companions.

"That is not what you told me when the Naskapi came to trade. You said that she was pretty. You wished that she had come with Chisasi," Grimr said. He laughed at his friend's discomfort. "You are just making excuses."

Thorkell glared at him.

Halfdan clapped the man on the shoulder. "Just think it over, Thorkell. I do not need your answer now. If you are interested, as Grimr has said, give yourself a chance. It might be your only opportunity. Winter approaches, a warm and willing woman will make all the difference to you."

"I will think about what you have said. By this time tomorrow I will decide."

"Fair enough, until tomorrow then." Halfdan nodded to the two men and turned toward his longhouse. He felt satisfied. *By Thor, this could be the beginning of something good for all of us.*

* * *

Gudbjartur's scouting party
150-leagues southeast of Halfdansfjord

Gudbjartur, at Deskaheh's suggestion, had decided to utilize two of the captured, lightweight, birch bark canoes rather than the much heavier ship's boats. He had many opportunities to be thankful for both the canoes and Deskaheh as the arduous journey continued.

Reluctantly, because of the bulk and added weight, Gudbjartur had made the decision to include a few items of trade goods with their meager supplies and he parceled them out with his men. They consisted of bright pieces of cloth, combs, glass bead necklaces, and a few of Ingerd's copper baubles. He hoped these few items would provide a means to communicate peaceful intent to the strangers they would surely meet on their journey overland to the sea.

As the expedition penetrated the interior, the beauty of the countryside struck them. Heavy forest, both hardwood and evergreen, interspersed with large open grasslands and fens, bisected by rivers, lakes, and small freshets too numerous to count, unfolded before them as they paddled rapidly along their way. Wildlife of every description abounded. In the interest of speed, Gudbjartur insisted they stick with the dried rations rather than lose time on a hunt. There would be plenty of time for that after they reached their objective.

Deskaheh knew the country intimately, having been on many forays against his traditional enemies, the Naskapi, who lived all over this land in scattered bands. For this was the Naskapi's Nitassinan or Homeland in their language.

Dawn of the sixth day of travel found the expedition nearing journey's end. The preceding day had seen them crest a divide after a long overland portage; the remainder of the journey to the sea was downstream.

Just before full darkness, they nosed the two canoes into the bank for the night. They found Naskapi sign in abundance. Deskaheh told Gudbjartur that the sign indicated they were close to a Naskapi village. Gudbjartur told his men he hoped to avoid discovery until they could approach the Naskapi openly during the hours of daylight.

The setting sun cast its shafts of intense light through the thick forest canopy as if to make one last effort to hold the long shadows of late evening at bay. Nevertheless, the darkness won out.

Without a fire to cast its glow over the campsite, the sharp outlines of the men scattered about the small clearing soon began to soften and blend with the surroundings. Gudbjartur relaxed against the upturned base of a downed pine tree. The campsite he had selected was near the center of a brush-covered island in mid-river. Just after they carried the canoes into the island's center, he personally checked the campsite's security from both sides of the river and saw no sign of his men or the canoes.

The men ate the dried fish, meat, and pemmican they carried. They sat cross-legged on the ground or reclined against a tree trunk, relaxing while listening to the wet gurgling of the river. The sound of the flowing water had a hypnotic quality about it and served to dampen the sounds of the night forest.

The masking sounds of the river also allowed the men to converse in subdued tones without fear of detection. "This pemmican is not bad, Deskaheh. I am beginning to get used to it," Snorri said, as he took another bite.

"That is good," Deskaheh said. "It is heavier to carry than dried meat or fish but it is tasty and filling."

"How far are we from the sea?" Gudbjartur asked.

Deskaheh turned toward Gudbjartur, barely visible against the dark tree roots. "Tomorrow morning we will enter a big lake. If the wind is not blowing and we paddle across the middle, we can be in the river that flows to the sea sometime after midday. By nightfall we should fetch up to the long saltwater bay."

"Good. We will make a kill tomorrow. Some fresh meat will be welcome," Gudbjartur said.

* * *

Gudbjartur had kept his two canoes in the center of the watercourse wherever possible, in the hopes of giving them a slight edge when the inevitable encounter with the people of this land occurred.

Just after midday of the seventh day of their journey, they encountered Naskapi in the wide, slow-moving river that issued from the big, almost circular lake they had crossed.

There were more than a dozen warriors in the group, both ashore or lounging in one of their canoes. They froze in various attitudes of surprise as the Northmen materialized in their river.

Gudbjartur was in the bow of the lead canoe as they rounded a bend in the river. He saw the Naskapi men with their three canoes pulled up on the opposite riverbank at the same time they saw him and his men.

"Naskapi!" Gudbjartur called the warning. "Paddle toward them. This is as good a time as any to make contact. Deskaheh, you do the talking. Tell them who we are and that we want to trade."

Deskaheh inclined his head in assent, his attention on the Naskapi as the Northmen's two canoes paddled slowly toward them.

* * *

The Naskapi warriors remained immobile, watching the Northmen as they approached.

Deskaheh stood erect slowly, bracing himself from side-to-side in the unstable canoe. He held a swatch of brilliant blue wadmal aloft for all to see. "I am with the men of the north. We come in peace, to trade," he shouted in his Haudeno tongue.

Beyond a slight stirring among the Naskapi, like dry leaves in a sudden wind gust, there was little response. The tongue of their enemies set them to talking. Although he was dressed as his companions, the man's language and distinctive features were plain to see.

The sudden movement among the Naskapi drew a warning from Deskaheh as he sat back down abruptly. "Watch out, some of them have put arrows to their bowstrings! They do not appear friendly now, Gudbj. I believe they will attack."

"Stop paddling," Gudbjartur hissed over his shoulder as the Naskapi scattered out along the shoreline. Suddenly an arrow thudded into the upthrust prow of Gudbjartur's canoe. Had it not been for the prow the arrow would have struck him in the chest. "Turn around to port, paddle back upstream," Gudbjartur shouted as he flailed at the water with his paddle, in a frenzy to turn the bow. Several arrows followed them as their canoes made the turn upstream, miraculously missing all aboard.

"Here they come!" Snorri shouted from the second canoe. "They are in all three canoes."

"Good," Gudbjartur called to his crew at large. "We might be able to stay ahead of them. I think we have more paddlers in each boat."

The pursuit by the Naskapi cut off any chance of continuing downstream to their destination. Hollering enthusiastically, the Naskapi tried to close the distance. A few well-placed arrows from the powerful longbows of the Northmen kept them at bay.

The grind of paddling against the current turned the chase into a grueling contest between both sides as the men settled to the task. With five men in each canoe, Gudbjartur and his men stayed ahead of their pursuers for the remainder of the day. The cloaking darkness ensured safety from pursuit, as Deskaheh had told them that the Naskapi disliked fighting at night.

Later that night another mid-river island provided the men with a short rest before they re-entered the big lake. The exhausted men lolled about in the thick brush.

Gudbjartur gathered them together for a quick, whispered, conference. "We will rest here through the night. I want to launch before dawn and make an all-out effort to get far enough into the lake so that we cannot be seen from the shoreline."

"Gudbj, it would be best if we split into two groups. They will use the night to get ahead of us. They will be waiting somewhere in the lake," Deskaheh said.

"Why don't we just travel at night? If they do not fight at night we might avoid them." The whispered voice came out of the gloom.

"We will not avoid them, Snorri. This is their land. They will use all their skills to capture us. Their leader will have sent a runner to warn the people. Other warriors will join them on the hunt. My people would do the same. If we stay in our canoes, sooner or later we will round a bend of the river, and they will be there," Deskaheh said.

Gudbjartur listened to his men without comment as most entered the conversation. His mind grappled with the extreme danger of their position as he cast about for the best course of action. His intent was to befriend the Naskapi, trade with them. Unfortunately, that did not seem to be a possibility given the hostility demonstrated by their pursuers. Silence came to the island; the conversation ebbed as individuals drifted into fitful sleep.

As before, a single guard remained alert, waking his relief when he could no longer stay awake.

* * *

Gudbjartur awakened with a jerk. A damp blanket of early morning haze and mist hung in the still air above the river. He was thoroughly chilled and damp with dew. He got stiffly to his feet and shivered as a chill coursed through his body. Peering around the small island to the limit of visibility, checking for signs of danger, he stamped his feet to drive the chill from his bones. Others began to stir, rising from the ground like specters. Deskaheh suddenly materialized at his side. *By the gods, the man's stealth is unnerving.*

"I have checked the island and the riverbanks. We are alone," Deskaheh said.

"Good. So far we have been lucky." He beckoned his men to gather round. "As Deskaheh suggested, it is probably best that we separate into two groups. This limited visibility may give us a better chance to make good our escape. I will take half of you and take the right fork. Snorri, you take the rest of the men up the other fork. I hope to elude pursuit and either regroup later or continue back to Halfdansfjord separately. Either way, head back to Halfdansfjord as quickly as possible."

Without further ado, the groups separated. The mist quickly swallowed the canoes as they rapidly paddled upriver.

* * *

Gudbjartur was unaware of the fate of the other boat crew after they separated, and was not able to waste any thoughts on them. His crew's bid for freedom in the cloaking river mist was short-lived. As Deskaheh had predicted, they rounded a bend in the river and almost ran into two canoes of Naskapi. The hostiles had drawn their canoes out of the water while they rested on the riverbank. Quickly recovering from their surprise when the Northmen surged by, they set off in pursuit. Although they managed to maintain their lead, Gudbjartur knew that escape by canoe was not to be. With two canoes of Naskapi in pursuit, it would only be a matter of time before more of them blocked the river ahead.

He quickly made the only possible decision. "Head into that small cove," he shouted. "Hide the canoe in the trees. Quickly! They are almost upon us. Each of you run in a different direction. Good luck!"

Gudbjartur watched a moment as his men melted into the forest. His heart thudded in his chest. *I hope that the natural gloom of the forest will aid their escape.*

He turned his attention back to the river, straining to hear any unusual sounds as his eyes swept up and downstream. He sighed in resignation and pulled the axe from its belt keeper so it would not bang against his legs. Quickly surveying the edge of the heavy woods, he picked out a course for his bid for freedom and ran straightaway from the river. He ran at top speed for a considerable time. Thoughts tumbled through his mind as he bobbed and weaved through the heavy undergrowth like a crazed bull. Branches whipped and plucked at him, seemingly in a bid to deny him passage. Too big and heavily muscled to be a good runner, he knew his enemies would catch him if they found his trail. His tremendous strength, endurance, and sheer will power had always stood him in good stead in life's games of survival. This would be different though. He did not underestimate the men who chased him. Although he came among them with little exposure or prior knowledge, he instinctively knew them to be tough, resourceful adversaries. *This is their land. Here they are the supreme predator.*

Abruptly he changed direction for a time, continuing his plodding run until his breath came in ragged gasps. He stopped and listened for sounds of pursuit, detecting none. Spent from exertion and the fear of capture, he knew he must rest. A windfall jumble of dead trees and brush presented itself, and he crawled into it and covered himself with the detritus of the forest floor. A concerted effort slowed his breath and racing heart. With a sigh, he closed his eyes and tried to empty his mind.

Beyond the natural sounds of the forest, he heard nothing, as he lay comfortably burrowed inside the windfall. In spite of a few bothersome insects, sleep finally claimed him.

Waking with a start, he did not know where he was for a moment. Realization came with the moldy smell of the rotten leaves that covered him. Stretching slowly to ease muscles cramped by long inactivity on the damp ground, he suddenly froze into immobility as movement caught his eye.

Materializing from the gloom of the forest, a Naskapi warrior glided soundlessly forward. Unconsciously placing each foot before actually settling his weight into the step, the man came to a halt directly in front of the windfall hiding place. He had heard, or sensed something.

Maybe he heard me stretch. Almost holding his breath in his effort to remain quiet, Gudbjartur averted his eyes out of fear the man might sense his gaze. The hot flush of fear that discovery could come at any moment caused his heart to thud in his chest. The blood beat wildly in each temple and against the backs of his eyeballs deep within his skull as it coursed through his veins. The pressure built in his ears until he thought the Naskapi would certainly hear the roaring.

The man stood within feet of his lair, his body rigid as he listened intently for a repeat of that which had drawn his attention. A ray of sunlight chanced to fall across the Naskapi's face at that moment.

Gudbjartur glanced quickly at the man, and then away, knowing that the Naskapi would detect his presence if he stared at him. The Naskapi, like he himself, was an animal. As such, he readily recognized the presence of another dangerous animal, one that watched or stalked him.

As the ray of sunlight moved over the Naskapi's face, Gudbjartur again glanced quickly at him, indelibly imprinting the man's features in his mind as the black eyes seemed to bore directly into his soul. As close as the man was, it was not possible for him to distinguish Gudbjartur from the mass of leaves and twigs that covered him. However, he stopped breathing nonetheless, and slowly closed his eyes. Resolving to attack the man now, rather than wait for the discovery of his hiding place, he gripped the axe tightly in anticipation. Slowly he gathered himself to lunge from the windfall.

The shrill call of a bird caused the Naskapi to turn his head toward the sound and away from Gudbjartur's lair. The man tilted his head back, cupped both hands around his mouth and an identical answering call came from his throat. He turned his head back toward the windfall once again, his body held rigidly as before. The black eyes minutely examined the pile of rubble for a moment. Then he turned and made off in the direction of the signal, as silently as he had come.

Gudbjartur slowly relaxed after the Naskapi disappeared from view. He stayed where he was for a time, still in a high state of anxiety from the close encounter.

Finally, he carefully extricated himself from his hiding place. Although loath to leave its safety behind, he knew he must distance himself from this place or the ordeal would never end. So he, too, moved off into the forest, with as much stealth as he could muster, knowing in his heart that escape depended on his skill and the luck of the gods.

His pursuers were a part of the forest itself. He was unsure if he could elude men who moved through the forest as silently as a wisp of smoke.

* * *

As sunlight brought its warmth to the south slopes and chased the chill of the night from his body, Gudbjartur watched the seven Naskapi warriors from his place of concealment near the highest point of the escarpment where he had spent a fitful night. The warriors had suddenly materialized from the dark forest and scattered out over the grassy meadow below his position. He knew they were casting about for his tracks from last night.

He was hungry and tired. The chase had left him few reserves of energy. Intuition told him the end was near. His pursuers continued to close in and he could not hope to avoid capture through the hours of daylight. He had been lucky last night and well he knew it. He had walked down the center of a small stream to conceal his tracks and hid inside a beaver lodge for a time. He smiled to himself as he thought about how agitated the two beavers had been at the intrusion. But the Naskapi dogged his trail no matter what he did, whatever deception he tried.

If they continue in their present direction they cannot fail. I must double back on them. Otherwise, I will have no chance of escape. He saw them clearly now as the intervening distance lessened. Sunlight glinted from their sweaty skin. The chase had not been easy for them either. As they crossed the meadow below his position, he ducked quickly as one of the warriors stopped to study the escarpment where he lay hidden. Suddenly a yell from below told him all he needed to know. They had found his tracks.

Gudbjartur crawled backwards until he was well below the brow of the escarpment, jumped to his feet, and ran rapidly down the back slope, dodging trees, and leaping windfalls, intent only on distancing himself from his pursuers.

Still at a dead run, he broke out of the dense forest onto the edge of a cliff that overlooked the open water of a large lake. He knew immediately his race was over. The cliff ended on a large outcropping far above the rocky shoreline, trapping him like a fly in a spider web. He stepped carefully to the edge and looked down. At the base of the cliff, a jumble of jagged boulders extended to the water's edge. He knew he could not hope to jump out far enough to reach the water. *If the fall does not kill me the water will, for I cannot swim. It is finished unless I suddenly sprout wings and fly like those two buzzards circling over the ridge,* he mused as he surveyed the area. *They have me trapped. I have no place left to run.*

He looked out over the open water. The choppy surface shimmered like a cascade of bright silver coins in the afternoon sunlight. With one last glance offshore, he sighed, and turned to confront his pursuers as they burst whooping in triumph from the forest.

* * *

The Naskapi warriors fanned out in a semi-circle before their prey, eliminating all avenues of escape.

The men studied Gudbjartur with childlike curiosity. Standing before them was a large, bearded man, clad in brightly colored red and blue-patterned clothing of a material unknown to them. He wore a short-sleeved, knee-length pullover tunic and ankle-high leather shoes. An ornately carved leather scabbard and pouch hung from the broad leather belt that encircled his waist. The bone handle of a long-bladed knife protruded from the scabbard. A broad, sweat-soaked headband kept a full head of unruly light brown hair from his eyes. He was unlike anyone they had ever before seen. A head taller than any of them and heavily muscled, the man exhibited a confidence and bearing that gave them pause; they saw no outward sign of fright or nervousness in his unblinking, pale blue eyes.

* * *

Gudbjartur examined the men who had him cornered with the same care they gave him. Slowly he shifted from side-to-side, keeping his eyes on all seven of them, alert for the slightest advantage. He gripped his long-handled battleaxe with both hands, holding it waist high, close to his body, with an easy familiarity born of long association. Sunlight reflected off the honed cutting edge of the wide blade, giving the fearsome weapon a mystical appearance.

He took careful note of the variety and extent of the Naskapi weaponry. Their weapons were inset with skillfully knapped, jagged-edged stone blades of varying shape and length: hatchets, wooden war clubs, knives, bows, spears, and other weapons unfamiliar to him. He also noted that none of his adversaries had any arrows left after the long chase and reflected he was fortunate in that regard, else he would already be dead.

The warriors were naked above the waist except for the colorfully decorated vests some of them wore. Hip to ankle leather leggings looped to a belt that also provided support, front, and back, for a breechclout between their legs, and leather ankle high shoes completed their attire. Their heads were shaven clean, except for a wide roach, or mane of hair, from front to back on top. They had smeared all their exposed skin with something that colored it a uniform light red, giving them a shiny, almost greasy appearance in the bright sunlight. Brighter red hand prints, alternating yellow, black, and blue decorative designs—circles, jagged lightning bolts, solid dots, triangles, wavy lines—were painted on their faces, arms, and chests. The body decorations made them appear larger than life and they conveyed a sense of impending danger and dread to an adversary.

One of the men facing Gudbjartur carried a spear with a long wicked-looking stone point with serrated edges, of a kind of red and yellow chert he had never before seen. The weapon was so magnificent he noticed it in spite of his predicament.

Interpreting their hesitation as an advantage, Gudbjartur's bearded face split into a broad disdainful grin as he glanced rapidly from one to another. The man with the red and yellow spear point uttered a short exclamation and suddenly charged at him, ignoring the shouted command of one of his companions.

Gudbjartur parried the spear thrust with the handle of his axe, and chopped down his assailant, very nearly cutting the man in half. The viciousness and power of the stroke sprayed blood and internal body fluids all over him, his other assailants, and the rocky surface of the cliff edge in a seemingly endless splash of red. For a heartbeat, the Naskapi froze in place, stunned into stillness as they blinked in disbelief at the rapidity and ease with which the axeman snuffed out their comrade's life. Then they began easing forward, careful to keep out of reach of the bloody axe held at the ready as the man awaited their next move, an unnerving smile on his face.

With a wild look in his eyes, the smile still rigidly in place, Gudbjartur darted glances at his adversaries.

"What is the matter? Has courage failed you?" His voice dripped with disdain.

Although the warriors knew not the meaning of the words, their surprised hesitation at the sound of his voice gave him the advantage he sought. Throwing his head back, he shouted at the top of his voice. The chilling, long drawn-out war cry of the Northmen burst upon the startled Naskapi.

"Odin!"

The war cry still reverberated along the rocky shoreline as he charged at his adversaries. The axe swept them aside like a great scythe through grass, as he continued calling on Odin, the god of war, to assist him. The six Naskapi scattered wildly, striking out with their own weapons in an attempt to fend him off, but two more fell in a welter of gore as he lay to among them.

With three of their number killed by the violence of the big man's attack, the others circled him warily. The contest became a battle of attrition as the four remaining Naskapi warriors kept the pressure on, wearing him down, never allowing him to catch his breath while they cut him to pieces with feints and short thrusts. He tried to keep the cliff at his back, but that was not possible as he pressed his attack rather than defend himself. Every time he attempted to close with one of their number, or escape from their constant probing, their changing tactics thwarted his action. However, one more came too close to the arc of the battleaxe. The blade of the axe, driven by powerful shoulder muscles, cut through the man's war club as though it were a twig, slicing a long, deep cut across his chest in the process. The Naskapi fell away, gasping in pain, while his fellows pressed all the harder at Gudbjartur.

Suddenly, three more warriors burst upon the scene from the forest verge. One was in the process of loosing an arrow that would have ended the unequal battle there and then, but a shouted command from their leader arrested him.

* * *

For some reason he wants me alive. He wants this fight to be hand-to-hand, no arrows, Gudbjartur thought.

With odds of seven-to-one, once again the battle would end when his adversaries tired of their sport. Unable to hold all his antagonists at bay and surrounded in spite of his best efforts to the contrary, Gudbjartur felt himself weakening. The inexorable pressure had worn him down. Bleeding from several wounds, but still pressing his attack, the big man's valiant effort ended when a war club crashed into the back of his head. Falling like a great tree, he slammed face down on the bare rock. The axe flew from his nerveless, bloody grip to skitter across the rock surface, falling into a wide fissure near the cliff's edge.

* * *

Gathered around their fallen enemy, the six able-bodied warriors regarded him in silent tribute. Each touched the body of their brave foe with a weapon to absorb his spirit and courage, as was their custom.

Surveying the carnage of the short battle, the men examined their three fallen comrades, in awe of the damage caused by the big axe. The wounded warrior lay off to the side, bleeding profusely and writhing in agony from the long diagonal cut across the middle of his chest, through muscle to the bone. His wound was not fatal; however, it required immediate attention to staunch the blood flow, and one of his comrades knelt to assist him.

Hiada bent down and turned the first victim over, exposing the full extent of the damage wreaked by the battleaxe. His voice full of loathing at the sight and smell of violent death, he turned toward Glooscap, "Come look at Pantoo. The cut is almost all the way through, from shoulder to hip. The only thing holding him together is part of his skin."

"I do not need to look; I have his blood all over me, and that is enough," Glooscap said. "Ukeen, find the axe. We must have this weapon."

"Where did it go?" Ukeen walked toward the edge of the cliff.

"I saw it go in that long crack after Miknap hit him," Kejo said as he joined Ukeen, who was down on all fours looking in the crack.

"It is too deep and dark down there to see it." Ukeen shielded his eyes from the bright sunlight. "Wait!" he exclaimed. "I see the end of the handle, but it is too far down to reach. Somebody bring me a rope, I might be able to get hold of the handle." Ukeen rose to a kneeling position.

Hiada took a coiled, braided leather rope from his belt and handed it to Ukeen, then knelt beside him to peer into the crack. "I do not think it is long enough to reach that far," he said, watching the other man's attempts to flip a tiny loop in the rope over the end of the axe handle.

Glooscap, standing beside the body of his foe, examined a large knife he had taken from the man's belt when an excited cry from the edge of the cliff distracted him.

"I have hold of it!" shouted Ukeen.

All gathered around to see the axe as Ukeen struggled to pull it from the crack. The rope was too short to provide sufficient advantage to get the job done and the frustrated man announced, "I need more rope. I cannot get it like this. Someone give me a belt or something." Glancing up at Hiada, he pointed at a braided rope belt around the man's waist, "Give me your belt, Hiada."

Ukeen tied the two lengths of rope together which gave him enough slack to stand erect. Bracing his feet apart on either side of the fissure, he heaved upward with a mighty effort. The rope stretched but the axe remained stuck in spite of Miknap joining the effort.

"Do not break my rope!" Hiada shouted.

The warning came too late. The rope parted and Ukeen and Miknap collapsed in a heap. Laughing as they extricated themselves, the two joined Hiada as he peered into the crack in a vain effort to locate his rope. Stretched to the limit when it parted, the rope had shot into the crack like an arrow from a bow, and except for the loop on the axe handle, he could not see it from the surface.

"My rope is gone," Hiada lamented, peering into the crack. "What are we going to do now?"

"Here is your belt and part of the rope," Miknap said, handing them over, still laughing.

"It is not funny. It took me a long time to braid that rope," Hiada said.

"Well, that one was rotten, I guess, so it must have been time to braid another," Ukeen said.

The good-natured banter over Hiada's misfortune suddenly stopped in mid-sentence when their fallen foe groaned and flopped over on the ground.

Rushing toward the man they had thought to be dead, the first to reach his body, Kejo, raised his club to deliver the deathblow, when a shouted command from Glooscap stopped him.

"Hold, Kejo!"

"He killed three of my friends. He is our enemy!" Kejo shouted, wheeling toward Glooscap.

"Yes, he is our enemy and I, too, am angry over the loss of our friends, but we have much to learn from him." Glooscap said. "He can tell us who he is, and where he comes from? How many others are with him and what they want here in our land? We can always kill him. For now, I think we should keep him alive. We will let Sachem decide. He would be angered if we did not show him this strange man."

"I want to kill him. We do not need him and we do not need to know anything about him. He killed my friends and he must die for that." Kejo glanced at Miknap and Ukeen for support. "Besides, he does not speak our language and we do not speak his, so how can we ask him these things?"

"Maybe he knows sign language." Miknap said with a grin, causing a few chuckles and defusing the tense situation.

"Why do you laugh? Our friends are dead and cannot laugh at such a stupid joke."

"Enough, Kejo!" Glooscap said. "I have spoken and it will be as I say. Sachem will decide his fate, not you, not me. Miknap did make a joke. He meant no disrespect to our dead friends. If Sachem spares him, we will teach him our language. Then we can find out these things." Leaning toward Kejo, he placed a conspiratorial hand on his shoulder. "Everyone knows sign language is not good for everything, even you," Glooscap said with a broad grin.

Snorting in disgust, Kejo shrugged off Glooscap's hand and wheeled away from the group to the sound of laughter at his expense.

Glooscap sobered as he looked at their prisoner. "Tie him up with what is left of Hiada's rotten rope before he decides to jump up and run away again. Let us make camp here. It will be dark soon."

Miknap and Hiada gathered stones, constructed a fire pit, and kindled a fire. Kejo and Atkaa unceremoniously dragged the semi-conscious man to a tree, set him upright against the trunk, and securely tied his arms behind it. Atkaa removed the heavy woolen headband from the prisoner's head and examined it curiously before throwing it on the ground. Bending over the man, he poked a finger at the largest cuts and examined the other wounds, pulling him forward to examine those on his back.

"Whew! He is very heavy, and he stinks. The only reason he is still alive is the headband and hair cushioned the blow. His head is split open and still bleeds, and he is bleeding from other wounds, but he breathes."

"Leave him," Glooscap ordered, glancing at Atkaa, the only one among them with any arrows remaining. "Divide your arrows with Kejo, Atkaa. We could all use fresh meat after this long day, so get us something before dark. The rest of us will attend to our dead while you are hunting."

Glooscap and the other four men busied themselves carrying rocks to cover their fallen comrades while Atkaa and Kejo trotted off in opposite directions to hunt. They covered the dead with rocks where they fell, their weapons at their sides, without ceremony beyond a respectful silence after completion of the task.

* * *

Gudbjartur regained consciousness unobserved and watched the activity curiously. They seemed to pay no attention to their wounded comrade, leaving him to fend for himself. The man carefully spread a greenish paste on his wound, gritting his teeth in pain. Thinking back to the battle with satisfaction, Gudbjartur recalled the axe barely caressing the chest of the man, but the razor-sharp edge did its job nonetheless. He shifted his uncomfortable position to ease cramped muscles, a deep cut on his shoulder reopened, and a slight groan escaped his blood-caked lips. Gudbjartur saw the heads of the warriors jerk around as all turned to glance in his direction. He wished he had kept his mouth shut. All four men walked over to look at him and he instinctively braced himself for what might follow. With face and clothing covered in blood from his head wound, he defiantly returned their stares with his one open eye, the other being cemented shut with dried blood.

* * *

Contemptuously, Hiada sneered, "He no longer looks dangerous, but we do not scare him."

"He does not look like he feels too good," Miknap observed dryly.

"Considering how hard you hit him, it's a wonder he feels at all," Hiada said. "From the way he looks, he may not make it back to the village."

"He will make it, and we will make sure of it," Glooscap said. "When the hunters return, some meat will revive him."

Gesturing in the direction of the cliff edge, Glooscap said to the two men, "You two get that axe from the crack. We must have it."

"We have no more rope, Glooscap. How can we get it from the crack?" said Hiada.

"Use your head. Between the two of you I am certain you will figure it out."

Laughing at this last statement, Miknap punched Hiada in the arm and moved toward the edge of the cliff, saying over his shoulder, "His fat head will not fit in the crack either, Glooscap. Come, Hiada."

"He did not mean that," Hiada said as he followed Miknap to the cliff edge. "He meant for us to think of a way to get the axe."

"Oh, did he, now? I am glad you explained it to me."

Glooscap smiled at this exchange and the efforts of the two men as they tried to snag the broken rope with a stick. He shook his head at their attempted humor and walked over to see how the wounded man, Eskanan, was faring.

* * *

Just before full darkness descended, Atkaa and Kejo returned with the butchered meat of two small deer. Each man sawed off a chunk of meat still warm from the life force recently departed, and dropped it in the coals of the fire to sear briefly. The wounded man, Eskanan, joined them. He moved slowly and deliberately so as not to reopen his wound. The others watched him without comment or assistance as he cooked some of the fresh meat, joining the others as they relaxed around the fire. Theirs was a hard life and each must shift for himself.

Conversation revolved around the axe that Miknap and Hiada had finally coaxed from the deep crack. Hiada sat scrubbing the gore of their dead companions from the blade and handle with sand. When finished he passed the axe from man to man and each had a chance to examine it before Glooscap took final possession.

"Here, Miknap, the knife is yours for bringing him down," Glooscap said, tossing the long-bladed knife to him. It was their way, this division of the spoils of war.

Deftly catching the knife by the handle, Miknap nodded without comment. Sitting cross-legged on the ground, he admired the heft and keenness of his new knife.

"Maybe he will show us how to make such a weapon. This axe is made of the same material as his knife. It is hard but not brittle like our stone and bone blades. Our enemies would have no chance if we had such weapons. The hairy one would show us how to use it," Glooscap said as he sat with the axe cradled in his lap.

The conversation rekindled Kejo's hatred of the captive. Snorting in derision, Kejo said, "What makes you think the hairy one can show us anything about fighting?"

Glooscap considered his friend for a moment before he answered. "He killed three of our men, one after the other, without pause. When the axe wounded Eskanan, there were only three of us to face him. If our other three men had not found us and attacked him when they did, I think you and I would have joined Pantoo and the others in death. I want to know how to use this axe." He held it aloft in both hands. "And I want to know how to fight like him."

"Well, he cannot teach me anything about fighting," said Kejo.

Shaking his head at his friend's refusal to see the obvious, Glooscap returned his attention to the heavy axe as he turned it repeatedly in his hands.

* * *

Gudbjartur's hands had been untied and he sat watching the heated discussion over his axe as he ravenously consumed the large chunk of half-raw meat one of his captors had thrown to him.

"Give him some water, Atkaa," Glooscap said, as he watched the prisoner tear at the meat.

Atkaa returned to the prisoner and dropped a water skin on the ground at his feet. Gudbjartur laid the remains of the meat on his outstretched legs and reached for the water skin, his single open eye locked on the impassive, black eyes of Atkaa, who watched him a moment before walking back to the fire. Slowly and deliberately, savoring each mouthful, Gudbjartur drank from the water skin, the precious liquid sent a coolness coursing through his ravaged body as he swallowed. Using what remained, he cleaned the caked blood from his eye and face as best he could.

* * *

Glooscap came to stand over his prisoner a little later. With a combination of words and sign language, using the axe for emphasis, he told him if he ran away, they would kill him. Glooscap finished his speech with a clear question, "Do you understand what I tell you?"

Nodding his assent at the obvious question, Gudbjartur gave the listening men no doubt as to his understanding of the situation in which he found himself. Glooscap nodded to him, handed the axe to one of his men, and placing both hands behind his back in demonstration, he indicated the tree at Gudbjartur's back with a lift of his chin, retying him securely without another word.

The men lounged comfortably around the fire while they recounted their individual accomplishments with exaggerated tales of participation in the day's events. The more outrageous the story the more appreciative the laughter accorded the storyteller.

Observing this behavior, Gudbjartur surmised from their elaborate pantomime that the topic involved the fight he had had with them. His people did much the same thing. While his captors celebrated victory, his mind grappled with his situation.

Believing they had spared him for some reason beyond his understanding, he viewed his capture and restraint with trepidation. His captors obviously intended to take him away the next day; otherwise, he would never have regained consciousness. Dawn was to be the beginning of an ordeal, of that he was certain.

Sleep eluded him for most of the long night. Tormented by mosquitoes from which there was no escape, a pensive mood claimed him as his mind wandered through the many events of this first summer in Vinland.

* * *

Chapter Four

Lysufjord, Greenland and Ungava Bay, Markland

Trade with the scattered farmers of the settlement had been brisk. Within two weeks of their arrival at Lysufjord, Greenland, the far-flung farmers had all received word of the trade goods available at the head of the fjord. So many people congregated that both loads of green logs from Vinland had been traded for an equally valuable cargo of barley, rolls of coarse linen and wadmal, rolled copper sheeting, forged iron bars ready for the smithy's hammers, and an assortment of lesser goods from the Homeland, normally unavailable to the settlers of Halfdansfjord. Plenty of cargo space remained to accommodate the expected bounty of walrus meat and hides. If the hunt was good the ships would be loaded to capacity for the voyage to Halfdansfjord.

Wind and sea conditions had combined to make the uneventful voyage from Lysufjord, a fast passage for the ships of Sweyn and Athils. The strong northwest wind had moaned in the rigging as the ships surged and plunged through the heavy swells in ideal sailing conditions as the strong wind and southerly current that swept out of the Greenland Sea had sped them to their destination in record time.

A cloudy sky and good steady wind out of the northwest had brought the ships out of the strait south of Helluland and into the huge bay on the coast of northern Markland where they expected to find Inuktuk and the Tornit people. Perfect sailing conditions died with the wind as the ships sailed further south along the west coast of the bay in search of the river's mouth where the Tornit people were to be found. Within a short time after the god, Njord quelled the north wind, the ever-present sea haze thickened and the Fog Giant covered the sea with his cloak. The ship drifted slowly on the current. An occasional breath of air moved the wet sail enough to provide momentary steerage-way for the ship before it sent accumulated moisture cascading from sail and rigging alike and onto the men aboard her. The rigging banged as the ship surged and rolled off the swells from out of the strait as they coursed in even progression across the wide bay.

Sweyn held onto the forestay of his ship, straining to see ahead. Water dribbled from his hair, into his eyes, and col-lected on every surface as the Fog Giant laid his wet, grey blanket over the ship. He stood with his thrall, Rolf on the bow platform, watching the man wield the plummet line while others of his skeleton crew busily worked the ship into the unknown and unseen shoreline. He felt the loom of the land suffuse his breast. A fogbound approach to any shoreline always made him nervous; to an unknown shoreline even more so. The back echo of the intermittent bullhorn con-firmed this feeling. He leaned forward, straining to pierce the haze and fog as his ship drew ever nearer the land.

"Thirty feet under the keel; the bottom is shelving," Rolf said as he coiled the plummet line for another throw.

"Drop the sail. Out sweeps," Sweyn ordered his waiting crew. He had waited until the last possible moment. With only four men at the sweeps, forward progress for the big ship was both slow and arduous. The ship lost steerageway before the sweeps began to move her slowly ahead once again.

"Give Athils two short horn blasts," Sweyn called aft. The fog quickly swallowed the two short blasts. He cocked his head, listening for the return signal. Faintly, two short answering horn blasts came to him from Athils' ship. He grunted and turned his attention forward.

"Ten feet on the line, Sweyn," Rolf said, all but invisible at the bow rail.

"That is enough, the fog thickens," Sweyn said. "Stow the sweeps," he called to his crew. "Anchor the ship." Three short horn blasts warned Athils. An answering three short horn blasts echoed back through the fog.

The way went off the ship quickly and Sweyn helped two crewmembers muscle the heavy anchor over the steerboard bow. The crewmembers snubbed the anchor rode to a cleat and the ship swung to the slight current he had noticed earlier in their approach. *The flood tide begins. I am glad to be anchored before full flood.* He knew he could expect the water depth to increase by as much as thirty feet as the tide surged into the bay. He looked aft in the direction of the long, echoing horn from Athils' ship as he, too, closed the shoreline before anchoring. "Give him a short horn so he does not ram us as he makes his approach." He turned aft. "Ormiga, Rolf," he called into the fog. He could no longer distinguish familiar parts of his own ship as the fog continued to thicken.

"We are here, Sweyn," said a disembodied voice from close by.

Sweyn chuckled. "I still cannot see you. No matter. You men take turns at the anchor rode so you can payout line as the tide comes in," he said as the two suddenly materialized at his side. "Have you eaten?" he asked.

"Aye, we ate on the way in." Rolf glanced at his companion. "I will take the first watch." The other man nodded, his attention turned aft as the wail of Athils' horn pierced the fog. A short, answering wail followed immediately from Sweyn's ship.

"He draws nigh," Sweyn observed. As if in anticipation of his thoughts, three short blasts came to him from Athils, with a like answer back. Sweyn sighed explosively, wiping collected moisture from his beard. "Good, he has anchored. Otherwise, he would be aboard in a few moments." His men dutifully laughed at his humor. All on the ship were relieved that the threat of collision was behind them.

* * *

Dawn found the ships still fogbound as the men awakened and climbed from their sleeping bags.

Sweyn sniffed the damp air as he relieved himself over the rail. Before he finished he heard his men doing the same. A slight breeze stirred the fog. He sensed that the ship had swung at her anchor in response to the changing tide and was oriented to the beach in the opposite direction. He made his way to the foot of the mast where his six-man crew had gathered at the food bags. He selected a long piece of dried cod and sopped one end in the communal bowl of whale oil, noting that little oil remained. Holding the bowl, he motioned with it toward a firkin nestled between the leather food bags. "Pour some more oil."

Ormiga, who happened to be the closest man, picked up the oil firkin, and pulled the bung with his teeth. "It is less than half full," he said, pouring a little oil into the bowl. The firkin of whale oil, a nutritious accompaniment to the dried fish and whale meat rations, would be empty soon.

"When the Fog Giant returns to his lair, we will find the Tornit and go walrus hunting. I fancy the firkin refilled with walrus oil before we make sail for Halfdansfjord." Sweyn sat down with his back against a food bag and tore at his morning meal. His men followed suit, either finding a comfortable seat or leaning over the rail to stare into the fog, each alone with his thoughts as they consumed the basic fare of life at sea. After a time, all busied themselves with small individual work projects or sail and rigging maintenance while they waited for the fog to lift.

"Rolf, go up the mast," Sweyn said. "Maybe you will see something from up there." Without comment, Rolf untied the halyard from the sail yard and tied a sling in the line's standing end that disappeared into the fog at the masthead. He stepped into the sling and held onto the line with both hands. "Hoist away," he said to two men who had taken hold of the halyard's running end. He sat in the loop he had tied while holding tight to the halyard as the men hoisted him slowly aloft by walking the halyard aft, as they did to raise the sail.

"Avast heaving!" Rolf called as he reached the masthead. The two men cleated the halyard securely. Silence prevailed for a time. "Deck there, Athils' masthead is sticking from the fog."

"Where away?" Sweyn called through cupped hands.

"Off the steerboard quarter. It is far, I can just barely see it above the fog. Wait, somebody just climbed to the masthead." The wail of his signal horn pierced the damp silence. A short time later, they heard a faint answer. "He sees me! He is waving!" Rolf called.

Silence descended over the ship for a time as the crew took up their tasks once again. The slap and gurgle of the sea against the ship's hull eventually lulled some to set their work aside and succumb to languor.

"Sweyn, the fog lifts off the water's surface," Ormiga called.

"About time." Sweyn, jerked awake by the hale, squeezed accumulated water from his beard as he got to his feet.

"The wind comes. The Fog Giant flees to his lair," Rolf called from the masthead.

"Aye, the ship is swinging to the wind," Sweyn said. He cupped his hands and shouted aloft. "We are bringing you down." He motioned to the two men standing by on the halyard.

When Rolf reached the deck, Sweyn gave his orders. "Hoist the sail. Standby to get underway." He stepped to the rail and looked toward where the land should be. The fog had begun to swirl in the freshening breeze, but he still could not see well enough to order the sail sheeted home. He absently pounded the rail with his open hand. *Soon, the wind comes. Be patient.* He strained to see. Suddenly he saw the ship's shadow on the water. *Finally, the sun comes through. It will not be long now.*

Without a sound to announce their presence, two long, slender, kayaks materialized in his field of view. "The Tornit have found us," Sweyn called over a shoulder.

His men gathered at the rail. The kayaks stopped two boat lengths from the ship. Each held a single occupant. The ship's crew and the two Tornit men watched each other silently through the heavy mist for a heartbeat.

"Inuktuk," Sweyn said. The name of the Tornit leader that they had met in the early spring, and that he had memorized at Gudbjartur's insistence, produced an immediate reaction from the man in the closer of the two kayaks.

A big smile split his face. He bobbed his head in animation. "Inuktuk." He pointed with his double bladed paddle back the way he had come. "Inuktuk," he repeated.

"Ha, we have found them!" Sweyn exclaimed. "As soon as this god-cursed fog lifts we will follow them to their village." He had hardly spoken when with a few flicks of their paddles the two men disappeared from view. With an oath, he marveled at how quickly they disappeared.

"Their kayaks are so low to the water they can probably see the shoreline." The men heard a faint horn signal in the distance.

"Athils is underway," Ormiga said.

"By Hel," Sweyn cursed. "He is further offshore. The fog has lifted offshore first." He bent over the rail as far as possible without falling overboard. "I can see a short distance, but not well enough to sail." He stood back up and looked aft. "I still cannot see the tiller arm of the steerboard."

"Why not use the sweeps?" Ormiga said.

Sweyn pondered his question. "All right, man the sweeps. We will up anchor. By then maybe we can sheet home the sail." He absently wiped a hand through his blonde hair and squeezed water from his beard while he watched his men go about their duties. *With four men at the sweeps, we might not be able to break out the anchor.* "All hands man the sweeps. Ormiga, take in the slack on the anchor rode as we overrun the anchor." He spit on his hands and joined his men at the sweeps. The four sweeps lay positioned in the water for the stroke, their blades forward. Each man braced for the effort. "Now!"

The ship slowly gathered way. Ormiga hauled in the anchor rode over the bow rail. "The anchor rode is up and down," he shouted over his shoulder when the ship passed over the anchor. With one final heave on the rode, he quickly cleated it to allow the forward momentum of the ship to break it from the bottom. The ship slewed slightly as the anchor almost arrested forward momentum. "The anchor is aweigh," he shouted, as he felt the hook lose its grip on the bottom. Heaving mightily, he struggled to lift the heavy iron hook off the bottom before it snagged again. Two more men quickly added their muscle to the effort, the anchor came over the side, and they secured it in its chock.

"Hold the stroke," Sweyn said. "Stow the sweeps."

The long sweeps rattled inboard, the crewmembers passed them across the beam of the ship to their opposite number on the other side. Because of their length, this was the only way to deploy or remove them from the rowing port strake in the ship's side. The crewmembers stowed the sweeps atop the t-supports fore and aft of the mast where they were off the deck and out of the way.

Sweyn peered over the side to watch the bubbles of their passage on the water's surface, gauging the drift of his ship in the current. "We are drifting slowly out to sea on the ebb tide," he said. "Sheet home the sail."

Three horn blasts echoed out over the water to signal Athils that they were underway. Crewmembers trimmed the sheet lines to the wind and securely cleated them. The ship slowly gathered way, answering the helm as the speed increased.

Sweyn could now see his helmsman Einar, standing at the tiller of the big steerboard. The fog was thinning rapidly. "Einar, come about as soon as you have enough speed," he said. His men waited to trim the sheets again after the ship reversed her course.

"Ready about," Einar called to alert the sheet handlers to the turn. The agile ship turned rapidly through the eye of the wind and gathered speed on the new downwind course.

Sweyn still could not see the shoreline through the mist and haze. He chewed on his mustache. "Bring her up into the wind a little. Let the sail luff so you just have steerageway," he called to his helmsman, not wishing to hurry about until he knew where he was going.

The wail of Athils' foghorn pierced the mist from some-where off their port side. Both ships would continue the in-termittent signal until the visibility improved.

Moments later, with the final wail of a foghorn, as if by prearranged signal, the north wind began to moan through the rigging and the last lingering tatters of fog blew away. The bay opened like a vast door before the ship.

"Athils is in sight off the port quarter," Einar shouted from the helm.

Sweyn turned to port in time to witness Athils' ship spring into full view as the mist cleared. Turning his attention back to the shoreline he saw a flotilla of kayaks paddling toward his ship from a wide river's mouth visible to the southwest. "Sheet home the sail. Steer for the river's mouth Einar," Sweyn shouted to his men. His eyes smarted in the freshening wind. He blinked rapidly to clear the tears as he narrowly watched Athils' ship and the oncoming kayaks.

"Those kayaks are lying across our course," Einar observed. "If they do not move, the ship will be among them."

"Maintain our course, they will move out of the way," Sweyn ordered.

As predicted, the Tornit boatmen parted enough to allow Sweyn's ship to speed on its way. The ship must have looked like a wall of wood to the Tornit as it tore by them. With the exception of Inuktuk and the three men who had been with him at Snorrisfjord, none had ever been this close to a Norse ship, if in fact they had ever before seen such a large vessel.

The Tornit boatmen shouted good-naturedly among themselves as they maneuvered their kayaks out of the ship's path with a few flicks of their double bladed paddles. They seemed to regard the threat posed by the ship as a game of tag, not unlike that played on land. Laughter swept the gaggle of boats, as each man tried to outdo the other. They could not hope to match the big ship's speed, although several tried.

Sweyn laughed in spite of himself at the boatmen's antics. "They have a sense of humor, I will give them that." He raised his arm in farewell as the kayaks fell far behind. He turned his attention to Athils' ship that had begun to head-reach on his ship as he came about on the steerboard tack. He cupped his hands and shouted to his helmsman. "Athils has the lead, Einar, follow him in." He turned to his crew who lined the rail watching in anticipation of challenging Athils. "This is not a race. If it was, Athils has won for he is close-hauled, ahead by three ship's lengths, and we cannot sail any closer to the wind's eye. He will fetch the shoreline on the north shoreline of the river's mouth with one more tack. We will have to tack twice to do the same thing."

"More kayaks are coming out from the river, Sweyn," Ormiga said, calling attention back to the river's mouth in the distance.

The river delta appeared wide and inviting from a distance. Sweyn beckoned to Rolf. "Go up the mast again and tell me if you think we can sail up the river to the Tornit village and beach the ship out of the wind." He watched the preparations to hoist Rolf aloft and then glanced toward Athils' ship. "Never mind, Athils has changed course for the river's mouth. He has already made my decision for me."

Everybody but the helmsman gathered at the bow with Sweyn to watch the cautious approach of Athils to the rocky shoreline.

Sweyn grabbed the forestay and hoisted himself athwart the bow rails. Balanced thusly, a foot on each rail where they joined together at the up thrust stem, he used the additional height to examine the river's mouth. He called aft, "Einar, follow Athils course exactly. I see rapids just upstream from their village, so there will be submerged rocks. We will row in at a speed of dead slow."

A moment later, the familiar clatter of the long sweeps told him that his crewmembers were preparing to beach the ship. He noted a small group of people gathering on the riverbank. Most of them wore the drab, earth-tone leather clothing that blended so well with the backdrop of the rocky, treeless landscape that they were difficult to see. However, two people wore blue and red parkas that had been made of the wadmal that Inuktuk had traded from Halfdan earlier in the season.

Sweyn gestured toward the small crowd. "It is hard to miss those parkas. One of them must be Inuktuk."

"Athils is heaving to, Sweyn. There goes his sail," Ormiga observed, calling attention back to the other ship.

In anticipation of Sweyn's command, Einar turned the ship more into the wind to take some of the weight off the sail as the other crewmembers prepared to lower the heavy sail.

"Heave to." Sweyn shouted the order that put the ship's helm into the wind. She came to a graceful stop and began to pay off downwind as the sail came down the mast. In due course the sail was stowed and the sweeps deployed. Sweyn joined his men at the sweeps for the short row to the beach.

"Athils has anchored," Einar called. Athils' ship could be seen swinging around as the anchor caught and she reacted to the pluck of the ebb tide.

Sweyn grunted as he strained into a backstroke. He then quickly made his way forward. "All right, raft up to his ship portside to portside," he called to Einar as he assessed the situation. One ship length away, Sweyn held his arm aloft. "Slow the stroke. Boat the port sweeps." The two steerboard sweeps continued their slow cadence. The ship swung slowly as Einar expertly brought her alongside the other ship.

A grinning Athils and his crew lined the port rail as the two ships were secured together.

"Well done, Einar!" Athils said as he swung aboard Sweyn's ship. "The water is too shallow in the river. I think it best to take the small boats in from here," he said as he and Sweyn shook hands. He gestured toward the river's mouth. "All those rocks sticking up in the river made it easy to decide. The ebb tide is still running, so it is certain to get worse."

"I agree," Sweyn said. With a lift of his chin he gestured toward the shore, "Here come the Tornit boatmen. It looks like there are only about thirty people in this village judging by the number of boats and that crowd on the riverbank." The two captains watched the approaching kayaks while the ships' boats were launched.

* * *

Sweyn's assessment of the Tornit band's numbers had been about right; all told there were thirty-six men, women, and children in the village. The women seemed to outnumber the men, a fact not lost on the Northmen.

Wolf-like sled dogs far outnumbered the human residents. Excited by the arrival of strangers in the village they set up a howling and barking that soon reached cacophonic proportions that frayed the nerves after a time. The Tornit seemed not to notice the din initially. That soon changed as even they tired of the noise. A few shouts, cuffs, and kicks by some of the Tornit men restored order, much to the relief of their visitors.

Lack of a common language presented a problem from the outset, but limited verbal and signed communication occurred nonetheless. The willingness to talk and the friendly demeanor—a smile seemed their universal facial expression—of all the Tornit soon overcame whatever communication difficulty existed. Given their circumstance, visitors were rare. Inuktuk and the hunters who had been with him were the only Tornit prepared for the arrival of the Northmen.

Especially exciting for the rest of the people were the men, strange in every way, which had arrived in giant wooden boats, to a land where wood was virtually unknown. Every man, woman, and child took a turn at crowding around the bows of the two ships to rub the wooden planks of the bows with a look of reverent ecstasy on their faces. Some of them even smelled the planks, exclaiming in their guttural language to the others.

The Tornit's simple delight at the ships and gear of the Northmen acted as a catharsis for the crewmen, many of whom had spent most of their lives at sea, away from the openness and pleasant demeanor of such guileless people.

Camaraderie naturally led to a feast, for what better way to become acquainted than to eat together. Stores from both ships became a part of the communal food prepared by the women. Soon the smell of stew wafted through the little settlement and the people gathered together with the Northmen in their houses to partake of the simple fare.

The four Tornit dwellings were dugouts, oriented along the south side of a low, rock-strewn spine, overlooking the river, which provided some protection from the incessant north wind. Each house site had been chipped from the permanently frozen ground, half above and half below ground level, which afforded the occupants excellent protection from the elements. Like people everywhere, the snug quarters housed an extended family and were constructed of readily available materials: rock walls were caulked with mud and lichen, driftwood and whale ribs became roof trusses that were covered with walrus hide, the thin soil and sod of the tundra were added to complete the house and protect occupants from the wind and cold. However, the windowless interiors, dimly lit by oil lamps not unlike those used by the Northmen, were dark as a cave when first entered. A kind of entry alcove or tunnel, with a piece of seal or walrus hide at each end, was oriented to the south, giving protection to the interior from a cold blast of wind during the comings and goings of the occupants. The low entry alcoves presented a challenge, as the Norsemen were considerably larger than the Tornit. Although the interior was roomy enough for comfort, the much taller Northmen could only stand erect near the center roof brace of spliced together whale rib bones. The only interior ventilation came from the entry alcove, as the structure was otherwise airtight. Interior heat was furnished by oil lamps and the packed humanity. Although warm and comfortable, the air inside the houses became somewhat odorous after a time.

The friendly Tornit showed the Northmen their possessions with obvious pride. Limited in scope they might be, being neither extravagant nor wasteful of precious materials, but patience and skill went into the construction of every item they possessed, from weapons and the tools of hunting, to their kayaks and the dogsleds of winter.

In a land without wood, save for an occasional piece of useful driftwood, each family unit seemed especially proud of a large platter or trencher from which they all ate. Intricately pieced together with splints of wood and bone, the artistry of the trencher drew the attention of the Northmen as they were shown the Tornit possessions.

"Look at this," Athils said, passing the trencher to Sweyn, who held it up to the nearest lamp for examination.

"They have glued wood and bone splints together. Very clever." Peering closely at the trencher, he added, "It is thin but strong, I can see the flame of the lamp through the sides. I wonder what they use for glue." Sweyn passed it back to Athils.

"Whatever they use is as strong as our glue." Athils tested the glued joint with his thumbnail. "I do not think the caribou get this far north, so they use something other than the hoofs we boil down." He passed the trencher to its owner with a nod and smile of appreciation. After a final look around, the two men got down on all fours and crawled out through the entrance alcove.

"I do not think we have the luxury of time on our side," Sweyn said, indicating the threatening look of the northern sky with a lift of his chin as he and Athils joined a group of their men.

A bank of dark gray clouds had begun to form in the distance. The north wind carried a chill that had not been so pronounced when the tour of the village had begun.

"Gudbj would say that snow will come by morning," Athils said. "And I would not disagree."

"Nor I," Sweyn said. "We have committed to stay until tomorrow. Unless we are fogged in after yon storm blows itself out, I think we had best load up Inuktuk, his men, and their kayaks and sail to hunt walrus while we still can. Ice is already forming along the shore. Winter freeze up is not far away."

"Aye, we are cutting this hunt close," Athils said.

* * *

The two ships sailed on the ebb tide the next day. With the exception of two old people who remained behind to care for the children, all the men and women of Inuktuk's village had come on the hunt.

The hunters found the bounty that they sought on a windswept island to the west of the bay of the Tornit, walrus beyond count. The beasts customarily used a stony, sloping beach on the island's south shore to haul themselves from the water and the Tornit knew that. A large herd had been trapped while sunning themselves ashore. Some had lumbered into the water in a bid for freedom only to die in the shallows as the hunters swept down on them without warning.

Sweyn, Athils, and their combined crews were in the thick of it. The spears, arrows, and axes of the Northmen were responsible for most of the hunting success. Although the Tornit certainly did their share with their harpoons and lances, especially with the animals in the water, the long range killing capabilities of the powerful bows and arrows carried the day with the prey trapped on shore.

The Tornit kayaks had never made the trip to the hunting grounds so quickly, nor had they ever been able to surprise their prey so completely and kill so many animals at once. Each kayak could tow but a single carcass a short distance. Because of their size and weight, the walrus, or avik to the Tornit, carcasses were dismembered ashore and the meat, usable offal, and organs were normally packed aboard the much larger umiak and the women paddled the open boat back home after the hunt. The ships of the Northmen made the umiak and the arduous paddle back home in the open sea unnecessary for them. Sweyn and Athils had insisted that none be brought on this hunt.

All went well until an enraged, mortally wounded bull lunged atop a kayak, drove his tusks as long as a man's arm down through the boat and its terrified occupant and disappeared through the wreckage into the blood-stained depths. Neither the walrus nor the unfortunate Tornit hunter was seen again.

* * *

Three days later, more intermittent light snow came on the brow of the north wind. The cold descended like a blanket over the island under the partially overcast skies. The face of the full Autumn Time Moon peeked through the clouds and bathed a scene of hurried activity on the island's single beach in light more brilliant than the summertime twilight of the polar night.

Both ships lay high and dry during the hours of low tide, propped upright on their keels. Meals were taken aboard. The ship's hold was the only shelter available from the wind to light the two charcoal braziers. The women cooked the simple stews that they all subsisted on, while others ate the delicious blubber raw while they worked.

Nights had also been spent aboard in comparative comfort and safety. Bears would be drawn to the smell sooner or later and both captains agreed that only the high sides of the ships, under the watchful eye of a guard, offered sufficient security for a full night's sleep.

The snow and icy wind brought an air of urgency to the hunters. Sweyn worked with a mixed group of Northmen and Tornit as they labored to remove the ballast stones from the two hulls. The stones were no longer necessary, as their weight, used to stabilize the ship at sea, was being replaced by the bounty of the hunt as fast as the switch could be achieved. Men dropped ballast stones over one side of the ships while others carried hides and frozen chunks of meat up the gang-planks. So far, the backbreaking work of loading had kept pace with the killing and butchering.

Athils and Inuktuk had taken charge of the butchering crews on the beach. The sheer volume of rich meat from a single animal soon had piles of freezing meat dotting the beach. As fast as the hide was stripped, the prize of ivory teeth was chopped from the skull with an axe to gather in a single pile for loading with the meat. As soon as blubber began collecting, one of his men kindled a driftwood fire in a rock alcove protected from the wind and boiled enough fresh blubber down to oil to replenish both oil firkins for the voyage south.

One of Inuktuk's men towed a big male narwhal onto the beach late on what they all hoped would be the final day on the island. People gathered around the prized animal and soon it was processed into its usable parts. The final meal of the day for all of them was the delicious muktuk and the whale meat stew that followed. Inuktuk insisted that Athils take the narwhal tusk to present to Halfdan.

Walrus carcasses, in various stages of dismemberment, dotted the rocky beach, with more floating in the shal-lows. The tide was in flood, making it unnecessary to secure the carcasses. The flood tide would bring them ashore and leave them stranded on the beach as the water ebbed during the next tidal cycle, where the butchers could do their work. Some of the bulls carried the weight of ten men and could not be hauled up on the beach without winches, which were not available. Most of the kill were mature bulls and cows, but many calves were also scattered about. The object of the hunt was to kill enough for the winter and that mission had been accomplished with alacrity, as evidenced by the piles of frozen and partially frozen meat piled atop the fresh hides spread for the purpose.

The Tornit men were skilled hunters, their survival as a people demanded it. The women were experts with their strange looking half-moon shaped knives, making short work of any meat cutting job. The typical ulu knife had a short, t-shaped bone or ivory handle, attached to a slightly longer tapering edge of the same material, into which a cutting edge of knapped flint, sharpened scallop shell, or fire hardened bone, was inset along the bottom edge.

Ormiga and one of the women were engaged in a good-natured race to complete the dismemberment and boning of a huge bull. The animal had died on his stomach and they had started the butchering process along the animal's backbone on each side. Their laughter and chiding was not lost on Sweyn and the rest of the crew who were loading the ship.

"She is going to beat him," Sweyn said, chuckling in appreciation at the speed and expertise of the young woman. Her ulu fairly flew through one long cut after another as she rapidly cut away the hide, leaving the thick fat and underlying muscle intact.

The men laughed and shouted encouragement to Ormiga.

"He has already lost more than this contest to her," Einar said.

Sweyn looked at him. "I know, he told me yesterday that he is thinking about staying with the Tornit."

"Do you approve of that?" Rolf asked.

Sweyn glanced toward the pair and shrugged his shoulders. "He is a freeman; he can do as he wishes."

"Well, I may want to stay, too," Rolf said.

"You cannot!" Einar punched him in the shoulder, his statement a reference to Rolf being Sweyn's thrall.

Sweyn looked at Rolf. Their relationship had always been one of mutual trust rather than that which is normally present between a freeman and his thrall; although you could not say that they were friends, exactly. Neither had ever stepped over the unspoken boundary that existed.

"Do you want to stay with the Tornit?" Sweyn asked.

"I might, if given the chance," Rolf said.

Looking directly at Rolf, Sweyn nodded and pulled at his beard. "All right, go ahead, stay if you wish."

Rolf was stunned. He looked at his companions. All had taken Sweyn's decree in the same way.

"Do you mean I am free?" Rolf asked Sweyn, looking closely into his eyes.

"Aye, you are."

Sweyn began dropping ballast stones over the side again, the matter closed as far as he was concerned.

Rolf and the others seemed rooted in place. After a moment, Rolf began dropping stones over the side, too. He kept glancing at Sweyn as they worked, mulling over in his mind the momentous happening.

The others returned to their work. Nobody said anything for awhile, but all of them glanced toward Sweyn and Rolf from time to time as one man passed the heavy stones to the other, who dropped them over the side.

Einar finally could not stand it anymore. He dropped a frozen chunk of walrus in the hold atop the layer of hides against the hull and turned to Rolf. "Well, are you going to stay with the Tornit?" he asked.

"No, I will go back to Halfdansfjord. I have been with Sweyn most of my life. It is what I know." He paused. "I am still free, Sweyn?"

Sweyn nodded. "Aye," he said, a slight smile on his face.

Rolf shook his head in wonder. The others crowded around, pounding him on the back in congratulations. Freedom for a thrall seldom happened. It was hard to digest so suddenly.

"We had better get back to work or we will all stay with the Tornit this winter," Sweyn said. The normally taciturn man did not share his reasoning with his men, nor did he say another word about what he had just done.

* * *

The next day found the hunters back at the Tornit village. Both ships were overloaded with meat, hides, and blubber so that the surplus could carry the jubilant Tornit through the long, dark winter.

The young woman's family had accepted Ormiga from the outset, like he belonged with them. The couple spent most of their time smiling at each other.

The transformation in the man was obvious to his workmates. The men's stoicism was their defense in matters that none understood. Their lives, of necessity, were normally led without the company of women, and most had come to accept that they had little chance to acquire a mate.

Sweyn, Athils, and Inuktuk, stood near the two gangplanks as the last of the meat and hides was offloaded. The flood tide had decreased to a trickle and the slack water that the two captains were waiting for was nigh.

Athils pointed at the edge of the water and explained the significance of slack water to Inuktuk. "We sail for Halfdansfjord, Inuktuk. When the tide is slack, we must leave so we can catch the ebb tide out of this bay."

Sweyn laughed and Inuktuk bobbed his head in apparent understanding, his face split in a huge grin as he looked at his two companions.

The captains were uncertain about his level of understanding but the explanation had been reinforced with elaborate pantomime in the hope he would know the reason for haste.

Sweyn waved his arms over his head. "Load up, men, we sail for Halfdansfjord!" The clatter of sweeps being readied brought the finality of departure to all within hearing. Sweyn stood on the bow platform as his ship was pushed out from shore.

Shouted farewells went back and forth as the two ships' bows turned toward the bay.

"We will return next summer, Ormiga, if you change your mind," Rolf shouted as he plied a sweep.

"And welcome you will be, all of you, but I will not change my mind. I belong here," he answered, his arm over the shoulders of his smiling mate.

Rolf waved in acknowledgment. He gave a shake of his head and bent to his rowing.

Sweyn cupped his hands at his mouth as the bow of his ship entered the bay from the river's mouth. "Stow the sweeps. Make sail for Halfdansfjord!"

Every person in the little village followed along the riverbank as the ships slowly rowed into the bay. They were still waving as the sails rose to the mastheads and the ships heeled to the press of the north wind and set a course for the strait.

* * *

Chapter Five

Gudrod's hunting party

Gudrod thought it odd that Ingerd gave permission for her sons to accompany him and eleven other men on a boat hunting expedition up one of the many unexplored rivers. She seemed to be unusually distant, almost uncaring, and he knew she was not like that, but he did not press her about it. He did not really want to know what the problem was.

"They will be all right with us, Ingerd. I spoke to Gudbj about taking them hunting. This will be a real adventure for them because we will be away for several days exploring a new river. We are departing as soon as I find your sons."

"Yes, he told me. It is fine. Take them. I seldom see them except at night anyway. They are no longer boys. They are the oldest of the boys here and they are rapidly becoming men, especially after all the hunting they have done and the time they have spent with you men. We women lose them too quickly," she said wistfully.

"Well, I do not have to take them hunting. I told Gudbj. . ." His voice trailed off as she held her hand up to interrupt him.

"Take them, Gudrod, and welcome. It is the way of things. This is their rite of passage and it has always been so." Her eyes held his. "I am only a woman, their mother, but I want them to be men and I cannot teach them that. My time with them is almost over and well I know it." Placing a hand on his arm, she smiled slightly. "Go. Find them and tell them they are leaving with you. They are always ready, so your departure will not be delayed."

Nodding uncomfortably, Gudrod took his leave of her. Glad to be away, he sighed and went to find Ivar and Lothar. Females were unfamiliar to him. He was a man's man and their ways had always been a source of confusion for him. From time to time during his younger years, he had enjoyed their company. Now he no longer sought a female, preferring the company of men. It was simpler and easier to get along with men.

* * *

The gossip of the settlement had alerted Ivar and Lothar that an expedition was afoot and slated to depart after the mid-morning meal. They knew Gudrod to be the leader and both had gathered their weapons and trail packs in anticipation of accompanying him. They spied him walking through the settlement before he saw them and turned toward them. This was all the encouragement they needed to meet him halfway.

"So, it looks like you are expecting me." Gudrod smiled at the two boys as they waited with anticipation.

Ivar, always the spokesman, replied hopefully, "We heard you were leaving today and we hoped you would take us."

"I am. Go down to the strand. The others are gathering there. Tell Helge you are going with us. I have something to do. Then I will join you and we will be off," he said, his eyes belying the smile on his lips. His conversation with Ingerd still rankled and it clouded what should have been anticipation of the expedition. *I refuse to allow her motherly instincts and opinions to spoil this expedition for those boys,* he thought, as he strode off in search of Thora, who had promised a pack of pemmican for the expedition.

* * *

Just after midday, the expedition entered the destination river from the bay. The weather could not have been better. The day was typically hot for this time of year, with sufficient clouds to provide intermittent shade from the intense sun, and light breezes to cool the paddlers and help keep the insects at bay.

The swarm of seabirds that had followed the canoes along the shoreline of the bay lost interest as the flotilla progressed farther upriver and the surrounding forest began closing in. Gradually, the sounds of forest and fen replaced their raucous cries.

The snap and buzz of insects and a flurry of activity from a nearby pond as flocks of ducks and geese took wing in alarm at the intrusion, served to provide a continual sound of warning to the denizens of forest and river. The warning cries of unseen birds watching from the brush and trees lining the riverbanks and the chattering squirrels that scolded the intruders as they glided past, broadcast their presence to all that would listen.

* * *

Unknown to the expedition, four Haudeno warriors, advance scouts for a raiding party, hid in the riverbank brush to await the source of the warning that they, too, had heard. From this place of concealment, within a matter of feet of the five canoes of Northmen as they paddled by, the enemy scouts watched and waited, before regrouping to confer. Two of their group then made off to report to the main body.

* * *

The expedition continued the leisurely trip upriver, blissfully unaware of their imminent danger. Gudrod's plan was to proceed upriver three days before they began to hunt, except to kill camp meat. As he laid it out, the expedition goal was twofold: explore the new river and hunt on the return downstream. Halfdan wanted to know the frequency with which others used the river.

The twelve men and two boys, dispersed in five canoes to allow sufficient room to haul home the expected fresh meat, had paddled easily along the north shoreline from

Halfdansfjord. Now that they had entered the river and paddled against the current, more effort was required to achieve
the same rate of forward progress. Knowing this beforehand,
Gudrod separated the boys so their presence aboard a canoe
would not cause the other canoes to have an unfair advantage. Although both were game to paddle, they could not
keep up with the men. Over the course of the trip, they were
to change canoes often.

Progress upriver was steady. The going became increasingly
difficult when rapids necessitated a portage of canoes and
supplies to the next stretch of relatively calm water. The two
boys could not help carry the canoes upside down on their
shoulders—being too short—but they helped carry supplies
and some of the weapons. Oftentimes, they made multiple
trips back and forth around the rapids, but they did this without complaint, much to the surprise of the men.

After negotiating a difficult series of three rapids, Gudrod
called a rest stop before they set out again, on what appeared
to be a long, welcome stretch of good water. The group lolled
on a grassy knoll at the edge of the dense forest, just back
from the river a short distance, eating pemmican and dried
meat or fish. Conversation ebbed back and forth.

"We are not the only people to come here, Gudrod. There
have been tracks around every set of rapids," Helge said from
where he rested against an upturned canoe.

"I know, and that is one of the reasons we are here. Halfdan
wants us to scout the river as we carry the canoes around the
rapids. We will check the north bank as we go upriver and will
check the south bank when we return downriver." Gudrod's
glance took in the group. "We must make contact with these
people. The reason for this expedition and the one Gudbj went
on, is to try to bring about first contact. Halfdan thinks, and
I agree with him, that if we go about our activities normally
these people may accept us without undue problems. We will
not strike the first blow. Do all of you agree with that?"

"Yes, of course we do," Helge, said. "If this is an expedition
to make contact with the natives, why did we bring Gudbj's
sons? If there is trouble they might get hurt or killed."

"This has been planned for some time, Helge. It was Gudbj's idea for the boys to accompany us. He felt it would show the native men that we sincerely want to get along with them. Putting our young at risk is the ultimate expression of a trustworthy motive. Gudbj used those words when he made the proposal. I just hope he is right," Gudrod said, glancing at the two attentive boys.

"We, too, hope he is right. We have talked of little else since we were selected for this expedition," Helge said.

Silence prevailed for a time after this last statement, until young Ivar stood and stepped toward Gudrod. "Can I be heard, Gudrod?"

A slight smile on his lips, Gudrod nodded appreciatively and gestured toward the assembly, indicating for the boy to proceed.

"Our father," he began, gesturing toward his brother Lothar, "felt our presence here with you men was valuable for our people. I do not know his thinking on this because he did not tell us, but I trust him, and I trust Halfdan, who agreed with him. Else we would not be here."

"We trust him too, Ivar. We have already talked over the reason for your being here, so we do not need to mention it again," he said, looking pointedly at Helge.

"I agree, Gudrod. It does not matter anyway, the boys are with us, and they are welcome. I just hope nothing happens to them. I would not want to be the one to tell Gudbjartur that we lost his sons."

"Nor I. Hopefully that will not be necessary. Gudbj knew the risks when he told me to take them," Gudrod said. "These boys knew the risks too, but I appreciate it did not stop them from coming with us."

A rumble of assent followed this last remark, effectively ending the conversation.

"All right, if there is nothing further," he said, his glance sweeping over his companions. "Let us be on our way. There is time remaining in this day to get farther upriver, at least until darkness or the next rapids, and then we will make camp for the night."

The banter between canoes, as the expedition set off up-river once again, did not last long as the men settled into the grind of paddling into the current.

* * *

The two remaining Haudeno scouts shadowed the canoes from the dense forest throughout the course of the day. The going through the forest was very difficult for the two men, but in spite of losing sight of the canoes many times, they caught up when the expedition stopped to rest after carrying canoes and equipment around the next rapids. The men would continue in this way until they departed to meet the main body of their raiding party as their canoes sped downstream on a collision course with those of the Northmen.

* * *

Gudrod called a welcome halt soon enough to set up camp and eat before full darkness descended at the end of the first day of upriver travel. Camped on the shore of a small lake, the men soon had a smokeless fire going and a kettle of water on to boil for stew.

Both boys eagerly helped by adding pieces of dried meat they cut into bite-sized pieces before stirring them in.

"Come with me and I will show you how to find onions to add to the pot." Bjarni, one of the men who stood watching the preparations, beckoned to them. The two boys finished their chore and rose to follow him into a grassy area close by.

"It is easy. Walk slowly through the grass until you smell them underfoot, like this." He bent down to separate the blades of grass until he found the two short cylindrical spears of the wild onion. Digging with the tip of his knife blade in the dark soil, he soon coaxed a small bulb loose and held it out to the boys. "Smell it, and you will always be able to find the onions. They add a good taste to the stew," he said, as both boys sniffed the plant. "Now, move slowly through the grass until you smell an onion, and then dig it up as you saw me do, until we have enough for our stew. Leave the tops on because they have the same taste as the little white bulbs."

Shortly thereafter, Bjarni and the boys washed their collection of onions in the river.

"So, you found some," Helge said appreciatively, as he approached the trio. "I just added some mushrooms to the pot, and others are collecting goosefoot greens and smartweed roots. We should have quite a feast tonight if everyone finds what they are looking for."

"Good. We will be ready to eat," Bjarni said, getting to his feet. "Here," he continued, handing Ivar his handful of onions, "you boys take these and chop them all up together with yours and throw them in the pot."

The two men watched the boys run off to do their bidding. "They are good lads, Helge, eager to learn and both do as they are told. That Ivar is something, though. I think he will be quite a man, like his father."

"Yes," Helge agreed, as he watched the boys kneeling beside the campfire using their knives to cut the onions into the stew. Chuckling as more than a few onions dropped into the fire, completely missing the pot, he continued. "Gudbj is proud of both of them. That is why I wonder if it is wise to expose them to the danger of a scouting expedition into unknown territory."

"We all worry about that, but they need to know what we are teaching them and this is the only way to learn the ways of being a man," Bjarni said. "There are enough of us that an enemy force might think twice before attacking."

"Aye, unless they have us outnumbered," Helge said.

"That is always a possibility, but I prefer to think they will be as curious about us as we are about them."

"Time will tell, Bjarni. Time will tell."

* * *

The two Haudeno scouts, concealed in the brush across the river from the Northmen's camp, watched the meal preparations with interest. The smell of the stew wafted across the river, causing the two men to salivate because all they had to eat was pemmican. The sound of the river hid their voices, allowing them to converse in almost normal tones, until darkness and a flickering fire across the river hid any activity from view and sleep gradually claimed them.

* * *

Dawn found the expedition members busily preparing to depart. They consumed the reheated remains of the stew. Bedrolls and packs, damp from the heavy overnight dew, lay stacked next to the canoes for loading, and Ivar and Lothar were receiving instruction in cleaning up the cookware at the river's edge.

"Why do we have to clean everything up?" Ivar asked, knowing the answer but defiant nonetheless. "I do not see anyone else working, just Lothar and me."

"Because I tell you to, Ivar, and I am a man, bigger, stronger, and tougher than either of you little boys," Helge said. "Now, scrub those bowls, spoons, and pot, out with sand like I showed you, so we can finish loading and launch the canoes."

Gritting his teeth, Ivar complied while Helge watched both of them with an amused expression on his face. *Lothar says nothing, but that Ivar, he is a fighter and is never bashful or hesitant with an argument.*

"You two will learn many things on this expedition, which is why you are with us—to learn. We will decide what you are to be taught, not you. We all went through these things, Ivar. Every dirty job that needs doing you will do. The most important thing you will learn is to obey. Remember that, both of you. It will make this time easy and fun. You are no longer boys. You are with us to learn to become men, so you can stand beside us as equals. No matter what we do, we will do it together. It is your father's wish that you be here. You will get out of it what you put into it. Do not fight against us. You cannot win. If you persist, somebody will get mad at you. Now, do we understand each other?" he asked, his glance going from boy to boy before coming to rest on Ivar.

Lothar simply nodded without comment, but not Ivar. Silent acceptance was not his nature. "Yes, Helge, we understand. I will learn carefully so when it is my turn to teach boys how to be men I will know how to do it correctly," he said, his unblinking eyes fastened on the face of the large man who towered over him.

Throwing his head back, the man guffawed at the pluck of the boy. "I will wager you will," he said. "Enough of this. Now, get this gear loaded. Let me see if you remember the *correct* way to load it. The others are ready to go, so let us be about it." Helge walked away shaking his head. *That boy definitely came from the loins of Gudbjartur Einarsson. Someday he will be every bit the man his father is. By the gods, he will make a chieftain,* he thought, as he stooped to take hold of one of the canoes to push it into the water.

* * *

The two Haudeno warriors were silent witnesses to everything that transpired in the camp of the Norsemen, including the obvious defiance of one of the boys. They did not understand the conversation, of course, but body language and facial expressions are universal. The two men glanced at each other and commented appreciatively over the courage of the young boy who faced up to the big hairy man who confronted him.

A short time later, the five canoes paddled upriver, and the two warriors rose stiffly from their place of concealment and shadowed them from the forest, as before. Both were damp and chilled from the heavy dew of the night air, but soon the sweat of exertion warmed them as they continued to keep pace with the canoes. This continued until the canoes beached below the next rapids and began another portage.

The river began a wide loop to the south and the two Haudeno warriors chose this time to set off overland, cutting off a half day's travel time to the agreed upon lake rendezvous point with their main body. They had much to report to their leader, and they set off at an easy lope into the southeast.

* * *

"From now on, two men will be on guard, one in front, and one behind while we are carrying around these rapids,"

Gudrod said, as the canoes beached below the same rapids. "I will take the lead and you, Helge, take the rear. We will trade off at the next rapids. Everyone stay alert. Eventually we will make contact with these people, and I want us to be ready. I doubt they will jump us, especially if they see we are ready, but when they do contact us it will be while we go around one of these rapids, for that is when we are the most vulnerable."

Unlike the other rapids they encountered, these coursed through country that was more open; the heavy forest gave way to a mix of river and fen. The openness did make for easier going if one did not consider the gluey mud of the fen they encountered if they strayed very far from the rocky riverbank.

Later that day the idyllic stretch of river the expedition had been paddling on for the past several hours narrowed appreciatively from the flat calmness they had found so enjoyable. The river suddenly deepened as it funneled through a narrow gorge. Although confined by the walls of the gorge, the river formed no rapids. Instead, a powerful smooth current flowed from a large lake at the top end of the gorge.

Gudrod, being in the bow of the lead canoe, decided to maneuver into the middle of the current pouring from the lake rather than remain near the wall of the gorge, in somewhat slacker water, as he, Ivar, and the two men with him attempted to shoot through the narrow opening of the gorge and into the lake itself. That this decision was the wrong one, given the conditions, became immediately apparent as the canoe spun like a top in the powerful outflow and capsized, dumping occupants and equipment into the icy water.

Shouts of consternation rose from the other boats as the occupants frantically grabbed packs, weapons, and people as they surged past. Both Gudrod and Ivar managed to stay afloat long enough to lay hands on a pack or other item of cargo—for neither could swim—as they surged rapidly downstream in the grip of the powerful current. Helge grabbed one man as he slammed into his canoe. The other man was not so lucky. He wound up under the overturned canoe, slipping under the surface to drown in the cold dark depths without anyone witnessing his demise. His water-soaked clothing dragged him under before he could utter a cry for assistance.

The four upright canoes, their occupants no longer paddling as they grabbed for floating equipment or weapons, spun out of control in the current as everything, including Gudrod and Ivar, floated downstream in the grip of the powerful current. For a time men shouted without purpose, all gripped by the need to do something, anything.

Finally, a shout from Helge restored a certain order to the chaotic scene. "Forget the gear! Go after Gudrod and Ivar!" he shouted at the top of his voice. "We will pick up as much as we can here."

Two canoes detached from the group and sped downstream in search of Gudrod and Ivar, both of whom were out of sight around a bend of the river. They found Ivar as he struggled out of the water and onto the rocks of the river's edge.

"I am all right!" Ivar shouted and waved as the two canoes swept past. "Gudrod is downstream somewhere." With that, he sagged to the ground, exhausted. He pulled the soggy pack that had saved his life across his outstretched legs and hugged it to his chest. His breath came in shuddering gasps as he glanced around and tried to regain himself. Downstream he saw the two canoes speed around another bend and out of sight. Looking upriver, he saw that he was quite alone for the moment. He stretched out full length to rest and wait for someone to come for him.

* * *

Four Haudeno warriors were in the forest behind Ivar. Two of them were the scouts that had shadowed the five canoes as they proceeded upstream. They viewed the chaotic upset in the gorge as assistance from the gods, for right before them was the brave boy they had mentioned to their chief.

As it happened, one of the four men hiding in the forest, a matter of feet behind Ivar had lost his only son the preceding winter. He viewed the appearance of this brave, pale-skinned boy, as a gift sent to him from the river gods. His companions tried to talk him out of it.

"The risk is too great, Odatshedeh. If the pale-skins see us. . .," one said.

"The gods have sent this boy. He is about the same age as my son was. The pale-skins are too busy to see us. We can grab him and be gone before they know we are here," Odatshedeh said. "Two of us can grab him while the other two keep a lookout for the pale-skins. Seawi, you help me," he lifted his chin to a companion.

The man, Seawi, glanced away toward the boy stretched out on the riverbank. Making up his mind, he nodded to his companions. "I will do this thing," he said with conviction.

"Good! It will take only a moment and we will be gone from here." Odatshedeh glanced at the other two men with a nod.

They reluctantly agreed with the scheme. "We will take this news to our leader. He will want to know in case we do not see either of you again," one of the men said. The two warriors set off to rejoin their main body.

Odatshedeh and Seawi sneaked out of the forest toward the supine Ivar. The gurgling of the river masked any slight sound of their approach. Ivar had no warning before they were upon him. The two warriors ruthlessly subdued his resistance, muffling his cries of terror. Quickly they whisked him away into the cover of the forest.

* * *

"Where did you last see him?" Gudrod asked, shivering in his soaked clothing. His eyes anxiously swept the passing shoreline from the canoe that had picked him up after his soaking.

"There!" exclaimed the man paddling in front of him, pointing at the nearby riverbank with an extended paddle. "I see the pack he floated to shore on."

The four occupants of the canoe, Gudrod included, grabbed weapons, vaulted into the shallows of the river, and surged for the shore. Securing their canoe out of the water, the men spread out, looking for tracks in the rocky soil.

"Here, I have found fresh tracks," Bjarni shouted, kneeling to examine a single print in the mud between two big rocks.

The others joined him. "This is like the other tracks we have been seeing along the river, not one of ours," Gudrod said. "Scatter out and look for more." Looking upstream, he saw the rest of his men come around the bend, paddling rapidly to join them. "Here come the other canoes. Bjarni, you stay here and tell them what has happened. It looks like natives may have taken Ivar prisoner. Come you men," gesturing toward the forest, to the remaining two, "we will try to cut their trail."

* * *

The raiding party clustered around the struggling boy, curious to see such a strange youngster. The meeting between Ivar's abductors and the main body of the Haudeno raiding party, some twenty men, was brief.

"Take him to the canoes. We will meet you there after we meet the pale-skins," Sakokaeah said, watching the two abductors tie Ivar's wrists and legs securely to a short pole. The main body of warriors scattered out in the forest concealing themselves on either side of the game trail that they expected the pale-skins to use.

Odatshedeh and Seawi picked up the pole to which they had trussed Ivar and loped away, the boy swinging suspended between them. They made off at the best possible speed for the lake where they had hidden their canoes. The two men paused to catch their breath a couple times along the way, undue haste unnecessary; for they knew the other warriors of the raiding party would cut off any attempt at pursuit.

* * *

Ivar endured the pain and discomfort of whipping brush and tree limbs, the constant jostling, and abrupt changes of direction for which he could not adjust as he hung suspended on the bouncing pole. Suddenly his captors burst from the dense forest onto the shore of a lake where they dropped him abruptly in the mud of the shoreline. The two Haudeno warriors began pulling the cut branches and brush from a group of canoes that lay concealed nearby, paying no attention to Ivar. The boy used the opportunity to worm his way loose from his bonds. He jumped to his feet and ran away toward the nearby forest.

His captors shouted at him and gave chase. One man caught him just as he entered the forest verge, cuffing him to the ground. The boy jumped up and flailed with his fists at his antagonist, managing to strike him on the side of his jaw. The man recoiled with an exclamation. The boy pressed his attack. The other warrior positively collapsed with laughter as his companion dodged away from the shrieking boy. An argument ensued. The two men, one of them still consumed with mirth, the other angry, stood out of range regarding their captive. The boy glanced from one to the other. Without waiting for a resumption of the brief struggle, Ivar stooped and grabbed a length of dry tree limb lying at his feet.

Without pause he shrieked the one word he knew his father used when attacking. "Odin!" The shrill war cry of his people burst from the boy's mouth as he ran at the two surprised warriors.

Both men leaped aside, easily avoiding Ivar's rush. The angry one swung a knobbed wooden club at the boy's head at the same time, hitting him flush above the right ear. The boy fell senseless to the ground.

The two Haudeno stood over the boy's unconscious form. One chuckled while the other exclaimed in anger over the pluck of the boy to attack him, a warrior.

"We should kill him," Seawi said angrily.

"You will not harm him. He will replace my dead son. He is young and strong; a brave boy to fight two grown men," Odatshedeh said, glancing down at the inert form. His eyes shifted back to his fellow.

Seawi locked eyes with him. He shifted his glance uncomfortably at the unmistakable warning in Odatshedeh's eyes.

"As you wish. He is your problem then. He will not bend easily to your will."

"He will bend or break as a branch in the north wind. I will give him this choice," Odatshedeh said.

Both men were still in conversation thusly when the boy stirred from his place on the ground.

* * *

Ivar sat up slowly. His ears rang and he felt dizzy from the blow. His head spun and he had trouble focusing his eyes for a moment as he rubbed the knot just swelling into prominence on the side of his head. His fingers came away covered with blood. He wiped his bloody fingers on his tunic. In spite of the defiant look he cast at his antagonists, unwillingly his eyes filled with tears at the pain.

One of the men knelt before him on the ground; not the one that hit him, the other one. Ivar made to strike at him, but the man grabbed his wrists in an iron grip, forcing them down, his eyes on Ivar's all the while.

The shape of the man's face and his hooked nose reminds me of Deskaheh. The lean, wolfish face and hooked nose was an arm's length away from him. A sheen of sweat glistened on the skin of the man's shaven skull. The black scalp lock made the man look dangerous. Ivar shuddered.

The Haudeno slowly relaxed his grip, his black eyes on Ivar's blue eyes. He wagged an extended finger in front of Ivar's face, then drew his finger across his throat, a clear indication to the boy what he could expect if he caused further trouble. The man raised his chin questioningly. Ivar nodded.

Getting to his feet, the man reached down and jerked the boy upright, pushing him toward the canoe.

Ivar glanced back in the direction they had come, a wild look on his face as his eyes desperately sought some avenue of escape. His face reflected despair at his plight. He paused a moment longer, the lake at his back. The two Haudeno warriors spread out before him blocking his way. The angry one motioned impatiently toward the canoe. With a shuddering sigh of resignation, Ivar turned and walked dejectedly to the canoe. *I do not know what they intend to do with me,* he thought, as he sat down in the center of the canoe. Gingerly his hand sought the knot above his ear. He looked at his bloody fingers with a kind of detached expression on his face. *I am still bleeding. Wound dew, my father would call it.* He closed his eyes and massaged his temples to still the wave of dizziness that activity had engendered. *At least I am still alive.* The enormity of the situation allowed the tendrils of despair to ensnare his fertile young mind.

* * *

The eleven heavily armed Northmen, with Lothar bringing up the rear, spread out into the forest. They proceeded cautiously, studying the ground until they cut the trail of the kidnappers.

"Hold up, men," Gudrod said, holding out both arms. "If we continue like this we may run headlong into an ambush. Skeggi, you go ahead and see what you can find."

Skeggi, the best tracker among them, walked in widening half circles out in front of Gudrod and the others, head down, examining the ground closely until he found where Ivar's abductors had joined up with a much larger group. He turned and waved Gudrod forward.

"How many, Skeggi?" Gudrod asked impatiently.

"It is difficult to tell exactly in these leaves and pine needles, but I would say at least twelve men." I think most of them are still close by, Gudrod. They were walking, not running. These two pairs of tracks here," he continued, kneeling down to point them out, "are following the game trail straightaway. They are trotting, carrying something heavy, probably Ivar, between them. These other tracks are over the top of them. There are two sets, and a large bunch of men made them. They may be between us and the two that have Ivar."

Pulling at his beard in silence, Gudrod looked out over the trail ahead, obviously thinking about a course of action.

"How do you know they are carrying something?" Helge asked, looking at Skeggi.

"The tracks are deeper than these others. The outside edges of each footprint are deeper still because they were leaning away from something they carried between them."

Kneeling down to examine the tracks, Helge snorted in derision. "You can tell all that from these tracks in the leaves? I can hardly see them."

"That is why he is the tracker and you are not, Helge," Gudrod said, his glance darting furtively through the forest ahead of where they stood. "Now enough of that. Scatter out on either side of this trail. Skeggi, you follow the tracks. The rest of us will follow you. I do not need to tell you all we must find Ivar before these men take him clear away so we never find him."

A strangled cry from Lothar, almost forgotten in the excitement, followed this pronouncement. "Do not say that, Gudrod! You must find Ivar and get him back," he blubbered miserably. "Our father will be very angry if you lose Ivar."

"Easy boy, easy," Gudrod said, placing a hand on the trembling shoulder of Lothar. "I did not mean we will not get Ivar back. We will certainly try. That is all we can do. Now, you stay right beside me, Lothar. We will do our very best. You can help us by keeping your eyes open for anything we might miss. Buck up now and pay attention," he continued sternly. "You will not help Ivar by crying."

Gudrod turned away from the boy and the two joined the line of advancing Northmen moving slowly through the forest, alert for the least movement, sound, or sign. Suddenly the shrill cry of some kind of bird, close at hand and not in keeping with the surroundings, caused Skeggi, followed closely by Gudrod, to crouch quickly behind the nearest clump of underbrush.

Several arrows zipped suddenly from the dense brush ahead. Two men behind Gudrod, a little too slow to react, went down. It fell to Gudrod, with nine men including himself and a young boy, to beat off the attack of a superior force of shouting warriors.

* * *

Chapter Six

Gudbjartur, prisoner of the Naskapi

As Gudbjartur languished during the final hours of darkness on this second day as a captive of the Naskapi, he pushed his problems into the distant recesses of his mind, choosing instead to dwell on pleasant memories associated with his peoples' short history in Vinland.

During the last half of the Lambing Time Moon, he recalled the decision by majority opinion to remain for the winter, or permanently. To that end, construction of the settlement began. Building material was nearby and profuse. While workers satisfied the demands for the project, he also ordered timber stockpiled for trade with Greenland.

During the Haymaking Time Moon, the vitally important summertime tasks began in earnest. Workers scythed winter fodder for the livestock. The grass of the lush meadows and fen matured a full moon earlier this far south. He and Halfdan suspected that the rapid growth of the grass—armpit high at maturity—would limit its value as winter fodder. Halfdan had turned to him with a twinkle in his eye. Gudbjartur chuckled to recall the thought, *It would be better than snowballs,* he had said with a straight face.

The cut grass cured rapidly in the hot midday sun, helped along by the unceasing wind. As soon as the grass dried sufficiently to be stored, workers raked the hay up and transported it to the byre end of each longhouse.

Others cured and stored the enormous quantities of meat and codfish brought in by the hunters and fishermen that would be required to sustain the people over the long winter. The larders bulged with processed whale and seal meat, always a mainstay. Great quantities of dried sturgeon meat and barrels of their salted roe rapidly accumulated from the easily caught fish. He recalled that when they came in from the sea their numbers literally choked the rivers as they fought their way inland to spawn.

After completion of much of the summer work, Halfdan sent him with nine others on a scouting trip far to the southeast. He had decided to take Deskaheh the Haudeno, their former prisoner—now an accepted member of their society—on the scouting trip because of his knowledge of the interior and his desire to participate. Halfdan had previously told Deskaheh, after his weeks of captivity, that he was free to return to his people, but Deskaheh had decided to remain until autumn, at least.

Now, after several moons among his former captors, it appeared that his stay might be permanent. He told them he might not be welcome among his people after losing so many warriors. Besides, he had told them, he had no family left and he rather liked his life among the Northmen, especially considering he and Thora had developed quite an interest in each other.

He chuckled over the thought of the two together. He could not imagine a more unlikely pair. For some reason, Thora, a woman avoided by men because of her sharp tongue, became enchanted with Deskaheh and him with her. No longer was she the woman of the sharp tongue, the reason being that Deskaheh had proven to be the man she needed and wanted. The change in her was profound. It became a favored topic of gossip whenever a group of women gathered. Because of their association, Deskaheh rapidly learned the Norse language and Thora, at the same time, became adept in the language of the Haudeno. A thoroughly useful and timely relationship had developed.

It seems like only yesterday. Now my men are probably captured or dead. Unwillingly his thoughts returned to the present as the Naskapi camp began to stir with the first faint lightening of the eastern sky. *The new dawn promises rain later in the day.* Gudbjartur glanced at the leaden sky. *Maybe some of the mosquitoes will drown.*

* * *

One of his captors dropped a chunk of meat and a leather pouch containing the dried ration all the Naskapi carried with them on the ground at Gudbjartur's feet. Freeing his hands, the man motioned at the food, and turned to his companions, "Look at him. His face is all swollen from mosquito bites. His eyes are almost shut."

"I do not care if they sucked out all his blood and he is blind," Kejo said disgustedly.

"Get him some more water. And the medicine leaves and wood ashes to stop the bleeding," Glooscap ordered.

Gudbjartur regarded the man who helped him from under painfully swollen eyelids as he cleaned himself up as best he could. The man did not seem hostile toward him. In fact he acted almost as if he was concerned, which he was not, of course. Stripping the leaves off a low-growing bush close by, the man gestured for Gudbjartur to put them in his mouth and chew them into a green paste to apply to his wounds. The leaves were very bitter, but he did as the man bade him, chewing the leaves into a paste, and then mixing them with ashes from the fire on a handy piece of bark. The resulting poultice, applied thickly to his wounds, provided an immediate coolness, and stanched the seeping blood. Nodding in satisfaction his benefactor rose and departed without having uttered a word. Gudbjartur looked curiously at the leaves and the bush they came from, resolving to remember their curative powers for later use.

The hostile one, Kejo, walked over and looked closely at Gudbjartur. Snorting derisively, he delivered a powerful kick to Gudbjartur's leg. A low groan escaped Gudbjartur's lips in spite of his effort to remain stoic.

"Leave him alone Kejo! He can not walk if you break his leg," Glooscap said. "And if he cannot walk you may have to carry him," he added for emphasis.

* * *

The day before Gudbjartur's capture, after a hectic day-long pursuit by a determined party of Naskapi, he had split his canoe crew up and the four men set off separately in the hope they could elude pursuit in that way. One of them, Deskaheh the Haudeno, finally eluded his pursuers by walking in the water of a small lake for a time and then hiding under a pile of flotsam against a tree that had fallen in the water.

He did not know what happened to the three men he had been with until he smelled smoke just before sundown. Using the cover of coming darkness, he followed the faint odor to its source.

The guttering campfire he found revealed few details except the men lounging around it on the rocky outcropping were Naskapi warriors. The failing light offered no clue as to the identity of the prisoner dimly visible at the outer edge of the available firelight tied to a tree, but he resolved to find out before continuing with his own escape.

After spending the night hidden securely within the low-lying brush above the Naskapi camp, covering himself with leaves and brush to ward off insects and the chill night air, he patiently awaited the coming dawn. Like most of his kind, he was content and stoic in the circumstance.

In the dim light of pre-dawn, he observed the Naskapi camp stir to life. Knowing they would set off without delay he concentrated on the prisoner who remained tied to the tree. One of the Naskapi untied him and jerked the man to his feet, where he swayed weakly back and forth, just managing to keep his balance. *It is, Gudbj,* Deskaheh thought excitedly, identifying the large muscular frame of Halfdan's lieutenant. *At least he is alive. They have a use for him; otherwise, he would be dead.*

One of the Naskapi said something to Gudbjartur and gestured toward the lakeshore. Without further discussion, the seven warriors, their prisoner in the middle, set off single file along the shoreline and out of his range of vision.

Deskaheh waited for some time to be certain he was the only one in the vicinity, then rose from his place of concealment and made off in the direction of the river that had borne the scouting expedition to this place. Halfdan would want the news of the expedition's demise as soon as he could make the long journey back to Halfdansfjord.

* * *

Gudrod's Hunting Party

As Gudrod's men pressed forward rather than retreating, the battle with the native warriors who had ambushed them raged back and forth for a time, literally from tree to tree, the combatants never coming to grips in hand-to-hand fighting. All the Northmen, armed with bows, a couple of heavy hunting spears, a like number of hand axes, and Gudrod's sword, gave a good account of themselves but the bow, being primarily a defensive weapon in these circumstances, offered no opportunity for the charge that had proven so effective against these men during the previous engagement. Nor did the outnumbered men have the heavy shields, battleaxes, and throwing spears, normally associated with offensive warfare, with them on this hunting expedition.

Gudrod finally called for a withdrawal as it became obvious they battled a superior force.

"Fall back slowly!" he shouted. "Keep the pressure on! If they begin to press the attack, shoot arrows as rapidly as possible! We must keep them off us or we are doomed!"

"They are not following us, Gudrod!" Helge shouted from the flank of the Northmen's line that extended into the forest. "They are leaving."

One last flight of arrows came from the well-concealed enemy as they melted into their forest fastness.

"Helge, Gudrod is hit," one of the men, shouted.

"So am I," Bjarni shouted, hopping over to lean against a tree. "I am hit in the leg."

Their comrades gathered around the two wounded men. Bjarni had already broken off the arrow shaft when Skeggi knelt down to examine the wound.

"You are luckier than Gudrod, Bjarni; he got an arrow in the neck. It looks like your arrow is stuck in just the big muscle of your upper leg. I do not think it is in deep enough to be stuck in the bone. The loose folds of your tunic probably slowed it down some. Do you want it out, my friend?" he said, looking up at the man.

"Yes, do it! I am ready," he answered through gritted teeth.

Skeggi grasped the stub of the arrow shaft, pushed the tip of his knife down along the shaft, slightly widening the entry hole in the process, until he felt it grate against the arrowhead, and jerked shaft and knife out in one motion.

Bjarni, gasped and grabbed his leg with both hands, "By the gods!"

"You will be fine. I will build a small fire," Skeggi said, grinning mirthlessly at the man. "You can heat your knife blade a little and burn that wound shut to stop the bleeding."

"Never mind the fire. I will tear a strip of wadmal off my tunic and bind it up. You had best go see about Gudrod," he said, with a lift of his chin indicating the group of men gathered around their fallen leader.

* * *

Gudrod was still alive, but shot through the neck as he was, all he could manage was a gurgle as the wound dew, his life's blood, poured from his mouth.

"Gudrod," Helge said, resting a hand on the man's shoulder as he knelt on the ground at his side. "I am sorry, you have a death wound. The Valkyries come for you; I hear their song."

The men grouped around their fallen leader glanced furtively at their surroundings, sure in their own minds that the handmaidens of Odin would materialize from the forest at any minute and bear Gudrod to Valhalla.

Helge placed Gudrod's sword in his hand, closing the man's stiffening fingers around the haft. Gudrod nodded slightly and blinked his eyes in silent thanks; passage into the afterlife with weapon in hand, the hope of all warriors.

They could do nothing further for him. His men waited silently for death to claim their leader. A few moments later Gudrod's eyes suddenly opened wide. A wet gurgle passed his lips. His legs stiffened out in a last spasm of resistance, and he died.

* * *

Sometime later, the nine surviving members of the expedition, gathered around the graves of their three fallen comrades, discussed their recent experiences. The mounds of river rock over each corpse bore testimony to the mood pervading the group.

"I would call our battle with those men a draw," Helge said, glancing at the others. "The river claimed Bersi, and we lost Gudrod, Ofeiger, and Sturla in battle. They lost five men from our arrows, but they had more to start with, so I think that makes us even."

"They took their fallen warriors with them so we do not know if they are dead or even how many there are for certain," Bjarni said.

"It does not matter, Bjarni, they are gone and that is all we need to know. They left when they did because they did not intend to do anything but delay us from pursuing them to recover Ivar. The two men who took Ivar were long gone when their comrades ambushed us. I think we were outnumbered two-to-one judging from the tracks we found when we followed them to the lake where they had their canoes hidden," Skeggi said.

"I wish I knew why they attacked us. We meant them no harm. We were just exploring," Helge said, thinking aloud.

"As I mentioned at the lake, I do not think they belonged here either. It was a raiding party and they were out to get whatever they could. When they saw Ivar alone, and saw he was only a boy, they grabbed him," Skeggi said.

"They look like Deskaheh did when we first captured him," Lothar said. The boy had stood off to the side of the group of men, largely forgotten as the discussion progressed.

Helge nodded in agreement as his glance shifted to the boy. He chuckled at this bit of information from one so young.

"I think you are right, Lothar. I guess the rest of us were so busy we did not notice that the men we were shooting at looked like Deskaheh. So, they were Haudeno, not Naskapi," he added as an afterthought.

"I saw Lothar shoot several arrows himself," one of the men said.

"And, I," another said.

"I hit one of them, too. I saw him fall down," the boy said proudly, happy to be the center of attention for a change. Looking around the group of men, he directed a question to Helge, who seemed to have assumed leadership. "Helge, are we going to go after Ivar?"

Shaking his head, the man glanced at his companions. "I do not think that would be wise, Lothar. We are too few and we do not know this country. If Deskaheh was with us we would probably go after them, but the eight of us here would not be able to get Ivar back without some help. If we push them, I am afraid they might kill him. What do the rest of you think?" Helge's glance took in the attentive men.

Nobody said anything for moment, most of the men apparently unsure what they thought at this point.

"I, for one, agree, Helge, and I think the others do, too," Bjarni shifted his eyes to his silent companions. "We know how Lothar feels about his brother being kidnapped. We all feel his loss, too, but getting Ivar killed by an attempt to recover him certainly would not be very smart."

Helge regarded the small group thoughtfully. "All right, so be it then. If nobody has anything further to say about all this, let us load the canoes and head for Halfdansfjord. We should arrive back there sometime tomorrow. If it was not so late in the day I think we could make the journey downstream in one day because we can shoot most of the rapids without carrying around them. But, I think it best to put some distance between this place and our camp tonight just in case some of the Haudeno come back."

"I have something to ask, Helge," Lothar said.

Helge and the other men stopped what they were doing and gave the boy their attention.

"When will we go after Ivar? We must try to get him back before winter," Lothar said in a hopeful tone of voice.

"That will be up to Halfdan and your father, Lothar. Gudbj is certain to want to go after him right away and he should return about the same time as us, so we will have an answer to that question right away, maybe even tomorrow."

Lothar nodded, but said nothing further on the subject as he helped load the canoes.

They decided to leave two canoes behind because with their depleted numbers they would not need them. They stored them upside down in a good hiding place and covered both with brush to both protect them from the elements and conceal them from the prying eyes of those using the river.

* * *

Lothar did his best to keep up his end of the paddling as the four canoes set out on their journey downstream. As time passed he lapsed into a silence that endured until they camped for the night. His misery over the loss of his brother and best friend was obvious to everyone. Although his companions attempted to include him in the banter between canoes, he remained taciturn.

After a time, conversation died for everyone. The unpleasant task of telling Ingerd and Gudbjartur of the loss of Ivar weighed heavily on everyone's mind, especially Helge, whose duty it would be to do the telling.

* * *

The Haudeno war party and their captive, Ivar Gudbjartursson

Ivar's captors had joined the main body of the war party near sundown the day before. The planned rendezvous occurred three days after his capture in a well-protected inlet off the large lake they had paddled through all day. A dogleg bend in the inlet's shoreline ensured the campsite remained hidden away from possible detection by enemies using the same lake for travel.

Ivar leaned against a sun-warmed rock watching the sixteen warriors mill about as they talked and tended to the two wounded among them. The fourteen new arrivals seemed curious about their strange captive at first. Now, beyond an occasional glance, the men paid little attention to him.

One of his captors and a particularly fearsome looking man, to whom he deferred, left the others and came toward him. They stopped in front of him and the man he knew as Odatshedeh talked to the fearsome one at length. He had no doubt that they talked about him.

"The boy is a brave one, Sakokaeah," Odatshedeh said. "He screamed his war cry and attacked Seawi and me with a stick." He chuckled at the memory, and then faced the other man, his expression gone serious. "He will replace my dead son. My wife, Nahcomis still grieves for my son. She will welcome this boy."

"The council will decide his fate, not you or I. His bravery will weigh heavily with them. Until they decide, he is an enemy, boy or not. We have all lost family. It is the way of things," Sakokaeah said as he studied Ivar's face.

Under the scrutiny of the man, Ivar pushed himself erect from the rock upon which he leaned. "I am Ivar, the son of Gudbjartur," he said, tapping himself on the chest with his thumb. "Ivar," he repeated.

The two Haudeno glanced at each other and then back at their prisoner. Both were silent for a heartbeat. Odatshedeh looked again at his companion and the corners of his eyes crinkled in mirth. He chuckled. "He has not spoken before." He looked at Ivar and tapped his own chest. "Ivar, I am called Odatshedeh." He pointed at his companion. "Our war chief is called Sakokaeah." The two men waited for a response. The other warriors overheard the exchange and watched the drama unfold.

Ivar eyed the two men before him. Then he glanced at the other warriors, gone suddenly silent as they waited. He pulled himself up straight and locked eyes with the man who had captured him. "Odatshedeh," he said in almost perfect mimicry of the strange name while nodding his head in acknowledgement. His eyes shifted to the hard black eyes of the war chief. The man scared him. He steeled his resolve. "Sakokaeah, I am Ivar the Northman," he said. He hoped his voice was steady.

The unblinking eyes traveled over Ivar's erect, rigidly held body as the man appraised this upstart who confronted him with such bravery for one so young. He looked full into the blue eyes that returned his regard without flinching. He inclined his head slightly without breaking eye contact. "Ivar," he said. "Grown men fear me, but you, a mere boy, do not." His eyes flicked to Odatshedeh. "This boy will be a great warrior one day. I will speak of this to the council. You have done the right thing, Odatshedeh." He again made eye contact with Ivar, and then without a word turned away to rejoin the others.

Odatshedeh's eyes followed his chieftain for a moment and then shifted to Ivar. Slowly a grin spread across the hard visage. He held Ivar's eyes, reached out slowly, and squeezed his shoulder. The boy held the man's eyes and endured his touch without flinching away. The touch was brief, the smile genuine. Odatshedeh nodded slightly and turned away.

Ivar watched him go. Slowly he exhaled. He chanced to look toward the others. All watched him; their faces no longer seemed hostile. *These Haudeno are just men, not unlike any others. For the first time since they captured me I am not afraid,* he thought, as he leaned back on the rock and crossed his arms.

* * *

The Naskapi and their prisoner

Moving rapidly northeast, paralleling the shoreline, the seven Naskapi alternately walked and trotted in single file with their prisoner at the center. They did not restrain Gudbjartur in any way, but his position in the center of the line made escape impossible. The Naskapi made no attempt at stealth. By nature, they moved quietly, giving Gudbjartur to believe this to be their home territory.

Later that morning the leaden sky began to give up its moisture. Sporadic drops of rain steadily increased to a downpour accompanied by brilliant flashes of lightning, gusts of wind, and ear-splitting cracks of thunder. *Thor is in rare form with this display. Perhaps the god of thunder has sent this storm to my aid*, Gudbjartur mused. However, no relief materialized, nor did the Naskapi seek shelter.

The grueling pace continued through the course of two long days, never slackening or halting. Men dropped out occasionally to relieve themselves and caught up when they finished. Their captive got no such consideration. Circumstance dictated that he relieve himself on the go. Beyond a splitting headache and the pain of his wounds, Gudbjartur had no difficulty maintaining the pace, knowing his fate without doubt if he could not.

They consumed food and water only when they halted overnight. With few exceptions, no conversation passed between the men, making their progress through the heavy forest virtually silent except for the occasional scrape of leather clothing on brush or the snap of a twig. Startled animals of all kinds, frequently surprised out of their reverie by this silent approach, scattered before them. Gudbjartur found he was developing a grudging admiration for his captors. He had become increasingly aware of their perfect harmony with the world in which they lived. They had the ability to glide through the forest like wraiths, unheard and unseen, making them deadly adversaries.

In many ways, they were similar in appearance to Deskaheh, although these men had darker skin tones and their faces were not as sharp and angular. Their clothing and weapons also were similar to Deskaheh's yet at the same time different. *These men are Naskapi and Deskaheh is Haudeno—different tribes.* Their languages did not sound the same to him either, although he thought them similar.

The advantage and utility of the short roach of hair down the center of their shaven heads, so in contrast to his long hair, the short compact weapons they all carried, and every item of clothing they wore, became increasingly apparent to him. He knew the reddish tint of their skin was not natural. They rubbed a red gluey mud on themselves to ward off mosquitoes. A lifetime of use left their skin stained permanently red. Deskaheh used the mud also. He had demonstrated how to use it and where to find it to the Northmen; many people now used it to avoid the clouds of insects that plagued every air-breathing creature. Glooscap finally offered it to him, demonstrating its use with elaborate gestures. It was the last time mosquitoes pestered him beyond buzzing around his face. The Naskapi thought it humorous, save Kejo, as he smeared himself, including his beard, liberally with the messy substance.

His people could learn much from these men, and given the opportunity both groups would benefit from the association. Of this, he was certain.

Finally, midday of the third day the pace slackened, and Glooscap sent Kejo and Eskanan ahead. Some time later, the haunting cry of a loon brought the group to a quick halt. Listening intently, they heard a repeat of the signal. One of them answered in like fashion, and the group set out toward the echoing sound without anyone having uttered a word.

They came out of the forest onto a high cliff overlooking a river. Kejo and Eskanan waited near two canoes that they had just pulled from the concealing brush. The men crowded around one another in animated conversation while Gudbjartur observed silently. He thought it curious that they ignored him for the most part. *Overt action on my part would no doubt attract immediate attention.* He smiled inwardly at the thought.

Free to examine the boats, he found them to be similar in appearance to those captured from Deskaheh's men. These, too, consisted of a rigid framework of split hardwood over which the builder attached a skin of white birch bark. The lengthwise internal framework, upswept at each end, and braced crossways with thicker, equally spaced wooden members, established the outer shape of the vessel. Thinly split, inner tree bark or roots—probably from the same birch trees the bark came from—laced all the various parts together. Pine pitch, a substance used by his people, too, sealed all the joints in the bark covering. Both ends being identical, it did not matter which direction the occupants faced. The bottom in the middle was flat, tapering, and curving upwards toward each end. Having lived with boats all his life, Gudbjartur knew these boats would be as functional as the

Haudeno canoes that had transported him and his men to this place.

* * *

Glooscap watched Gudbjartur's examination of the boats. He surprised him by offering what sounded like a brief explanation.

"They are called canoes," Glooscap said. "We will use them for the rest of the journey to our village."

"Canoes," Gudbjartur repeated, nodding in understanding. *Perhaps later, providing I still live, I will tell Glooscap how I came to know of the canoe.*

Soon after he had recovered sufficiently from his mauling to pay close attention to what occurred around him, he realized that Glooscap was the same man who had stopped in front of the windfall where he lay hidden. Considering this man had spared his life after his capture he felt fortunate that he had hesitated before attacking him that morning. *It is funny how things turn out. My fate is ordained by the gods,* he thought, as he looked into the black eyes that had searched the windfall for him. *If I had killed him, I myself would be dead now. One day, if I survive, I will tell him of these things. We should get a good laugh out of it.*

The two men regarded one another without another word passing between them. Glooscap returned to the others. As the Naskapi turned away, Gudbjartur noticed a slight softening of his facial expression with the addition of a few crinkles around the eyes. *Not a smile exactly, but a welcome change from the stern expression he normally uses when he looks at me.* With the exception of Kejo, who remained taciturn and antagonistic, the Naskapi's hostility toward him had gradually changed to one of indifference.

The canoes were large enough for four or five men. Each had bulrush mats on which to kneel while plying the paddles.

Glooscap motioned for Gudbjartur to help launch one of the canoes. They easily lifted the canoe and launched it into the river. The delicate maneuver of boarding required a certain amount of teamwork to prevent its capsizing.

Gudbjartur boarded first while the others held it stable. Then Kejo, Eskanan, and Glooscap followed suit. Each boarded by gripping the sides and springing in, settling easily onto the bulrush mats spread in the bottom. The two canoes moved off upstream with everyone paddling.

* * *

Before his capture, Gudbjartur had marveled at the ease of paddling a canoe and the speed it attained without undue effort. Now he found the constant flexing of shoulder muscles as he paddled reopened the wounds in his upper body, causing considerable pain and discomfort as the days wore on.

Frequent rain showers gave them relief from periods of hot muggy sunshine, but on more than one occasion, Gudbjartur bailed rapidly with a bark scoop tossed to him by the scowling Kejo.

For the next two days they paddled steadily up river, carrying the canoes around rapids encountered, stopping only as the daylight faded to darkness. They subsisted on dry rations while the men lounged for a time recounting the day's events before sinking into an exhausted sleep. They tied Gudbjartur securely to a tree each night, but not with his hands around the trunk as before. Instead, the rope passed around his waist and his back rested against the tree trunk.

Midday of the next day they sighted three canoes as they paddled along the shoreline of one of the many lakes. At first sighting, Gudbjartur's captors allowed their canoes to drift, hugging the shoreline closely to avoid detection until they confirmed the identity of the others. Strangers or enemies frequented this area almost as often as members of their own tribe did.

Against the backdrop of the rocky cliffs and dense forest the two canoes would have been all but invisible from their position ahead, which proved to be the case given the surprise a wild whoop of recognition from two of his captors caused among the new arrivals.

As the three canoes drew rapidly inshore toward them, Gudbjartur recognized two of his men among the paddlers, Snorri, the small boat captain of times past, and Gaut, one of the hunters. Both slumped dejectedly in the canoes until Snorri caught sight of Gudbjartur and shouted in recognition. A club crashed into the side of his head wielded by the Naskapi behind him, effectively ending further attempts at communication. The two Greenlanders huddled silently in the canoes. Snorri held his head in both hands; fresh blood dripped through his fingers from his split scalp. Gudbjartur and Gaut observed the interplay between the two groups of their captors. That the topic of discussion was the prisoners was apparent. The anger directed toward them by the various speakers gave the three silent prisoners considerable trepidation.

While the Naskapi obviously knew one another, their captives could not know they were members of different bands and were bound for different villages. When the two groups separated as they continued their journey, although they were in sight of one another for a time, it was apparent to Gudbjartur they had different destinations as the other canoes turned north into a smaller tributary river and soon disappeared from view. Thoughts of the other two men and his people in general occupied his mind the remainder of the afternoon. Not having the opportunity to talk with Snorri and Gaut, not knowing the fate of the rest of his men, left him downcast. This condition stayed with him until Glooscap called a halt at dark. He disdained the dry ration, sinking instead into the sleep of exhaustion.

* * *

On the morning of the seventh day, the camp awakened to a gentle rain and light wind. His captors busily prepared for another day of travel. Left alone with his thoughts, Gudbjartur enjoyed the feel and smell of early morning. The calls of awakening birds, the sudden slap of a fish's tail as it rolled on the lake's surface, and the patter of raindrops on the leaves of the trees, made him happy just to be alive. His thoughts gradually returned to the events of the previous afternoon. He decided dwelling on them would change nothing for him, so with an effort he put them aside for the time being.

Already soaked by the rain, his reverie broken by a call from Glooscap, Gudbjartur shuddered at a sudden chill brought on by the increasing wind-driven rain. He rubbed the last vestiges of sleep from his streaming face and turned to do Glooscap's bidding.

Glooscap studied his prisoner as he moved about the campsite, knowing the effect the previous afternoon must have had on him. Although Gudbjartur's feelings were of no concern to him, as a leader he was aware that a man's innermost feelings could cause him trouble at some point in the future, and it was that which sparked his interest in Gudbjartur's actions this day.

The wind-driven rain made for miserable travel for the occupants of the two canoes as weather conditions steadily worsened. Gudbjartur thought Glooscap might call a halt as the north wind increased, causing the lake to get too choppy for the canoes. However, they hugged the shoreline closely, gaining some protection from the onslaught. Frequent bailing gave Gudbjartur a welcome break from the tedium and discomfort of paddling.

Late in the afternoon, the stormy weather left the struggling canoes in its wake. Gradually the lake's surface calmed and the world reawakened to brilliant sunshine. The wind brought respite from the heat, and stormy skies quickly gave way to the same heavy, still, humid air as steam rose from every drying surface into an atmosphere made fetid by the smell of leaf mold from the forest floor. The lead canoe turned up a small river to the north and the solid forest wall of both riverbanks soon engulfed them.

After a time, the river split in two around a large tree-covered island before rejoining in a section of rapids where the waters issued from another lake. They carried the two canoes around the rapids and dropped them into the shallows of the lake. Forward speed increased dramatically as the pull of the river's current lost its hold on the canoes as they paddled into the lake itself, straight across the center, setting a course direct toward the distant shore rather than along the shoreline as before.

The tired men increased their effort upon sighting smoke in the distance and entered into excited and animated conversation. Gudbjartur lapsed into a pensive mood as the rising smoke plumes jolted him back into the reality of his position once again. Either his treatment was about to get worse or better he realized with mounting anxiety, as their approach evoked frenzied activity ashore.

* * *

Chapter Seven

The Naskapi Village of Glooscap

The smoke Gudbjartur had first noticed as a smudge on the far shore, separated into the plumes of many individual fires. The last vestige of hope remaining to him disappeared as he realized the size of the Naskapi village along the lake's north shore. *There must be many scores of people living here. Moreover, this is just one of several of their villages.*

Several canoes came out to meet them from the broad sandy beach in front of the village and the occupants became both excited and agitated at sight of the prisoner. Curiosity at this strange man was evident on most of the faces. Some of the Naskapi were openly hostile until warned away by Glooscap.

The constant milling of the many canoes, as the occupants jostled for a closer look at the stranger, reduced progress toward the village beach to a crawl. Several capsizes were narrowly averted in the process. Gudbjartur watched the play of emotion across the many faces. That these people regarded him as an enemy was obvious. The press of humanity gathered at the shoreline made landing difficult. The situation would have gotten out of hand had not the crowd suddenly parted in front of Gudbjartur like a sea of grass knocked aside by a wind gust.

Standing alone in this open space was an old man whose bearing indicated one accustomed to the respect paid him by all those present. He was clad in very pale, unadorned buckskin clothing, which served to accentuate his presence by its very simplicity. His build was slight, almost thin, and he was of medium height. Shoulder-length black hair streaked with gray framed a deeply lined dark brown face dominated by piercing black eyes that studied the stranger come among them.

Gripped in his right hand he held the grounded haft of an ornately carved and decorated crook. Atop his head sat an elaborate headdress fashioned of two matching deer antlers—the trappings of the supreme chief of all the Naskapi. Affixed to the tip of each antler tine were streamers of twisted animal hair, moving restlessly in the slight breeze. Taken altogether, his simple yet effective clothing and trappings served to intensify the aura of his presence.

Not a sound came from the throng as all expectantly strained to catch the first words spoken. Gudbjartur stood unmoving. He could not help but be impressed by the power flowing from this man. The dark eyes studied every detail of the Northman from head to foot. He had no doubt that this man held his fate in the palm of his hand.

Shifting his gaze to Glooscap, the old man's questioning look got an immediate response.

"We captured him six days ago, Sachem, after a long chase. He killed three men before Miknap clubbed him from behind."

This revelation brought an angry growl from the crowd that died out as the old man raised his hand and nodded for Glooscap to continue.

"He is a great warrior and the first of his kind that we have seen closely. I brought him here for you to see and to talk to, Sachem. I wanted to seek your wisdom on what can be learned and let you decide if he is to live or die," Glooscap said in a deferential tone of voice.

Hearing the old man called Sachem, Gudbjartur knew that he looked upon their supreme leader, the leader of all the Naskapi bands. Although Sachem's gaze was disconcerting to him, Gudbjartur did not flinch or cower in any manner. Such conduct would indicate cowardice to Sachem and the assembly at large. His fate was uncertain. Gudbjartur stood proudly erect, gazing directly at Sachem, his seemingly outward calm belied by the turmoil felt within. Feeling the warm flush of excitement and fear course through his body steeled his resolve to present a brave front to this man.

Sachem said in a deep strong voice, "You have done the right thing, Glooscap. I will think on this and decide what to do with this stranger. Take him into the village and tie him to one of the prisoner posts so that all may look upon him. Until his fate is decided, do not mistreat him. We may have need of him."

Sachem stood silently for a moment, his dark eyes disconcertingly fixed on Gudbjartur's face. "Call the elders to the council fire, Glooscap. You and your men will tell us of the capture of this stranger." He turned away without waiting for a response and walked toward the village gate.

* * *

In spite of a high state of anxiety, Gudbjartur found his entrance into the village to be both surprising and enlightening. These people had a highly developed society similar to the Greenlanders. The quality of their longhouses and the organization of the village within a log palisade indicated a high degree of planning. He was being taken to what he assumed was the village center. A large roundhouse—the only such building that he could see—occupied this prominent space alone. Sachem and his entourage walked directly into this building, followed by a great number of other people until it filled to overflowing.

Arrayed in a circle near the entrance of this roundhouse were posts higher than the tallest man, the purpose of which became apparent as they led him to one and tied him securely.

Gudbjartur suffered the scrutiny of what he assumed must be everyone in the village. He was relieved not to have come to harm yet, but the noise and dust kicked up by the crowd jostling for position to look at him was intimidating nonetheless. He had no way of knowing that a council meeting to decide his fate was convened nor did he know he was under the protection of Sachem for the time being.

Loud voices, some of whom he recognized as belonging to his captors, came from inside the roundhouse. Realizing they were probably discussing him—relating the circumstances of his capture judging from the angry tones—he strained to hear the speakers to judge their feelings.

The crowd around him gradually thinned out as people grouped near the entrance to listen to the proceedings from within came and went. Several small children remained sitting near him on the ground chattering like squirrels at this new and exciting addition to their daily lives. Gudbjartur, amused at their antics in spite of his situation, smiled and winked suddenly. His action took all of them by surprise. They squealed and ran away laughing, as children will. Sensing a new game in the offing the bravest among them soon returned, darting in to touch his foot before running away. Their actions toward him became increasingly bolder until an old woman bearing food and water approached, her strident voice scattering them like chaff before the wind.

Gudbjartur watched her approach as he sat with his back against a post. They had tied his hands in front and several loops of leather rope secured him about the waist and chest against the post.

The woman sat the food containers on the ground and freed his hands. He rubbed circulation back into his wrists and gratefully accepted the proffered food, a kind of stew in a wooden bowl. She also handed him a bark container of water. Noisily he slurped the mixture of vegetables and meat into his mouth.

The old woman remained for a time. "The council will be finished soon. Glooscap will come to take you before them," she said, gesturing toward the council hall.

Understanding the gesture, and recognizing the name, Glooscap, Gudbjartur replied, "I am ready for whatever happens." His words belied the turmoil he felt.

The old woman collected the empty containers and turned away without comment.

The lengthening shadows of approaching darkness caused Gudbjartur's sense of despair to deepen. Voices from the council hall were limited to a rumble of normal conversation, giving him to believe the storytelling time was over. *They are discussing my fate.* The tone of the conversation rose and fell as the topic changed. Watching the reactions of the listeners near him provided Gudbjartur with a gauge of the conversation within the roundhouse. A comment or exclamation from within drew a glance or muttered comment from the assembly without. A voice he recognized as Sachem caused all movement outside to cease as the onlookers strained to listen.

* * *

A short time later, just before full darkness, the assembly in front of the council hall entrance parted as two men walked out and turned toward Gudbjartur. The council had ended. They had made their decision.

Bracing himself for what he felt was the end, Gudbjartur calmly regarded Glooscap and Kejo standing before him. Those who had remained throughout the council grouped around the trio to bear witness, although they already knew the outcome, having overheard Sachem.

"Untie him Kejo," Glooscap ordered, his gaze locked on Gudbjartur.

Roughly untying him and jerking Gudbjartur to his feet, Kejo shoved him toward the council hall entrance. Gudbjartur stumbled and almost lost his balance on legs numbed by inactivity.

Blinking in the light of the council fire, Gudbjartur stood uncertainly before a group of men who sat studying him intently. They were the elders of their people. Now that they had reached a consensus, they studied the man before them without visible emotion.

Gudbjartur, determined not to show fear, returned their scrutiny with a calmness that he did not feel. In spite of his outward calm, he had no spit; his mouth and throat had gone dry as dust. He glanced from face to face in a valiant effort to control his racing heart. Each heartbeat drummed in his inner ears. He fastened his gaze on Sachem, knowing he would speak.

Sachem rose from the pile of mats he sat on and approached Gudbjartur, stopping directly in front of him. Gudbjartur towered over the slightly built man, but feeling no advantage whatsoever because of it, he stood calmly and returned the gaze directed at him. Once again, Sachem subjected him to a silent examination, first looking into his eyes, as before, and then walking in a slow circle around him before returning to his place in the council. Gudbjartur, heart pounding from pent-up emotion and tension, stood rooted in position looking straight ahead over the council members, his mind a jumble of anticipatory thoughts.

Gesturing toward Glooscap and Kejo standing to either side of Gudbjartur, Sachem began to speak slowly and clearly to the three men, reinforcing and illustrating every statement with sign language. As he spoke, a slow awareness came over Gudbjartur as he realized the impact of what Sachem was saying.

"Glooscap has brought you to us so that we may learn why you and your people have come to Nitassinan. Bands of Naskapi live in all of this land. We do not welcome strangers. I have agreed with Glooscap and most of the council that we may learn valuable things from you and that is why you are still alive. Many here are not happy with this decision, wanting to burn you at the stake for killing three of our men. One of those wanting you dead is Kejo, who stands beside you. I have made him and Glooscap responsible for you. They will teach you our language and customs. Given time, you will become a member of our tribe, one of the people. You will live in the wigwam of Glooscap first. After one moon has passed you will be in the wigwam of Kejo for one moon, changing with each new moon. You will live with us in peace. You must learn our language and our ways. You will teach us about your people. If you do not do these things, or if you try to escape, we will hunt you down. We will not spare you then. Heed my words, or you will die many times before death comes for you. Now, go in peace with Glooscap," Sachem said, sweeping his right hand out before his body, palm down. "I have spoken. It will be as I say."

Gudbjartur understood few of Sachem's words but reinforced with sign language the intent of the deliberate, forcefully delivered speech was obvious. Relief flooded through him when he realized he was to survive. A glance at Glooscap revealed his acceptance. Kejo remained taciturn, his body tight with hostility.

The council hall went from relative quiet to animated conversation as the council members rose to depart.

"Cheer up, Kejo. This will be a challenging time for all of us. It will not be easy to teach him our language and learn his, but with everyone helping we can do it," one said.

"Yes," another said who stood next to Gudbjartur. "The men he killed were our friends, too. It is best for all the people to learn from him first. We can always kill him later. For now a warrior such as he is a welcome addition."

"Did you understand any of what was said to you?" A tall stately old man asked Gudbjartur. Turning slightly toward the speaker, Gudbjartur found himself facing a man as tall as he, with an open, friendly expression on his face.

"If you are asking me if I understand," Gudbjartur said smiling, "I understand a little, but I am confused about what is expected of me. All that matters to me now is that I am alive. The rest will become clear with time."

The sound of his voice and the guttural intonation of the strange language he spoke attracted the attention of every man within earshot. With the exception of Glooscap, Kejo, and the other men who had captured him, none had heard him speak before. Smiling at their reaction, Gudbjartur was surprised to find himself the center of attention. Questions came at him from all sides. Most of the faces were new to him, as men crowded into the roundhouse from outside. Some he recognized as his captors.

"What is your name?" one said, pointing at him.

"He doesn't know what you ask," said a man he recognized, "you must tell him your name first."

Tapping his chest, this man said in a clear voice. "I am called Miknap. I split your head with my club. Miknap, M-i-k-n-a-p," he emphasized, tapping his chest. "What is your name?" he asked, tapping Gudbjartur on the chest.

Suddenly understanding the question, Gudbjartur said loudly enough for all to hear, "I am Gudbjartur, G-oo-d-byar-tur," he repeated, sounding out his name while tapping his chest.

"You are Miknap," he said, tapping the man on the chest. This last brought appreciative laughter from the group.

His name was difficult to pronounce and strange sounding for these men, though they tried with varying degrees of success. To simplify matters he said to the group at large, "Most of my people call me Gudbj, G-oo-j," he emphasized, tapping his chest. From that day on, until they gave him a Naskapi name, people called him Gudbj.

Marveling at the speed of his acceptance, Gudbjartur allowed himself to relax for the first time in many days. He did as they bade him. He had survived. Whatever turns his new life took with these people he would gladly accept them.

* * *

Chapter Eight

Haudeno Village of the War Chief Sakokaeah

After six grueling days of canoe travel the Haudeno war party and their captive entered yet another lake in a seemingly endless string of rivers and lakes. Ivar had often wondered how the men knew where they were. It all looked the same to him.

Less than seventy leagues straight north, on a lake not unlike this one, was the large Naskapi village where Gudbjartur languished as a prisoner. Fortunately, neither son nor father knew that they shared a similar life-changing event.

Ivar sulked for several days. He did not understand his captors' language, which would have helped his outlook somewhat, and he missed his family, especially his brother Lothar. The two were inseparable. They talked of things that he would have mentioned to no other person. Each confided in the other his most intimate thoughts. He smiled and chuckled under his breath as he remembered the two of them lying hidden in the brush watching Sigmund and Genevra couple in one of their frequent trysts.

Lothar had put his mouth against his brother's ear and asked, "Where is he putting that big thing? I cannot see where it goes, but he has it buried inside her."

Ivar almost strangled at the question. He choked off the laughter that threatened to burst from his mouth, hissed a warning, and held his finger to his lips in an attempt to silence Lothar.

His brother covered his head with his arms as a paroxysm of mirth shook his shoulders.

Later, after they had crawled away, Lothar took up the thread. "Do you know which hole he was putting it in?" He asked through their laughter.

"What difference does it make?"

Lothar would not let it go. "I think it makes a difference. Which hole does the baby come from? Maybe that is the right hole to stick it in?"

Ivar punched Lothar in the arm as the two staggered back and forth, their arms linked, almost collapsing with laughter.

"You do not know either, do you?" Lothar said. A look of cunning revelation crossed his thin face.

They laughed together as they walked through the forest back toward the settlement, their arms over each other's shoulders.

"Maybe the girl will tell us which hole she wants it in when our time comes," Ivar told his brother.

Lothar stopped, disengaged himself from Ivar, and looked at him. "Well, I hope so, because I will want to do it right." This time they did collapse in laughter.

Ivar laughed aloud at the memory. The Haudeno to his front turned around at the sound in time to see the smile on Ivar's face. Not able to understand what was going through the boy's mind he simply nodded. Crow's feet softened the stony face.

Ivar looked away to study the passing countryside. They were drifting with the current in a slow-moving river. Beyond an occasional flick of their paddles to direct the bow of the canoe, paddling was unnecessary. Inevitably, his mind began to wander again. The voice of his father, Gudbjartur, kept intruding into the jumble of his thoughts. For the first time he wished his father were here to tell him what to do. Now, he regretted standing up to his father every time there had been an opportunity to have some kind of discourse. He had done it on purpose, to feel superior somehow, to experience a sense of being grown up. *I hope he comes for me.* A feeling of sadness, of loss suffused his breast.

If such is possible under the circumstances, he mentally dealt with his plight, correctly deciding sulking was not in his best interests. *I must not dwell on the past. My mother always told me to be positive, to accept life as it comes, to make the best of it.* He thought it easier said than done. Nonetheless, he began to settle into his new role with all the adaptability of the young. His captors treated him well, he had enough to eat, although the sameness of the diet bored him, and the constant paddling through the initial stage of muscle soreness at the unaccustomed activity had begun to harden his well-proportioned young body. The man Odatshedeh kept the boy close, shared his food with him, and seemed to mediate with his companions in Ivar's behalf. They all watched him because he was different from them, although the differences became less with the passage of each day.

Ivar began to look at the warriors as men, individual men, not unlike his people. With the exception of their looks— light brown skin, black hair and eyes, and the sharp features of most of them—they were much like his people. The men argued, laughed at jokes played at each other's expense, and talked about their surroundings, or whatever caught their fancy, exactly like his people. He especially admired Odatshedeh. Although his face appeared stern, he had found that a different sort dwelt within. The man acted as if he actually had Ivar's best interest at heart. When the river had passed through a bog earlier, a cloud of mosquitoes disturbed from their torpor during the heat of the day assailed the canoes. Ivar swatted ineffectually at the pests as they settled in to feast on his exposed skin.

"Here, Ivar," Odatshedeh said, tossing him the bag of red ocher. "Smear the mud on your skin. The mosquitoes will not bother you." The man demonstrated by rubbing his face and arms.

They had not offered Ivar the greasy red mud before today. He recalled having seen Deskaheh use the mud but he did not know that it repelled the pests until now. After a rain shower or a day of exertion, the moisture on their skin dictated that they renew the protection, so the bag made the rounds as the men reapplied the ocher. Ivar nodded his thanks to his benefactor and began to apply the ocher as he had seen them do. He knew from watching his captors that it would take little of the greasy stuff to cover his skin. Dipping a small ball of ocher from the bag, he rubbed it over the palms of his hands, as they did, and starting with his legs, soon covered all his exposed skin, except his face.

Odatshedeh indicated the boy's face with a hand gesture and a lift of his chin.

Ivar closed his eyes and carefully rubbed the ocher all over his face and neck. He resumed paddling. Watching his greasy arms flash in the sunlight he realized for the first time that except for his blonde hair and blue eyes he was almost the same color as the Haudeno, a little lighter because of his white skin, but not much. Unlike the mud of the earth, ocher did not dry in the sun; pulling at his skin and making him itch. Rather, it maintained its greasy feel. He decided that he liked the way it felt, the way it made him look.

They left the mosquito swarm in their wake and Ivar was no longer pestered by them. He looked back at Odatshedeh and smiled.

The man grunted an acknowledgment and called out to the others. "You see, now he no longer looks like a pale-skin. He looks more like one of the people."

"He is not one of the people," Seawi said petulantly.

"He will be my son. Be warned," Odatshedeh said. The anger on his face was plain to Ivar as he watched the exchange.

"The council will decide what is to be done with him, not either one of you," Sakokaeah interjected from the lead canoe, effectively stopping the exchange.

Ivar did not understand, but he glanced at the war chief when he spoke. The man's hard black eyes looked at him impassively. The stony face conveyed not a flicker of feeling.

Sakokaeah was plain scary. Ivar admired that trait about the war chief. He was a leader and the boy recognized that he would be a dangerous adversary. He determined that he would try to learn from him and do his best to stay out of the man's way.

Each of his captors had their own distinctive traits, differing personalities that made them what they were, good and bad. He watched them as much as they watched him, finally deciding their faces were different after all. At first, he had thought they all looked like Deskaheh. Although many of them did have the same sharp features, some had faces that were more like his people, rounder, with high cheekbones. The distinctive hooked nose seemed common among them. All had a kind of smell about them. He did not find it unpleasant; rather it was more like a wild smell, of the earth, campfires, the leaf mold of the forest floor, a faint scent of pine, the humid heat from a fen, all of these things. They were well-formed men, lean and muscular. Nothing escaped their notice. Their eyes saw everything in their world. He realized they did it without effort, like animals. *That is it. They are like the animals of this land, a part of the forest.* He decided that he admired them for this innate trait.

The lead canoe had stopped paddling, wordlessly calling an infrequent halt. The occupants of all four canoes stretched cramped muscles and rested on their paddles laid across the low sides as they drifted slowly toward the shoreline on the slight breeze. A mutter of low conversation passed between the canoes as the warriors visited.

Ivar occupied the front position in one of the canoes. He turned his flushed face toward the breeze. Its caress dried the sweat from his brow and refreshed him. A fish rolled on the surface near the shoreline, calling his attention. A raft of ducks scolded and quacked in the distance. A sigh escaped the boy's lips. He stretched tired shoulder muscles, closed his eyes, and luxuriated in the cooling breeze. He had found kneeling on the bulrush mats that covered the canoe's bottom to be difficult in the beginning. After six days, he no longer thought about the discomfort. As it happened, the leather bag containing the trail rations that they all shared laid close to hand. He untied the thong securing the opening and transferred a handful of the dried mixture to his mouth. He did not know what it was, but he rather liked the faint sweet taste of the crumbly mixture. It was all he had eaten since his capture. Chewing contentedly, he turned and passed the bag to the man to his front. They made eye contact. The man nodded slightly. Again, Ivar noticed a slight softening of his features.

Sakokaeah uttered a clipped phrase and they began to paddle again. The speed built to a comfortable pace. This continued through the heat of another day without pause until the time of lengthening shadows. The hot sun passed from view as its face dipped behind the treetops. Coolness came to the air.

The four canoes beached in a cove on the shoreline. The men had been here before as evidenced by a small, oft-used fire pit concealed from prying eyes in a large depression created by a downed tree. Ivar helped with odd camp tasks as Odatshedeh directed. They always carried the canoes above the high water mark at day's end, but not today. One remained in the water, nosed up on the shore.

* * *

"Come, we are going to hunt for fresh meat," Odatshedeh said to Ivar, motioning him toward the canoe. Seawi stood silently by while Ivar looked from one to the other.

He knew they were going to try for some fresh meat by their actions. *They are tired of the dry rations, too.* He looked out over the lake. *It will be dark soon. It is a good time to hunt, but we will not have much time.* He shrugged, as boys will under such circumstance, and waded into the water to help launch the canoe. The two men laid their bows and quivers of arrows in the canoe and pushed it from the shore. The three boarded the unstable craft without mishap, Ivar in the middle, and paddled away along the lake's shoreline.

The men chose the direction of travel so as to paddle directly into the slight breeze stirring the lake's surface, giving them the advantage of a downwind approach to prey coming out of the forest to water.

Odatshedeh turned to Ivar and held a finger to his lips. The boy nodded his understanding, emulating the soundless paddling of the men as the canoe glided silently along the shoreline within easy bowshot.

Odatshedeh guided the canoe in closer as they approached a rocky outcropping jutting into the water. He stopped paddling and held a hand up. The canoe continued slowing forward of its own volition, rounding the bend silent as a shadow.

A cow moose and her big calf fed on bulrushes in the cove created by the rock outcropping. Both had their head underwater as they fed on the lake bottom, unaware of the imminent danger.

Odatshedeh made eye contact with Seawi, indicating the calf with a lift of his chin. Both men raised their bows, pulled to the arrowhead, and released in the same fluid motion. The arrows sped the short distance to the calf, slicing into the animal's ribcage a hand's breadth apart.

The calf jerked its head from the water at the impact and churned for the shore. The sudden activity and terror of the moment pumped its lifeblood from the mortal wounds and it collapsed in death.

In the commotion, the cow raised her head from the water, bulrush dangling from her mouth, to gaze stupidly at the canoe a matter of feet away. Realization dawned and she fled from the lake into the cloaking forest, oblivious to the fate of her calf.

Ivar laughed aloud, appreciative of the finesse, the expert execution of the hunt, and the kill. Odatshedeh smiled. Seawi did not.

The calf had conveniently collapsed on the shore above the water's edge. Ivar did not know what the men were doing, but each dipped a finger into the calf's blood and swiped it across their foreheads uttering a short phrase at the same time. Odatshedeh gestured to Ivar. He froze, knowing what was to come as the man marked his forehead with blood in similar fashion. Much later, he came to know of this custom among the people, to thank the animal for releasing his spirit to them.

Born in the early spring, the calf weighed more than the largest buck deer. The men quickly stripped the hide, spreading it out on the ground fleshy side up. Then they rolled the carcass up onto its chest and stomach leaving the backbone upright on the hide. They began to butcher the best meat.

Ivar pitched in where needed without Odatshedeh's guidance, a fact not lost on either man. He watched the rapid process curiously. They did not separate the large meaty leg portions at the joints, as his people did, but rather they deftly removed the long cylindrical muscle groups, leaving the heavy leg bone intact. Odatshedeh likewise stripped the back strap, along each side of the backbone, away in two long cylinders of meat covered in the thick back fat of the bountiful summer forage that the animal had eaten. He handed the back straps to Ivar, indicating he wanted him to pile the meat on the hide, which he did. This continued until nothing remained but a skeleton with the paunch intact. Only then did they gut the animal, setting aside the stomach, liver, and heart. Odatshedeh and Seawi each cut a generous piece of warm liver and stuffed it into their mouths. Ivar salivated. Odatshedeh cut off another piece and passed it to him on the point of his knife blade. Ivar stuffed it into his mouth, chewed a few times and swallowed. "Nothing tastes better than liver warm from the kill," he said, knowing the men would not understand. He belched contentedly.

That they understood.

Seawi turned the head upside down and made two deep cuts along the inside of the lower jawbone from front to back. Then he carefully cut around the narrow front end of the jawbone, grasped the loosened flap and ripped the tongue loose. Cutting where necessary he deftly pulled it out intact and tossed it on the pile of meat.

Ivar whistled in appreciation.

Seawi's emotionless eyes flicked to Ivar for a heartbeat before he looked away.

He does not like me, no matter what I do.

The men picked up the skeletal remains and threw them aside, leaving a pile of meat, usable innards, and fat on the hide.

Odatshedeh handed his bloody knife to Ivar and motioned him toward the lake. Both men froze in attitudes of expectation, especially Seawi, who did not trust the boy.

Ivar looked from one to the other. He shook his head once, looked at the knife, and back at each man. Smiling slightly he walked down and knelt at the water's edge, scrubbed the clotted blood loose with sand, and rinsed the flint blade. He examined the knife curiously. A wooden handle secured the dark, reddish quartz blade with rawhide whippings. He noted the short, wide blade, thickened at the top, tapered to the edge and point with a series of finely knapped scallops. He tested the keen edge with his thumb. Getting to his feet, he handed the knife back to Odatshedeh.

Without taking his eyes off Ivar, Odatshedeh spoke to Seawi. "Give Ivar your knife."

Seawi made to object, but swallowed his words when he saw the look Odatshedeh directed at him. He handed his knife to Ivar, who cleaned the blood away as before and handed it back. The two locked eyes, the warrior, and the boy. Ivar did not blink or flinch. Seawi said nothing, turning away. *Perhaps one day he will like me, but not this day.* He glanced at Odatshedeh. A slight smile smoothed the perpetual scowl on the man's face.

I have been tested, Ivar thought, as he helped the two men load the hide and meat into the canoe. *I am not certain why, but Odatshedeh does not treat me like a prisoner. Perhaps I will know the reason when we arrive at their village.*

* * *

The slight breeze had died with the sunset. The heavy, humid air carried a faint smell of wood smoke as the hunters traveled the short distance back to the campsite. The waning crescent of the Harvest Time Moon gave little illumination to the shadowy lakeshore and even less to the forest depths as darkness enveloped the land. Their eyes adjusted with the failing light and presented them no problems insofar as threading the fragile canoe through the rock outcroppings as they closed the shoreline by their campsite.

The mournful cry of a loon echoed over the lake. Ivar turned his head toward the sound. The breeze that died with the darkness left the water's surface shimmering in the weak light of the moon. He could just make out the unmistakable snake-like head and neck above the low, partially submerged body of the loon at the apex of the twin triangular ripples of its passage on the lake's surface. Suddenly the bird dipped below the surface on its eternal quest for fish, leaving hardly a ripple to mark its passage.

An owl hooted. Instinctively Ivar knew that the perfect mimicry did not come from an owl, but rather from the campsite's sentry, hidden from view in the darkness of the forest. His suspicions were confirmed when several warriors came out of the tree line to meet the canoe as it came to rest on the shoreline.

Two men carried the hide and meat away. Odatshedeh handed Ivar his bow and quiver. The boy held the man's eyes a moment. With a lift of his chin, Odatshedeh motioned him toward the camp. Seawi said something in an angry tone. Odatshedeh answered with a single word, again motioning Ivar in the direction of the camp. Seawi said nothing further.

Ivar strolled toward the campsite, invisible in the darkness of the forest ahead, the leather bow case, and integral quiver clasped in his hand. He leaned them against the root ball of the downed tree, near the flickering light of the small cooking fire. A whiff of cooking meat brought saliva into his dry mouth. The rich smell made him realize that he was hungry. He glanced back toward the lake and saw men backlit by the weak moonlight on the shimmering surface of the water as they carried the canoe into the tree line for the night.

* * *

A thin pall of smoke hung in the hot still air along the distant south shoreline of the long narrow lake. The flotilla of canoes had made their way directly across the lake's center rather than along the shoreline as before. A steady increase in the normal pace set by the lead canoe, as features of the shore became more distinct, indicated to Ivar that the long journey would soon end.

The palisades of a large village began among the thinned trees of the mixed hardwood and evergreen forest some distance back from the shoreline. Smoke rose into the still air from the smoke holes of many longhouses, their rooftops just visible over the pointed upright poles of the palisade.

Ivar saw dozens of canoes drawn up on the beach. Several put out to meet the returning raiding party. He watched curiously, trying to take in the spectacle about him as the people exchanged shouted greetings. The gaggle of village canoes did not impede their progress unduly as they followed Sakokaeah's lead straight for the landing beach. The new arrivals could not help but notice him as they paddled through the milling canoes. Although the ocher stained his exposed skin a uniform reddish hue, his blonde hair was a dead giveaway. *I am not afraid. These people do not look hostile to me. I do not feel that I am in danger.* This assessment surprised him.

Sakokaeah's status among the people became obvious as the raiding party waded from the shallows to deposit their canoes on the beach with the others. That the large crowd deferred to him was immediately obvious to Ivar as people greeted him respectfully and then got out of the way.

Sakokaeah stopped as a boy about Ivar's age walked up with a smile on his face. The two greeted one another. He tousled the boy's lank black hair and handed him his weapons. The boy locked eyes with Ivar. His face was impassive as the two studied each other briefly.

Sakokaeah turned to Odatshedeh. "Bring the boy to the council hall. I will meet you there." His attention focused on the sound of a squealing little bit of a girl as she ran into his outstretched arms. The cruel face of the man Ivar thought to be the meanest looking man he had ever seen melted into a broad smile as he lifted the little girl above his head and then tenderly hugged her to his breast.

A slight smile crossed Ivar's face at this out-of-character display.

Odatshedeh gestured toward the receding back of the war chief as the man walked toward the village gates. The boy carrying his weapons walked at his side while the man engaged in animated conversation with the boy and the child in his arms. "She is his youngest daughter," he said, watching Ivar closely. "His son carries his weapons."

Ivar looked into his eyes. Although he did not understand exactly, he made his own assumption of what he had just witnessed. He nodded in apparent understanding, which seemed to satisfy Odatshedeh. The man gestured for him to follow and they headed for the village gates.

People continued to come from the village and the nearby vegetable fields until a large crowd of the curious walked along with them toward the open gates of the village. Most seemed only curious about the strange pale-skinned boy as word passed that he was there. There was no open hostility. Not until now, that is.

A boy slightly taller than himself purposely blocked the way. Ivar halted a few paces in front of him, knowing trouble when he saw it. The crowd obligingly formed a cordon as the two looked each other over. Ivar darted a glance at Odatshedeh, who stood to the side, hipshot, with his arms crossed and an expectant look on his face. Strangely, the crowd was silent as people shuffled for position.

Ivar felt no fear. He realized that the boy had probably chosen the sandy beach area to start his fight. *I would have done the same,* he thought, as he looked the other boy over from head to foot. *He is taller, but I think I am stronger and meaner.* He hoped he had his upper lip curled in contempt. *This is another test. I cannot let him beat me.*

Their examination of each other and the inevitable posturing boys will do before a fight, ended abruptly when the Haudeno boy attacked. He came in low, trying to grab Ivar around the legs to throw him to the ground.

Bystanders goaded them on. The excitement of single combat and the expectation of bloodletting gripped the crowd. Shouts of encouragement came from all sides as the onlookers encouraged their champion.

Ivar had always been fast on his feet. He used the other boy's momentum to push off him, sidestepped, and grabbed the outstretched arm of his adversary, spinning him off balance. His clenched fist slammed into the side of the boy's head as he lunged by.

Already off balance, the blow sent the Haudeno boy to his knees in the dust. He scrambled quickly to his feet, none the worse for wear. The look directed at Ivar conveyed a certain respect that had not been there before. He came at Ivar again, with more caution this time. They grappled, straining to throw each other to the ground. Ivar found himself flying through the air as his adversary feinted, grabbed him around the head, and rolled him over his hip. The boy tried to follow through with a scissor hold around Ivar's waist. Ivar lunged free and caught the other boy full in the pit of the stomach with a satisfyingly solid head butt.

A whoosh of escaping air briefly left the boy light-headed and gasping for air. The two warily circled one another.

Ivar let the other get his breath back. A mistake, he would later recall, as the other boy, feigning breathlessness, suddenly attacked again, arms flailing.

A clenched fist crunched into Ivar's nose. Stars darted before his eyes, tears welled up from the pain and humiliation, and blood spurted into the dust. He wiped at the blood, tasting the salt as it trickled into his open mouth.

The crowd went silent for a moment as the two circled warily, their open mouths sucking air like beached fish.

Ivar lunged suddenly. The crowd erupted again. Ivar ducked under a flailing fist, grabbed the other boy above the knees, and slammed him into the dust on his back. He jumped astride the other's waist, pinning both arms with his muscular legs. Sensing victory, he pummeled the other's unprotected face. Odatshedeh dragged him off, still swinging. Odatshedeh exclaimed as he blocked Ivar's fist, his voice all but inaudible in the noise of the crowd. He held his open palm to Ivar. That and the single shake of his head made the boy realize that the fight was over.

Ivar's breath came in ragged gasps. He glanced at his adversary in the dust as the boy rolled onto his knees and got to his feet, never taking his eyes off him. Ivar looked wildly around the sea of boisterous faces while he fought to control his emotions.

The disheveled Haudeno boy stood a few feet away. Blood seeped from a cut over his left eye. He swiped irritably at it. The black eyes watched Ivar.

The noise from the crowd subsided as people watched expectantly.

Odatshedeh still held Ivar by the arm. He gestured for the other boy to approach and took him by the arm. Looking from one to the other, he squeezed their arms to get their attention on him. "Shake hands. The fight is over," he ordered. The hard eyes looked from one to the other. His glance stopped on the Haudeno boy and he lifted his chin.

Reluctantly the boy extended a hand to Ivar. His manner did not convey acceptance that the fight had ended.

The pursed lips and expressionless black eyes of his erstwhile adversary gave Ivar pause until Odatshedeh squeezed his arm. He glanced up at the man and once again, the chin gesture indicted what he wanted. He briefly gripped the other boy's hand.

Odatshedeh released them. "Good fight," he said. "You will be friends one day." His statement got a snort from the Haudeno boy.

Ivar still had his eyes on the other boy. "I am Ivar," he said, tapping his chest. "I am the son of Gudbjartur the Northman. What is your name?" The gestures and tone of voice made the question obvious.

"Tell him your name," Odatshedeh said.

"I am called Otetiani," he said. No expression crossed the young face.

Ivar nodded. "Otetiani." He looked at Odatshedeh. "I understand, Otetiani," he repeated. He glanced back at the other boy and bobbed his head once. The blue eyes bored into the black eyes.

Both boys had taken the measure of the other.

"Come, we go to the council hall," Odatshedeh said. He glanced at the two boys again and gestured in the desired direction, satisfied that the encounter between the two had accomplished something good. "The council of chiefs and elders will decide what is to be done with you, Ivar." He glanced at Otetiani. "You, too, will go."

Ivar glanced up at Odatshedeh in time to see a look of satisfaction cross the stony features. Both boys dutifully fell in behind the man as he walked through the village gates.

* * *

As he followed along, Ivar glanced occasionally at his former antagonist, giving him little regard, for the village began to draw his full attention. Its similarity to Halfdansfjord surprised him. Even the longhouses had the same basic shape as those built by his people, although each seemed a different size to his unpracticed eye. The longhouses of the Northmen surrounded a central common area in which artisans built shelters to fashion and trade their wares. At one end, the common also provided a place for livestock pens and shelters. By contrast, the Haudeno longhouses seemed scattered indiscriminately about the space inside the palisade. With the exception of dogs, he saw no other animals.

A sort of common area occupied the village center. People of all ages performed various tasks. He noticed that the Haudeno were a healthy, happy, good-looking people. All the people he saw seemed well formed. Except for their varying shades of brown skin, he thought them much like the Northmen. It seemed that only warriors and some of the boys shaved their heads to create the distinctive roached scalp lock down the center from front to back. Most of the people he saw had shoulder length hair, some braided, others not. All had black hair, shiny like the wing of a raven. Children ran about or played at various games, just like he, Lothar, and their friends. He swallowed the sudden lump in his throat as his brother briefly came to mind. With an effort, he put the thought aside for another time.

Women clustered in groups making baskets, leather clothing, scraping or tanning hides, and many other tasks that he could not identify. Like his people, the Haudeno stayed busy with tasks associated with everyday life. He liked what he saw.

Odatshedeh entered a large, rounded house standing apart from the others. He turned at the doorway and beckoned the boys to enter.

Otetiani entered without hesitation. He was on familiar ground.

Ivar did not know that this was the council hall of the Cokanuk band of the Haudenosaunee. He entered with trepidation, as he had no idea what to expect. He steeled himself with an effort. *I will not show them fear,* he vowed. He found the interior of the longhouse to be cool and gloomy. There were no lamps to light the interior. No fire burned on the large central hearth. Weak sunlight filtered in through two smoke holes near the center of the dome-shaped roof and through the single doorway. As his eyes adjusted to the poor illumination, he realized that he stood in the midst of a large group of silent people seated around the open center of the house. He saw both men and women.

Odatshedeh had halted before a small group of men seated on hides and bulrush mats. He motioned Ivar to his side.

Ivar wiped sweaty hands on his tunic as he walked to Odatshedeh. He hoped that nobody noticed. He recognized the grim face of the war chief, Sakokaeah; the other men were all strangers to him. He drew himself up tall, licked lips gone suddenly dry, and tried to still his heart as it thudded against his ribcage.

An old man, his lank hair streaked with gray, his face deeply lined, looked Ivar over slowly from head to foot. Finished with this examination he called Otetiani and gestured for him to stand at Ivar's side. The council examined the two disheveled boys.

Their silent appraisal, albeit brief, did nothing to dispel the disquiet coursing through Ivar's body. His eyes fastened on Sakokaeah as the man rose from the mats.

Sakokaeah stepped over to the two boys. He took first one and then the other by the arms to turn them back and forth in the dim light while he examined their cuts and bruises. The cut over Otetiani's left eye had stopped bleeding, but the eye had swollen shut. The dried blood of a split, swollen lip gave the thin mouth a misshapen appearance.

Ivar froze when the war chief took him by the arms. Their eyes locked, and then the man examined his swollen nose. Dried blood all but closed both nostrils. A darkened swelling had risen over his right cheekbone.

Sakokaeah held Ivar's eyes for a heartbeat, the cruel face expressionless. He glanced at Odatshedeh who stood impassively beside Ivar. "I am told they fought well," he said. "Who won?"

"They did fight well. It was even until Ivar pinned Otetiani. He was pummeling his face when I dragged him off. You sent your son to test the courage of this pale-skin boy. Both of them have much courage. I am proud of them," Odatshedeh said.

Sakokaeah held the eyes of his son. The stony expression slipped a little. He held the blue eyes of Ivar. "I, too, am proud of them." He turned and took his seat on the mats with the other council members. The cutting sign indicated that he was finished.

The old man with the lined face spoke. "I, Deganawida, and the council have decided to take the brave pale-skin into our band. You may make him your son. He will be one with the people," he said. His eyes fastened on Odatshedeh. He inclined his head slightly.

Odatshedeh nodded and looked at Ivar. "Deganawida has spoken."

Ivar did not understand the words but he glanced at the old man. The man's black eyes watched him closely. Young he might be, but he recognized that this man was the Haudeno chief.

Odatshedeh turned to the silent assembly. "Nahcomis," he called. His eyes searched the gloom. A woman rose from her place and walked to him. They held each other's eyes for a moment while he spoke softly to her. At first, she shook her head as she looked from him to Ivar.

That they talked about him was obvious to Ivar as he watched the exchange. He did not know what was happening, but the woman kept glancing at him while Odatshedeh talked to her. She came to stand before him. As they studied each other, he saw that she, too, was nervous. She clasped and unclasped her hands as she searched his face. He thought that she had a kind face, but her scrutiny and silence began to unnerve him.

"Ivar, this woman is called Nahcomis, she is my mate," Odatshedeh said. As always, speech included elaborate hand signs.

Ivar looked from one to the other. With his eyes on Odatshedeh's face, he used the hand sign he had seen them use for two people together. Holding his hands toward them, he extended his index fingers and bumped them together, to signify a joining.

The ghost of a smile transformed the stern visage of Odatshedeh. He nodded.

Ivar's eyes fastened on Nahcomis. "I am Ivar Gudbjartursson, the son of the Northman Gudbjartur. You are Nahcomis, the mate of Odatshedeh." He spoke slowly and distinctly, using elaborate hand signs to emphasize and clarify his speech, as they did.

A radiant smile chased the anxiety and nervousness from the face of Nahcomis. She looked at Odatshedeh. "This paleskin cannot replace our son. Perhaps he will fill the hole in my heart one day. He will be welcome at our fire," she said.

Ivar held her eyes. She reached out slowly and rested her hand on his arm. He did not flinch away.

Odatshedeh's arm encircled Nahcomis' waist. They held each other's eyes for a heartbeat. His other arm encircled Ivar's waist. The boy endured his touch because he knew that something profound was happening.

Suddenly, the silent assembly became boisterous. By the simple gesture of encircling his mate and Ivar, Odatshedeh gave the people to know that the boy had become one with them.

Ivar's mind was in turmoil as the people crowded around them. No longer were they stoic Haudeno. Something had transformed their regard of him. He did not know the full extent of what had just happened or he would have known that an intense change had occurred in his life.

* * *

Chapter Nine

Naskapi village of Glooscap

D arkness came to the village before Glooscap took Gudbjartur into the wigwam in which he and his family lived. Gudbjartur soon became aware, as he moved about, that many people lived in the wigwam in addition to Glooscap and his family. *There are at least five family groups, judging from the five hearths down the long central floor that live together here.*

One of the people watching his progress through the throng in the wigwam with Glooscap was the old woman who had brought him food while he lay tied in front of the council hall. Her name was Ekuanit. She had a smile for him, and she treated him well. Surprisingly—he found out as he met the others—she was the mother of Glooscap. This revelation gave him to know that her treatment of him had not been by chance; rather Glooscap had ordered her to feed him and treat him well. He found this a perplexing way to treat a prisoner, especially one recently captured. For this reason, he found himself observing Glooscap closely as the man led him through the wigwam, hoping to obtain some insight into his status. *They do not treat me as a prisoner. Either they intend to adopt me as one of their band or I am a slave. Either way I am alive. I guess my future with these people and what they expect of me will become apparent eventually. Most people treat me with in-difference. I expect nothing less. After all, I am their prisoner. But, they have all received orders about my treatment. Of that, I am certain.* He pursed his lips as he grappled with this dilemma.

* * *

Gudbjartur awakened the following morning to the sound of Glooscap's wife, Meshika, busily stirring the fire to life. Other women performed similar tasks down the length and breadth of the longhouse as people awakened and began stir-ring from the comfort of the sleeping platforms. He watched and listened with interest as the normal noise and activ-ity of early morning began, thinking it all so similar to his people.

The trills and calls of awakening birds heralded the ap-proaching dawn before a glimmer of light penetrated the gloom. The sun was well up before sunlight flooded through the east-facing entrance of the longhouse as dawn burst upon the Naskapi village.

Glooscap and his family occupied the area around the curved end of the longhouse and on both sides of the last hearth from the single doorway. The other four hearths, and the people living around them, were backlit by the sunshine flooding through the entryway. The sun's rays also pierced the gloom of the interior through the three smoke holes in the top of the longhouse's roof. Dust, kicked up from the dirt floor by the morning's activities, shimmered in the bright sunlight as he watched from the sleeping platform.

He did not know what to expect on his first full day. *I will lay quietly on this sleeping platform until somebody comes by to tell me otherwise.* He stiffened his body, stretching out full length, luxuriating in the unaccustomed idleness. A sudden chill brought on a shudder. He sighed and clasped both hands behind his head. Blinking in the gloom and smoke of the morning hearth fires, he let his eyes play over the bustle of ac-tivity. He took in details of the interior of the longhouse that had not been apparent the previous night when Glooscap brought him here after the council meeting.

From the outside, the longhouses—he now knew them to be called wigwams—appeared to have low roofs, which they did when compared to the surrounding ground, but the inside was actually a roofed-over, chest-deep dugout. Headroom inside was over ten feet, including the portion below ground level. The dugout portion also provided the added warmth and protective qualities of the surrounding earthen wall, adding to both the security and utility of the wigwam.

The fire pit hearths sat atop a raised dirt parapet down the center of the wigwam. They had removed the dirt between each hearth site, creating five waist-high areas down the center on which to construct the stone hearths. The cooks did not need to stoop over while cooking. *This arrangement is better than our floor level hearths.*

From his place on the sleeping platform, he viewed the construction and design of the wigwam with interest. The framework consisted of poles buried in the ground, in an oval approximately thirty feet wide and eighty to a hundred feet long—sizes seemed to vary from house to house. The thin top ends of each pole were tied securely together over the roof. Smaller diameter branches woven tightly together horizontally between uprights above the top half of the walls further buttressed the structure and formed the distinctive loaf shape of the wigwam. Additional small diameter branches, woven horizontally through the main uprights along the bottom half of the walls ensured that the internal framework maintained sufficient rigidity to withstand the weight of the rolls of bark roofing, wind gusts, and the weight of the Time of Whiteness snows. Each step of the construction increased the overall strength of the wigwam, resulting in a house in which many people could live in comfort and security from the weather.

The Naskapi eat when they are hungry. There is no set mealtime, not unlike the Thalmiut that Halfdan told me about. He had noticed a cold haunch of cooked meat hanging from a peg and stew set aside on the hearth in case someone needed food.

He watched Meshika stir up the fire, adding fresh firewood to the still hot bed of ash and coals. She pushed two soapstone pots to the edge of the hearth nearer the flames to reheat for the morning meal.

As he continued his observation of the wigwam and its occupants, he could not know that he would soon have much more than a passing knowledge of wigwams and these particular occupants.

He rolled out of the comfortable confines of the pile of soft fur bedding and sat on the edge of the sleeping platform, rubbing the sleep from his eyes and stretching cramped muscles. The old woman, Ekuanit, walked up to him with the ever-present smile in place.

The first words out of her mouth were obviously a greeting—they included her version of his name—so he responded in kind.

"Good morning, Ekuanit," he said slowly, emphasizing each word.

"Good morning, Gudbj." She handed him a wide-toothed comb and bowl and gestured for him to follow her. They walked from the wigwam toward the nearby lakeshore, the short brown woman with the hulking Gudbjartur in tow.

Many people were scattered along the lakeshore in both directions, washing and grooming themselves. Beyond a simple lift of the chin, Ekuanit spoke not a word. She knelt on the coarse sand-and-pebble beach to begin her own morning ablutions. Gudbjartur glanced around to see if anyone had taken notice of him. He found that they had not. With another look around, he shrugged his shoulders and knelt to join the old woman.

The cool morning breeze and the icy lake water combined to wring a gasp from him as he splashed water on his face. As he sat on the beach combing the water from his streaming beard and hair, he had to chuckle to himself over the way his first day of captivity was taking shape. *I wonder if I am to follow this old woman around all day,* he thought as he got back on his feet.

A wave of dizziness and nausea came over him and he sank back on the beach. He bowed his head onto his fingertips, closed his eyes, and waited for it to pass. *I have gotten to my feet too rapidly. No, my ears are ringing. I cannot ignore the head wound any longer. I am afraid Miknap cracked my head and it will take a long time to heal, if it ever heals.*

Ekuanit finished her ablutions. She looked up in time to see Gudbjartur sitting on the beach with his head bowed, massaging his forehead.

"What is the matter, Gudbj?" she asked, bending toward him.

Gudbjartur waved a hand in the universally understood sign for dizziness. He kept his eyes shut until the attack passed. *They are more infrequent now, so I must be healing.* Slowly he got to his feet, swaying slightly in spite of his best efforts to the contrary. He stood a moment gathering himself. Ekuanit watched him carefully. She examined the still-oozing wound in the back of his head. Clucking in apparent sympathy, she gestured for him to follow and walked back toward the village.

He snorted in irritation as she walked off without a backward glance. However, he did as she directed and followed. In spite of occasional waves of dizziness, he took the opportunity to examine the large village. Beyond a few glances from passersby, nobody paid him the least attention.

They do not regard me as a threat. To the contrary, they do not regard me at all. Most simply ignore me. I am not accustomed to this kind of treatment. He chuckled to himself.

* * *

Gudbjartur trailed behind Ekuanit back to the wigwam. He found people clustered around the hearths, dipping their bowls into the stew pots. He looked at the bowl he had just used to wash his face and hair and then looked around for a clean replacement or guidance from someone. When neither materialized he shrugged his shoulders and dipped his bowl into the stew.

Sometime later, after he had finished the meal, he sat alone on the sleeping platform watching the interplay between people. He thought the occupants of each wigwam might all be members of an extended family, as was customary with his own people. *There must be fifty people in this wigwam.* Assuming a similar number lived in each of the six wigwams he had seen there were about 300 people in this village. *That is about the same numbers that live at Halfdansfjord. There are many villages of Naskapi and many villages of Haudeno with all their related tribal bands. That means hundreds; perhaps thousands of natives already live in this land.* He found his conclusions sobering. *I hope that they allow my people to live among them. Otherwise, our dream of a new home is impossible. Perhaps my capture just might prove to be a way to accomplish this.* His mind grappled with the endless possibilities of a peaceful existence for everyone. A gesture from Glooscap interrupted his thoughts.

* * *

Gudbjartur walked over to join the animated group around the hearth. Glooscap introduced him to all of them except the children who were already outside doing whatever it is that all children do. He dutifully repeated each of the unfamiliar names as best he could. His attempts caused good-natured comments and laughter.

With a slight smile wrinkling the corners of his mouth and eyes, Glooscap nodded his satisfaction.

"Good. You try to talk to us. That is why you are here, to learn our language and customs. All of us will teach you." His gesture encompassed the smiling crowd.

"You are a member of my family and one of all the people who live in this wigwam. They will treat you as one of us. You will live and work with us. Everyone works and so will you. For now, you will work with the women. Ekuanit will help you to understand what to do. In this way, you will quickly learn our language because all of the women will have a hand in teaching you. Do you understand what I tell you?"

Gudbjartur nodded in the affirmative at the obvious question. Although he understood little of the conversation, Glooscap had spoken slowly and clearly, emphasizing each word and phrase with signs. Gudbjartur held his open palm toward Glooscap with a quizzical expression on his face. "Am I a prisoner?" he said, clasping his hands firmly together.

Glooscap regarded him with narrowed eyes for a moment. He shook his head. "No," he said.

"Then, am I free to go?" He smiled slightly at his own question, already knowing the answer.

"You are not a prisoner, but you are not free. Sachem has commanded that you learn our ways and our language. Kejo and I are charged with you. We are responsible. It will be as Sachem has said. Do you understand?"

"Aye, I understand some of what you say." He nodded to Glooscap and glanced at the faces of all those listening so intently to their exchange. "I do not understand why I am alive or why you treat me as you do. I fought you and killed three of your men, yet you accept me into your wigwam as a member of your family. This I do not understand. Perhaps understanding will come as I learn more of your language." He chuckled, shrugged his shoulders, and held his hands out, palms up, clearly conveying his confusion. Not understanding why, several onlookers joined in his mirth, but not Glooscap. His grim expression did not alter. Gudbjartur held his eyes and bobbed his head, sweeping his hand forward at waist height as he had seem them do.

"I understand a little, Glooscap. I will not violate your people's trust in me."

Glooscap's expression softened somewhat. He inclined his head slightly and gave the cutting sign with the edge of his hand. The topic had concluded. He beckoned Gudbjartur to follow and stepped over to one of the wigwam support poles. Crouching down he scooped some of the dirt aside. His meaning became clear as he spoke.

"After about five seasons, the poles making up the support framework of the wigwam rot off at the ground. You will help the village women build a new, larger wigwam, before the Time of Whiteness, to replace this one. Gudbj, this post is rotten all the way through," Glooscap said. He dug some of the rotten wood out and crumbled it between his fingers. "The posts are all rotten. We need a new wigwam. Do you understand?"

"Aye, I understand the wigwam post is rotten. But I am not yet certain what I am to do about it," Gudbjartur said, almost as an afterthought to himself. He glanced at Glooscap. "But I think I am to do some of the work to fix these posts."

Glooscap inclined his head in assent and then continued. He gestured to include the group of women. "You will help Ekuanit, the women of my family, and the women of Kejo's family to build a new wigwam. In this way, you will learn our customs from the women who do all the work. You can also hear all the gossip about everyone else," he said. He smiled at the group of women with Ekuanit as they dutifully laughed. "Now, go with Ekuanit and these women and they will show you the work that is to be done."

Glooscap rose and walked from the wigwam. Gudbjartur watched his retreating back a moment, shrugged, and followed. Glooscap turned when he saw Gudbjartur following. He realized that Gudbjartur did not understand what he was to do or with whom he was to do it. The women found this to be humorous—thinking a man working humorous enough—and laughed. Even Glooscap, at the urging of Ekuanit, smiled at the misunderstanding. Gudbjartur finally realized the joke was on him and stood waiting for Glooscap to clear it up for him, his jaw clenched in exasperation.

Glooscap took Gudbjartur by the arm and pointed him toward the site for the new wigwam. "You stay here, Gudbj," he said, making it clear that he was to stay and help the women.

"All right. I understand that I am to stay here, I think," Gudbjartur said. A slight smile pulled at his mouth.

Glooscap clapped him on the back, gestured for him to follow the chattering women with a lift of his chin, and turned away.

* * *

Gudbjartur watched him walk away. He turned with a sigh and followed the women. *I will make the best of this. I will work beside them on whatever job needs doing.*

In the beginning, everyone save Ekuanit treated him with reserve. That did not last long as he pitched in to help them with the myriad tasks expected of Naskapi women. His interest in their daily lives—no man had ever expressed an interest before—his charming personality and his strength and huge size soon won them all over.

Over the course of many days, about half the time between new moons, he worked with the women gathering materials from the forest and transporting them laboriously to the site where others prepared them for the actual construction of the wigwam. The process was very time consuming, not un-like the building of Norse longhouses.

No warriors guarded him. He knew that he could just slip away, melt into the forest. *I would not get far before they would come after me. I do not think I would get a second chance. These are good people. Our two peoples can learn much from each other.* He began to understand the women well enough to be of some help. The almost constant chatter as they went about their various tasks, and his responses, caused gales of laughter as they mimicked his language, some of them quite well. He began trading words with them as they worked; a Norse word for a Naskapi word and so on. He had never tried to learn an-other language, but found, much to his surprise, that he had a natural facility.

All the young women had babies in cradleboards with them. He watched, with growing admiration, the care given the babies while their mothers performed a variety of difficult tasks, yet their children received all the attention required. He became aware that the cradleboard for the papoose, as they called babies, was the secret. The cradleboard was a wood, rawhide, and soft leather affair about two feet long with a footboard at the bottom and a wide, thin, wooden bow at the top, right above the child's head. Shoulder straps on the back of the cradleboard allowed the mother to carry the papoose like a pack on her back. Over the top bow was a soft leather hood that attached to the backboard part of the frame and served to protect the baby from sun, wind, and rain. The bow also furnished a place to hang noisemakers, bits of leather, or a shiny rock or seashell to keep the occupant from becoming bored or troublesome. Amazingly, the babies did not seem to have such problems. He found this especially admirable because cranky babies always grated on his nerves.

Each morning the mother dressed her child in a full-length, long-sleeved, soft leather pullover, a miniature of that worn day and night by most of the women. Then she placed the child on his back in the cradleboard. He observed that they utilized the same absorbent moss for bodily waste that his people used, changing it as need be. They laced the child up in the soft leather covering that served to both protect them from the elements and confine them in the cradleboard. The only parts of the child not restrained were the head and arms. Because of the way the cradleboard was constructed the child could be completely relaxed, kick its legs, stand erect by pushing on the footboard, or do almost whatever amused it while propped against a handy tree trunk or hanging from a limb, while the mother worked nearby.

* * *

Gudbjartur understood the basic building techniques of the Naskapi after all the materials had been gathered and prepared and actual construction began. They asked his opinion on the inevitable problems associated with any large construction project.

He was amazed at the rapidity with which the new wigwam took shape after they sited the new beside the old. Ekuanit scratched the shape and desired size in the rich black earth of the forest floor with a stick, to the accompaniment of loud suggestions from her helpers. They used live trees for the support posts where possible, digging shallow postholes along the periphery of the oval to plant freshly cut posts where necessary. Each post spanned a hand's breadth at the base, tapering to a supple, slender top. With more women arriving, it grew into a community project, a social event, rather than hard work.

Gudbjartur helped strip branches and bark from the full-length birch trees selected for support posts. He scored the bark from top to bottom with a knife that Ekuanit gave him, worked it loose around the base, and stripped it away in one long piece while holding the post with his foot. Working with two helpers who bent the supple standing trees over, he peeled the bark away. Others split the peeled bark into thinner strips that they needed to tie the framework together.

Two days later a completed wigwam framework stood ready for the next step. Impressed with its strength and rigidity

Gudbjartur stood back and admired its shape and symmetry. He had helped tie peeled branches and saplings to each horizontal support post with the slippery birch bark strips. The result was a loaf shaped latticework structure with rounded ends. Three, square-framed smoke holes spaced along the curved top, a single entrance alcove, and doorway framed in the south end completed the intricate framework of the wigwam.

Gudbjartur climbed to the rounded top of the wigwam to help finish the three smoke holes. *Their smoke hole design is better than ours. Rain cannot get in around the rain cap. Any breeze will suck the smoke right out,* he thought, as he used supple bark strips as whippings to secure the framing of the square smoke hole to the wigwam framework. On another part of the roof, he observed two women build a small upright frame over the middle smoke hole and fit the rain cap. They laid a long, wide piece of bark over the frame and pinned each end to opposite sides of the smoke hole. He shook his head at the simplicity and obvious functionality of the simple rain cap, seeing how well they would work with the draft doors he had helped build earlier. The three small draft doors—one in each sidewall and one in the rounded end—provided a means of easily regulating the draft air for the hearths. He admired the simple, yet effective design that had several improvements over the Norse longhouse.

* * *

While Gudbjartur helped build the wigwam framework, other workers collected and stockpiled the birch bark necessary to cover it. He began helping them after completion of the framework. *It is fortunate that birch is so plentiful. They do not have to travel far to get all they need.* They selected suitable birch trees, as free of knots as possible, then cut and peeled large rectangles of bark from the living tree. It came away easily, usually in one piece. They pinned the resulting rectangular slabs together, end to end, with sharpened willow withes, rolling the bark loosely as it accumulated. These rolls were then stacked in the lake shallows, to keep them from drying out, until the time came to begin lacing them to the finished framework with thongs made of the limber inner bark of the same trees. These rolls of inner bark thongs joined the roof rolls in the lake shallows until roofing time.

* * *

Gudbjartur had a hand in every phase of the construction, including the final—digging out the interior—before they laced the roof rolls in place. The time-tested digging methods of the Naskapi entailed loosening dirt with a sharpened digging stick, scooping the dirt up, and carrying both dirt and an occasional rock away in heavily constructed baskets woven especially for that purpose. There were many people so this method had always worked and, in fact, still worked now, but Gudbjartur decided to show them a better way.

Casting about in the surrounding forest, Gudbjartur found a suitable piece of green birch and with the willing assistance of two young women, he fashioned wooden wedges of dried birch with his flint knife. Then he dropped to his knees at one end of the birch log and picked up a handy rock to use as a hammer stone. "Now watch," he said, grinning at his two helpers. Carefully, he drove the wedges into both ends of the birch log until it split in two lengthwise, creating two halves with relatively smooth surfaces.

His helpers exclaimed in admiration as the log split evenly in two.

"I need your help to split it into planks," he said, demonstrating what he wanted them to do. Butting one end of the half-log against a handy tree, he used the hammer stone to carefully tap the wedges into the other end at a point that would yield the thickness of plank he wanted. As the plank began to split from the half log, he drove another set of wedges into each side to control the split as evenly as possible. One of his helpers held the half-log in place on the ground with her foot, grasping what she needed to do. As he hammered the wedges in, the log crept to the side.

He gestured to his other helper. "Hold it down on the other side. I cannot recall your name," he said, looking up at her.

"What is your name?"

"I am called Mishta," she said, in a small voice.

"Mishta," he repeated. "All right, hold the other side down with your foot."

"I am called Nutashkuan, Gudbj," the other young woman said.

He looked up at her and chuckled at the serious expression on her face. A grin softened his bearded face. "All right, Nutashkuan it is, then. I do not know how long I will remember your names, but remind me if I forget." Still grinning, he shook his head and resumed hammering in the wedges.

The green, knot-free wood split easily into a plank as long as his leg and two hand's breadth wide. He held the resulting plank out in his hands to examine it for defects. His two helpers stood quietly by while he roughed out the desired tool, the green wood curling easily from the edge of his keen blade as he whittled out the shape of a digging shovel. He put the final touches on his creation, spending the most time scooping wood from the blade to create a depression to hold the dirt. *I wish I had Jorundr's tools. I could make this shovel so much faster, and the end result would certainly be better than this crude thing.* He held it out at arm's length as he got to his feet.

Nutashkuan, thinking he had made a canoe paddle, mimed a paddling motion.

Gudbjartur shook his head. "We call this a shovel. You can use it to dig in the soft ground inside the wigwam. It should work well enough," he said, handing the shovel to Nutashkuan.

He stood and stretched cramped muscles while his helpers examined the strange tool. Mishta handed the shovel back to Gudbjartur and he beckoned them to follow. He walked over to where the others plied their digging sticks, stepped into the shallow trench, and began to dig. Everybody stopped scratching with their sticks and watched him in amazement as dirt flew from his efforts.

Without warning, an arrow thudded into the back of one of the young women nearby as she stepped unknowingly into its flight path. Her pretty, young face collapsed in shock and surprise as she fell from the edge of the excavation into Gudbjartur's outstretched arms. Quickly lowering her to her side on the bare ground, he examined the arrow protruding from the area of her right shoulder blade.

"I think you will be all right. The arrow did not go through the bone of your shoulder," he said, patting her arm in an attempt to comfort her.

"I will return for you," he said, gesturing for one of the women crouched down in the safety of the excavation.

"Take care of her until I return," he said with feeling.

"Ekuanit, keep them here. I will return," he shouted for all to hear, as he gestured for the others to take cover in the trench and behind the dirt piles.

Standing slowly, he looked over the dirt piles to see what was happening. Without doubt, the village was under attack. Groups of strange men were moving quickly toward his position, killing everyone they met along the way.

The attackers came through the part of the stockade removed to accommodate the new wigwam. He did not see many warriors, but the surprise of a hit-and-run attack worked to their advantage. As the attackers ran out of victims in their immediate vicinity, Gudbjartur suddenly vaulted from the excavated area with a shout that paralyzed the war party for a moment. That was all the advantage that he needed as he smashed into the surprised men.

"Odin!" The bloodcurdling battle cry seemed to reverberate from the walls of the wigwams as a huge crazed man, the like of which they had never before seen, suddenly lay to among them, swinging a wooden shovel. Four men went down before the others recovered sufficiently to protect themselves.

Clutching the broken handle of his erstwhile shovel like a club, he battered his enemies aside. Spittle flew from his mouth. His eyes were those of a demon as he screamed his battle cry.

A Haudeno thrust a spear at him with both hands, the man's shoulder and arm muscles corded with the effort. Gudbjartur twisted desperately aside; the keen edge of the flint spear point caressed his ribcage, opening a cut like a grinning mouth as it deflected from a rib.

The Haudeno's momentum carried him forward into the splintered, upthrust point of the broken shovel handle as the

Northman drove it into the man's body with all his strength. A whoosh of air blew from the man's mouth, his face collapsed in agony, and he fell to the ground, transfixed by the shovel handle.

Weaponless now, Gudbjartur ducked under a vicious backhand swipe of a Haudeno war club and drove his unprotected head into the midsection of the man, bearing him to the ground and crushing the wind from his lungs with a knee. At the same time, he repeatedly smashed his elbow and forearm into the man's throat, leaving him rolling on the ground to choke in his own blood.

Gudbjartur leaped to his feet and stooped to tear weapons from the fallen before crashing forward on his berserk attack into another group of Haudeno warriors. He literally foamed at the mouth as he screamed his war cry. Although he alternately lost or used the weapons at hand, he pressed ever forward on the attack, sometimes with his knotted fists as his only weapons. His imposing size and the ferocity of his relentless attack began to unnerve his adversaries. Brave warriors, forged in the crucible of many hand-to-hand battles, began to recoil away from his onslaught. In the next few minutes, he felled five more warriors before the Haudeno rearguard came under attack from the village warriors.

Under the fury of this combined attack, the remaining warriors broke off the engagement and ran for their lives. Naskapi warriors killed the enemy wounded where they lay on the ground or took them prisoner.

Gudbjartur joined another group of warriors led by Glooscap as they chased after their attackers fleeing into the forest. After a time, Glooscap called a halt when it became obvious that the Haudeno men had given them the slip.

"There will be another day." He gasped for air as he looked over his men. His eyes came to rest on Gudbjartur. "You saved our village from being completely overrun by the Haudeno war party," he said as he appraised the man.

Several other warriors added their comments before Gudbjartur answered Glooscap.

Gudbjartur's breath came in shuddering gasps. He glanced at the men grouped with Glooscap. "I must return, Glooscap.

There is a wounded girl who took an arrow meant for me," he said, gesturing toward the village with a gore-covered enemy war club. He waited for a nod from Glooscap, and then moved off in the general direction of the village. Breaking into a lope, he wove his way through the forest.

Glooscap, understanding only a part of what Gudbjartur said to him, watched the man's back recede from view in the cloaking forest. He shook his head at the jumble of thoughts coming to the fore concerning Gudbjartur. He glanced at his men, who seemed as perplexed as he did over the actions of the man who had so recently been their prisoner. He muttered under his breath and walked away toward the village, his men following behind.

* * *

After Gudbjartur and the Naskapi warriors chased the enemy from the village, women gathered the wounded into groups, caring for them as best they could while waiting for the medicine man and his helpers to get to them. The medicine man came in due course and cut the arrow from the young woman's back. He applied a soothing poultice to stop the bleeding and went on to others needing his services.

Gudbjartur scarcely gave the five enemy captives a glance as he hurried by; his mind occupied only with the young woman who had stepped unknowingly into the path of the arrow meant for him. As he burst on the scene, her companions had just helped her to her feet. The crowd parted to allow him to approach her directly. Several of them reached out to touch him as he passed. He was later to realize their touch was a tribute to him.

Bending down slightly, he placed a hand gently on her shoulder and looked into her dark eyes. She was somewhat pale, although her facial expression as she looked at him conveyed no sign of the pain she must feel. "Are you all right, my friend?" he asked, concern obvious in his tone of voice.

She nodded at the question. "Yes, Gudbj, I am well. The medicine man broke off the tip of the arrowhead in my shoulder blade. He said it would not matter to leave the tip in my bone."

A woman handed him the bloody arrow. He examined the missile, seeing that about half of the point was missing. *Thank the gods this did not come from one of our bows. The arrow would have gone clear through her,* he mused, returning the arrow to the woman.

Gently he placed his hands on the young woman's shoulders and turned her around so that he could have a look at the wound. A gooey poultice and wad of absorbent dry moss secured in place by a thin leather strap over her shoulder and down across her chest excluded the actual wound site from view. *There is no blood from the wound. That is good. I hope the poultice will cause the wound to heal rapidly without infection. I do not think Asa or Thorkatla could have done better.* He turned her around to face him. His hands rested on her shoulders. Bending forward, his pale blue eyes searched her face, on her black eyes. "By stepping in front of that arrow, you may have saved my life."

She bobbed her head and smiled at his sincerity, knowing not what he said.

He took another tack. "What is your name?" he asked, using the sign he had only recently acquired.

"I am called Ashua," she said, smiling up at him.

"Good!" he laughed. "I understand. You are Ashua."

The others crowded around. Because of the animated conversation and sign language, Gudbjartur realized his facility with the Naskapi spoken language and signs increased daily. The women expressed their appreciation for his part in routing the enemy from the village.

Ekuanit restored a bit of calm to the boisterous group when she arrived with a bark bucket of water and insisted on cleaning the enemy blood from Gudbjartur. In the process she found that not all the blood belonged to the enemies he had slain. Some came from wounds he had sustained in the short, fierce battle. Moreover, using his head like a battering ram during the attack had reopened the troublesome head wound.

"Blood is coming from your head, Gudbj. Here, set down and let us clean you up," she said, guiding him to a seat on the top edge of the trench.

He realized that he felt a little dizzy now that the rush he always felt from combat began to subside. As tensed muscles relaxed, he also found that he rather enjoyed being the center of their attention, a feeling to which he was unaccustomed of late. *Considering that I am the man of the day to these women I have worked with,* he chuckled to himself, *I am taking their praise well and with the required amount of humility.*

As it happened he would never fully recall what he did that day, but others would.

* * *

Chapter Ten

A Northman is reborn

Gudbjartur took his leave of the chattering women and strolled through the scene of battle in an attempt to sort the jumble of his thoughts. The details seemed foggy to him. His brief examination of the area helped little, although he did find the blood-soaked blade of his shovel near the section of missing palisade. He did not find the handle. He stood turning the blade repeatedly in his hands, so lost in thought that he missed Glooscap's soundless approach until the man was right behind him.

Wheeling around rapidly, Gudbjartur came up short as Glooscap extended his hand palm outward toward him.

"Whew!" he exclaimed, smiling at the man while willing his tensed muscles to relax. "You should not sneak up on me that way."

"Perhaps you are getting careless, beginning to relax with us," Glooscap said, sweeping his arm around to encompass the village. "Come with me, Gudbj, there is a council meeting. They want you in attendance."

Gudbjartur nodded, idly tossing the shovel blade on the ground without a thought, as he prepared to follow Glooscap.

"Bring that with you," Glooscap said, pointing at the discarded shovel blade.

"Why? It is no longer of any use."

"Just bring it. The elders will have questions about what you did and how you fought our enemies."

"All right. I understand that you wish me to bring it, but I do not understand why," Gudbjartur said, stooping to retrieve the blade.

The two men walked to the council hall side by side, in silence, except Gudbjartur caught Glooscap glancing at him from time to time. When he did catch him, Glooscap simply nodded, as if Gudbjartur should know the reason for the glances. He did not. *Whatever it is, he agrees with something. Of that, I am certain.*

To reach the council hall entrance, one passed through the circle of prisoner posts arrayed before it. *I remember how I felt tied to one of them. I also remember that they treated me well, not like these men.* Five Haudeno men, bound hand and foot, hung head down from the posts. Every person, from the very young to the very old, who happened by, took a moment to hit one or all five men with something, be it a stick, club, a hand full of dirt and stones, or a clenched fist. Everything imaginable to torment them, for that is what it was, pure torment.

Gudbjartur paused a moment to study the prisoners. He hoped that the men were not of Deskaheh's people, not that it would matter if they were. Their fate was sealed. They were already dead, actually. Nothing could save them. The manner of their death would fit their crime against the Naskapi. *I will not be called on to decide their fate. I am amongst a strange people. Their thoughts, beliefs, and customs are alien to me. I do not know how they expect me to act.* As he contemplated his own situation ruefully, he looked up into the expressionless eyes of Glooscap. The man beckoned him to follow with a lift of his chin. As they continued toward the council hall entrance Gudbjartur's thoughts tumbled through his mind. *I am unsure of my status, but it seems only a step away from those prisoners.*

Glooscap motioned Gudbjartur ahead of him into the interior of the council hall.

As before, it took a moment to become accustomed to the gloom of the interior after the brightness of the cloudless day. Glooscap walked over and sat down in the council circle opposite Sachem and the council of elders. Gudbjartur stood uncertainly near the entrance until Glooscap motioned for him to join him. *Thankfully, they have not laid a fire. I already sweat. It is too hot in here with the press of bodies.* He nodded a greeting to several of those he recognized. He took a seat beside Glooscap, aware that every eye followed his movements. *I am unsure how to take their attention.* The murmur of voices gradually died out. Each council member waited for Sachem to speak.

* * *

Sachem did not rise from his place on the rush mats. He addressed Glooscap.

"Begin the story of the enemy raid, Glooscap. I see you have brought many of the participants here to talk to us. That is good," he said. The black eyes shifted to Gudbjartur.

Glooscap rose to his feet and walked slowly around the council circle as he gathered his thoughts. "These Haudeno are not of the band we usually have trouble with. I do not know them. The five prisoners will say nothing, knowing they are to die. I had two guards at the hole in the palisade. Both are among the dead. One of the prisoners killed a young mother and her papoose, running his spear through both of them as they tried to run to safety. That man lies badly wounded. Gudbj got him," he said, gesturing in the direction of Gudbjartur. "We had three killed and ten wounded." He pointed at Gudbjartur. "If he had not fought for us there would have been many more casualties." Glooscap turned to his mother and waved her forward. "Ekuanit will tell you what happened. She and these others were there, I was not."

Ekuanit rose from her place in the group of women, among them Meshika, the wife of Glooscap, and Ashua, the young woman who took the enemy arrow meant for Gudbjartur, and strode to the center of the council chamber. She faced Sachem and began telling her version of the attack.

"A large group of us were digging out the floor of our new wigwam. Gudbj was showing us the new shovel that he had made. We were all amazed at how quickly he dug out the dirt. Ashua happened to move in front of Gudbj, to better watch him dig, when an arrow hit her in the back, knocking her into his arms. The Haudeno attacked through the hole in the palisade where we took the logs down to make room for our wigwam. We all saw them and began to run hither and yon, but Gudbj yelled at us in his language and used sign language. He gestured for us to join him in the trench where he had been digging. He pulled us into the trench and pushed us down, talking all the while in a mixture of his language and ours." She paused a moment, looking out over the council members, who had thus far remained silent except for an occasional guttural sound of anger as she relayed her tale. She then pointed to Meshika, the next in line of seniority among those women present. "I have told my tale," Ekuanit said. "Meshika will be able to add more, I am certain." She smiled at the woman she regarded as a true daughter as she walked back to her seat.

Meshika waited until Ekuanit regained her seat. She glanced briefly at Glooscap, then addressed Sachem and the council.

"Ekuanit has told a good tale," she said, acknowledging the smiling woman. "What I will say now concerns that man." She pointed at Gudbjartur.

Gudbjartur watched her. He knew that her tale was to be about his attack. *Perhaps I will understand enough of her tale to remember what I did because I remember little of the battle.*

Meshika continued in a strong, sure tone of voice. "If he had not been with us in the first few moments of the attack, I believe the enemy would have killed or captured many of our women. The Haudeno poured through the hole in the palisade. All of sudden Gudbj stood up. He jumped from the trench roaring his war cry, and ran at the attacking warriors armed only with the digging tool he had just made that morning. The Haudeno were so surprised at his appearance and even seeing him here that they paused for a moment. By the time they recovered, Gudbj was among them, screaming all the while in his language, some word, I think, a single word, but his screaming and roaring of that one word and the ferocity of his attack stopped them. One of our young women stopped to grab her papoose up as she ran toward the trench. A Haudeno warrior threw his spear and killed both of them."

She paused for a time as she walked around the fire pit before the grim council members. The people were more silent, more circumspect, than they had been during Ekuanit's tale. Meshika stopped in front of Gudbjartur, who sat on the bulrush mats looking up at her. She continued. "Gudbj felled the warrior who killed the mother and papoose with his digging tool. That man hangs from one of our prisoner posts now," she said. A growl, not unlike a wolf bearded in its lair, rose from the assembly. "I saw a pile of enemy dead and wounded around him. Every man who drew near him he either killed or wounded enough to put them out of the fight. He broke the wide part of his digging tool from the handle when he struck one warrior, nearly cutting off the man's head. All he had left was the handle but still he fought. I saw a warrior attack him with a spear. He parried the man's spear and drove the handle of his digging tool completely through his body. He used that warrior's spear to kill another, then taking his weapon to kill or wound another. Never in my life have I seen a man fight as he does. He is like Night Wind, the demon of the forest." Her rapt listeners glanced fearfully into the shadows at mention of the mythical apparition of the nighttime gloom of the forest.

"The Haudeno warriors broke and ran because of his ferocity. Our men fought bravely beside him and counted many coups on the enemy. However, their methods of fighting are not what won the battle so quickly for us. It was him, Sachem!" she exclaimed passionately, pointing in Gudbjartur's direction. "Gudbj! He who fights like a demon!" Her face reflected the intensity of her passion as Meshika turned to the council. Her eyes paused on the face of each council member before coming to rest on Sachem. He watched her without expression for a heartbeat, before she broke the brief eye contact with him, gave the cutting sign to signify that she had finished, and turned away to resume her place among the women. Before taking a seat, she helped the wounded Ashua to her feet.

The young woman reluctantly took her place in the council center. Embarrassed to be under the scrutiny of the council elders and the many onlookers, the young woman stood for a moment with eyes downcast, her hands tightly clasped, and her thoughts in turmoil.

Kejo spoke to her from his place among the onlookers, behind and to the side of where Glooscap and Gudbjartur sat before the council. "Tell them your part of the story, Ashua," Kejo said softly.

Gudbjartur turned and looked in Kejo's direction when he spoke. Their eyes locked. For the first time Gudbjartur detected no hostility in the man's eyes.

Attention drew back to Ashua as she began to speak. "I do not have a long story to tell. As you have heard, we were watching Gudbj dig with his shovel. I was standing to one side, but I could not see the digging well so I moved closer. Suddenly an arrow hit me hard in the back and I fell into the trench. Gudbj caught me and lowered me to the ground. He laid me on my side and then he stood up to look at the enemy warriors. A moment later, he leaped out of the trench and began yelling his war cry. I did not see any of the battle, but I could hear Gudbj yelling. Later, after the battle was over and the medicine man had taken the arrow from my back and worked his magic, Gudbj returned just as the others helped me to my feet. He was all bloody. He still had a bloody war club in his hand. He threw it to the side as he came up to me. I do not know everything he tried to tell me. I think he thanked me for stepping in front and taking the arrow meant for him. He told me he was sorry I had been hurt. He seemed very concerned." Pausing for a moment, her eyes sought Gudbjartur, and she finished directly to him. "Thank you for catching me after the arrow hit me. Falling into the trench would have hurt me even more and might have pushed the arrow in deeper." She held his eyes briefly, and then glanced at Sachem and the elders.

"That is all I can remember, Sachem." Receiving a slight inclination of his head, she demurely returned to her place, thankful not to be the center of attention any longer.

And so it went until everyone having a story to tell about the battle had his or her opportunity to tell it. It was the way

of the people, and one of the favored forms of public enter-
tainment. The warrior's tales were always the most favored,
especially when they won the battle, because they purposely
exaggerated their part in the telling. The more outrageous
the tale, the more elaborate the pantomime, the greater the
applause accorded the teller.

Now Kejo was the center of attention. His tale did not concern him. It was all about Gudbjartur.

It took some time before Gudbjartur realized the man was
telling a tale of his part in the battle. Until that moment, he
did not realize that any of the warriors had observed his performance. He chuckled to himself at the thought. *Their warriors, I guess they are my warriors, too. I have been accepted as one
of the people.* It sobered him somewhat, but the prospect for
the future of his own people, the Northmen, excited him.

He turned his full attention to Kejo. Atkaa had just handed
him the splintered handle of Gudbjartur's shovel. Kejo approached Gudbjartur and motioned for the shovel blade
lying on the mat between him and Glooscap. Gudbjartur
glanced at Glooscap, uncertain what Kejo wanted of him.
Glooscap pointed at the shovel blade and Gudbjartur picked
it up, still covered in dried blood and gore, and handed it
to Kejo.

The two men held one another's eyes for a moment in
time, the pale blue and obsidian black of the two warriors.
Kejo wheeled away quickly and jumped into the air, repeatedly yelling his version of Gudbjartur's war cry.

"Odin!" The war cry reverberated in the confines of the
council hall. He wheeled and dodged this way and that, slash-
ing at the air with the two sundered parts of Gudbjartur's
shovel held in his clenched fists.

The crowd clapped and cheered, gradually quieting down
so Kejo could continue.

"Odin!" He shouted at the top of his voice. Spittle flew
from his open mouth. He slashed the air repeatedly, finally
letting the blade of the shovel spin from his hand. Grasping
the handle in both, hands he mimed violently ramming the
splintered shaft up into the chest of an enemy warrior, as he
had seen Gudbjartur do.

The assembly oohed and aahed appreciatively, finally break-ing into thunderous applause. The people outside the council hall echoed the applause from within.

Kejo retrieved the other piece of the shovel and handed both to Sachem, who placed them at his side.

Kejo glanced once again at Gudbjartur as he returned to his place in the group of onlookers.

Gudbjartur felt humbled by what he had witnessed. He had no clear recollection of his part in the battle, yet he knew that Kejo's actions were a tribute to him personally. *Kejo no longer regards me as his enemy. I do not know why. I think the Naskapi have carefully prepared for this council. Before Glooscap came to bring me here, certain arrangements were made. The tales that they told are normal for them. But it is leading up to something. I think it has to do with me. Kejo suddenly changed his attitude toward me. I hope to learn the reason today.* Thinking back on what he had observed, he suddenly remembered that Kejo alone had spoken to Ashua when she hesitated in the telling of her tale. *The change in Kejo has something to do with her.*

A gesture from Sachem stilled the buzz of conversation.

"Glooscap, bring Gudbj before the council."

Gudbjartur darted a quick look at Glooscap as they rose from their sitting position and approached the council elders. He gleaned nothing from the man's expressionless face.

As a council member, Glooscap normally sat with Sachem and the eight elders comprising the council, but today, be-cause Gudbjartur was with him, he was to sit on the other side of the central fire pit directly opposite Sachem.

This arrangement was not lost on Gudbjartur.

As Glooscap and Gudbjartur approached, Sachem and the elders got to their feet, surprising Gudbjartur. He made eye contact with each council member in turn. His eyes came to rest on Sachem. *The council did not confer on their decision. They have already made it.*

The hush in the council wigwam was palpable as all waited for Sachem to speak.

Sachem nodded to Gudbjartur in greeting and his entire demeanor conveyed openness and friendliness, unlike their first meeting. "Gudbj, this council was called to honor you.

The Naskapi people give you their respect and gratitude for fighting our enemies. You did not have to fight them. Your status was not that of a warrior. But you did not hesitate, attacking them with only your digging tool."

He motioned for someone to hand him the digging tool. He examined the two pieces of the shovel, turning them in his hands. The magnetic black eyes lifted to study Gudbjartur's face. Suddenly, Sachem's face split in a wide grin, catching Gudbjartur completely off guard.

"I am told this digging tool works much better than ours, for both digging and fighting; a very useful tool. What do you call it?"

"We call it a shovel, Sachem."

"Shovel," he repeated, in an almost perfect copy of the guttural Norse word. "We will need more of these. You can show us how you make them."

It was not a question.

"I will show the people how to make the shovel, Sachem," Gudbjartur answered, returning the smile.

Sachem seemed to consider a moment. His head bobbed slowly. He continued to examine the broken shovel, and then raised his chin to indicate an area of the wigwam wall for the prominent display of weapons.

"This shovel will be tied in place with our other weapons of honor."

Dropping the broken shovel on the sitting mats, Sachem turned his attention back to the two men standing before him.

"What is Odin?" Again, he watched Gudbjartur closely.

He misses nothing. "Odin is the god of war for all Northmen," he said simply.

Sachem raised his chin to indicate Glooscap. "He has told me of this war cry. Why do you call on Odin when you attack your enemies?" Sachem said.

Uncertain of the meaning of all the words and signs, Gudbjartur glanced from Sachem to Glooscap. He gleaned nothing from the face of Glooscap. Taking a breath, he collected his thoughts before answering. He looked into Sachem's eyes. "I call on Odin to alert him that I am fighting, perhaps to the death. If I am slain, Odin will send his handmaidens, the Valkyries, to take my spirit to Valhalla, to his Hall of Heroes, to abide with him and his slain warriors forever." Gudbjartur spoke slowly and distinctly, with elaborate pantomime, feeling that his explanation would be impossible for Sachem and the others to grasp.

Sachem, too, paused while he seemed to consider. He glanced at his council. Beyond a nod or two none spoke. Sachem's eyes shifted back and forth from Glooscap to Gudbjartur. "Naskapi have this abode for slain warriors. I think we have many of the same beliefs."

Gudbjartur chuckled aloud. *Never again will I be surprised at the depth of this man's understanding.* He glanced at Glooscap in time to see the man's mouth and eyes convey his feeling, something that rarely occurred.

The ghost of a smile played around the corners of Sachem's eyes when he saw Gudbjartur's reaction to his words. "Glooscap has kept us informed of everything you have done since he brought you here. You have lived among us for almost one moon and during that time, you have been willing to learn our customs and language. We can communicate now. We have learned much about your people while you learned about us. That was our intent. We are well pleased with the results," he said, pausing for a moment to allow other council members to speak. Beyond a noncommittal grunt or nod none spoke.

"Before we finish this council meeting we want you to know what has been reported about your people, the Greenlanders. Chisasi, the war leader of another band of Naskapi, has traded with your village. He has been there twice. Your Greenlanders have completed their village and are hunting and fishing to prepare for the Time of Whiteness. Two of their big canoes remain at the village. The other four are gone. What do you call these big canoes, Gudbj?"

Gudbjartur smiled at the question. He spoke slowly, enunciating each word of his answer.

"They are called ships or knarrer."

The pronunciation of *ship* came easily, not so for *knarr*. For the first time, others tried the strange words with varying degrees of success. Their attempts had many of the onlookers laughing until Sachem raised a hand.

"Where have the four ships gone?" Sachem asked, his eyes intent, unblinking.

Sachem's knowledge of his people and their settlement surprised him. Gudbjartur answered truthfully.

"They sailed to Greenland with logs for the settlements. Then two of them will sail to the far north to hunt walrus with the Tornit." He watched Sachem closely to gage the extent of his understanding.

"Walrus?" Sachem shrugged his shoulders.

"Walrus are giant animals with long, white teeth." He put his hands to his mouth with two fingers hanging down in what he hoped resembled the teeth of a walrus. "The Tornit call them avik."

"Avik, yes. That is easier for us to say," Sachem said, looking at his council members. He nodded.

"Avik," he repeated the strange word. A wave of his hand indicated that Gudbjartur should continue.

"One ship will sail directly back to Halfdansfjord. The fourth ship will sail to the village of the Thalmiut to trade with them."

Sachem spoke briefly with the elders. The men turned their attention back to Gudbjartur.

"Tell us of the Tornit and Thalmiut," Sachem said.

Gudbjartur paused while he grappled with how to answer the question, given his limited language skills. He glanced at Glooscap. Not a sound came from those in the council hall as they waited expectantly for his reply.

"The Tornit are people of the far north. They hunt the animals of the salt sea from small boats. My people have made friends with them. My chieftain, Halfdan, has ordered two of our ships to hunt and trade with them. They are with the Tornit now." He paused, giving his listeners an opportunity to speak.

"We do not know of the Tornit. It is good to hear of them." Sachem lifted his chin indicating that Gudbjartur should continue.

"The Thalmiut are the people of the deer. They, too, live in the far north. They hunt the reindeer of the tundra. My chieftain made friends and traded with them. One ship is to trade with them on the return voyage from Greenland."

"Naskapi and Thalmiut are neutral now. Some northern bands of our people have fought with them over hunting grounds." Sachem eyed his council.

One of the elders spoke to Gudbjartur. "Can your Northmen be friendly with all the tribes of this land?"

"I do not know. We have already had a big fight with a Haudeno tribe from the south."

Sachem interrupted. "We know of this fight. I will speak of it later." A hand sign told Gudbjartur to continue.

"We want only to live in peace. War is not a good way to live. The Northmen have always known war. We have come to Nitassinan to live in peace with you, to trade, to raise children. That is our hope."

"It is difficult. Peace is elusive between different tribes. We shall see," the elder said.

Sachem and the elders seemed satisfied. The extent of their understanding was difficult to tell, given the limitations of the communication methods.

I believe the wily old man is testing me. They all are, he mused, glancing at the other council members.

Sachem rose to his feet and walked back and forth before his expectant people. He stopped in front of Gudbjartur and studied his face a moment before speaking.

"The Greenlanders live in peace in Nitassinan. We know about all the trouble that you have had. Chisasi has sent word of how your chieftain solved some of this trouble. That is good. If your people continue as they are, they are welcome among us. Your people hunt many animals in the salt sea and we do not, so there is enough for all. Later we will have council meetings together to talk and trade. We have much to trade with your people," Sachem said.

"They have much to trade as well, Sachem. Things you have never seen before, but that will be very useful to the people," Gudbjartur said enthusiastically.

"You and Glooscap are responsible for this new opportunity for our two peoples, Gudbj. Glooscap was very wise in bringing you here as a prisoner. Had he killed you we would have lost our chance to forge a friendly relationship with your people. The chance meeting between the two of you and the knowledge we have gained by having you here is the only way you would have been allowed to remain in our land."

Gudbjartur caught Glooscap's eye.

A smile curved the man's mouth, the hard face softened.

Gudbjartur smiled in return. His brow furrowed in question and he turned back to Sachem.

"What of my men, Sachem? Nine men were with me."

Sachem looked at Glooscap and raised his chin.

"Another Naskapi band captured five of your men after a fight. The Haudeno eluded my men in the forest. Three men in a canoe also got away," Glooscap said.

Deskaheh and three others are free. They will take word to Half-dan. His mind raced.

"Tell me about the Haudeno," Sachem said suddenly.

There are no secrets from this man. He already knew about Deskaheh. He waited for this time to ask me. They planned all of this carefully.

"His name is Deskaheh. He and more than one hundred of his warriors attacked my people for no reason. We won our fight with them. He alone survived and we spared his life. Over time he fell in love with one of our women. He is accepted by my people."

"And you?" Sachem asked.

"He is my friend now," Gudbjartur said simply.

Sachem said nothing. Once again, the black eyes bored into his.

Gudbjartur held Sachem's gaze without flinching or blinking while he waited respectfully for the man to continue. A tangible silence developed. *I cannot lie to him. He will know.* His eyes felt dry with his need to blink.

A barely perceptible nod from Sachem indicated his acceptance of Gudbjartur's words.

Gudbjartur blinked, exhaled slowly, and turned to Glooscap. His need to know more about the fate of his men overrode his natural caution among these people.

"What of the five men captured by the other Naskapi band?" he asked.

"Two men will stay with the people of that band. Sachem has ordered that they be well treated, that they will learn our language and customs, as you are," Glooscap said.

"Just two men? What of the other three?" He asked. Tightness clamped his chest and a roaring came into ears as the heat of emotion rose in his head. He already knew the answer.

Glooscap shook his head slightly.

They were good men. Sadness overcame him as he thought about their loss. *They have joined many other good men in Valhalla.* He glanced at the council. All leaned forward slightly, attentive. He turned back to Glooscap.

"Thank you. I wanted to know," he said. Glooscap answered with the cutting sign, closing the matter.

An expectant hush fell over the crowd. All eyes were on Sachem. They knew that something important would follow. Sachem's silence told his people that he had reached a decision.

Sachem had continued his study of Gudbjartur over the past moments. He shifted his position somewhat on the rush mats, straightened his back, and began to speak.

"We have all listened to the accounts of the enemy attack. Your part in it surprised us. You are a great warrior, Gudbj. Our men can learn much from you about warfare. The Time of Whiteness will soon be upon us. You will remain here, as one of the people, until the Time of Green Grass. Then we shall see. I know that you have a family. You must remain here to strengthen the bonds between our peoples. Your family will understand this. We will get word to them of our decision. Perhaps, they can visit you here. Later you may journey to visit them. We shall see. In the meantime, you will continue as I told you. Our peoples have much to learn about each other. Glooscap, Kejo, and you, are important to our success." He glanced pointedly at Glooscap.

"Come, Kejo," Glooscap said, waving him forward.

Kejo, with Ashua in tow, stepped up to Sachem and handed him a leather-wrapped bundle secured with a thong. Sachem laid the bundle on the mat at his side.

Ashua hung back. Kejo turned and motioned her forward. He placed his arm around her shoulders and they turned together to Gudbjartur. Kejo searched Gudbjartur's face. Before he spoke, the two men held each other's eyes.

"Ashua is my sister, Gudbj. What you did for her means much to me. I will not forget. If you had not gotten the women into that trench they would have been killed or captured, her among them." A slight smile curved Kejo's hard mouth.

"We were lucky, Kejo. Ashua probably saved my life. I will not forget that, either," Gudbjartur said humbly. "Perhaps, we can be friends, you and I, and put the past behind us."

"Pantoo was my friend. It was a fair fight. If he had not been impulsive, he might yet live. From this time on, let us be friends, Gudbj," he said simply, thrusting his right hand forward.

Gudbjartur grasped the hand extended to him. A chill coursed through his body. He threw his head back and laughed. Everyone laughed, including Sachem. "Yes, you might call it a fair fight. It is one of many fights. They are all over for now, a part of the past. I welcome your friendship, Kejo," he said, smiling at the man and his sister. "We may once again fight side by side. I would like that, to fight shoulder-to-shoulder with you."

The gallery of onlookers inside the council hall burst into infectious cheering and clapping that quickly spread to the listeners outside. It had become a happy day for the people and all were in a festive mood. They had much for which to be thankful.

* * *

Glooscap, turning slowly with both arms extended above his head, got the crowd back under control for Sachem.

"There is one more thing for us to do as a people. We have come to honor the man who fought for us. Sachem has a few more words to say to him, and to us."

He took his place beside Gudbjartur. To Gudbjartur's other side was Kejo. The three men stood before Sachem.

The council rose to their feet. Sachem regarded Gudbjartur in silence for a heartbeat. There were the tiny wrinkles of a smile around the eyes, and his face was altogether open and friendly, a departure from the normally expressionless visage.

"Gudbj, you came here as a prisoner, your fate yet to be decided. You are now one of the people and are fully accepted by all," he said, glancing at Kejo, who stood straight and proud at Gudbjartur's side.

"We have a custom of naming among the people that begins with the name given a child and usually ends with the name given that child as an adult. We have bestowed a name on you. It is one of honor, and this name comes from your performance in battle, protecting this village, and is the kind of name given to a warrior only."

He held a hand out, and a council member passed him the beautifully decorated leather bundle Kejo had given him earlier. The people made not a sound in the council lodge as Sachem stepped up to the three waiting men. He handed the bound leather bundle to Gudbjartur.

"Gudbj, take these weapons, for they are yours. We return them to you in gratitude for what you did for us against our enemies. From this day hence, we will call you by your Naskapi name. It is a name of honor. You have earned this honor. You are Nipishish. It means Axeman in the language of the people."

A great cheer rose from the people assembled in the council hall, gradually swelling to include all those outside. It was a great day.

* * *

Nipishish, formerly Gudbjartur, had talked to and been congratulated by so many people he expected he would be confused for a long time. He never forgot a face, but names came and went in his mind, except the names of those close to him. *It will take me some time to accustom myself to my new name, but I like the sound of it—Nipishish.* His right hand rested on the head of the battleaxe, once again at its place on his belt, as his mind sorted through the events of this day.

* * *

The people mourned and buried the dead the following morning. As in all societies, custom dictated the ceremony. The women had prepared the bodies the night before by applying red ocher to every surface, including the hair. Red ocher also covered the tokens, tools, food containers, and weapons, everything that lay in readiness for the journey to the afterlife.

Virtually the entire population of the Naskapi village participated in transporting the bodies the short distance to the knoll overlooking the lake where the burial ceremony was to occur. The bodies of the warriors, women, and baby reposed on leather robes adjacent to a like number of waist deep graves on the east slope of the knoll, toward the rising sun.

Nipishish observed the preparations with more than a passing interest. As an accepted member of their society, he felt honored to join with them in their solemn farewell to their dead. He found more similarities than differences between the Naskapi burial practices and those of his people, the Northmen.

As he stood among the silent warriors, watching the women finish their work, he thought of what had transpired earlier. Out of respect and at the friendly urging of Glooscap and Kejo he, too, had prepared himself in a fashion similar to the other warriors. He stood hipshot, his hand resting atop the head of the battleaxe. Except for his imposing size and neatly trimmed beard, he did not look that much different from the other men. His hair was done up in a queue and bound neatly with a leather thong. He had carefully greased all his exposed skin with red ocher. Kejo had personally painted designs on his face, arms, and chest. His relatively hairless body, a family trait, made the result look satisfying to everyone, judging from the admiring comments. Naked to the waist, he wore the same breechclout, leggings, and moccasins common to all the men. His wide, heavily muscled shoulders and arms were in contrast to the lean hardness of most of the other men.

Ekuanit had proudly presented his new finery to him that very morning. Just as proudly, she took his smelly, frayed, and torn wool clothing outside on the end of a stick and set fire to them. He chuckled as he recalled the chiding and laughter in Glooscap's wigwam as Ekuanit carried his worn clothing out the doorway. *I thought she would wash them, not burn them.* His mouth curved in a smile at the thought.

The soft buckskins felt good against his skin. His suit of new clothing included a knee-length, long-sleeved pullover of the same soft buckskin that he set aside for the Time of Whiteness cold that would soon descend on Nitassinan.

His eyes shifted to the group of warriors whom he accompanied. All had armed and prepared themselves as they would for battle. Each sported favored painted designs on their faces and bodies meant to strike fear into an enemy. Most carried rawhide shields on an arm or over a shoulder. He saw a wide variety of weaponry: spears, bows, and quivers of arrows, tomahawks, and assorted war clubs of every size and shape. Tufts of deer or bear hair around the edges of the shields and on the hafts below the spear points fluttered in the light breeze off the lake. As he gazed over the gathering, he thought the tableau of the two to three hundred people arrayed over the slope to be an impressive site.

Sachem, the tribe's shaman, Pessamit, and the council occupied the forefront of the assembly. Sachem was resplendent in a full suit of pale, almost white buckskin. The deer antler headdress and feather-decorated, gaily painted, deer antler staff of his station completed his attire.

Nipishish felt a chill course through his body as he studied Pessamit, the shaman, the medicine man of this band of Naskapi. A skull mask concealed the man's face and he wore a full suit of buckskins painted in white with an excellent likeness of a human skeleton. The effect was eerie, given that Nipishish had never before seen the like. He shook himself to dispel the feeling of dread, man's innate fear of death, and contemplation of the afterlife.

All eyes fastened on Pessamit as he began to chant and shuffle slowly to the beat of drums and rattles. People began to sway to the rhythm as the primal beat consumed them, including Nipishish, much to his surprise.

Not unlike the burial customs of the Northmen, the Naskapi ceremony was brief. Beyond the chanting of the shaman, not a word came from the assembly. Men picked up the corners of the leather robes and lowered the bodies into each grave. Processions of individuals from the assembly placed tokens, amulets, small baskets, bark boxes of food, weapons, and favored possessions beside each body. Several people began filling in the graves, tamping the dirt down, and replacing the sod. Others scattered the leftover dirt down the slope, blending the gravesites into the landscape. That done, Sachem led his people back toward the village.

Nipishish glanced over the burial site one last time. *One rain and these graves will disappear.*

The whir of rapid wing beats drew his attention as a large flock of ducks flew overhead and settled into the lake shallows at the edge of the rice grass. The flock scattered through the rice and began to feed on the seed heads. He pursed his lips as he turned away to follow the others. *Life always goes on,* he thought as he watched his footing on the slope.

* * *

Later that day, Pessamit attended the wounded once again. The women of each extended family had made them comfortable and time would heal the wounds of most of them. Others repaired the hole in the palisade that had facilitated the attack in the first place.

Many of the women and young girls busied themselves gathering garden produce and preparing for the feast planned for that night in honor of Nipishish. Most of the men did not stoop to help the women with their chores, feeling their tasks were women's work and best left to them. Nipishish was not one who felt that way, nor did he have a male ego to salve. The people had seen him in action; he had nothing to prove to anyone, so he accompanied them, much to their delight, to the gardens.

Several small garden plots were scattered at random throughout the nearby forest clearings and along the riverbank. Each was fenced with a tangle of self-supporting willow withes and interwoven sticks from the forest floor in an attempt to exclude the deer and moose.

The primary crops were corn, beans, sunflowers, and squash, all planted randomly together. The beans climbed the cornstalks and sunflower stalks in their quest for their share of the life-giving sunlight. Squash vines seemed to be everywhere underfoot. Groups of women tended the gardens daily: watering, chopping unwanted weeds away, occasionally fertilizing the plants by burying rotted fish guts at their base, and harvesting the ripened produce in baskets.

Vegetables and other garden produce had never been a part of his diet; most did not grow in the northern climes of his world. He had never before seen such a variety of delicious food that he did not have to hunt. There even seemed to be enough for the insects, deer, and rabbits. He learned early on that lying in concealment near a garden plot always produced a fat deer for the stewpot just before full darkness as they walked the fencerow seeking a hole through which to climb.

Squatting down, he twisted a corn ear off at the stalk and peeled the husk away, revealing a small ear of corn slightly longer than his thumb. He put the ear in his mouth, cob and all, and chewed contentedly while he looked for ripe squash hidden under the large leaves of the vines. The ear was tender and milky, pleasing to his palate. The corn had become one of his favorites. He smiled at the thought of the roasted cakes made from the meat of the squash, the delicious roasted squash seeds, and beans. Why, a stew made of corn, rice, and beans in a broth of deer bones, seasoned with maple sugar, had to be the best of all. *It is hard to decide what I like the best. It is all delicious.* He listened to the women chattering and laughing as they worked. *They like having me help them,* he thought, topping off the basket at his side with other produce. *And, I enjoy working with them. It is calming and satisfying to grub in the dirt and reap the harvest for our efforts.*

Meshika grinned down at him as she picked her way through the squash vines carrying a large basket of mixed vegetables.

"Here, let me have the basket. I will carry it for you," he said, getting to his feet. He transferred her basket to his shoulder and gestured to his own full basket. "Pick up that one for me. I will carry both to the wigwam."

* * *

Meshika picked up his basket, grunting slightly with effort as she boosted it onto his other shoulder. To her, the heaped baskets seemed too heavy for him to carry both, but she knew that he would consider them a trifle. She smiled up at him. Framed and backlight by the late afternoon sun as he was, she could not see his facial expression, but she knew he was smiling behind his beard, for he always smiled at them. "Thank you, Nipishish. I am not accustomed to having the help of a man," she said, shifting to the side into his shadow and shielding her eyes from the glare.

"I will always help you when I can. All of you," he said, gesturing toward the others with his chin. "I am also here to protect you while you work."

"We all know and appreciate that. Others have protected us, too. You are the first to help at the same time."

He nodded and turned away.

She watched him weaving a path through the vines, easily balancing his burdens on his shoulders. The head of his axe hung down between his shoulder blades on a broad strap looped over a shoulder. She had not noticed it before, because it seemed such a part of him. *I am glad that my husband captured him. Otherwise, my people would not have the benefit of friendship with him and his people. I think all of us are better off. We have enough enemies; it is good to have friends, too.* She shook her head at her thoughts and with a sigh returned to her work.

* * *

At the height of the feast that evening, just before sundown, the five prisoners confronted their fate before the wrathful council. With extreme malice, Glooscap paraded before the hapless men, making known in gory detail the way they would die. Four would burn at the stake. The fifth man, the one who had mercilessly driven his spear through a young mother and her baby, would receive a death in keeping with what he had done.

Nipishish had broken his wooden shovel over the man's head, nearly killing him with the force of the blow. He was alive enough to feel the pain that would soon enfold what remained of his mind.

Revelers poked and prodded the prisoners, making wagers over which of them might last the longest in the fires. After all, this was a festive event attended by everyone, and anything and everything was cause for a wager among the people.

Nipishish and Miknap stood at the rear of the crowd that milled about, tormenting the condemned. They were engaged in a serious bout of wagering over which of the prisoners would outlast the others.

During the council meeting, Miknap had returned Gudbjartur's knife to him, the same knife that Glooscap had given him after the fight with Gudbjartur. However, he coveted the knife and tried to cajole Nipishish into parting with it.

"I want to trade for that knife, Nipishish. What will you take in trade?" Miknap asked.

Nipishish smiled inwardly at the look of cunning and avarice on the man's face. He did not understand the subtleties of the exchange, but he gleaned enough from Miknap's facial expression to refuse. Wishing to drive a hard bargain if they agreed on an exchange, he shook his head.

Miknap jerked his knife from its scabbard.

"I will trade you this knife!" Seeing the doubt on Napishish's face, he included the club that he had used on Gudbjartur when they captured him.

"Ah! I will take the knife scabbard, too," Nipishish said, knowing that he had the better of him.

Miknap quickly nodded, sealing the trade before Nipishish changed his mind.

Nipishish threw his head back and laughed.

Miknap was all smiles, too. The two men returned their attention to the execution of their enemies.

* * *

Four newly planted execution stakes occupied the central commons of the village. Each had a large pile of wood around the base. People were carefully wetting the wood down so the fire would not burn too quickly. They wanted the prisoners to last as long as possible, slowly steaming atop the damp pile of firewood, thereby maximizing their suffering. Burning enemies at the stake was the favored way to kill prisoners and everyone looked forward to the spectacle with anticipation.

Warriors dragged each of the four prisoners from the council hall to the stakes and quickly trussed each man atop a pile
of firewood. Resistance was futile, although each tried, no
doubt hoping they would be clubbed unconscious so they
would not feel the flames. But that was not to be.

All were fully conscious when the flames began to lick at
the firewood parapet they stood on. Steam rose into the still
air of the evening as the damp wood began to burn. Super-
heated steam began to scorch their bare feet. The men danced
from one foot to the other to the limits of their restraints.

Last-minute wagering over the prisoner seen to be the toughest had the boisterous crowd in a frenzy. Dust rose into the
air as they milled about for a better vantage point. The sound
reached a crescendo, not unlike the snarling of a beast.

First one and then another prisoner began to scream as the
flames reached out for them, becoming unbearable. Blackened feet stopped all movement. Legs crisped, blackened, and
split open as the heat crept higher. Their torsos hammered
against the stakes in a paroxysm of agony, the mind still conscious of the symphony of death that rushed to lay claim to
the spirit that remained alive.

The crowd went crazy as the prisoners' confining ropes
burned through and the blackened corpses of their enemies
slipped down into the flames. An oily black smoke rose into
the air and drifted about through the screaming people as the
bodies burned. The smell was horrendous.

It all ended too quickly for everyone, but then, it always
did.

Nipishish and Miknap remained at the rear of the crowd as
individuals danced around the place of execution. Nothing
remained of the stakes, for they, too, were consumed. Miknap
shook his head and grinned at his companion.

"They all died well," he said.

"Who won?" Nipishish asked. "Here, take the knife, I think
it is a draw. As you said they all died well."

"Good! A draw it is," Miknap said, accepting the steel knife
while passing his weapons to Nipishish. He pulled the steel
knife from its ornate scabbard and tested the keen edge with
his thumb. "A good trade," he said a big grin on his face.

At the same time, Nipishish tested the edge of the beautifully knapped chert blade of his new knife. *It is every bit as sharp as my steel knife. If it makes my new friend happy to make the trade then I, too, am happy.* He did not mind losing the knife a second time. *I know that one day I will win it back in another wager. On the other hand, perhaps I will return to Halfdansfjord and obtain another just like it.*

Glooscap's loud voice rose above the hubbub, demanding attention. As the many voices of the crowd died away, he directed everyone's attention to the forest verge, some distance from the village entrance through the protective palisade. The people quickly gathered to witness the fate of the fifth prisoner, he whom they referred to as baby killer.

The badly wounded man, held tightly by two men, stood naked, stripped of his clothing. At a nod from Glooscap, the men dragged the prisoner to an upright sharpened stake. They lifted him into the air above it, and rammed his body down, through his anus, over the stake until it penetrated well into the man's guts. An inhuman scream tore from his throat, briefly overpowering the noise of the crowd gathered round.

The stake, its diameter that of a man's forearm, stood high enough that the prisoner's feet could not touch the ground as he struggled. His untied hands flailed in the air weakly.

Nipishish shuddered slightly and glanced at Miknap. The man grinned and shrugged.

Nipishish watched the struggling Haudeno in fascination. *He looks like a moth caught in a spider web. But for the will of the gods, and fate, I could have endured a similar end.*

The weight of the prisoner's body ensured that the stake's sharpened end slowly, inexorably, pierced his vitals. The man's continual screaming began to grate on peoples' nerves as the sound reverberated out over the lake until late into the night. Gradually the screams weakened to an occasional squeak. In the end, the manner of his final demise was satisfying for all; a fitting end, considering his crime against the people.

The Haudeno's body remained on the stake, food for the birds of the day and the skulking night creatures. One day, what little remained would fall to the earth, to become a part of the dirt, trodden underfoot and forgotten by passersby.

* * *

Several days later, toward the end of a warm day of bright sunshine, a troubled Nipishish sought the solitude of the lakeshore. He found a secluded niche in a rock outcropping near the bustle of the village, yet apart. He took a seat on a narrow ledge facing the lake and rested his back comfortably against the warm, moss-covered, rock. Two canoes among the rice grass drew his attention. He watched the women and young girl occupants harvesting rice for a time. Their laughter floated over the water, bringing a brief smile to his trouble-clouded face.

The first time he had seen women harvesting the rice from canoes he knew they were harvesting something, but he knew not what. Later he asked Ekuanit. She showed him a bark box of the rice and then painstakingly, with elaborate signs to reinforce his limited vocabulary, explained the process of carefully bending the seed heads into the canoe with a stick and knocking the seed loose with another stick.

While the women worked, they pulled the canoe through the thick stands of rice grass, chattering all the while. Inevitably, they missed some grain and some fell into the water, ensuring that the crop reseeded itself from year-to-year. When they had what they needed, he saw them return to the village, carry the canoe from the water, and upend it over the fleshy side of a spread hide. The rice cascaded onto the hide and they spread it evenly over the surface. Over the next few days, the grain would cure, drying out in the sun. The work would continue through the late summer until the ripe grain was all harvested, dried, and winnowed. Excess to present needs were stored for the long Time of Whiteness.

Rice was a staple for the people, much as barley was for his people, and he found that he rather liked the nutty taste of the grain. A savory mixture of boiled rice and beans to which he added a generous dollop of honey or maple sugar was a favorite. He salivated at the thought and glanced toward the village. Columns of smoke rising straight up into the still air, as the women stirred the hearth fires, made him realize that it would soon be time to eat.

The recent past tumbled through his mind. Thoughts of Ingerd and his sons dominated as he sorted images of Halfdan, his people, Glooscap, the Naskapi, and a veritable flood of less important trivia.

He missed Ingerd most of all. His sons were important, but Ingerd was not only his mate, she was his friend, a part of his soul. A flush coursed through his chest and heat rose to his face as longing gripped his mind.

Thoughts of his chieftain followed. Halfdan was more than his chieftain; they were close friends. Like the brother he wished he had, the two men shared everything, and both were intuitively aware of each other's thoughts and desires.

The axe lay across his lap; he polished the keen edge with a whetstone, an activity that he always found to be mentally stabilizing. He held the axe head in one hand and plied the whetstone with the other. His eyes followed the movement of the hand, but this ingrained act was automatic from long practice to the point he seemed unaware of his surroundings. But he was not unaware, as Glooscap saw when he stepped soundlessly to the small ledge on which Nipishish sat and saw the man's eyes snap in his direction and the muscles of his body coil in readiness.

"I thought I might be able to sneak up on you," Glooscap said. He chuckled as he saw the tightness leave his friend as quickly as it had come.

"You almost did. I did not hear you." He smiled up at Glooscap and gestured to the ledge. "I think I sensed you. Have a seat."

Glooscap sat down with a sigh and looked out across the lake. Except for the occasional ripples left by fish as they began to feed in the lengthening shadows of the forested shoreline, the lake's smooth surface was unruffled. Nary had a puff of wind stirred the heavy, humid air. The azure water reflected the trees and rock outcroppings of the shoreline and the scattered soft clouds drifting by against the bright afternoon sky. The two men reflected in silence on the bounty of the gods.

Nipishish glanced at Glooscap. "I have wanted to tell you something. I had to wait until I knew more of the language of the people. I also have a question to ask. It is a good time now and this is a good place." A wave of his hand encompassed their surroundings.

Glooscap silently regarded his companion's face.

"Before you captured me I saw you in the forest from where I lay hidden in a brush pile. You materialized so silently and suddenly that I almost swallowed my heart. You were so close I was afraid to look at you, knowing that you would feel my eyes. My heart drummed in my ears and I scarcely breathed for fear you would hear me. I resolved to attack you before you found me. As I coiled myself slowly to leap out at you, one of your men signaled. You answered him, looked carefully again at the brush pile, and stole away as silently as you had come." Nipishish searched Glooscap's face for some sign of his thoughts. Finding none, he asked the question that he had lived with since that time in the forest. "Did you know that I was there?"

Glooscap's eyes smiled and he chuckled. "No, I did not know it was you or I would have called my men to me. I knew that something, a presence, perhaps the demon, Night Wind, was in the brush pile, or nearby. I have remembered that time, too. I am glad to know that I sensed only you. I can fight you, but a demon? That I would not wish to do," he said.

"Nor I," Nipishish said, his eyes locked on the other man's. "Now, I am glad that I did not attack you."

"I feel the same. You have become one with us, Nipishish, and that is good, for everyone. Now, what is your question?"

"Why did you attack us that day? We came in peace."

"Men of another Naskapi band attacked you. My men and I did not get into the fight until we joined these other warriors later. You were strangers in our land. That is all we knew in the beginning."

"Do the Naskapi always attack strangers?"

"No, not always, but we always attack Haudeno. When the other warriors saw Deskaheh with you in the lead canoe that is all the reason they needed to attack you. We came to help in the fight."

The two men held each other's eyes for a heartbeat. Nipishish nodded his acceptance of the explanation and looked out over the lake again.

"I watched you before I came up here," Glooscap said, his eyes searching the man's face. "You are troubled by something."

"Aye, I am troubled. I have thoughts of my wife, Ingerd, and my sons, Ivar and Lothar. I miss them. Ingerd is troubled. I am certain that she knows that I live, for I feel her thoughts," he said, looking out across the lake. "I miss my chieftain, Halfdan, who is also my friend. We have shared much together. Life would be good with you, and your people, if they were here too."

Glooscap sat with his hands clasped around a knee. He turned to Nipishish. "I came here to tell you something that Sachem has done, as he said he would. He has anticipated your need, as he anticipates all things. He has sent Kejo, Miknap, Atkaa, and Manshipit, to the village of your people. On the way, they will stop at the village of Chisasi so that he may show them where your village is located. Your chieftain, Halfdan, knows Chisasi so there will not be trouble." By the time he paused, he had Nipishish's full attention. "Sachem ordered Kejo to tell your chieftain that you live and that you are one with the people. Your chieftain may come here to trade with us before the Time of Falling Leaves. He may bring your family with him on this journey. If they wish, they can stay here with you until the Time of Green Grass next year, so that they may know the people and learn our ways and language with you."

"When did Kejo go on this journey?" Nipishish's thoughts tumbled in confusion at the magnitude of what Glooscap told him.

A hand sign indicated that the question was of no consequence. "They are there now."

"But. . ." Nipishish began, as questions came to the fore. The cutting sign stopped him.

"Sachem has spoken. It will be as he says. Be patient, my friend. You will see that he has anticipated everything. Now, I feel the stew pot calling me. Let us go to the longhouse, for the shadows lengthen." The two men got stiffly to their feet and stretched.

As they walked back, Nipishish smiled. Glooscap saw the smile, nodded, and clapped his friend on the shoulder.

"You see, I told you that Sachem knows all things," he said. "He knew that you were ready for this news."

Nipishish glanced at Glooscap, his face again split in a smile. *Aye, I think he does know all things. I was in despair, and now. . .*

* * *

Chapter Eleven

Halfdansfjord—a bearer of bad news

Halfdan awakened from a sound sleep, unsure of what had aroused him. He rubbed the sleep from his eyes, looked toward the foot of the sleeping platform, and saw the guard, Gisli, gesturing to him in the flickering lamplight. He got up quickly, pulling on a tunic as he swung his legs off the platform. Gisli gestured for him to follow and hurried toward the council chamber portion of Halfdan's longhouse.

He stopped just before the entry door to the council hall and turned to Halfdan.

"Deskaheh is back. He just got here. He is really a mess. He came overland. He has not eaten in three days because he did not want to risk stopping to kindle a fire. Thora is feeding him now. He has bad news," he added, glancing at Halfdan.

Halfdan swept past Gisli. He halted before a thoroughly disheveled and exhausted Deskaheh. The man dropped the cold meat joint he had been eating back on the trencher and rose to speak to his chieftain.

"Set back down, man. Continue eating, it looks like you need it. Tell me your tale while you eat."

"No, I will tell you standing, while we face each other, Halfdan. I am the bearer of bad news."

Halfdan's eyes narrowed. He folded his arms and waited for the man to speak.

"Four days ago we were deliberately and savagely attacked by parties of Naskapi warriors. They were very hostile from the outset, already thoroughly incensed for some reason. I think their hostility was because of me. I do not know that for certain because we did not have a chance to parley. We tried until it became obvious that they would not talk to us. Then we tried to flee. We were in our canoes and we stayed together for some time until Gudbj decided we might have a better chance if the two crews separated. Those of us with Gudbj took a different fork in the river. The other canoe went upstream in the main river channel. I do not know what happened to them. There were several Naskapi canoes full of men and some of them stayed after us. I assume the rest of them went after the other canoe. Snorri and five other men were in that one, I think." Thora handed him a drinking horn of hot broth. He smiled gratefully at her.

"Let him eat, Halfdan. He is so weak he can hardly stand," Thora pleaded, looking beseechingly up at Halfdan.

"I am not keeping him from eating, Thora. He wanted to stand." He turned to Deskaheh.

"Set down before you fall down," Halfdan ordered. "Eat, drink, relax! Tell the story slowly. Miss nothing. I want to hear all of it." He glanced back at the entrance as people filed into the council hall and quietly sat down. *Word has passed quickly. Soon everyone will be here.*

"It looks like the word of your return is out. Here, eat! Wait a little while for the others to get here before you continue with your tale." Halfdan pushed the trencher of meat toward Deskaheh. The man wearily sank down on the bench and began gnawing on a joint of boiled meat.

Halfdan turned to his people, now streaming through the entryway. Hands on hips he watched them enter. He waited for the shuffling to cease as the new arrivals sought vantage points around the walls of the big council chamber. The growing crowd gradually lapsed into silence, facing the central hearth and fire pit, where Halfdan, Deskaheh, and the others waited patiently.

"Deskaheh had only just begun to tell me his story when everyone began coming in here. I decided to wait so everyone could hear his tale first-hand. When he left off, hostile Naskapi, many of them, were chasing the two canoes of Gudbj's scouting party. Now, you know as much as I do."

Bedlam reigned for a time as people voiced concerns or belabored some point or other.

Halfdan held his arms up to restore quiet. "Let Deskaheh speak without interruption. As you can see, he is not in good shape. He walked and ran through forest and fens for the past three days to get here so he could tell us his tale." He gestured for Deskaheh to continue.

Deskaheh and Thora sat side-by-side. His hand rested on her knee. She had hold of his arm. He smiled wearily to her and rose to his feet. He walked slowly into the center of the council chamber.

Every eye followed him. Absolute silence, so pervasive the occasional snap of the burning wood in the fire pit was the loudest sound in the room. His dark eyes swept the crowd, paused briefly at a familiar face, before continuing in their sweep.

"Halfdan, I need Thora at my side," Deskaheh said, turning to face the man directly. "She speaks Haudeno well. I still have trouble with some Norse words. She will be able to help me."

Nodding at his request, Halfdan took a seat next to Frida and Ingerd. He caught Ingerd's eye for a moment. His look conveyed the depth of his anguish, for both knew what was coming. He turned his attention back to the front. Everyone waited for Deskaheh to gather his thoughts and continue his tale.

Deskaheh loosed a great sigh. He glanced at Thora. Her nod seemed to give him strength. He spoke slowly at first, seeming to grapple with the right way to present what he had to say.

"Four days ago our scouting party met several canoes of Naskapi warriors. We tried to parley, but they became hostile as soon as I greeted them."

Inevitably, a few chuckles and humorous remarks greeted the serious beginning of his tale.

"They did not like you as we do, Deskaheh," said a voice from the crowd. Other comments followed as people tried to add a touch of lightheartedness to Deskaheh's somber demeanor.

Deskaheh smiled weakly without comment. He glanced at Halfdan, and then turned his attention back to the crowd as the people stopped fidgeting and quiet descended. All seemed to lean forward, attentive.

"My Norse is not so good," he said apologetically. He whispered something to Thora before continuing. "Thora helps me when I do not have the words." He paced, collecting his thoughts. When he began, the words tumbled from his mouth. "Gudbj split the two canoes up when the river forked, thinking we would have a better chance of getting away if we separated. It seemed to us that most of the pursuing canoes chased after us. I am not sure how many went after our other canoe. I do not know what happened to Snorri and the men with him. We barely kept ahead of our pursuers. After a time the Naskapi stopped screaming, saving their breath for the chase. One of their canoes got close, within easy arrow range. A warrior shot twice at us, one of his arrows glanced off the upthrust stern of our canoe. Before he could shoot again, Gudbj shot him and he pitched over the side, upsetting the canoe and holding up the others for a time. We all hollered and laughed when this happened. We used the time to put a little distance between us and them." He paused to take a drink from the bucket of fresh water the thrall, Halla, set on the hearth. He smiled his thanks to her.

"We remained ahead of them until full darkness. Gudbj ordered the canoe beached so we could scatter out and hide in the forest. They would have caught us all if we had stayed on the river. Our best chance was to hide in the forest until just before dawn. We hid the canoe. It was very dark that night. The silver face of the moon lay hidden behind clouds. We remained in hiding until just before dawn, as Gudbj had planned. We met back at the canoe and set off upstream. It was a very. . ." he paused to ask Thora something in his own

language. He smiled in recognition of the word that had escaped him. "It was very foggy that morning. The dense fog
along the river helped us stay hidden, but not for long."

He again paused for effect. Being a natural storyteller he
used the moment to gather his thoughts before plunging on,
knowing the tension in the council chamber built with his
every word as he took his listeners with him on the journey that very nearly cost him his life. "We did not know the
Naskapi had used the darkness to get ahead of us up the river,
although I told Gudbj that they would probably do just that.
I do not know whether they slipped by in the forest during
the hours of darkness or paddled their canoes upstream at
night. But either way, the next morning we nearly ran into
two of their canoes not long after we set out. The fog saved
us that time. We heard them before they heard us and we
hid against the riverbank in the high rice grass and let them
pass. The first canoe went by and Gudbj whispered for us to
each pick a target in the last canoe and loose one arrow into
them when they came abreast of our hiding place. It worked
very well, we hit most of the men with our one volley, but
that was not the last canoe. We paddled away as quickly as
possible and ran into three more canoes up river of our position. Gudbj ordered us back into the bank, we abandoned
the canoe and all set off in different directions at a dead run.
I knew they would expect us to run away so I hid close to the
riverbank downstream of where we left our canoe. There were
seven Naskapi in the two canoes and they set out on the trail
of my companions into the forest interior. They did not find
me because I walked in the water of a small lake for a time
and then hid under flotsam near a tree that had fallen in the
water. One man walking in the water along the shoreline almost stepped on me, but they did not find my tracks."

"Do you know what happened to Gudbj?" Halfdan asked,
as he and several others got to their feet to stretch.

"Yes, and I am getting to that point in the story, Halfdan,"
Deskaheh said. "I do not want to miss anything. It is difficult
for me to tell such a long story in your language." He indicated Thora, who had never left his side as he strode back and
forth in the telling, offering a word here and there when he

got stuck for the right word or phrase. "I could not tell this story without her."

Glancing around the still silent crowd, Halfdan spoke for all of them. "We know that, Deskaheh. You are doing a good job. Continue at your own pace, but tell us about Gudbj soon. Some of us grow impatient to know what happened to him."

"I will Halfdan, and Ingerd," he said, acknowledging her as she sat quietly beside Frida. Her only response was a slight inclination of her head. He looked directly at her for a moment before he continued. "I was freezing in the water so I got out and hid under a pile of leaves and sticks. I stayed in my place of hiding all that long day, never hearing, or seeing another Naskapi. Not long before the end of the day, I stood from my place of concealment and began following the trail of the man who almost stepped on me. The Naskapi split up. Some followed sets of tracks while others cast about looking for tracks. It was obvious, after a time, that they had lost the trail of their quarry in the trash of the forest floor. They all began casting back and forth trying to cross the tracks once again. In the distance, through a clearing in the forest, I saw a long ridge, so I made for that thinking I might see where everyone was if I got to higher ground. If I had not been on the ridge I would not have seen the smoke of a campfire just before darkness."

Deskaheh again paused a moment. The crowd seemed captivated by his tale. A palpable silence gripped them. People strained to catch every word and inflection of what he had to say next. "I crawled toward the smoke and just before total darkness I found the Naskapi camp and saw a prisoner tied to a tree. By then it was so dark I could not tell who it was. The flickering firelight was the only illumination and soon that faded. The Naskapi scattered out somewhat and began to turn in for the night. I covered myself with leaves and sticks and went to sleep. A sound awakened me later and I realized I had slept the night away. It was first light. They were busy breaking camp and would soon set off wherever they were going. Two of them got the prisoner to his feet and stood talking to him. I crawled as close as I dared while they were all busy.

It was Gudbj, Halfdan. He was all bloody, but he was alive, standing on his own."

Pandemonium broke out at this announcement.

Deskaheh, his eyes downcast for a time, perhaps reliving the moment he identified the Naskapi prisoner, finally looked up. He waited for the people to quiet down. Halfdan did not move nor did he say anything. Frida had her arm around Ingerd's shoulders. They had their heads together as Frida whispered to her friend. Ingerd sat stiffly erect, just barely in control of her emotions. A tear escaped from one of her brimming eyes and slowly wound a course down her cheek. Her eyes never left Deskaheh's face, although she nodded dumbly at something Frida said to her. "He is alive, Ingerd!" Deskaheh exclaimed. "He is alive! They wanted to keep him alive for some reason; otherwise, he would be dead. We must not forget that. When they set out, he was in the middle of the column, untied. I followed them to where they had hidden their canoes. Then I went back to their camp to look around. From the sign I found I can tell you the story of the fight. I found the graves of three warriors Gudbj killed. I also found the blood of one badly wounded man. He almost fought them to a standstill judging from the sign I found. There was blood all over the rim rock along the cliff edge where the fight took place. They had trapped him there. That is when he turned to fight, when they had him trapped and he had no escape. He wiped out half their number and badly wounded another. Three more men joined the fight later. I found their trail from the forest; otherwise, I think Gudbj would have killed all of them. There were only three able-bodied men left when the other three joined the fight." He paused. The crowd remained silent, attentive to him as he paced back and forth, his eyes downcast as he grappled with the torrent of thoughts tumbling about in his head.

"What happened then, Deskaheh?" Halfdan asked softly, after a few moments of silence.

Deskaheh stopped his pacing directly in front of Halfdan. The gods spoke before he could answer.

At that moment, an incandescent flash of lightning illuminated the entry doorway and the people assembled within.

The brilliant light flickered and pulsed through the roof smoke holes and doorway of the longhouse, as a living thing. The flash lent a surreal quality to the assembly, temporarily freezing all movement. Immediately thereafter, a tremendous crash of thunder shook the longhouse to its foundation. The gathering storm manifested itself directly overhead. The soft patter of raindrops increased to a crescendo as the roar of the tempest engulfed Halfdansfjord and all its environs.

Continuous sheet lightning bathed the settlement as Thor, the god of thunder and lightning, hurled his bolts from the heavens. A mutter of subdued conversation swept through the people as individuals shared words of superstitious awe at this visitation from the gods. Some less affected by superstition or fear of the gods, expressed their concern at the violence of the storm.

Ashes from the hearth blew all over the council hall as the wind changed direction. All those still seated watched a small group of men at the entry doorway struggle against the violent wind gusts to close the double entry doors. The moment this was accomplished the room became a secure enclave from the elements once again. More than one individual had occasion to give thanks that they had this secure town to dwell in rather than the tents of a short time ago.

People gradually settled down from the interruption and Deskaheh continued with his tale. "This is all I know about Gudbj. I think he is still alive. I think we will find this out for ourselves before another moon passes."

"Why do you say this?" Halfdan asked.

"It is a feeling I have. They normally kill all their enemies on the spot. They wanted him for something. That is why I believe he still lives."

Halfdan sat in silent contemplation of Deskaheh's answer before rising from his place. He offered his opinion in a loud enough voice that all within heard his words.

"I was visited by the gods recently when I chanced to walk by Yggdrasil. They made me believe that Gudbj has a great mission to accomplish for all the people in this land. Now that Deskaheh has told us this story, the meaning of my visitation from the gods is clear to me. I, too, am certain Gudbj lives."

Pandemonium again swept through the crowd. Everyone spoke at once. Halfdan did not attempt to calm them down. The events affected him in the same manner as they.

A semblance of order returned after a time. Halfdan gestured at Deskaheh to continue.

"After the Naskapi paddled away with Gudbj, I found one of our canoes and began my journey back here. I could have returned in about two days by canoe but this was not to be. Later that day I chose the smaller of two streams around a mid-channel island. I do not know why. It was not the better of the two courses but it seemed to be natural from where I was in the river. Suddenly I heard something. I stopped paddling and hugged the bank. At least one Naskapi canoe passed on the other side of the island, paddling upriver. I did not see them because of the island's dense brush cover. If I had not taken the small stream around the island, they would have caught me. I immediately hopped out of the canoe in the shallows, pushed it off downstream and took to the forest, believing it to be safer than travel on the open river. Three days later, I finally got here. You all know the rest. This is the end of my tale." His hand chopped down in the cutting sign. He turned to face Halfdan.

"Good, Deskaheh," Halfdan said, getting to his feet. "We all thank you for telling your tale. We are all happy you made it back here. Probably not as happy as Thora is, though."

Laughter swept though the crowd as Deskaheh and Thora took a seat once again. Deskaheh picked up the joint of meat he had been working on before he began his story.

Halfdan's eyes swept the room. His wife came to stand at his side. "Frida and I are going to our sleeping robes now. We have no choice but to wait and see what happens. In any case we certainly cannot do anything more tonight." The couple turned toward the doorway leading to their quarters.

People milled around the hearth for a time, seemingly reluctant to leave. Many had a need to speak to Deskaheh as he sat beside Thora drinking warm broth and eating chunks of boiled meat. All seemed genuinely happy he had returned safely. The crowd gradually thinned as individuals and small groups braved the steady rain outside as they walked or ran toward their own longhouses.

* * *

The violent, storm-shattered, stygian night proved to be caused by much more than a few passing thunderstorms. Halfdansfjord awakened the next morning to skies filled with low, dark, moisture-laden clouds. A stiff wind blew from the west, bringing wave after wave of violent squalls. For the next three days, the clouds gave-up their moisture in a steady downpour, the first major storm since the settlement's completion. The site proved to be ideal as far as drainage was concerned. The animal pens became a sea of mud, but excess moisture drained away nonetheless. The log walkways kept the people high, if not dry, and because of the slight slope of the ground to the south, no running water entered any of the longhouses. The people worked on various projects in a warm comfortable atmosphere.

By the time the storm began to abate during the morning of the third day, Ingerd had sunk into despair. Frida's best efforts to cheer her up came to naught. Daily life for her became a series of automatic activities. She ceased joining the others in conversation as she went about her duties. Without conscious participation or enjoyment, her tasks became drudgery. Her mental outlook was about to take a turn for the worse.

* * *

Late that afternoon the sun finally shone through ragged holes in the overcast, bringing welcome warmth to the settlement. Steam rose from every surface as the countryside began to dry out.

A lookout's warning horn announced the arrival of three canoes, inbound from the east. Word soon passed that the three canoes hugging the north shoreline, taking advantage of the calmest water of the choppy bay, was Gudrod's hunting expedition.

Those working on the landing beach knew immediately that the expedition had run into trouble. Just the three canoes, with eight men, and one boy landed.

"Where are the other canoes? Where is Gudrod?" The questions came from all sides.

Helge shook off the questions. He and his men strode into the settlement toward the council chamber. "We will tell everyone at once. Someone get Halfdan. Tell him I want a council."

A group of women, among them Frida and Ingerd, had been sitting on the benches along the outside of the council hall, taking advantage of the last warming rays of the setting sun while they spun wool yarn. The soaked, disheveled group of men walked through the village gate and headed for the council hall. Ingerd immediately saw Lothar, but not Ivar. She stood slowly, realizing that several members of the group were missing. Unconsciously she dropped her spindle whorl and staff on the bench. She and her companions, work forgotten, walked slowly to meet the new arrivals. Everyone in the village observed the men's arrival and knew something was amiss. People from near and far began converging on the council hall.

An emptiness beyond description gripped Ingerd as Lothar strode directly to her. "Mother," he began, his words arrested by Ingerd's interruption.

"Where is Ivar?" she asked, her furtive glance darting to the gate in the hopes his tall form would suddenly materialize and still her fluttering heart.

"He was captured," Lothar blurted. He came to a halt in front of his mother. "We were attacked by Haudeno. He is still alive! We know he is!"

Ingerd's shoulders sagged at the news. *First Gudbj and now my only blood son.* She looked about in confusion.

"Come, Mother, Helge wants to tell the story only once," Lothar said softly. He placed an arm around her waist and guided her as they followed the gathering crowd into the council hall. Ingerd glanced at Lothar as he took charge, trying to comfort her. *He called me, Mother. I do not recall him ever calling me that before. Perhaps he has.* Her thoughts tumbled in disarray.

* * *

Halfdan arrived with the last group to enter the council hall. He examined his disheveled men closely as he walked up to them. *It seems that our luck has turned for the worse. For the second time in the recent past, I see some of my people like this.* He greeted his men with a nod, his eyes shifted to Helge.

"It is hard to know where to start, Halfdan. I have thought of nothing else for two days," Helge said.

"Start at the beginning. Take your time, you are home now," Halfdan said, his glance shifting from man to man before coming to rest on Helge.

Helge looked over the people waiting for him to speak. *They are all here, I think.*

"All went well until three days ago. Bersi drowned in the river when the canoe he was in upset in a swift current that flowed through a narrow gorge. Gudrod and Ivar were also in that canoe, but both made it to shore by holding on to some of the packs that floated by. Before we collected everyone from the upset canoe, the Haudeno captured Ivar while he sat on the riverbank waiting for us."

"How do you know they were Haudeno?" Halfdan asked.

"We did not know until later. Lothar mentioned after the battle that he thought that they looked like Deskaheh did when we first captured him. He was right. The rest of us did not make the connection until he did."

People glanced toward Deskaheh when they heard this. Thora held his arm possessively.

Halfdan gestured for Helge to continue.

"Where was I?" Helge pulled at his beard.

"You said that Ivar was captured," Ingerd said from her seat beside Frida.

Helge's eyes quickly shifted to Ingerd. He looked away just as quickly, uncomfortable under her unblinking stare. "Anyway, Skeggi tracked them and we went right after the men, there were two of them, who had captured Ivar. They had him trussed to a pole between them and Skeggi followed their tracks without difficulty. Right after we started out after Ivar, we crossed the tracks of more Haudeno. There were twelve to twenty men in this bunch. We could not tell how many because of the ground cover. Shortly after that, the Haudeno ambushed us. Two of our men, Ofeiger and Sturla, went down from the first flight of arrows. We fought the Haudeno until they withdrew. I think they attacked to keep us from going after the men who had captured Ivar." He paused to catch his breath. "Bjarni fell with an arrow in his upper leg, and Gudrod was hit in the neck by the last flight of Haudeno arrows. We could not help him. The Valkyries came for him soon thereafter. He was a good leader, we will miss him."

"I, too, will miss him. He was a good friend to all of us," Halfdan said, gesturing for Helge to continue his tale.

"The Haudeno withdrew then. I made the decision not to give chase. His captors might have killed Ivar if we had pressed them too closely." He looked at Halfdan for a moment. "We buried three men back there, good men. We will miss all of them. We could not find Bersi in the river. I thought you would want to know about this as soon as we could bring the news. Gudbj will want to go after them." He looked around the room until he saw Deskaheh. "Where is Gudbj?" he asked, his eyes on Deskaheh. Confusion furrowed his brow.

"Deskaheh brought more bad news three days ago. Hostile Naskapi have captured Gudbj. So far, Deskaheh is the only one of the ten men in the scouting party to make it back here," Halfdan said. "Gudbj is alive. Deskaheh watched the Naskapi take him away. That is all that we know."

The men with Helge all began to talk at once.

Lothar had remained at Ingerd's side. The two held each other, speaking in subdued tones.

Helge spoke for all of those in Gudrod's hunting party when he confronted Halfdan. "By the great Loki, what are you going to do?"

"I have thought of nothing else since Deskaheh brought us this news," Halfdan said. He spoke loud enough that everyone heard him. "Now that you have returned with more news of hostility with the natives, I can see only one option open to us. We must nip this trouble with the Naskapi in the bud. I must know why hostile Naskapi attacked Gudbj and his men. I thought that we could be on friendly terms with them. Now I do not know. I must have an answer to this, so tomorrow morning I will depart for the village of Chisasi. They will know what has happened." He walked back and forth in front of the hearth for a time, his mind grappling with the turmoil within. Nobody intruded on his thoughts, knowing that his decision would be forthcoming. He stopped in front of Deskaheh. "I will want you to accompany me if you think you have recovered enough from your journey."

Deskaheh stood. "I will go, Halfdan," he said. "I am recovered."

"He is not recovered. But, it does not matter, he cannot refuse you. He cannot go without me. I could not stand that Halfdan, not after all of this," Thora said. She held onto Deskaheh's arm possessively.

Deskaheh shrugged. "I do not need her to talk to the Naskapi, but I do need her to talk to you, Halfdan."

Thora shoved his arm and snorted.

Halfdan looked from one to the other; the crow's feet at the corners of his eyes began to deepen. He chuckled. "So be it then. I need both of you." His eyes sought Ingerd and Lothar. "You, too, may go, both of you if you wish. This is a mission of peace, to find out if Chisasi and his people know what happened to Gudbj."

Ingerd looked into Lothar's eyes. He nodded. Words were unnecessary between them. "We will go, too," she said.

Frida caught his eye.

He smiled at her. "Aye, Frida. I knew that you would want to go if Ingerd went." He looked at the small party he had selected. "Good! We leave at dawn. I expect to be there by nightfall according to what Chisasi has told me. We will travel light and fast, in two canoes. I need four men to accompany us." His eyes traveled around the room.

"We will go Halfdan," Helge said, stepping forward with three of his men.

Halfdan nodded, his eyes traveling over the disheveled group.

"We are fine. A good night's sleep and clean clothes is all we need. We will be ready at dawn."

"As you wish," Halfdan said. Again, he looked over the assembly. "Tostig!" He called.

"I am here." The man stood to make his way toward Halfdan.

Halfdan turned to him. "You are in charge while I am gone. We should return in three, maybe four, days." He held the man's eyes a moment. "I am giving you Gudrod's ship until Thorgill returns. He is next in line for command before you."

Tostig, briefly at a loss for words, finally managed to mumble, "I understand. You will not have occasion to regret your decision, Halfdan. I will do a good job."

"I know you will. Gudrod would approve. You will soon have your own ship."

Tostig nodded and turned away.

Halfdan's eyes traveled over his people. He took Frida's hand. "Now, if nobody has anything further, I think we had best find our sleeping robes. Tomorrow will be a long day."

* * *

Chapter Twelve

Halfdansfjord—messengers from Sachem

The encroaching light of dawn softened the deep shadows of a moonless night; at the same time details of the settlement and countryside began to sharpen. A slight onshore breeze rustled the leaves of a stand of birch within the palisade walls, bringing with it the heavy smell of seaweed left high and dry by the ebbing tidewaters of the bay. Gulls squabbled over newly discovered tidbits left by the receding water. Their brethren of forest and fen trilled the morning greeting to their kind.

Halfdan and Frida sat eating soup with their thralls. Normal morning conversation was missing. Halfdan had been awake much of the night as his mind grappled with the problems of his people. That his mood was circumspect was obvious to all. Both he and Frida were ready for the journey to the village of Chisasi as soon as it was light enough on the river to avoid the risk of hitting a snag or rock with the fragile canoes.

"We would like to go with you Halfdan," Finbar the Thrall said tentatively, breaking the silence. He usually did the talking for his companion Ewyn, who seldom spoke in the presence of his chieftain, holding Halfdan in awe.

Halfdan looked at the man, and then turned his regard to Ewyn. "You want to go with me Ewyn?"

Ewyn jerked at the sound of Halfdan's voice. The meek little man always tried to avoid the attention of his chieftain if possible.

Frida placed her hand on Halfdan's arm, always mindful of the unpredictability of her husband. She knew that Ewyn lived in fear of most things in life. Halfdan occupied the pinnacle position of the thrall's extensive list of fears.

Halfdan glanced at Frida. The look in her eyes, and the hand that lightly rested on his arm conveyed her thoughts to him as surely as a spoken word.

"Aye, Halfdan, he wants to go. We both do," Finbar reaffirmed.

Halfdan held up a hand, his eyes on Ewyn. The man looked up from his soup bowl straight into the eyes of his worst fear.

Halfdan bade Ewyn to speak with a lift of his chin.

Ewyn glanced quickly at Finbar who jerked his chin at his friend, imploring him to speak.

"Aye, Halfdan, I would go if you want me to," Ewyn managed, his voice trailing off.

Halfdan laughed aloud. "I have never heard so many words from you. You should speak more often. You have no reason to fear me. Have I ever mistreated you, Ewyn?" Halfdan leaned forward, waiting for an answer. "Have I?"

"No, never," the little man said.

"All right then, enough of this. Both of you can go. Get your packs together and each of you bring a spear. We will leave shortly," Halfdan said. Getting to his feet he stretched, and winked at his wife. Her smile said it all.

* * *

Suddenly, the repeated bellow of a warning horn from the north guard tower shattered the normal sounds of morning, bringing armed men running to the north parapets from every longhouse.

Halfdan came to an abrupt halt near the gate. He cupped his hands and shouted to the man in the guard tower. "What is it?"

"The Naskapi are back. Six men are walking across the barley field toward the gate. The one in the lead looks like Chisasi, but there is not enough light to tell," the guard shouted back.

Halfdan waved an acknowledgement. "Open the gates, Tostig," Halfdan said to one of several men clustered at the north gates. He turned to the gathering crowd, and called out. "Deskaheh, Thora, are you here?"

"We are here, Halfdan," Deskaheh said. He and Thora worked their way through the crowd to his side.

"Good, I will need both of you to talk to the Naskapi."

"Here, Halfdan, I have your talisman and sword," Frida said as she ran up to him.

He turned to her. "The talisman is a good idea." He bowed toward her so that she could put the Naskapi talisman of life, the gift from Chisasi, on over his head. He smiled his thanks. "I will not need the sword," he said, turning to walk toward the gates, as they swung open.

She followed him. "I will be nearby if you do."

He waved a hand to her as he and his retinue walked from the gate to meet the visitors.

* * *

The six Naskapi had almost crossed the barley field when the group of Northmen exited the north gates. Halfdan came to a halt and waited for them to approach. When he recognized the lead Naskapi in the dim light, he stepped toward him with a welcoming smile in place.

"Chisasi, good morning, welcome," he said.

The Naskapi and Northmen came together and the two leaders shook hands.

"These men bring word from Sachem," Chisasi said without preliminary. His eyes shifted to Halfdan's talisman of life. He nodded in approval. The ghost of a smile transformed his features.

The four Naskapi strangers saw the talisman, too. Their demeanor opened.

When Deskaheh began to translate for Halfdan, the Naskapi strangers cast hostile glances at him. His Norse clothing did not detract from the fact that they easily recognized him as Haudeno.

Chisasi greeted Deskaheh with a curt nod and spoke to his men.

"He has told these men who I am, that Thora is my wife, and that I am one of your people," Deskaheh said.

"Good, I hope they accept that." Halfdan eyed the four strangers.

"They will accept it, Halfdan, for Sachem has sent them to talk to you," Chisasi said, looking from Halfdan to his companions.

Deskaheh provided a short translation.

Halfdan nodded. "Good. Tell Chisasi that word of our presence in Nitassinan traveled fast; it did not take Sachem until next summer to make his decision, as he thought. Let us go to the council hall for food and drink. We can talk there."

Deskaheh translated and the group began to walk back toward the gates. As they entered the settlement proper, the four strangers looked up at the mass of armed men arrayed along the parapet with obvious trepidation until a few words from Chisasi calmed their anxiety. Trepidation soon gave way to curiosity as shouted greetings went back and forth.

Frida and Thora hurried ahead of the men to get the council hall ready for the arrival of their guests, only to find their haste unnecessary. The early morning arrival of the Naskapi happened to fit nicely with preparations for the first meal of the day. Ingerd, Rannveig, Halla, and Genevra, had everything ready when Frida and Thora walked in.

Frida and Thora made straight for Ingerd, noticing immediately that their friend bustled about happily with the other women. A transformation had occurred. They had not seen this much animation from her since she had descended into her funk over Gudbjartur.

"Ingerd, you look so happy," Frida said, a big smile curving her lips as she held her friend at arms length.

"Of course I am happy. The Naskapi have brought good news about Gudbj," she said with exuberance, swinging Frida wildly in a circle, scattering a laughing Thora aside.

"We do not know that, Ingerd. They have not told us that they are here with good news about Gudbj, only that they have news for us," Frida said. "Tell her Thora, what we heard out there."

Thora made to answer until arrested by Ingerd's raised hand.

"*I* know," Ingerd said fiercely. "That is why they are here. I know it as sure as I know both of you; *all* of you." She swept an arm out to encompass the group of women at the hearth. She laughed aloud and then threw her arms around both Frida and Thora, hugging them tightly.

"We will know soon, here they are," Frida said.

Ingerd stepped over to confront Halfdan. "I must know." Ingerd's intense blue eyes reflected her concern as she searched his face.

Uncharacteristically, he held her a moment. "I cannot answer that now, Ingerd. I do not know yet why they are here," he said, holding her at arm's length. "We cannot hurry this meeting. Sachem has sent these men here. They bring word from their leader that is very important for our people." The intensity of her eyes, as they searched his face was uncomfortable. "Be patient, please. Soon we will know."

None of this was lost on the Naskapi. "This is the woman of your war leader." Chisasi said, having seen Ingerd on his last visit.

"Aye, this woman is the wife of Gudbj, our war leader. She is called Ingerd," Deskaheh said.

Ingerd recognized her name, her eyes fastened on the face of the tall Naskapi leader. She pushed by Halfdan and stepped up to him. "Please, do you know something about Gudbj?" she said, looking up at the man.

Before he could answer, one of the men beside him repeated a word that he had recognized. "Gudbj? Yes, we know this Gudbj. We call him Nipishish, now. Sachem has bestowed this name on him," the man said.

Ingerd looked at him in confusion. She turned to Deskaheh and Thora. "What did he say? Somebody tell me," she pleaded.

"He called Gudbj, Nipishish," Deskaheh said.

Ingerd grabbed Deskaheh's arms, her obvious level of confusion increasing. "But what does that word *mean*?"

"Nipishish means Axeman," Deskaheh said to her.

"Axeman? But why. . ." her voice trailed off in confusion.

The man who had identified Gudbj as Nipishish took that opportunity to talk, even though he had no idea what she had just said. He spoke to Chisasi first. Chisasi bade him to continue with a lift of his chin. The man then addressed Halfdan.

"We fought him, took him captive to our village. He was our prisoner." A wave of his hand included his three companions. "Sachem spared him. He was to live in the wigwam of Glooscap to learn our language and our ways. He worked with the women, doing woman's work. We were attacked by Haudeno one day." He looked pointedly at Deskaheh. "Gudbj fought them, killing many. He saved many of our women. One of them was my sister, Ashua. I will not forget that he did this thing. Sachem gave Gudbj the name Nipishish to honor him as a great warrior and one of the people." The cutting sign indicated that he was finished talking.

Deskaheh chuckled and shook his head at the way of things. He looked down at the floor and scuffed his foot in the loose dirt. He looked up at Halfdan with a smile. Halfdan answered with a scowl and lift of his chin, indicating that he did not understand.

Deskaheh sought Ingerd's eyes. "These men have come from their Sachem to tell you of Gudbj. They honor him as a great warrior with the name Nipishish. Three of these men are the ones who captured Gudbj and took him to their Sachem."

Ingerd looked at the Naskapi who had spoken previously. She glanced at Halfdan with a question in her eyes. He answered with a slight nod. She glanced at Deskaheh and Thora.

"Help me. I want to talk to him," she said, stepping forward without waiting for an answer. She stopped before the Naskapi. Her lively blue eyes locked on his expressionless black eyes.

"I am Ingerd. Nipishish is my mate, my man, my life," she said. "I must know how he is. He is alive. I know this. But why is he not here with you? I do not understand." Her eyes searched his face.

Deskaheh started to repeat her words to the man. Ingerd interrupted.

"Wait! What is his name? What are their names?" she said, gesturing at the other men, but not taking her eyes from the Naskapi's face.

Deskaheh asked.

The Naskapi answered her directly. "I am called Kejo. These men are called Miknap, Atkaa, and Manshipit." He indicated each in turn.

Ingerd's eyes followed his hand as he introduced the others. She understood without translation.

"Kejo," she said. "Kejo," she repeated his name, feeling, almost tasting the strange word on her tongue. "Is my man well, Kejo?"

"Nipishish is well," he said. His hard features softened as he held her eyes.

She nodded slowly. A slight smile curved her mouth. "Thank you, Kejo." He inclined his head slightly in acknowledgement.

She smiled at the other Naskapi and turned to Halfdan. "Thank you, Halfdan. I am satisfied, for now." With a toss of her head, she returned to her place at the hearth.

Halfdan watched her go. He shook his head, his mouth battling with the smile that rose unbidden to his lips. "Well, I could not have done better myself," he said, beckoning to the group at large. "Chisasi, Kejo, men, let us sit down and have some food. We can discuss the details while we eat."

Deskaheh repeated his words and the group congregated at the hearth for bowls of stew.

* * *

Having finished eating, Halfdan and Frida sat side by side across the table from Chisasi, Kejo, and the others. Ingerd, Thora, and Deskaheh sat nearby.

The Naskapi seem to have accepted Deskaheh. I imagine in a different setting such neutrality would not occur. Halfdan picked bits of meat from his teeth with a sharpened splinter. He chuckled under his breath and shook his head as he remembered some of the unintended humor during the meal.

Frida glanced at him, her mouth curved in a smile. She raised a questioning eyebrow as she caught his eye.

"I just recalled Kejo stabbing a chunk of whale meat from the stew with his knife. He looked at it, smelled it, and asked what kind of animal it came from," Halfdan said, laughing aloud. "When you told him it was whale meat, he sniffed it again, popped it in his mouth, and three bowls of stew later he was full. I doubt that he knows yet what a whale is." He looked across the table at Kejo, made eye contact with the Naskapi, and smiled at the recollection.

A slight return smile flashed across the man's face, he bobbed his head once, as if in agreement, and then leaned toward Chisasi, who sat beside him, for a muted conversation.

Chisasi indicated Halfdan and Ingerd with a hand sign, and then turned toward Deskaheh.

"Deskaheh, help them to understand the words of Sachem. Tell them first who Sachem is to the Naskapi. Then Kejo will speak Sachem's words," Chisasi said.

Deskaheh nodded, rose to his feet, and stepped over to Halfdan's table. "Chisasi asked that I help you to understand who Sachem is and to tell you his words. I know that you already know this, but he asks that I tell you now."

Halfdan held up a hand to Deskaheh and called to Ingerd. "Come, sit beside me," he said, patting the bench. She walked over and took a seat with him. Halfdan looked at Deskaheh. "Before he starts talking I want you to ask him why the Naskapi attacked Gudbj's scouting party. Tell him that Gudbj and his men came to trade, to make friends, not make war." Halfdan indicated Chisasi with a wave of his hand.

Deskaheh turned to Chisasi. "Halfdan wants to ask you why we were attacked by Naskapi when we came to trade. We meant no harm."

"The men who attacked you did so because you are Haudeno. They thought the Northmen were enemies, too. They did not know that you lived with the Northmen," Chisasi said. "These men were not with those Naskapi. Those men are from a different band."

Deskaheh translated.

Halfdan locked eyes with Chisasi. "Will the warriors of some of these other bands be hostile toward us?"

"Yes, many Naskapi warriors will be hostile until they all receive the words of Sachem," Chisasi said.

Troubled now, Halfdan asked him a question that had begun to nag him. "Tell me more about the people of this land, all of them, not only the Naskapi. Will we always have war with some of them?"

Chisasi glanced at the other Naskapi when Deskaheh made known Halfdan's question.

"Tell him about the Anishinabeg," Kejo said.

Chisasi held Kejo's eyes a moment, silent, made up his mind, and turned back to Halfdan. "There are many bands of Naskapi scattered throughout Nitassinan. Most are east and north of here. Other people, the Anishinabeg, live to the south between your village and Kitchi-Gami. These people do not know that you are here." He watched closely the effect his words had on the Northman.

Deskaheh translated Chisasi's words and a buzz of conversation swelled as people put their heads together.

Halfdan recognized two words that he had not heard before. He looked to Deskaheh for answers. "Who are the Anishinabeg and Kitchi-Gami?"

"They are kinsmen of the Naskapi," Deskaheh said. "There are many bands of Anishinabeg. Most live along the northern shore of Kitchi-Gami, a big lake. It is one of five great lakes. All are much bigger than the saltwater bay where my people live. Their warriors will eventually discover that your people are here in Nitassinan. They might attack. I do not know their hearts. We will have to wait until we make contact with them. Word travels slowly over this land. Some people will not have heard and others might not listen to the words of Sachem." Deskaheh seemed uncomfortable as he translated. Thora stood at his side. Although she tried not to show it, people nearby knew she had understood Chisasi's words before Deskaheh spoke to Halfdan.

Halfdan looked at Frida, who sat across the table. Her face reflected his feeling of inner turmoil. He shook his head and sighed. A half-hearted smile curved his lips. "Maybe it is not as bad as it sounds," he said. Her raised eyebrow provided an answer.

Halfdan was silent for a moment, his eyes traveled over his people as they digested this new, troubling insight into the land that they now called home. "Ask him what happened to my other men that were with Gudbj."

"We were ten men. Halfdan wants to know what happened to his other men." Deskaheh watched the Naskapi as Chisasi conferred with them. Kejo was the most vocal of the five warriors. Chisasi bade him speak with a wave of his hand.

"Five men were captured with Nipishish. Other Naskapi bands captured them," Kejo said.

Deskaheh spoke to Halfdan.

"Five captured, that is a total of seven men accounted for. What about the other three men?" Halfdan said.

Deskaheh asked Kejo directly. Kejo held his fists out together in front and turned them sideways, as if he were breaking a stick.

Halfdan caught Deskaheh's eye. "Does that mean what I think it means?"

"It is bad. He does not know for certain," Deskaheh said.

Chisasi spoke to Deskaheh. "We do not know if any of those men are alive. It will be sometime before Sachem knows their fate."

Deskaheh began to speak until stopped by Halfdan.

"I understand him," Halfdan said. He got to his feet and his eyes traveled around the room, pausing here and there on a particular person. He pulled at his beard and nodded, accepting that over which he had no control. "All right. We will hope for the best until we get word about them." He turned to Deskaheh. "I still want to know if the Naskapi warriors from the other band who captured five of my men are hostile toward us, or will they follow Sachem's lead toward peaceful coexistence? Another thing, I would not allow you to go after Ivar, or find out what happened to him. It was too dangerous for you. Now, ask the Naskapi if they can help, or perhaps tell us what happened to him." He gestured toward Kejo. "Ask him these things," Halfdan said to Deskaheh, again indicating Kejo with a lift of his chin.

Deskaheh spoke at length to both Kejo and Chisasi. A lively discussion ensued, eventually involving all of the Naskapi warriors.

Halfdan listened intently trying to follow the gist of what was happening. Thora came to stand beside him. The two put their heads together in whispered conversation as Thora did her best to help Halfdan understand.

Conversation within the Naskapi group ended abruptly and Deskaheh turned toward Halfdan and Thora. Halfdan held up a hand to Deskaheh and turned toward the silent throng watching the proceedings. His eyes sought Ingerd and Lothar. He motioned for them to join him. Ingerd held his eyes, a question on her face. Halfdan smiled slightly and nodded, as if to assure her that everything would be all right. He put an arm around her shoulder and gently pulled her into his side. Lothar stood tall at her other side. Halfdan turned his attention to Deskaheh. "Go ahead with what they want to tell us."

Deskaheh nodded and waited while the Naskapi gathered around. The two groups formed a loose circle, waiting for him to translate. He made eye contact with Halfdan and began to speak. "Sachem is the supreme leader of all Naskapi," Deskaheh said. "He is more than a chief; he is also a Holy Man. His decisions are final to all of their people. A word from him can start or stop a war. Kejo will tell you the rest of the story. I will fill in if need be."

"We understand," Halfdan said. He made eye contact with Kejo and bobbed his chin.

"These are the words of Sachem," Kejo said. He spoke up so that all would hear his words.

"Nipishish is not our prisoner, but he cannot leave us for Sachem has given him a task. Because of Nipishish, Sachem will allow the Northmen to live in Nitassinan. If he fails, you all fail. Nipishish is now one of the people. He fought for us and shed his blood for our village. He will stay with us until the Time of Green Grass, during the Planting Moon, to learn our language and our ways. We will learn his ways. Some of us will learn his language. Nipishish lives in the wigwam of Glooscap, our war chief, until the new moon. Then he will live in my wigwam until the following new moon. And so on. Then Sachem will see how much Nipishish has learned. He will decide then what is required. Sachem may free Nipishish to do as he wishes, or not. I do not know. Glooscap and I are responsible for him while he remains in our village. We must be certain he learns what Sachem has decreed." His eyes shifted to Ingerd. "Deskaheh has told us about the loss of your son, Ivar. We will tell Nipishish of his capture by the Haudenosaunee. Before the Time of Whiteness we will try to find out about him. You, Ingerd, and your other son Lothar, may come to our village during the Time of Falling Leaves, to see Nipishish. You, too, may live with us, if you wish. Sachem has said that you will be welcome. The decision is yours. If you want to make this journey, I will take you, or Chisasi and his men will take you," Kejo said. He paused, watching Ingerd.

Ingerd's eyes had filled as Kejo spoke. She held his eyes without blinking. A tear weaved a course down her cheek. She nodded dumbly, not trusting her voice. Lothar's arm encircled her waist. The boy held Kejo's eyes a moment, then he nodded slightly and turned his face away to kiss Ingerd tenderly on the cheek. She smiled at him and the two hugged, their shared relief all but consumed them.

Kejo watched them impassively. He looked at Halfdan and gave the cutting sign. "These are the words of Sachem. It will be as he has said."

Deskaheh translated. He kept his eyes on Halfdan.

"I understand. Tell them that I will tell my people of this decision for it is of concern to all of us," Halfdan said. He got to his feet and shook hands with each of the Naskapi while Deskaheh translated. Halfdan's eyes swept the room as he looked for Tostig. He motioned him over. "Pass the word to the rest of our people. They will need to hear about our plans. Tell them that I will take Ingerd and Lothar to the village of Chisasi when the time comes," Halfdan said, his hand on the man's shoulder. Tostig made his way through the milling crowd toward the doorway, to do Halfdan's bidding.

Halfdan turned to Deskaheh. "Tell Chisasi that I will bring Ingerd to his village during the Time of Falling Leaves. I want to see the village, meet the people, and trade with them. I will want you to lead us there, so find out how to get there."

"I will tell him. I already know how to get to his village," Deskaheh said.

Halfdan indicated Chisasi with a lift of his chin. "You have been to his village?"

"Aye, I have been there."

Chisasi was talking to Kejo and did not notice the exchange.

"Will anyone recognize you when we go to the village?" Halfdan asked.

"Nobody in the village saw me. I have been there only once. I saw him there, but he did not see me." He indicated Chisasi with a lift of his chin.

Halfdan looked at Deskaheh, thinking over what he had just heard. "All right, if you think it is safe for you there, I need you to go with me."

"I will tell Chisasi that you want me to interpret for you when you take Ingerd. If he does not wish me to go to his village, he will tell me. If he agrees, I will ask him how to find his village," Deskaheh said. A slight smile creased the corners of his eyes.

"Good idea," Halfdan said, "Tell him whatever is necessary to arrange our visit and then come back and tell me what he said. I will be talking to Ingerd."

Deskaheh nodded and walked toward the Naskapi grouped around Chisasi.

* * *

Chapter Thirteen

Halfdansfjord—shadows in the night

In the final hours of darkness, the quarter crescent of the waxing Slaughtering Time Moon cast its feeble light upon Halfdansfjord. In the north guard tower, the slumbering guard did not see the six shadows rise from the edge of the fen. Although he periodically jerked awake he also did not see the shadows glide across the open ground a moment later to merge into the darkness of the palisade wall and disappear from his field of view. It is doubtful that he awakened enough to feel the war club crush his skull as one of the shadows materialized into a man who had invaded his post without a sound.

A similar event occurred with the guard of the south tower, although he managed a strangled cry as he died.

A female dog and her brood, sleeping in a tight group for warmth at the foot of the palisade, awakened at the unaccustomed sound. Her woof awakened every dog in the settlement. The alarm began as low woofs. By the time the dogs assembled to investigate the sound that had awakened them, several were barking.

Fang, Halfdan's big wolf-dog, peacefully asleep on the same platform on which Halfdan and Frida slept, raised his head at the first woof. He listened intently, senses on full alert. A growl began deep in the great chest.

Halfdan came wide-awake at the first growl. He sat up, his hand sought Fang, just an outline in the flickering lamplight of the longhouse. "What is it, boy?" he said, scooting to the edge of the platform as Fang jumped to the floor and trotted toward the closed door. Halfdan shrugged quickly into his tunic, donned a vest against the morning chill, and grabbed a spear as he hurried to open the door.

"What is the matter?" Frida asked as she, too, arose and hurriedly dressed.

The sound of barking dogs was now plain to hear as Half-dan threw open the double doors. Fang lunged through the opening and disappeared into the darkness outside.

"I do not know," Halfdan said as he hurried outside.

Frida quickly strung her bow and positioned a quiver over her right shoulder as she trotted after Halfdan. She nocked an arrow to the bowstring as she approached the north gate where the barking dogs had congregated. She stopped. Holding the bow at the ready her eyes swept the parapet, noticing that nobody manned the guard tower. "I do not see the guard," she shouted to Halfdan. The crowd of armed men milling around the gate swelled rapidly as more ran up to join them.

Halfdan glanced at the guard tower. "Open the gates! Loose the dogs!" Halfdan shouted. He rapidly mounted the guard tower ladder. A moment later, he descended just as rapidly.

Tostig met him at the foot of the ladder. "Steinn should be up there," he said.

"He is. He is dead. The back of his head is craved in," Half-dan said through gritted teeth, his rage barely contained. His eyes played over the crowd of armed men. A kind of growl swelled from them as they heard his words. "Tostig, Helge, each of you gather men and circle this palisade until tracks are found. I want to know what happened here."

His men hurried to comply. Grimr ran up to Halfdan, grab-bing his arm to get his attention. Halfdan swung angrily to-ward him.

"Easy Halfdan," Grimr said, taking a step back. "The south tower guard is dead. His throat has been cut."

"By Hel, what is going on here?" Halfdan yelled. He stormed toward the open south gate just as Grimr's friend, Barthur, ran through the gate from the outside. He turned toward Halfdan when he saw him.

The man came to a breathless halt before his chieftain. The look of intense fury on Halfdan's face gave him pause. He drew back.

"Speak man! What is it?" Halfdan roared at the unfortunate.

"Skeggi has found their tracks," Barthur blurted.

An impatient wave of Halfdan's hand bade him continue.

"He said there are six men. They came by canoe. He found where they landed. They are already gone," Barthur said, watching his chieftain closely.

* * *

A crowd of men, Skeggi in the lead dragging a man tethered by the neck, interrupted Halfdan's response. "The dogs stopped this one long enough for us to capture him," Skeggi said, pushing the prisoner forward. "We saw the five men with him get away in a canoe."

Halfdan's cursory examination revealed the man to be bleeding from several serious bite wounds.

"If we had not pulled the dogs off they would have torn him to pieces," Skeggi said.

Halfdan held up his hand to interrupt. "Wait," he said shortly. His fury was plain.

Frida stepped to his side. Her hand on his arm caused a transformation. The rage consuming him subsided, became contained. He exhaled audibly as he regained control. He looked at her.

"We need you Halfdan. Your people need you. More than ever in the face of this new threat," she said in a measured tone of voice. Her eyes searched his face.

He nodded slowly, and then he turned back to Barthur and Grimr. "Find Tostig. Tell him to search the bay with his ship for the others. Go with him. If they are out there somewhere I want those men captured or killed," he shouted at their retreating backs as they ran to do his bidding. He turned back to Frida. His eyes played over her face as he examined her in the scant illumination of early dawn. Her flaming red hair, tousled from sleep, lay heaped and tangled in an uncharacteristic dark mass. The clothing she had thrown on hung in disarray. She gripped a bow in her hand. He smiled in spite of himself. *By Freya, she is beautiful.*

"They have escaped, you know?" she said. She studied her man.

"They probably have. But, I want them to know that we are after them." He turned his attention back to Skeggi and the others. "Tie him to one of the trees near the council hall. I will be there shortly."

Without comment, Skeggi and the others took the man away.

Halfdan looked out over the commons area of the settlement. "Have you seen Deskaheh?"

"No, but I see Thora. I will ask her," she said. She placed her hand on Halfdan's arm and again searched his eyes.

"Go, I need him," he said, with a lift of his chin. "I am in control."

She nodded, squeezed his arm, and turned away.

He watched her wind her way through the people and out of sight. He shook his head. *She is something. I cannot imagine what life would be without her at my side.*

* * *

Just before midday, Tostig's ship returned. He found Halfdan talking to Deskaheh and Skeggi in the council hall. The men were just finishing bowls of stew when Tostig and his crew walked in.

Tostig came toward Halfdan to report.

"Get some stew first." Halfdan motioned them toward the hearth.

The hungry men made straight for the stew kettles on the hearth. Thora and her helpers ladled the steaming fare; the men tore off chunks of flat bread and found places around the tables.

Tostig and Helge sat down across the table from Halfdan.

"We did not see them, but I will wager that they saw us," Tostig said.

"What makes you think that they saw you?" Halfdan said.

"We sailed straight east from our beach, along the north shore of the bay," Tostig said. "They were not in the bay or we would have caught them. They turned up one of the rivers before the bay narrows into the fjord east of here. We think they paddled up the first river flowing from the north. The crew made lots of noise. I wanted them to know we were coming after them. They knew all right."

"We were close behind them," Helge said. "We could not go up the first river with the ship; the water is too shallow. But we could see upriver to the first bend." He glanced at Tostig. "We thought that they were hiding in the brush along the riverbanks, watching us."

Halfdan studied the two men in silence for a moment. "I wish you had caught them."

The two men exchanged a glance. Neither offered further explanation.

Halfdan turned his eyes on Deskaheh and Skeggi. "Bring the prisoner in here," he ordered. "Assemble the men, Tostig."

Word passed quickly that Halfdan had called for the prisoner. Men and a few women began filing into the council hall in response to Tostig's summons. All knew why their chieftain wanted them in attendance. With four of the five remaining ships' captains away at sea, Halfdan did not have his council available. He would hold council with the men of Halfdansfjord, his warriors, in their stead. Women, too, could speak at such a gathering, but they had no vote, if it came to that.

* * *

The prisoner presented a forlorn appearance in the face of the threat emanating from the crowd of bearded men who glared at him. In spite of that, he stood erect and faced his inevitable demise like the warrior that he was.

Skeggi sought a convenient bench. Deskaheh remained next to the man, holding the neck tether, while the assembly made their examination. He well remembered how he felt under similar circumstance.

The sound from the many voices of the assembly died abruptly when Halfdan rose from his seat and walked the few steps toward Deskaheh and the prisoner.

The black eyes of the prisoner followed Halfdan as he approached. That he faced a chieftain was immediately apparent to him. The large, bearded man standing an arm's length from him was possessed of an almost overpowering presence. A diagonal scar ran from his cheek through the corner of his mouth—the beard along the edge of the scar gone white from the shock of the sword cut—and down across his chin. It made him appear fearsome. The prisoner returned the gaze from the steady blue eyes without flinching, in spite of the fear that suffused his breast. Rage and hatred emanated from the big man.

Halfdan said nothing while he examined the prisoner. Blood had stopped seeping from all but the most extensive wounds. The dogs had stripped the leggings from one leg and ripped chunks of flesh loose from the exposed leg. Numerous bite wounds were widespread on his limbs. He wore the moccasins, leggings, and breechclout common to the native peoples of this land. Unlike most of the others that he had seen, this man's lank, black hair hung in two thick braids down his back. A decorative roach of stiff porcupine bristles, woven into his hair, stood erectly down the center of his head. Painted symbols of unknown significance decorated his face and chest.

"Who is he?" Halfdan asked Deskaheh.

"He is Anishinabeg," Deskaheh said.

"The same people Kejo told us about?" Halfdan said.

Deskaheh inclined his head in assent.

Halfdan's eyes played over the prisoner.

The man felt their caress like flames that sought to consume him. He tried to swallow the lump that rose in a throat gone suddenly dry. Thinking his time nigh, he began a low chant.

Halfdan's eyes flicked to Deskaheh with a question in them.

"He sings his death song. He thinks you will kill him," Deskaheh said.

"He will get no wagers on that score," Halfdan said. "Ask him why they killed my men."

Deskaheh spoke briefly to the prisoner. The man ignored him. "Look at me," Deskaheh spat out, jerking the neck tether. "Answer my question."

The man stumbled, almost losing his balance when the tether jerked his head sideways. For the first time he looked directly at Deskaheh. The hatred in his expression matched that which Halfdan had directed toward him a moment before. He knew Deskaheh to be his traditional enemy in spite of his Norse garb.

"Why did you kill our men?" Deskaheh repeated forcefully, the tether holding the man less than an arm's length away.

The man did not respond for a heartbeat. He shrugged. "To show you that we could," he said. His voice dripped with sarcasm.

Without taking his eyes off the prisoner, Deskaheh translated. "He said that they killed our guards to show us that they could."

Halfdan chuckled. The prisoner noted that his facial expression and the look in his eyes did not change.

"I can appreciate that. They caught us unawares. Steinn and Àn died because they were probably asleep," Halfdan said. He looked at the man again, then turned aside to pace. While he thought, he pulled at his beard. After a moment, he stopped in front of Deskaheh and the prisoner. "Where do his people live? I know he is Anishinabeg. But what tribe does he come from? What is his name? You know what I want to know, Deskaheh. Ask him," he gestured impatiently.

The prisoner watched Halfdan closely as he made his requests. He licked his dry lips, not knowing what was to come.

Halfdan held up a hand to Deskaheh. "Wait!" He turned and motioned to Thora, who stood nearby in case Deskaheh needed her help with the Norse language. "Get him a dipper of water," he ordered. "Perhaps water will help loosen his tongue." He motioned to Deskaheh. "Cut his bonds."

When his bonds fell to the slash of Deskaheh's blade, the man glanced without comprehension at his enemy. He rubbed the circulation back into his wrists and upper arms, wincing slightly as the blood surged back into his limbs. To confuse him further a buxom redheaded woman stopped an arm's length away and proffered a dripping dipper of water.

"I give you water, drink," Thora said. She spoke to the prisoner in the Haudeno language, which was similar enough to Anishinabe that he understood.

Surprised at this kindness, the man accepted the water gratefully, slaking his thirst slowly as he studied Thora and Deskaheh over the dipper's rim.

Thora indicated Deskaheh with a lift of her chin. "I speak Haudeno because Deskaheh is my man, my mate."

The prisoner handed the dipper back to her without a word, but his eyes studied her face.

"All right, that is enough," Halfdan said.

As Thora brushed past him to return to her place, she could not resist a quick lift of her chin to match the twinkle in her eye.

Halfdan snorted and shook his head. "After that I doubt I have much to add," he said loudly enough for all to hear. A few chuckles and low comments from the assembly swept through the council room. He turned and motioned for Thora to return. She came to stand beside him, knowing he wanted her help with translation. Halfdan waited a moment for quiet and then he nodded to Deskaheh.

He began questioning the prisoner. At first, the man said little beyond single words or clipped phrases. Gradually Deskaheh's methods produced more animated responses. After a time Deskaheh made eye contact with Halfdan, who had his head together with Thora as she tried to follow the rapid conversation for him.

"Go ahead." Halfdan gestured to Deskaheh. "I have part of it, now tell me the rest."

Deskaheh glanced around the room at the attentive assembly before he began. He spoke loudly enough for all to hear. "He is called Migisi. It means Eagle. He is Anishinabeg.

The Anishinabeg tribe is kin to the Naskapi, but they are not always on friendly terms with them. They call themselves Shinabeg or Shinabe for short. His band lives northeast of Kitchi-Gami on a big river that flows into the south side of our bay here. His people call themselves Kitchi sipi Anishinabeg. Those words mean Big River People." He paused, thinking Halfdan would be overwhelmed with the strange words. He was wrong.

Halfdan nodded thoughtfully. "I understand. Ask Migisi, why they make war with us? Not because they can, I want the reason they attacked."

"I know the reason," Deskaheh said. "They attacked to show us they could, just as he said. They do not want us in their land."

"Their land!" Halfdan's voice filled the room. He glanced at Frida, noting her arched brow. She got to her feet and moved toward the doorway that separated the council chamber from the other half of the longhouse. He looked back at Deskaheh. "This is Nitassinan, the homeland of the Naskapi. Chisasi would have harsh words for such a claim." He began pacing again, his agitation obvious as he struggled to regain a semblance of control.

Frida returned and walked up to him. She held the Naskapi Talisman of Life, given to him in friendship by Chisasi, in both hands. "Wear this, Halfdan. It might make all the difference while you negotiate."

"Negotiate!" He exploded in exasperation. "I am not negotiating. I will probably kill this man. My men will demand it." He waved a hand at the silent men watching the drama.

She shook her head slightly, her words for him alone. "They will demand nothing of you." Again, she held the talisman out to him. "Please, wear this. I have a feeling. The great god Thor will hold council with the god Frey. In concert, they will guide your thoughts and you will make the right decision, as you always do."

His hand rose unbidden to the Hammer of Thor at his throat. Halfdan, if he believed in any such thing, held both Thor and Odin in the highest esteem.

She smiled slightly at the gesture.

He bent toward her and she slipped the talisman over his head. "Thank you. I love you, Halfdan," she whispered in his ear.

A chill coursed through him at the words. He watched her return to her place. Only then did he turn back to Deskaheh and the prisoner, Migisi.

Deskaheh, of course, was aware of what had transpired between Frida and Halfdan. The prisoner was not.

When Halfdan turned, the man's eyes widened at sight of the talisman. His eyes shifted to Halfdan's, but he could not look upon the malevolence he saw in the piercing blue eyes.

Halfdan said nothing for a heartbeat. His eyes traveled over the prisoner's body. "Take him away. I will speak to my men," he said to Deskaheh.

Skeggi arose from his bench at Halfdan's words and he and Deskaheh led the prisoner from the council chamber.

* * *

Halfdan sat atop a table facing the assembly while he listened to his people vent. He had planted both feet solidly on the table's bench, leaned forward with his elbows propped on his upper legs, and tried to focus as first one and then another offered their opinion. For the past hour he had tried several different positions, including pacing back and forth while all had their say. It was the way of things. He wanted their opinions. Some had voiced more than one opinion. *That is why this always takes so long.* He found this tendency to be wearing.

Getting to his feet again, he raised his arms to restore quiet. "I want a consensus. What is the fate of this Anishinabe, Migisi, to be? Should we kill him?" An animal-like roar rose from the assembly. "Or should he be turned loose to take the word of our forgiveness and understanding back to his people?" The answer rivaled those wanting the man killed. He let them express themselves a moment more.

Tostig raised both arms over his head. Gradually the bedlam subsided. "Halfdan, I have a solution for both sides in this," he said from his place at one of the tables.

Halfdan gestured for him to speak.

Tostig stood so that all could see him. His eyes traveled around the room, stopping on his chieftain. "We are about split. I think Deskaheh should tell him that we are turning him loose. Return his weapons, give him a head start, and then four volunteers from our hunters will go after him. They will kill him if they can. If he gets away, he can carry that message to his people. Tell him our plan before he is released."

None of the listeners said a word. All knew that their chieftain would like the idea. Halfdan chuckled as he looked around the room; a big grin split his face. "That stopped them, Tostig. I like your idea. It will provide some sport for our hunters, and it gives the prisoner more chance than he gave our two guards." He glanced at Tostig. "So be it, then." He gestured to the room at large. "You pick the four men, Tostig." He turned to Skeggi and Deskaheh. "Bring in the prisoner," he ordered. As he looked around the room at the faces of his people, his eyes paused on Frida. She smiled her approval.

* * *

Late afternoon found the four hunters no closer to their Anishinabe quarry, the warrior Migisi. Grimr happened to be in the lead as the men moved quickly through the forest.

Thorkell called out from the rear. "Let us stop and rest, Grimr. I do not think we are going to catch this man."

"Good idea," Grimr said shortly. The group flopped on the ground, lay back in the tall grass, and caught their collective breath for a time.

"I keep expecting an arrow. I wish Halfdan had not returned the man's weapons," Thorkell said.

"I do not know what he will do, but I would not shoot at four men when all I had to do was stay out of sight to escape from them," Grimr said.

"Halfdan always has a good reason for everything he does," Barthur said. "Tostig was right, half of us wanted to kill the prisoner on the spot, the others wanted to let him go. Halfdan turned him loose to give him an even chance. I think he hopes the man escapes from us, to carry the word of our justice back to his people."

"Well, I want to catch him. He is making a fool of us. We only saw him that one time," Thorkell said in a disgusted tone.

Skeggi chuckled from his place in the grass. "He keeps doubling back on us. We have gone in circles. He does not want to be driven inland, so he hides, we pass his position, and he jumps up and runs back toward the bay."

"You are the tracker, Skeggi; figure a way to catch him," Barthur said.

His statement brought a period of silence as the men thought it over.

"Barthur is right." Grimr got to his feet. "We should not be together. If we split into pairs and he doubles back he will run into the pair that follows."

"That should work," Skeggi said. "Come on Barthur, we will push him hard. He may make a mistake and try to double back again. Thorkell and Grimr will have him then."

Their quarry's trail through the tall grass was easy to follow as the pair trotted away leaving their companions to conceal themselves separately while they awaited the expected return of the Anishinabe warrior.

* * *

The plan could have worked had not their quarry been watching their every move from his place of concealment under the fallen leaves and detritus of a large oak tree, a matter of feet from the tall grass that concealed the four men.

Migisi had doubled back and hidden to allow his pursuers to pass him once again. He smiled to himself, enjoying the flush of satisfaction and excitement that alluding them had brought to him. He regarded the chase as a game, a dangerous game, indeed, but one that never failed to get his blood up. Killing his pursuers would be satisfying, but to do so might compromise his escape, so he discarded that choice from the beginning. Thoughts of the big chieftain of these men came to mind while he listened to the muted conversation of his pursuers without comprehension. When the Haudeno had told him that his weapons would be returned, that he would be given a head start, and then four men would hunt him down to kill him, he recalled looking into the malevolent blue eyes of the chieftain with what must have been surprise written all over his face. The Haudeno explained that the rules were few: elude the pursuers and live, or be caught and die. If you live, the Haudeno told him, tell your people of our justice. Tell them that we gave you more of a chance than you gave our slain guards. Another man then handed him his weapons and the chieftain pointed to the open double doors of the longhouse. The Haudeno had then told him to go. Once more, he had looked into the blue eyes of the chieftain and found no feeling there. He remembered looking around the room at the silent bearded men watching him before he turned and walked from the doorway. Nobody had moved to stop him as he walked from the gate and trotted into the nearby forest where he turned to look for pursuit. Four men had just walked from the settlement's gate and stood looking in his general direction. He had known that they would come for him soon, so he turned and ran away.

He frowned suddenly as he realized that the ants had found him as they crawled through the moldy leaves in their eternal search for food. So far, they had not bitten or stung him, but he knew that could change at any moment. He froze in anticipation, gritting his teeth and steeling himself for the first sting; not daring to move. His concealment was perfect but the four men were too near; they might hear a rustle of leaves.

Suddenly the four men rose from the tall grass, stood conversing for a moment, and separated into pairs.

At that moment, an ant closed its jaws on Migisi's skin and began to sting him. He tensed, knowing its companions would follow suit, and they did. He was powerless to swat at them or brush them off so he remained as he was and endured the discomfort stoically.

He watched two men trot away to the north, on his trail. The other two conversed shortly and then separated to each side of the spoor they had been following. One man headed right for where he lay hidden. He tensed in readiness as he narrowly watched this new threat unfold. The ants forgotten, he held his breath as the man passed within the length of a

spear haft from him and out of his field of vision. He listened
to the swish of parted grass and the crunch of dried leaves
underfoot until the sounds made by the man who hunted
him faded into the distance. Only then did he carefully raise
his head from under the leaves and turn to look. Neither sight
nor sound of his pursuers did he perceive.

He cursed under his breath; the ants were literally eating
him alive as more of the pests came to the call. *The blood
of my wounds has attracted them,* he thought desperately,
squirming slightly as several ants began dining on the large
rip in his leg. Ignoring the pain of the feeding ants for the
moment, Migisi slowly got to his feet, his body unfolded
in stages as he shuffled in a circle, carefully examining his
surroundings. Discovering no sign of his big, hairy pursuers, he scooped up a handful of dry leaves and scrubbed the
feeding ants from his body. With one last look around, he
stooped to retrieve his weapons from under the carpet of
dry leaves and then jogged away along his back trail toward
the bay.

* * *

The sun set on the long day of pursuit without word of
the success or failure of the mission. Halfdan had just arrived
in the council hall to find that several others had the same
idea as he. A warming fire burned on the big hearth and a
large kettle of stew and a basket of fresh bread stood ready.
He filled a bowl, tore a piece of bread off a loaf, and joined a
group nearby.

"They should be back soon. It is dark as the inside of a
cow's belly out there," Tostig said as his chieftain sat down
across the table from him.

At that moment, the long wail of a guard's horn shattered
the quiet of the night.

"I told the north tower guard to sound a horn periodically
until their return," Tostig explained.

Halfdan nodded, his attention on the bowl of hot stew. He
stopped chewing and pulled a long cod bone from his mouth.
Contemplating its length ruefully, he said, "I can save this
one to pick my teeth."

The sounds of hungry men eating filled the room. Nobody spoke for a time.

"Throw me a piece of bread, Ring," Helge said to a man bent over the stew kettle. Without comment, the man threw a whole loaf of round, flat bread down the length of the table where it rapidly disappeared as those closest tore off a piece.

Four disheveled men walked wearily through the open doorway and made for the hearth, discarding their weapons on the way.

Those at the tables scooted over to make room as the four joined them.

The tired men ate rapidly. Nobody had spoken.

"Gisli almost jumped out of the guard tower when I spoke to him as we walked through the gate," Grimr said. "It is so black out there he did not see us coming."

Laughter went through the group.

Halfdan was sopping up the last of his stew. He stretched his shoulders and directed a glance down the table at his hunters.

Grimr heaved a big sigh. "He got away, Halfdan. We dogged him all day. We only saw him once."

"If he had kept running we would have caught him," Skeggi said. "He circled back and hid. Then he let us pass his hiding place and he jumped up and headed back toward the bay. There was no driving or pushing him, he always circled back because he wanted to stay near the bay. We almost stepped on him several times, but he was so clever that even I did not see his hiding places until we found where he circled back each time." He shook his head in exasperation.

Thorkell snorted in anger. "I wanted to kill him. He made fools of us out there. I do not think we ever came close to catching him."

"I think he knows a lot more about the forest than we do," Grimr said. "I have been a hunter all my life, but that man got the best of me fair and square. Good riddance to him, I say."

Barthur had been watching Halfdan as his companions told of the day's hunt. "I think you wanted him to get away. You had a reason to hunt him this way rather than just free him."

Halfdan watched Barthur for a heartbeat, and then his eyes flicked over his men. "Aye, I gave him a chance to live. It is not your fault that he escaped; rather his bid for freedom is the will of the gods. He knew that I could kill him because I wanted to. Giving him a chance to live, even a slim chance, was something he did not expect from me. That is why I did it. Something Frida told me influenced my decision. She said that she had a feeling that Thor and Frey were working in concert to guide my decision. Because of their influence, this man will take the word of our justice and fairness to his people. We do not need more dead bodies in this land. Sometimes we are too quick to kill. When there is a chance to show these people by our example that we want to live in peace, we must take it."

The guard Gisli walked in at that moment. "One of the canoes is gone, Halfdan, just as you thought it would be. We did not see the man in the darkness because you told both of us not to watch the canoes too hard. It had to be him because the canoe was there at sundown."

Thorkell shook his head and smiled without comment. Others were not as reticent as Gisli's report sank in, although the comments were between the men. To a man, none wished to disagree with their chieftain. The matter was closed for them.

* * *

Migisi the Anishinabe rested on his paddle athwart the canoe. When he had stolen the canoe, he thought it odd that nobody guarded them, especially since they had men who had hunted him all day. He did not have to spirit the canoe away either. He just walked up to the first one he found in the darkness, shoved it into the water, and jumped aboard. He had paddled rapidly away from the beach of the pale-skinned, bearded men. He thought that they would pursue him, but they had not. As he paddled farther out into the bay and away from the shoreline, the canoe came under the influence of the north wind. Except for an occasional flick of his paddle, he had little to do during the trip to the far shore of the bay as the steady north wind blew the canoe ever south.

The faint glow from the lamps and fires of Halfdansfjord came into his sight as the canoe turned naturally sideways to the wind. His treatment at the hands of the strangers in his land perplexed him. *Why did the big chieftain spare me?* His mind sorted through the events of the long day. No answer to the many questions came to him. *The other warriors will have returned and told everyone that I am dead.* He chuckled to himself. *The people will be surprised when I paddle up to the village beach. A council will be called to welcome me and to hear my tale.* He grew serious. *The council of elders will know what is to be done with the pale-skins.* He carefully studied the surface of the bay back the way he had come. To the limit of his vision, he saw no sign of pursuit. A crushing weariness descended. He heaved a big sigh, placed his paddle across the thwarts and tied it in place, and then stretched his aching muscles. The delta of his home river acted like a funnel to the bay that he crossed. He knew the steady wind would blow the canoe into the river delta as surely as if he had paddled. With that final thought, he gathered the bulrush mats from the bottom of the canoe for a pallet, settled himself down out of the wind, and fell instantly into an exhausted sleep.

* * *

Chapter Fourteen

Loon Lake Naskapi village

Three weeks had passed since the escape of Migisi the Anishinabe from the four hunters of Halfdansfjord.

Longer nights had gradually overrun the days as the land and its inhabitants prepared for the change of seasons. At night the cold of the far north crept ever southward like a slow moving river; each day the sun's zenith slipped lower in the southern sky.

The feeble light cast by the crescent of the waxing Autumn Time Moon grayed the deep shadows along the riverbank as two canoes paddled upriver from Halfdansfjord. A moderate breeze out of the north rippled the smooth surface of the deep, slow moving river.

At first light the birds began to awaken. Those denizens of forest and fen trilled their greetings, while the raucous calls of gulls could be heard out over the bay as they took flight to begin their daily patrol of the shoreline to see what tidbits the tide had left for them. The calls of all the birdlife reached a crescendo as more and more added their voices, heralding the coming of a new day to the northland.

A decided chill hung in the air. The morning breeze stirred the leaves of birch and oak trees on the banks of the river.

A swishing, rattling sound filled the air as the drying leaves scraped and pelted against one another. They had gradually changed color, dressing the forest in a blaze of orange, gold, and red hues. Leaves had only just begun to fall as the trees' sap retreated to the roots in response to the changing season. They accumulated in the river, gathered in rafts against fallen logs at the water's edge, piled up against a projecting boulder, or in a back eddy. The breeze made a few leaves skitter and dance their way across the water's surface until reaching an obstruction, or sinking, soaked through. Deep shadows along the river softened with the rising sun and its warmth thinned the morning mist. From its current position lower in the southern sky the sun still warmed the land, but it took longer; the cold seemed to hang in the air until almost midday.

* * *

Later that afternoon the two canoes from Halfdansfjord continued to work their way upriver toward the end of a long day. All day long the canoes' bows had sliced through rafts of leaves, briefly marring the placid natural beauty, which filled in behind them as they went on their way.

In response to the intruders the alarm spread among the wildlife of the riverine world: birds called, squirrels scolded, moose and other deer escaped into the cloaking forest, and rafts of mallards, geese, and eider ducks took flight.

A black bear foraging for morsels concealed in the detritus of the riverbank stood erect at the intrusion and watched the canoes glide by. His sensitive nose caught the hated man scent borne on the breeze. With a woof of alarm, he dropped to all fours and made off into the forest in his shambling gait.

* * *

The lingering cold had not been a factor of comfort for the eleven occupants of the two canoes. The continual effort of paddling guaranteed that. Halfdan, Frida, Ingerd, Thora, and Deskaheh were in the lead canoe. Helge, Grimr, Thorkell, Finbar, Lothar, and Ewyn followed. All three women and some of the men wore winter mittens because of blisters raised on their fingers and the palms of their hands by the incessant scrape of the wooden paddle handles on surfaces unaccustomed to such prolonged abuse.

Halfdan had enjoyed the journey. In spite of encountering six sets of rapids that they had to carry the canoes around, the trip had not been difficult. The utility of the canoes in these conditions continued to impress him. Such a journey would have been more difficult and taken considerably more time had he chosen to employ the larger Norse boats. They, too, were often carried. But the job required several stout men and even they could only support the weight for short distances in the rugged terrain. *No, canoes are the only real option here. They have developed over the years to fill a need and I am glad we have them.* He glanced out over the passing countryside, thinking it truly beautiful. This daylong canoe trip to the Naskapi village of Chisasi was his first opportunity to travel from Halfdansfjord since the moose hunt with Gudbj and the boys. The death of young Yola came to the fore; a kaleidoscope of color and scenes from the moose hunt cascaded through his mind. He pushed them aside, forcing his thoughts to the here and now.

He wielded his paddle easily without conscious thought; his powerful muscles pulled the paddle's blade through the backstroke without apparent effort. Frida, Ingerd, and Thora sat to his front. He watched the women paddle. The pace had never slackened because all knew that they would not arrive at the Naskapi village before dark if they did not maintain the pace set by Deskaheh. He smiled to himself as he watched the rhythmic flow of their stroke and the ripple of muscles along their tanned arms. In spite of the pain and discomfort of their blisters, the three, tough women held their own without complaint. He was proud of them. Ingerd and Lothar were the main reason for this journey, so they had to go, but he had told Frida and Thora of the difficulty in paddling all day, that they might want to reconsider going. Thora just shook her head and glared at him. Frida's arched eyebrow was her answer. *It is amazing what she can tell me with her eyebrows.* A smile twisted his mouth into a wide grin. He watched her in silent appreciation. A heat rose in his loins. She made his mouth water. He shook himself. *There will be time for that later.* To change his focus he glanced back at Lothar in the other canoe. Ivar's capture had forced the boy to mature. That he pined for his brother was obvious to everyone. He took special pains with Ingerd, referring to her as mother, sharing her grief at the loss of Ivar. Lothar was no slacker. After the long day of wielding a paddle, he struggled to maintain the pace set by the men, but maintain it he did. When I assigned the canoe positions, Lothar took exception to staying with Ingerd. *Why, he said that he wanted to be with Helge and the other men.* He smiled at the thought of the boy looking up at him and expressing his opinion. I expect he and his brother will be good men. And why not, their father is Gudbj? His thoughts turned to his friend. *I miss his council. By Thor, I miss him by my side.* He looked at Ingerd's back. *She and Lothar will be with Gudbj soon. Perhaps they will stay the winter with Sachem's band. Their absence will leave a void in our settlement. I know that Frida will miss her best friend most of all.* He glanced at his wife. *It will be worth it, to cement our friendship with the Naskapi. When all three return together in the spring, the celebration will be something to behold.* His thoughts returned to the present as Deskaheh directed their attention forward.

"The river forks just around the next bend. Chisasi's village is not much further. We will be there just before dark," Deskaheh said. He stopped paddling and pointed ahead with his paddle.

"Good," Halfdan said from the stern. "I think everyone is ready to get there." He turned to glance at the other canoe, seeing that they, too, had heard.

* * *

The canoes took the left fork, turning to the north, and soon entered a large lake. A faint smell of wood smoke came on the stiff breeze. Deskaheh headed the canoe's bow north across the western half of the lake, close inshore to avoid the worst of the chop whipped up by the northerly breeze. Cold spray occasionally came aboard. With the end of their journey nearing, the occupants endured the discomfort without comment, saving their breath for paddling as Deskaheh picked up the pace in a sprint for their destination.

The lake's near shoreline was rocky, ending on low cliffs interspersed with short stretches of broken rock, gravel, and sand beach at the water's edge. Heavy forest of mixed pine, birch, hazelnut, ash, and scattered oak began just back from the cliff. The far shore toward which they headed remained indistinct in the distance and gathering shadows of late afternoon.

"This is a beautiful lake," Frida observed in an attempt to break the long silence of her companions.

Beyond a grunt from Ingerd as she pulled through a stroke, no response came.

A few moments later, Deskaheh spoke over his shoulder. "Naskapi come," he said shortly, with a lift of his chin toward the north shore.

"Naskapi." Halfdan passed the word to the occupants of the other canoe.

Naskapi sentries had obviously detected the intrusion. Several canoes filled with warriors raced toward them from the shadows of the far shoreline. The distance separating the two groups diminished rapidly.

"Hold the stroke," Halfdan said. He fingered the Naskapi talisman hanging from his neck as his two canoes began to drift downwind. He watched the oncoming Naskapi canoes through narrowed eyes. "Keep us pointed at them," he ordered as the bow began to swing downwind.

"I hope somebody in that lot knows who we are," Helge said. Silence swallowed his understatement as the Northmen waited apprehensively.

* * *

Several days had passed since the arrival of the Northmen at the Loon Lake Naskapi village. The full Autumn Time Moon was on the wane. The Time of Falling Leaves was drawing to a close, sped along by the unceasing wind that people felt was unusually cold for the season.

The mingling of the two peoples was reserved at first. Although some already had prior contact with their visitors, the majority had not. It was hoped that with the passage of time their differences would become unnoticeable. The women experienced no difficulty, easily adapting to the new circumstance by their shared interest in children and crafts. The two different languages and the signs used by the Naskapi offered a minimal barrier to the women's chatter, as attested by frequent laughter from wherever they happened to be gathered. Thora could communicate without difficulty and Frida's abilities increased with exposure to the language. Ingerd understood more than she could speak, but she worked hard at gaining facility.

For the men, acceptance of the situation was much harder; the Northmen's presence among the Naskapi was difficult for the warriors to accept at first. Had a respectful friendship between Halfdan and Chisasi not already existed, doubtless the process of assimilation of the two cultures would not have occurred at all. Perhaps friendship for the other men would come later. In the meantime, the forced association was good for all of them.

Halfdan's two thralls, Finbar and Ewyn, took to the new circumstance better than the freemen did. The villagers did not know that they were thralls. The Naskapi kept slaves, too, but that fact was not apparent because they were a part of a strange culture and blended in with all the others, just as Finbar and Ewyn did with the Northmen. Both thralls were armed, so it was easy to see why the Naskapi could not tell the difference. To them they were the same as the other Northmen. Familiarity gained with the passage of time would more clearly define the cultural status of individuals for both peoples.

A nubbin of friendship began to develop between Helge and a Naskapi called Utshima. The two men seemed drawn to one another and could be seen with some frequency inspecting one another's weapons and possessions, or simply sitting in the shade engaged in various tasks, talking and gesturing while they worked. Neither would have known why this came about, nor did either examine the question, but their association smoothed the way for the others. As Helge later told Halfdan when the subject was broached over the campfire,

Utshima had an open, pleasant personality that made conversation easy. Helge being a garrulous man with manner-
isms similar to Utshima's ensured the two would become fast
friends with time.

Deskaheh's presence among the Naskapi, a man who was
their traditional enemy, was especially hard for them to
swallow. Chisasi purposely engaged Deskaheh in frequent
conversation as a way to demonstrate to his people his acceptance of the Haudeno among them, although both men
were taut as a bowstring in one another's presence. Chisasi
did not ask anyone's opinion when he sent four warriors to
hunt with Halfdan and his men, one of whom was Deskaheh. He issued his orders to them and they complied. Chisasi
and Halfdan had concluded that working in close proximity might be the best method to foster acceptance, perhaps
even a begrudging admiration for one another's expertise. It
was thought that they might just learn from the experience
and come away with an understanding that had never had
a chance to exist throughout the generations of hatred and
warfare.

Halfdan did not belabor the point with Deskaheh, knowing that the man was intuitive and would follow his lead
with the Naskapi. The occasional need to translate for Halfdan ensured that Deskaheh was always close by. With continual exposure to the combination of signs and verbalization
used by Deskaheh and the Naskapi, all the Northmen found
their understanding and facility with the language and signs
increasing rapidly.

* * *

Kejo and his men had hunted with and visited among
their kinsmen for several days before the arrival of the Northmen. They were now rested and anxious to begin the journey
to their own village with Ingerd and Lothar. Long distance
canoe travel was an accepted summer enterprise, whether it
be to war against enemies or for transport. Given Nitassinan's
vast fens, rivers, and connected lakes, with dense forest in
between, travel by canoe for any distance was often the only
viable option.

The trepidation normally associated with an arduous, even dangerous journey, did not manifest itself among the Northmen. Ingerd's joy and anticipation of her reunion with Gudbjartur saw to that. She helped her friends with the trading and crafts with the Naskapi women, but she chafed to go. Her enthusiasm affected their new acquaintances among the Naskapi women and girls, for all knew that Kejo and his men would be taking the two to the village of Sachem. And so it came as no surprise for anyone late one afternoon when Ingerd abruptly stopped talking and fastened her attention on Kejo as he made his way toward the gathering of women working at various tasks.

"Kejo comes," Ingerd said, getting to her feet. Frida and Thora rose also.

Kejo came to a stop and his eyes traveled over the three women who stood in frozen anticipation, each with their work still in hand. In spite of himself he chuckled. "We leave with the dawn."

"You leave at dawn," Thora told her friend.

"I know, I understood him," Ingerd said. She dropped the willow withe basket she had been working on and threw both arms around Kejo. "Thank you, Kejo. We will be ready." Knowing her embrace no doubt made him uncomfortable; she stepped back, holding his eyes.

He said nothing, but the crow's feet around his eyes were answer enough. With a nod, he turned away.

Ingerd turned on her friends, her face split in a huge smile. "Oh, thank you Thor, Frey, Freya, and Loki, all of you!" she exclaimed, thanking the appropriate Norse gods. "Now, where is Lothar? I must tell him the news," she said, looking around the village.

Frida pointed out in the general direction of the lake. "He is fishing with his new friends. I saw the four of them in a canoe paddle out along the lakeshore earlier. They should be returning soon."

"Oh, good, I am happy about that, they have kept him busy. He has spent every day with those boys." She paused in thought. "I am going to set down by the lakeshore; enough of work for today." She looked at her friends. "Want to come?"

"I will go. This is our last day together for who knows how long," Frida said, glancing at Thora, who nodded.

The three women gathered up their handiwork, told their new friends what they were about, and walked together toward the lakeshore.

* * *

A few days' later four heavily laden canoes with a mixed group of Naskapi and Halfdan and his men returned to the village after a long hunt. All were tired and footsore from the shared efforts of the last few days. As always, killing the game was the easy part. Skinning and boning the carcasses, and then lugging the heavy hides of moose, bear, and deer meat to the water's edge to load aboard the canoes had taken a toll.

After giving the meat and hides into the capable hands of the Naskapi women, the protruding roots of a large pine at the water's edge seemed to beckon. Halfdan leaned his bow and quiver against the tree, removed his knee length boots, and waded out to take a seat on one of the large roots. As he sat rubbing and washing his feet, many of the others joined him.

Their close proximity made conversation easier than the return canoe trip and for a time they talked of the hunt, as men will. This soon gave way to lethargy from their first inactivity since the hunt began.

Hands clasped in front, forearms resting atop his knees, Halfdan leaned forward, relaxing as his gaze traveled out over the lake. His mind wandered back to their arrival among these people and his initial impressions of both the people and their village. Although he had no basis for comparison at the time, later he would know that each Naskapi band exhibited slight differences in clothing and housing construction details from other widely separated bands.

This village consisted of twenty-two large, loaf-shaped, bark and hide covered lodges and a centrally located council house or hall behind a protective palisade. They had chosen a southern exposure on the north shoreline of the lake. The forest along three sides of the village had gradually been cut back as needs dictated. This open ground provided building materials and served to add to their overall security from enemy war parties. He estimated there were at least 220 people. After several days among them he knew them to be happy, productive, and secure.

The abundance of game and fish at every hand ensured the Naskapi could dry, smoke, and store enough surplus food to live through the long winter without the need to follow the annual migration of the woodland caribou and other large game animals that headed south in search of fodder.

The hunters of the people traditionally spent the Time of Darkness making new equipment, weapons, and working their trap lines to catch the prime furbearers on which much of their winter clothing and trade with other bands and tribes depended. Nothing was wasted. The carcasses of fox, fisher, marten, mink, and beaver became fresh meat for the stewpots.

In addition to the meat and fish products, berries of all sorts, edible roots, tubers, wild rice, and grass seeds were gathered in sufficient quantities by the women to provide a surplus for winter. Like the Haudeno, the Naskapi also preserved pemmican in large quantities. Stews of meat or fish, cooked in their excellent clay pots with whole grain seeds and seasonal greens were the Naskapi dietary mainstays. A pot of stew was always ready for anybody who was hungry.

The natural curiosity of the children about the strangers in their midst ensured that any reservations the adults harbored would be short-lived. The Naskapi children had helped so much with the budding relationship between the two peoples that he vowed to bring more children on the next visit. Chance alone brought Lothar on this trip and his friendship with the three Naskapi boys had proven invaluable.

He thought the efforts of Grimr and Thorkell would also prove beneficial. Both had decided to come on the journey, Grimr for his own reasons and Thorkell at his urging because of the two maidens who had been raped. Grimr and Pishikat, the maiden who was with child, were attracted to one another. Grimr's interest in Pishikat had been established at their first meeting. He obviously wanted the young woman for a mate. Although that remained to be seen, his efforts to establish a relationship with the young woman, and her budding interest in him, helped the overall situation immensely. Thorkell and the other maiden, who was not with child, were a different matter entirely. The young woman seemed afraid of Thorkell, and understandably so. Although he had done nothing to her, his long hair and beard made him look like the man who had raped her. That fact would be difficult to overcome. Thorkell seemed earnest in his attempts to befriend her. The two were spending time together and that was all he could ask.

His thoughts returned to the afternoon that they had paddled their canoes toward the village several days ago. He felt completely at ease here now, but he recalled that he did not feel at ease as he watched the massed Naskapi canoes full of silent warriors, none of whom he recognized, descend upon them. He chuckled at the memory, because now he could.

Helge and Deskaheh glanced at him questioningly.

"What is it?" Helge said.

Halfdan shook his head and smiled. "Nothing really, I was just thinking about how I felt when we first saw the Naskapi bearing down on us."

"In spite of your words of caution we were all afraid, I know I was," Helge said. "Until they saw your talisman and began to mill around our canoes, I thought we were doomed. It was daunting to watch those warriors coming toward us without doing something."

"Imagine how I felt," Deskaheh said. "After our time among them, this band has accepted me as one of your people, but most of them only do so because of Chisasi."

Halfdan nodded in agreement as he turned to look out over the Naskapi village. He only half listened to the conversation between the two men as they continued to talk about the first few days among the Naskapi. He saw the tall figure of Chisasi as he talked to two of his men near the village gate. Again he thanked the gods for their chance meeting. A chill coursed through him when he thought what could have happened had not Chisasi decided to confront him with the rape of his young women rather than return to his village to tell his chieftain. *Our first meeting and the justice meted out to the rapists is probably the only reason that Halfdansfjord is not a burned out ruin, the end result of a war to the death, and why we have a chance to live in this land.* His thoughts returned to the present at mention of their women.

"Thora and Frida will have spent most of their time in the company of Chisasi, helping with the trading," Deskaheh said. "He will want to have a feast with all the meat we have brought in, for he knows you will leave soon."

"Aye, let us go and find the others," Halfdan said. "Our women will be waiting. We must return home tomorrow. I should think Kejo and his men will about have Ingerd and Lothar with Gudbj by now."

Deskaheh glanced at Halfdan. "Gudbj is called Nipishish now. The Naskapi have bestowed this honor on him, for he is a fighter with honor. The people respect these two attributes in a warrior above all else."

Halfdan stopped and faced his men, while he considered Deskaheh's statement. Thoughts of his friend came to mind; the fight with the Haudeno war party, the attack of the great white bear, the Einvigi, the killing of Ulfar and Gisli, all the other everyday things that Gudbjartur took care of for me. *Aye, Gudbjartur Einarsson is a fighter. His honor and his loyalty to me and to our people make him what he is.* He looked directly at Deskaheh, and then Helge. His eyes traveled over the others and back out over the rippling waters of Loon Lake.

"As you know, I have thought much about this. The gods have selected my friend, Gudbj, or Nipishish as the Naskapi now call him, to join our peoples together as one. This I believe," Halfdan said with feeling.

His companions grunted in agreement, saying nothing, each instead with their own thoughts.

As they continued toward the village gate, Helge shook his head at the rush of memories occupying his mind that involved Halfdan's lieutenant. "As always, Gudbj is involved whenever a problem arises. I, too, believe the gods have chosen him for greatness."

Deskaheh chose that moment to return to the previous topic. "Ingerd and Lothar are close to journey's end, one or two more days, maybe. Kejo will have called a halt for a day of rest; it is a hard journey for a woman and a boy."

"I can attest to that, Halfdan," Helge said. "Ingerd and Lothar are tough, but seven days of paddling and portaging around rapids wears the toughest man down."

Halfdan sorted the thoughts that tumbled through his mind. He chuckled. "I would like to be a little bird sitting on a branch above it all when Gudbj first sees them. That would be something to witness."

Chisasi had joined the group of traders; Halfdan saw Frida's red hair as she talked to the war chief. "There they are, let us join them." The men turned toward the crowd of people gathered in the shade of a longhouse.

Chisasi saw them coming. He said something to Frida, and she and Thora, who was at her side, both turned to greet their men.

After the hugging was over, Halfdan, with an arm over Frida's shoulder, made eye contact with Chisasi. He nodded a greeting, holding the man's eyes. A slight smile pulled at the corners of his mouth.

The Naskapi's face reflected the hard life of the Northland and what he had experienced and done as the war chief of his band. His resolve and stern demeanor had not been altered by contact with the Northmen, but a friendship, trust, and mutual respect had developed between him and the chieftain whose eyes he now held. That he considered Halfdan a friend was obvious by the smile and softening of his features.

"I am told that the hunt was good. Our chieftain has called a council. We will feast together," Chisasi said.

Taken aback at the first mention of the chieftain, whom he had hoped to meet before leaving the village, Halfdan paused, using the slight delay to formulate the correct response. "I will be honored to attend a council and meet the chieftain of the Loon Lake Naskapi. How is he called?"

"He is called, Antanak," Chisasi said.

"Antanak," Halfdan repeated, hoping he would remember. "The hunt was good and there is much meat for a feast tonight. It will be good because we must return to our village tomorrow."

* * *

Sometime later, as word of the Northmen's departure passed through the village, Grimr and Pishikat sought out Halfdan.

Frida saw them coming before he did. "You were right," she said, indicating the pair with as lift of her chin. "I think we will soon know what they plan."

"I think we already know." He turned toward the two as they stopped; a slight smile twisted his mouth.

Grimr looked from his chieftain to Pishikat, who seemed uncertain and nervous before the towering Halfdan.

Frida's face lit up with a radiant smile and she stepped forward to embrace the young woman. "Do not fear my husband, Pishikat. He is our chieftain and you will find that he wants only what is best for us," Frida said, her hands on the woman's shoulders as she stooped slightly so they were eye-to-eye.

"I know, Frida, but it is hard to leave my people," Pishikat said.

"You will not be leaving them permanently. They are our friends. It is our hope that our two peoples will become one. In any case, our two villages are close enough for frequent visits."

A smiling Grimr put his arm around Pishikat. "I gave all my trade goods to her father and told him that I wanted her to be my mate and that I would care for her. He seemed satisfied, even relieved, I think. Her mother was not happy, but I told her we would visit to trade and she could come to visit us. A small roll of wadmal made her smile, so I think she accepts me too."

"Good, I am happy for both of you," Halfdan said. "Welcome, Pishikat. Sadness should not be a part of this for it is not an ending for you; it is a beginning for all of us."

She looked into Halfdan's eyes and for the first time smiled. "Thank you, Halfdan. I will look forward to this new beginning."

* * *

The return journey downstream was anticlimactic compared to the feast and open air council. After Halfdan was introduced to Antanak, he recalled seeing him several times beforehand, but he was not identified nor was there any indication that he was the chieftain of his band. Halfdan thought him cordial, considering the strangers in his village, but reserved nonetheless. The festive air of the feast that followed the brief council dispelled the last of the chieftain's reservations about the Northmen.

Prodigious quantities of roasted, half-raw meat were consumed by all. Dancing and chanting began after the feasting. Naskapi warriors and boys sat on the ground around a big drum. Favored chants to the accompaniment of the primal beat of the drumsticks, rattles, flutes, and horns of the Northmen soon had everybody swaying and dancing. The Northmen fit right in, becoming all but indistinguishable from the Naskapi. A thick pall of dust hung in the still air from the shuffling feet.

Much later a comparative silence lay over the village as the crowd thinned. Individuals had their fill of both the food and dance and staggered away to collapse in various attitudes of repose. Many people could be seen snoozing comfortably, their distended, meat-stuffed bellies sticking up like hillocks.

As the twilight of the northern darkness came and the fires burned to embers, a damp cold settled over the land. The satiated people begin to stir from their slumber, arising singly and in groups to seek the warmth and comfort of their lodges.

* * *

Thinking about the night's orgy of eating, Halfdan rubbed his stomach as his eyes searched the river ahead for possible hazards. The slight movement disturbed Frida whose head rested on his lap.

She chuckled throatily. "Are you still full?"

"I am stuffed; how about you?"

"Aye! I could not set up anymore. My stomach feels better when I am stretched out."

"Deskaheh, head into that grassy bank there," Halfdan said, pointing his paddle ahead. "I think we all need to walk around a bit."

They pulled the canoes from the water and walked through the high grass in an attempt to quell the lethargy all felt from the night's overeating.

"Thora and I will climb to the top of that hill, Halfdan," Deskaheh called.

Halfdan raised a hand in response. He and Frida walked for a time until he tired of it and sat on the riverbank to examine the rocks washed from the dirt by the current. Frida went on without him. Absently he skipped flat rocks into the river. He was satisfied with the way of things. This journey had produced a steadfast friendship with the Loon Lake Naskapi. Grimr had gained a mate and Thorkell, after a conference with Chisasi, had decided to stay in the village to further his blossoming friendship with Keshika, the other young woman wronged by the two rapists. He looked about for his wife.

Frida had lain down nearby in the sweet smelling grass, dozing off in the warmth of the sunshine. Sounds of her staccato snores came to him. A smile came to his lips. The pair was thus occupied when a shout from the nearby hillock caused Halfdan to lurch to his feet.

"Wake up, Frida, something is wrong," Halfdan said over his shoulder as he bounded through the tall grass in the direction of the hill. Frida leapt to her feet to follow the others as everyone ran after Halfdan.

"Smoke rises from the direction of Halfdansfjord," Deskaheh shouted as the others ran up the hill.

Halfdan came to an abrupt stop beside Deskaheh. He shielded his eyes with his hands as he studied the smoke that smeared the eastern sky. "That is a lot of smoke. If it is the settlement it may be under siege," Halfdan said. "The smoke is spread out like it is not coming from a recent fire."

"We are still about half a day away," Helge said. "Whatever is burning will be out before we can get there, I hope."

"All right, let us be on our way," Halfdan ordered. The group filed down the slope to launch their canoes. "Helge, you, Deskaheh, Ewyn and Finbar take the smaller of the canoes and go as fast as possible to scout out the source of that smoke. The rest of us will follow. There are two sets of rapids between here and the settlement. Find out what is happening without being seen. Come back and wait for us at the bottom end of the last set of rapids. I will decide what to do after we know the situation."

* * *

The sun had dipped below the tree tops by the time the travelers completed the portage around the last set of rapids. The half-light of fall would illuminate the rendezvous point for several hours before the darkest hours of the night. With the sun no longer holding the cold at bay a chill descended and the air along the river grew heavy and thick as mist formed. The only sound beyond the gurgle and rush of the river was the voices of the winged multitude as they sought their kind in roosting places.

"They are not here yet," Frida observed as they set the canoe down in the tall grass.

"No, I did not expect them to be. They were not that far ahead of us," Halfdan explained. "By the time they get to the settlement, thoroughly scout the area, and get back here, it might be after dark."

"I do not smell any smoke. The evening breeze, if there is any, usually comes off the bay, so we should be able to smell smoke if our settlement is still burning. Maybe the fire went out," Thora said hopefully, her head tilted back as she tested the still air.

"I agree, Thora. I do not smell anything either," Frida said.

"We will know before dawn, one way or the other," Halfdan said. He looked at his companions. "Grimr, you and Pishikat go down river and keep watch. I will relieve you after a time. Thora, you go watch our back trail. Frida will relieve you."

As they collected their weapons and moved away, Frida called, "Here Pishikat, you might have need of this." She held out a spear.

Pishikat met Frida's eyes and nodded, her mouth twisted in a slight smile.

Halfdan smiled at his wife as she turned to him. *There goes that eyebrow*, he thought appreciatively. "That was a good idea, Frida. You have a friend there."

"Of course, what else did you expect?" She looked at him, the expressive eyebrow still arched. A smile transformed her face.

He shook his head. "Let us move the canoe further into the grass. I do not want unwelcome passersby to know we are here."

Without further ado they picked up the canoe and moved it out of sight, then busied themselves returning the cloaking grass to its original, undisturbed state.

Frida stretched out full length in the grass beside the canoe. She caught Halfdan's eye and patted the ground at her side.

He took one last look around, heaved a big sigh, and settled down with her to rest.

* * *

The guard had changed and the gathering mist had cut visibility to almost nil. Halfdan kept nodding off in spite of vowing to stay alert. Sitting with his back against the bole of a large pine tree, and covered with a buckskin robe to ward off the chill, he was all but invisible in the mist off the river. He felt as though his eyes had just closed when the scrape of a paddle against the side of a canoe jerked him fully awake. Slowly he got to his feet, freezing in position as a canoe with four men materialized from the mist. Confirming their identity he whistled to draw their attention, swept his arm upriver, and trotted back toward the others.

"Thora, go get Frida, they are here," Halfdan said, waking up his slumbering companions. He turned as the four men hopped from their canoe and carried it ashore.

Helge was the first to approach the trio waiting at the river's edge. Momentarily distracted by the breathless arrival of Frida and Thora, he turned back to his chieftain. "It is as we thought, Halfdansfjord is under attack. Gudrod's ship and several of our boats have been burned to ashes and they tried to set the south palisade wall afire."

"Who are *they*?" Halfdan said through gritted teeth.

Helge glanced at Deskaheh.

"Anishinabeg," Deskaheh said, watching Halfdan as his answer engendered an instant rage in the big man.

"The same people as Migisi?"

Deskaheh nodded.

"How many?" Halfdan asked as Frida took his arm. He glanced at her, his rage unabated by her touch.

"We counted more than sixty canoes, with more coming all the time. I do not know how many warriors, but there are many," Helge said.

Halfdan was so enraged that everybody but Frida drew back from him. He turned on her and uncharacteristically, wherein she was concerned, lost what little control remained. "I should have killed Migisi. Sparing him did no good. His people probably regarded it as weakness. Nothing is ever solved by offering quarter to an enemy. Perceived weakness always invites another attack. Kill them as long as they come at you, it is the only way. It is our way," he spat.

Frida said nothing, her eyes downcast in the face of his rage.

Halfdan threw the buckskin robe to the ground and turned his back on them as he began to pace.

Helge glanced at his companions. "Our people have held them off, Halfdan," he said. "They cannot breach the defense that Tostig has organized. They have not even been able to scale the palisade."

Halfdan stopped and looked at him. He heaved a big sigh. "All right, tell me everything that you observed." He waved an arm at them. "All of you. You too, Finbar and Ewyn. If you saw something that Helge and Deskaheh did not see, tell me." His eyes shifted to Helge.

The man visibly drew himself up before he continued. "We climbed the hill to the west of Halfdansfjord, so we could watch without being seen. They have attacked at least three sides of the palisade. We could not see the east wall. But saw no activity over in that direction. It looked like only the south palisade was damaged by fire."

"The Anishinabeg have paid dearly. There will be much grieving in their village," Deskaheh said. "Empty canoes have floated ashore and are drifting east with the incoming tide."

"Dead bodies are lying on the landing beach and along the south palisade. We could smell them burning," Finbar said.

A meek sounding voice drew Halfdan's attention.

"I saw bodies floating in the water," Ewyn said.

Halfdan looked at the little man in surprise. He glanced at Frida in time to see the slight lifting of her beautiful mouth in the beginnings of a smile. He felt his tension ebb like the tide as he and addressed his thrall. "You saw bodies floating in the water?"

Ewyn nodded, unsure of his voice.

Halfdan threw his head back and laughed out loud. "Good Ewyn! I have told you that you can talk to me anytime. See, it is not difficult." He clapped the man on the shoulder.

Ewyn staggered a step to the side, his two-handed hold on the grounded haft of his spear the only thing that kept him on his feet. He looked up at his smiling chieftain.

"Relax, Ewyn, I appreciate your observation. You have done as I asked."

The man could only nod. A slight smile played about his weak, collapsed face.

Everybody laughed at the levity of the moment, a welcome respite from the anxiety that simmered just below the surface.

* * *

Several hours later, in the dim light of the midnight hours, Halfdansfjord lay in full view of the seven Northmen lying along the brow of a ridgeline to the west of the settlement. All slumbered comfortably in their robes, save one. Halfdan had not slept a wink. He had carefully observed everything they did, making note that activity among the besiegers gradually declined as the night wore on. It now appeared that the only ones awake were sentries hunkered down over small fires at points along the three walls of the palisade that he could see.

The plan he had laid out previously was simple, use the forest and the fen to avoid detection, and sneak to the settlement in the fen's outflow rill which flowed past the east wall of the palisade before running into the bay. If the Anishinabeg had in fact concentrated their efforts along the other three walls of the settlement, leaving the east side open for them to attempt their infiltration, then the plan should work.

Halfdan glanced at the eastern sky. *The darkest time is just ahead.* He awakened Helge, who lay at his side. "It is time, wake the others."

Moments later, the group stealthily made their way back to the river and paddled their canoes to the other side. Concealing the canoes in the brush at the river's edge, they stole off single file into the dark forest, weapons at the ready.

Deskaheh ranged ahead to the limit of sight. His natural stealth and nocturnal acuity something the others could not match. Halfdan watched him carefully, alert for a warning hand signal.

They entered the shallow waters of the fen, keeping to the deep shadows along the shoreline as they made their way to the outflow rill north of the settlement. The water of the fen was ice cold. Walking through it without making a sound became an exercise in concentration and discomfort as their feet and lower legs lost feeling from the numbing cold. This was the critical time. When they exited the fen and turned toward the dark mass of the settlement palisade they were in the open, exposed, and shielded only by the low banks of the tiny rill. Crouched as low as possible about a boat length apart, the column gingerly picked their way through the loose rocks of the rill. Stealth became impossible as people's feet slipped and tripped over the rocky bottom.

Halfdan's worst fear was detection by the north tower guard before he and his companions were close enough to make a short run on numb feet to the north gate and gain entrance before being overwhelmed by Anishinabeg warriors. *Just a little further,* he thought, gritting his teeth in the tension.

The blast of the tower guard's horn shattered the stillness, alerting all within hearing. Halfdan cursed under his breath. "Run," he shouted to his companions as he lurched from the cold water.

Deskaheh led the run into the north palisade. His shouts in the language of the Northmen got a quick response. The small walk-through gate creaked open and armed men surged out to cover the arrival of Halfdan and his company.

Laughing with relief they were quickly surrounded by their people as everybody gathered to welcome them home.

"You made it," shouted a jubilant Tostig as he shook hands with Halfdan. "I thought you would probably be returning in the middle of this little fight."

"It is good to be here. Tell me all about this 'little fight', as you call it," Halfdan said as they all moved toward the council hall.

Wet clothing was replaced with dry and copious amounts of hot chowder were consumed. Over the course of the time remaining to dawn, Tostig brought his chieftain and the others up to date while the hearth fire thawed them out.

"They came at dawn three days ago. More and more warriors arrived the first day. That is when they lost most of their men. I do not know why they are still here because they must know they cannot win this fight," Tostig said. The look in Halfdan's eyes gave him pause. "Ten men and three women have arrow wounds. All will recover. Nobody has been killed."

Halfdan nodded and bade him continue with a lift of his chin.

"The Anishinabeg cannot get close enough to inflict any real damage. Our wounded were all from arrows shot at long range that came over the palisade. Most of the wounds are not deep. Their losses have been high. We stopped shooting arrows at them yesterday to give them a chance to gather their dead and wounded. They did nothing. The dead and wounded are still lying out there. The worst part of the attack happened the first day when they burned Gudrod's ship and several boats with fire arrows. The wind came up in the afternoon spreading the fire to the south palisade wall, but the logs are still too green to burn well so the fire had smoldered out by sundown."

"How many arrows remain?" Halfdan asked.

Tostig chuckled. "We have a good supply because we have been shooting their arrows back at them. Herjolf and his mates are making more arrows, so we should end this fight with more than we started with."

"Good. You have done well, as I knew you would." He lapsed into silence for a time while he ordered his thoughts. "Later I will decide how we are to end this attack on our settlement. In the meantime, a little sleep will be welcome." He caught Frida's eye. "I will return here with the dawn."

"I will meet you here," Tostig acknowledged.

* * *

Chapter Fifteen

A cove west of Halfdansfjord

Unbeknownst to the citizens of Halfdansfjord, Brodir and Thorgeirr, their voyage from Greenland at an end, had seen the smear of smoke from the settlement fire on the horizon the previous afternoon. At the same time Tostig was making his report to Halfdan the two ships lay at anchor in a small protected cove two leagues west of Halfdansfjord. Brodir had sent a ship's boat under cover of twilight to reconnoiter the source of the smoke. That boat had only just returned with word of the attack by unknown natives.

The two ships had rafted up; riding at anchor with their beams together. Thorgeirr and some of his men had boarded Brodir's ship for a planning session.

"It looks like you men will have to fight to join our settlement," Brodir rumbled in his deep voice.

"It will not be the first time," Thorgeirr said. "We have always taken or defended our homes from someone."

"Thanks to you, there are enough of us to cause some real damage to those who have attacked our people," Brodir said. "Your people are about equally divided between our two ships so we each have a similar force. My scouting party has told me the situation at Halfdansfjord. The settlement is under siege by a large native force. The enemy warriors came by canoe and most are ashore attacking the settlement. They have burned one ship and several boats. Part of the palisade is still smoking, but the fire cannot destroy the green logs."

"Canoes?" Thorgeirr asked, shrugging his shoulders.

"They are light, bark-covered boats that all the natives of Vinland use. We use them, too. They are easier to handle on the rivers and lakes than our ship's boats," Brodir explained.

Thorgeirr nodded his understanding and Brodir continued.

"Warriors are still arriving from wherever they came from, so there are many canoes scattered all along shoreline. Many others are drawn up on the landing beach. If you are agreed, I think we should charge through their canoes in line astern, crushing those that stand in our way. There is an island just offshore from the settlement's landing beach and it will shield much of where we are going until we are closer inshore. I will pass the island on the west side. Just follow me in; I will wait to the last to drop my sail. The channel between the island and the landing beach is plenty deep enough for our keels, but it is narrow, and that is why our attack must be in line astern. Our attack should trap their new arrivals between the island and the landing beach. I intend to beach our ships right over the top of them. Plan to beach your ship on my steerboard side. Halfdan will attack them from behind as soon as he sees our ships. We will have them trapped between our two forces."

"I will follow your lead, Brodir, it sounds good to me," Thorgeirr said. "Every man and woman who can draw a bow or throw a spear will line the rails. We are heavily armed and well equipped so running out of spears and arrows will not be a problem."

"Good. At the first light of dawn we will wait for the on-shore wind to launch the attack."

"It takes too many men to man the oars, so I hope Njord brings the wind," Thorgeirr said.

Brodir nodded, his features set in a grim line.

* * *

Attack of the Northmen

At dawn, Halfdan and Tostig stood with a large group of men on the south parapet. All were fully equipped for battle. Frida had pressed the talisman of life given by Chisasi on a reluctant Halfdan, telling him that it might help. The beautiful piece hung on the outside of his chain mail jerkin in plain view.

Puffy white clouds scudded by against the brilliant blue sky; the onshore breeze freshened. Halfdan's eyes squinted in the breeze and the brightness of the rising sun as he closely watched the enemy activity off his landing beach.

"They finally decided to collect their dead and wounded," Tostig said with disgust. "Perhaps they are going to go back home."

"No, they are going to attack again," Deskaheh said from Halfdan's other side. "They are just clearing the field. I think that man standing in the canoe right there in front is their chief." He indicated the man with an outstretched hand.

Halfdan's eyes fastened on the man as he absently fingered his talisman. The Anishinabeg chieftain was too far away to discern facial expression, but the man was watching everything that happened around him. After a time he raised his arm over his head and shouted. A man in the canoe with him raised a horn to his lips. The long, drawn-out wail of the signal pierced the morning air and reverberated from the palisade wall. Warriors began to gather at the summons. Canoes converged on his position and warriors ashore began to mass along the beach.

The guard manning the south guard tower had an overall view of the settlement vicinity that the men clustered along the south rampart of the palisade did not have. "Halfdan, warriors are leaving the north and west walls of the palisade," called the guard through cupped hands, "they are moving toward the landing beach."

Halfdan waved in acknowledgement and turned to Tostig. "Gather one hundred men, full battle array with axe men. I will lead," he ordered tersely. His eyes went to the men nearest him. "Helge, stay close to me. You take command of our force if I fall. Deskaheh, I will need you at my side as well. Perhaps they will want to talk before we kill all of them."

The trio joined the men gathering at the gate and Halfdan jumped atop a handy bench, in full view, to issue his orders.

Quiet fell over the men as they watched their chieftain. Halfdan's eyes played over them. Their battle ready appearance and grim facial expressions swelled his breast with pride. These same men who every day performed the countless tasks of their society were now transformed into something else, something to be feared; to a man they had become Vikings, overcome by the primordial instincts of the natural warrior.

Deskaheh, although an accepted member of the society of the Northmen, shivered inwardly as thoughts of another time came to mind, when he had experienced firsthand the ferocity of these grim, bearded men. He put the thoughts aside as his chieftain began to speak.

"I wish it had not come to this," Halfdan said, looking out over his men. "We all hoped to avoid confrontation. They started this. We will finish it, one way or the other. If I fall, Tostig is in charge of the settlement until you all decide on a new leader." His eyes landed on Tostig. "Deploy our bowmen along the south rampart, Tostig; keep them back out of sight until I signal you. There will be time for only one volley of arrows before our charge places us among the enemy. There are not enough of us to wipe them out, but we might put them to flight. If not, I will call for a pullback. Your bowmen will cover the withdrawal."

Tostig rushed away to do his bidding.

Halfdan continued. "Helge, if I have fallen, you call for the pullback. Get our people to safety."

The man nodded without comment.

"The shield wall will charge through the gate en masse, axe men at the rear. Spread the wings of the shield wall when there is room, just before we crash into them. Work in pairs to smash an opening in their front rank to let them taste our axes."

He saw that Deskaheh and some of the others kept glancing aloft to the rampart, so he naturally turned slightly to see what had drawn their attention. Bowmen were climbing the

ladders to the parapet, some, already in position, were looking down at him, listening to his words. Among them were
Frida, and Thora. He locked eyes with his wife. A wordless
message passed between them. Frida pursed her lips, forming
a kiss. He nodded slightly and turned back to his men; the intimate contact with his mate broken. "Are there questions?"
he asked, knowing there would not be. His eyes played over
the silent men. He nodded. "Let us be about it then." He
strode to the forefront of his men. He glanced up at Tostig,
who watched him from the parapet, a clenched fist raised
aloft. The bowmen were in place along the parapet, arrows
nocked on bowstrings. He nodded to Tostig.

"Loose arrows!" Tostig shouted to the bowmen. The bowmen leaped forward to the palisade wall to shoot between the
pointed upright logs. A veritable shower of deadly missiles
fell among the unsuspecting Anishinabeg grouped along the
landing beach, killing and wounding many of them.

The moment Tostig shouted his command the settlement
gates were thrown open by four men standing at the ready.

At the vanguard of his screaming men, Halfdan led them
in on the attack. From the many mouths the war cry of the
Vikings of old further confused the Anishinabeg. "Odin!"
echoed out over the waters of the bay.

Dead and dying warriors, some transfixed with arrows
like the quills of a porcupine, littered the landing beach. The
massed warriors still standing milled about in disarray from
the surprise arrow attack when the screaming Northmen
burst upon them.

The shield wall crashed into their massed formation, knocking warriors aside like barley before a scythe. The axe men
darted through these gaps. Blood sprayed friend and foe alike.
Pieces of dismembered limbs flying about bore testament to
the destructive power of the Norse bearded axe when wielded
by the corded sinews of the stout, half-crazed axe men.

The initial flush of fear succumbed to an anger that fueled
a demonic rage and bloodlust. The wounded were killed by
whoever came up to them, without mercy or regard.

Known as a berserker among his people, the bloodlust had
overwhelmed the normal reasoned mind of Halfdan. He cast

his shield aside and swung his heavy sword with both hands, cutting down all who stood before him. Spittle flew from his mouth as he growled like a beast and screamed the incomprehensible epithets of the battlefield. The white streak of hair in his beard, around the cruel scar across his face, made him all the more fearsome to the enemy who had never before seen the like. Warriors fell away from him, pushing their mates aside in their attempts to avoid an almost certain death. The great sword chopped off arms, legs, and split heads asunder of all unfortunate enough to fall within its arc.

Neither Helge nor Deskaheh could stay near Halfdan as he plowed through his adversaries. Both men had their own problems as the battle fragmented into the many close struggles common in toe-to-toe single combat over the field of battle.

The big Anishinabeg war clubs and axes were sore pressed to match the keen iron weaponry and the ferocity of the men who wielded them. More than anything else the ferocity of the Northmen became the dominate factor in engagements between almost equal antagonists, for they did not defend, they knew nothing but the attack. And attack they did.

Gradually the Anishinabeg warriors fell back before the onslaught. Some regrouped quickly and gave a good account, pressing their fight forward as evidenced by fallen and wounded Northmen. But the general trend was to the rear for them and this continued until their rearguard had entered the waters of the bay. Some of these, perhaps not so accustomed to such protracted combat, availed themselves of the many canoes and sought to escape.

A horn sounded and the Anishinabeg chieftain began to exhort his men, beaching his canoe to join the battle. Those few trying to escape were finished and out of the fight. Panic is contagious and the chieftain could not prevent those who were cowardly or just plain scared from leaving the beach and taking to the first handy canoes to present themselves. Most of the Anishinabeg host was ashore with their chieftain, however, and these continued the battle with honor.

Inevitably, as the fighting surged back and forth the Anishinabeg chieftain and Halfdan would find themselves faced off against one another. Both leaders knew no other recourse. Theirs was the fight itself, that and what they owed their warriors. It is why they had been chosen to lead.

Halfdan confronted a painted warrior who surged forward, raised his shield arm, and stabbed from underneath with a short spear that took him full in the chest. His chain mail jerkin stopped the spear from entering his chest, but he staggered back a step from the force of the man's thrust, his chest pricked by the keen point of the spear blade. Recovering quickly, Halfdan swung his sword with tremendous force, cutting down through the warrior's shield, arm, and neck, ending his life in a spray of blood. As he jerked his sword free of the fallen enemy, he wheeled to face his next adversary, the Anishinabeg chieftain. The two men faced one another, both coiled for the attack, but neither taking the initiative as recognition, one for the other, occurred simultaneously.

Neither was aware of the reason for their hesitation, still gripped as they were by the frenzy of battle.

Halfdan took a deep breath; his shoulder muscles corded for the stroke relaxed slightly as recognition of his foe dawned, giving him pause.

The Anishinabe chieftain reacted in a similar way. His eyes flicked to the talisman of life hanging on Halfdan's chest. His eyes widened. He lowered the broad, flat-bladed battleaxe somewhat and stepped back. Raising his arms over his head, he shouted to his men. A signal horn sounded, his warriors stopped fighting and withdrew slightly.

Halfdan immediately followed suit. "Hold!" he shouted to his men, waving the bloody sword over his head.

The distinctive wail of Helge's signal horn stopped the fighting as the Northmen warily drew back, watching their adversaries.

The antagonists lowered their weapons and stood a matter of feet apart, primed to continue. Their breath came in shuddering gasps as they came down from the killing high that gripped them.

Without taking his eyes from the Anishinabeg chieftain, Halfdan spoke out of the corner of his mouth. "What did he say, Deskaheh?"

"He saw your talisman. That is why he paused and why he told his men to stop fighting," Deskaheh said.

The chieftain's eyes flicked to Deskaheh when he spoke to Halfdan. Recognition of his traditional enemy came at that moment. A look of confusion momentarily clouded his face as he looked from Deskaheh to Halfdan. Quickly, hatred suffused his face. With a final glance at Halfdan, he called to his men again and they all began to withdraw toward their canoes.

"Let them go!" Halfdan shouted, grounding his sword. "It is finished."

* * *

The words were hardly out of Halfdan's mouth before two Norse ships hove into view, their signal horns blaring.

The two ships had the full measure of the onshore wind as they rounded the point. Both made the turn to port, coming up close hauled on the port tack. Heeled to the wind, they surged toward the landing beach, in a line astern position from one another.

The giant, fearsome, Brodir stood on the bow platform of the lead ship. Bright morning sunlight flashed from his helmet, chain mail jerkin, and the sword that he swung overhead. His long, unruly black hair and beard blew in the wind and his deep voice boomed the Viking war cry out over the water. His men banged their weapons on their shields, the otherworldly din certain to strike fear into the enemy's heart.

Consternation gripped the Anishinabeg warriors ashore. They had just begun to gather their dead and wounded when they heard the blaring horns and looked up to see the ships. The first of them to sight the two ships happened to be those who had taken to their canoes to escape the field of battle— the cowards. Fate placed the ships in their avenue of escape, the west channel of the island. Although they could not have accurately described that which was coming at them, the ranks of screaming Northmen, bristling with weapons, arrayed along the ships' rails were in full sight, their intent obvious. The sound coming from the ships, amplified by the water, was chilling. Not a single canoe escaped the onslaught.

Many of the fleeing warriors, frantically wielding paddles to get out of the way of the huge ships, were ground to pulp with the wreckage of their canoes, or transfixed with arrows as the ships sped by.

The gods of war smiled on the carnage, as cowards are not favored among them.

* * *

As his ship entered the channel between the island and the landing beach it was apparent to Brodir that the situation ashore had changed. Several Northmen were running along the beach, waving and motioning him back. Without hesitation he ordered his helmsman to come up into the wind. Thorgeirr followed suit. The two ships, their sails acting like a brake, came to a stop a ship's length apart. "Drop the sail," Brodir shouted. "Out oars, we will row in." He cupped his hands and shouted to Thorgeirr. "The need for haste has passed. It looks like the battle is over."

Thorgeirr waved an acknowledgement and his sail came down the mast.

The rattle of sweeps could be heard as the ships were readied for the row ashore.

A short time later Brodir eased his ship into an uncluttered area of the beach, followed closely by Thorgeirr's ship. "Be alert, until we find out what is happening," Brodir called to the other ship.

The men, and many of the women from both ships, jumped into the shallow water at the bows and waded ashore. All carried weapons at the ready.

Before them lay the chaos of battle: scattered remnants of clothing, equipment, and discarded weapons attested to the ferocity of the confrontation. From the beach, around three sides of the settlement palisade, a similar situation met the eye of the beholder. The smoking remains of a ship and several boats had scorched the sand and gravel. Wisps of smoke curled from some of the upright logs of the south palisade as the fire demon sought purchase in them. Wounded and dead Northmen were being helped or carried toward the settlement's open gates by the people who had flooded onto the beach when the battle ended. Those newly arrived from the ships slung their weapons and pitched in to help bring order to the chaos and comfort to the wounded.

At the far end of the beach the attackers finished gathering their dead and wounded. Shortly thereafter they launched their canoes without interference from the spent Northmen who watched the Anishinabeg dispassionately as they paddled out into the bay.

"There is Halfdan," Brodir said to Thorgeirr as the two men strode toward the crowd of Northmen milling on the beach.

Halfdan would have been unrecognizable to anyone who did not know him well. Beside him stood two men, one a disheveled Helge, obviously a Northman, and another, equally disheveled, Deskaheh the Haudeno. The three were facing away, watching the Anishinabeg activity further down the beach. Deskaheh was talking to Halfdan and gesturing toward the Anishinabeg.

Halfdan turned at their approach. Thorgeirr's eyes fastened on the chieftain he had heard so much about, for this man would hold the destiny of him and his people in his hands. Before him stood a big, thoroughly exhausted man, covered in the gore of battle. He was bent forward slightly, both hands rested atop the pommel of a grounded, blood encrusted broadsword. *Even now, as tired as he is, I would not want to cross this man. The gods have led my people to this place, to him. This is what we have sought. Here we will make our home. To this man I pledge my fealty, before the gods, so long as we both shall live.*

Halfdan nodded to Brodir, his breath escaped in a gust. As he exhaled, his fatigue was apparent. The intense blue eyes flicked to Thorgeirr. "Welcome home, both of you."

"This is Thorgeirr the Hortalander. He brings his ship and people to join with us," Brodir said.

"You are welcome, Thorgeirr. We built our settlement for more people than we have. There is plenty of room," Halfdan said, shaking Thorgeirr's hand. The blue eyes bored into him, taking his measure. Halfdan nodded, and sighed again, his fatigue seemed to drop away. This simple act of acceptance by Halfdan made Thorgeirr and all those in his company, one with the Northmen of Halfdansfjord.

Halfdan indicated the two men standing with him. "This is Helge and Deskaheh. We fought side by side in this battle."

Brodir rumbled a greeting to his friends and each man shook hands with Thorgeirr.

Helge was familiar to Thorgeirr, for he was a Northman, but Deskaheh was definitely of a different cut. He gripped Deskaheh's hand; his pale blue eyes looked into the black eyes of the man. "I have heard about you, Deskaheh."

The man nodded. "We welcome more people," Deskaheh said, gesturing out over the field of battle. He sighed tiredly. "We were outnumbered by the Anishinabeg."

"Perhaps they will not return. They lost many men here," Thorgeirr said, his eyes traveling down the beach to the departing warriors.

"Deskaheh was answering that question when you men arrived," Halfdan said. With a lift of his chin he bade Deskaheh to continue.

Deskaheh looked at each of the Northmen before his eyes settled on Thorgeirr. "The Anishinabeg are many; they are like the blades of grass. The Naskapi are their kinsmen, too. Anishinabeg bands are everywhere south of here, along all the rivers, lakes, and on the shores of Kitchi-Gami."

"Kitchi-Gami, what does that mean?" Thorgeirr and Brodir voiced the question at the same time.

"I forgot, Brodir, you were gone when the Anishinabeg attacked the first time," Halfdan said. He chuckled. "So you do not know about them either. We will tell you all about what has happened in your absence, later while we rest and eat. And there is a lot to tell. Let Deskaheh tell you about right now."

Deskaheh and Halfdan exchanged a glance. Halfdan nodded to him and he continued with his tale.

"Kitchi-Gami means big water. It is a big lake, one of five that I know about." Deskaheh said. He always used copious hand signs when he talked, making it easier for the others to follow his rudimentary Norse. "I have not been that far south, but my people, the Haudenosaunee, know about this big water. This war party is small compared to what they can bring against us. They were probing to see how strong we are. I told Halfdan that they will be back in the Time of Green Grass. There will be many more of them, then." He paused, watching the stragglers among the Anishinabeg as they paddled their canoes to the south. The other men were similarly drawn to the spectacle of the enemy's departure. Canoes stretched from near the landing beach all the way to the southern horizon where they disappeared into the ever-present mist of the bay.

"Tell them the rest," Halfdan said.

Deskaheh's eyes fastened on Halfdan for a moment before he glanced at the talisman. Halfdan's hand rose to finger the talisman.

"Two things might save us from further attacks by the Anishinabeg, that talisman of life that Halfdan wears, or Sachem," Deskaheh said. He gestured vaguely.

Brodir and Thorgeirr made to interrupt until Halfdan raised his hand. "Let him finish. There will be plenty of time for questions later."

"The Anishinabeg war chief saw the talisman and paused," Deskaheh said. "Halfdan's wearing of the talisman surprised him. Otherwise he would not have pulled back his warriors and called off the attack. I do not think it alone will stop them from coming back in the Time of Green Grass. They do not want you here and there are enough of them that they will overwhelm Halfdansfjord and kill everyone but the children and some of the women. It is their way. We cannot stop them."

It was hard to miss the reaction this last statement engendered in Brodir and Thorgeirr. Their faces clouded with anger as they looked in the direction of the departing canoes.

Halfdan gestured toward Frida as she wound her way purposely through the crowd on the beach toward Halfdan. "Frida comes," he said, straightening his back he sheathed his sword and turned to greet her, a tired smile on his face.

She presented quite a sight to the men as they watched her approach Halfdan. She was still armed with a bow and quiver of arrows. However, the heavy leather jerkin and leather arm guard on her bow arm, could not conceal her obvious feminine attributes.

Thorgeirr seemed smitten by her, to the point that his quiet regard of this warrior woman drew a snort from Brodir.

She tossed her head at this unabashed display of approval from a man whom she did not know. Although her long, flaming red curls were somewhat restricted by the confines of the leather helmet she wore, the movement was so typical of her, that the other men smiled. She flashed a brief, radiant smile of greeting to all of them and then glanced over her mate's body for wounds before her eyes settled questioningly on his face.

"I am well, just tired," he said. With a twinkle in his eye and a lift of his chin he indicated the stranger to her. "This new admirer of yours is Thorgeirr."

She turned her eyes on the man. "Thorgeirr, welcome to Halfdansfjord," she said. "Later, we will have a feast of welcome for all of you."

Thorgeirr nodded wordlessly. He was suddenly uncomfortable to have the smiling Halfdan looking at him.

Halfdan ignored the situation for it was of no consequence to him; instead he threw an arm over Frida's shoulders and hugged her close. They turned and walked toward the open gate of the settlement. He spoke over his shoulder to the others, "Come; let us go to the council hall for some food. It will be good to set down, eh?"

"Some food would be good," Brodir rumbled, hitching his belt up higher on his ample belly. "This talk and all the activity has given me a powerful hunger. Come, Thorgeirr, I will show you our settlement."

* * *

Much later, thoroughly satiated men and women lolled about at the scattered tables inside the large council chamber room and overflowed into the commons in the settlement center. Prodigious amounts of fresh meat and fish had provided the fare for the communal meal for the more than three hundred people, including Thorgeirr and the 46 people with him. The new arrivals pitched right in with all the tasks associated with the close-knit social network already in place to the point that they became indistinguishable from the others.

The council members present, Brodir, Thorgeirr, and Tostig sat at Halfdan's table near the central hearth, facing the length of the council hall. As was customary in such circumstances, Halfdan and the others readily accepted Thorgeirr for his leadership as the captain of his own ship. While they ate, Halfdan brought Brodir and Thorgeirr up to date. Thorgeirr took it all in without comment, being unfamiliar with the whole situation. Halfdan regarded the man's reticence with favor, thinking that a man who keeps his mouth shut when faced with information of such import about which he knows nothing might, just might, be a valuable addition to the settlement.

Brodir had been especially angered at the capture of Gudbjartur and Ivar. However, eventually he had come to see the value these two separate incidents had for the future of his people in this land. News of Gudrod's death weighed heavily on him. Helge joined them to provide Brodir with the details as only he could. Afterwards, Brodir withdrew within himself for a time, in contemplation of his friend.

Later on, Tostig mourned the loss of Gudrod's ship, his first command. This seemed to awaken Brodir from his dark mood and his chiding of Tostig had provided the only moment of levity for the otherwise serious discussion.

Their hard life did not lend itself to protracted periods of sorrow or remorse, no matter the reason. Initial anger and then their ability to find the humor of a situation never failed to sustain them.

After their questions were answered, Halfdan led the discussion to the new situation that the settlement faced, given the open hostility of the Anishinabeg. He had listened to their suggestions, talking out all the various aspects of each possible solution. Now, it was left to him to make the final decision.

The others talked among themselves or held their own council, leaving their chieftain with his thoughts

He sat comfortably in his high seat at the center of the long trestle table, picking his teeth with a freshly cut wood splinter while he watched his people. Many had their heads together. The buzz of conversation filled the hall. He knew they talked about the same thing as their leaders; that they were anxious about the future in this savage land, as he, himself was. The people knew that he would talk to them soon. For now, he preferred to let them relax after their meal.

As his eyes played over the crowd in the long chambers, he let his mind wander a bit. Inevitably, he thought of Gud-bjartur, his friend and strong right arm. *By the gods, I miss him and his council. He is the only man who ever argued with me on a regular basis.* He smiled at the thought. *He will return with Ingerd and Lothar one day. Until then, he is doing the work of the gods for his people. I must remember that when I begin to miss him at my side.*

He glanced toward Helge and Deskaheh. He thought good thoughts of them and all the other men who had fought be-side him on this day. They had never faltered. All of them fought like the berserkers of old; fighting and dying for him and their people. He could ask nothing more of any man, but to give his all, to lay down his life for his fellows. As his eyes played over all those who had so recently engaged in close quarter combat, a feeling of pride suffused his breast. He smiled inwardly and stretched tired muscles.

They had all been refreshed by the food and a recent cycle through the steam bath, as had he, himself. The steam loos-ened or dissolved the blood and body fluids of the carnage and the quick dip in the bay that followed, washed away the remainder of the accumulated grime. There were those who were unaware of their many superficial cuts and con-tusions until this cleansing. He was among them. A visit with the wounded had also gotten these cuts and scrapes at-tended to. Thinking of the wounded depressed him initially, but he took heart in the knowledge that it could have been much worse. He thought of Frida, Thora, Asa and her ca-pable daughter Thorkatla, as well as all the others who toiled over the wounded even now. Tostig reported that 18 men had been slain and 25 wounded. Almost half of his attack-ing force had been lost, a serious butcher's bill to pay for an unresolved battle. He had given orders for the dead to be prepared for their journey to Valhalla. The ceremony would take place at sunset. During this twilight time of the northern night the Valkyries would come to spirit the slain to Odin's Hall of Heroes.

Deskaheh's words returned to his mind as thoughts of the battle flitted about in his head. *"They will kill everyone but the children and some of the women. It is their way. We cannot stop them,"* he had said. *"We cannot stop them,"* rolled through his mind, pushing all else aside, like the bow of his ship as she cleaved through the sea. He caught Deskaheh's eye and beckoned to him.

The two men faced each other across the table. Halfdan said nothing for a heartbeat, his blue eyes on the unblinking black eyes of this man who had become his friend and trusted advisor in all matters that involved the natives of Vinland.

"What would you do in my place? You know these An-ishinabeg and I do not. Tell me what is in your heart, what is in their heart. Tell them," he commanded, waving his hand to the room at large.

"I would do better with Thora here to help with the words," Deskaheh said without preamble.

Halfdan considered that. "So be it." He glanced down the length of the table. "Send somebody to fetch Thora. I need her," he said to Tostig.

Tostig and the others at the table stopped talking when he beckoned to Deskaheh. They knew that he had reached a decision and all leaned forward, attentive. "If Asa is finished dressing the wounds and can spare them, everybody should come to hear what Deskaheh has to relate and what I have decided."

Within moments, Thora strode through the door, wiping her hands on her apron. Her brief glance at her husband's face told her all she needed to know; something important was afoot. Her eyes shifted to Halfdan.

"Are the others coming?" Halfdan said.

"Aye, just as soon as possible, they are finishing with the last man now," she said.

He nodded and glanced at the door in time to see Frida enter, followed closely by Asa and Thorkatla. The rest strag-gled in a moment later. With their arrival and except for the wounded and the two tower guards, every adult was in attendance. Tables and benches had been moved to the outside walls so those in back could stand atop them to see the speaker. The heat and smell of the close-packed humanity filled the long hall. An expectant silence descended like a curtain.

Halfdan stepped up to the table top and looked out over the upturned faces. "I have not had an opportunity to meet many of you that came with Thorgeirr. That will come later, for now I bid you welcome."

His eyes sought Thorgeirr, who inclined his head in thanks for his people.

Halfdan continued. "We have known peace here in Nitassinan, and war. You have arrived in a time of war. With our combined efforts a time of peace will follow in this land. It will not be easy to achieve. From now on, all berry picking, fishing, and herb gathering forays are to be accompanied by armed guards. Everybody, men, women, and older children cannot leave this settlement unarmed. Until this war is finished we must be vigilant to survive. Deskaheh will tell you about the attack that we have beaten off. He will tell you what we face. For the benefit of our new people and those who have been away on the voyage to Greenland, he will tell you about the hostile natives that we now face. Thora will help him with his words." He added this last for Thorgeirr and his people. "He has already talked to me about this matter. Now he will tell you. When he is finished I will tell you what we must do, as a people, to survive." He nodded to Deskaheh.

Deskaheh and Thora climbed to the table top to stand beside Halfdan. Deskaheh glanced out over the crowd and his eyes turned to Thora, at his side. She smiled reassuringly. He took a deep breath and in a clear strong voice began to speak.

"The warriors who attacked Halfdansfjord are called Anishinabeg. The six men who attacked during the night awhile back are from the same tribe," he said. "There are more of them than all the other tribes combined, including my own people, the Haudenosaunee." He paused and clarified something with Thora. "The Anishinabeg are kinsmen of the Naskapi, who are friends with you Northmen. I do not think that they knew of this friendship before they attacked. I do not think that alone would have stopped them. They do not want you in this land. They withdrew for only one reason. Their war chief saw the Naskapi talisman of life that Halfdan wears. It surprised him. He did not expect to see such a powerful talisman at the throat of his enemy. That is why he ordered the retreat, not because he was beaten." The cutting sign followed his last statement. He was finished.

"Are there questions?" Halfdan asked his people.

Surprisingly, nobody said anything right away.

"Will they attack again?" Brodir finally asked for all of them, although he and Thorgeirr already knew the answer from their previous conversation with Halfdan.

"Aye, I am told they will," Halfdan said. "Deskaheh has told me that there will be many more warriors next time."

"When will they attack?" Brodir asked.

"Maybe not until next spring," Halfdan said. "They call it the Time of Green Grass. We do not know. It is getting late in the year, snow will come soon, but the weather is perfect for an attack right now. Because it is late in the year, they may decide to wait, to gather their forces for one all-out attack in the spring. Who can say?" Halfdan shrugged his shoulders.

Another brief silence, a time of introspection, followed his answer. Subdued conversation between individuals began as the implication of what people had learned began to sink in.

Halfdan let them talk.

"How can we stop these attacks, Halfdan?" Thorgeirr asked. "I know nothing about these Anishinabeg, but there must be some way to win."

Halfdan looked at Deskaheh and lifted his chin.

"Only Sachem can convince them to leave us in peace," Deskaheh said.

The obvious question for Thorgeirr died on his lips as those close by told him who Sachem was.

Halfdan held his arms up to settle the crowd down as people talked over this new information. "At dawn tomorrow, I will send a canoe with four men to the village of Chisasi. He will send men to tell Sachem what has happened here."

"What if this man, Sachem, will not help us?" Halfdan did not know the man who asked the question although he stood near Thorgeirr.

"Who speaks?" Halfdan said.

"I am Hrafen Ormersson, kinsman to Thorgeirr," the man answered.

"Hrafen," he acknowledged and deferred to Deskaheh with a hand wave.

Deskaheh met Halfdan's eyes. Then he answered the question, his voice dead of feeling. "If Sachem will not help, then this land will run red with blood. The Anishinabeg will come at you until you are all dead. The only ones they will spare are some of the women and children, who they will carry off to slavery."

Thora looked at her husband in shock. Bedlam swept the hall as everybody tried to talk at once.

Halfdan did nothing to stop them. His eyes sought Frida. Their eyes locked. Halfdan's heart thudded against his ribcage. An intense flush of heat rose through his chest and head at the full implication of what might befall them. *I have led them here,* he thought in anguish. As he glanced over the crowd his grim expression belied his feelings. *I have found this woman I love above all else. To be faced with this when I thought that we had found a place to live in peace, a place to raise our children, is too much to bear. By the gods, this cannot happen.*

* * *

GLOSSARY OF NORSE TERMS

Brattahlid—the farmstead of Eirik the Red near the inland end of Eiriksfjord, Greenland.

Einvigi—duel to the death. Challenger chooses the weapons. Usually swords and shields but can also be knives. Usually fought on hides staked to the ground, with both men clenching a length of leather strap in their teeth.

Eiriksfjord—site chosen by Eirik the Red, in 986, for the first of the two known medieval Norse settlements on Greenland's southwest coast.

Freemen—largest social order among the Norse. Men capable of owning land. Women could be freemen but could not vote or own land.

Frey—god of fertility, crops, peace, and prosperity. Freya—

goddess of love. Sister of Frey.

Furdustrandir—wonder Beach or Marvel Strand. Thought to be the forty-mile stretch of white sandy beach located south of Cape Porcupine, Labrador, Canada.

Gotar—people of Gotland. One of the two main Germanic tribes, the other being the Svear, which became modern Sweden.

Hel—goddess of death and the ruler of the realm of the dead. Daughter of Loki, who rules the abode of the dead. Hel lives among the roots of the world-tree, Yggdrasil, and has the appearance of a rotting corpse.

Helluland—flat stone land, Baffin Island, Canada.

Leifsbudir—Leif's Booths or Leif's Camp. Found in 1962 on the northeastern tip of Newfoundland, Canada, by Helge and

Anne-Stine Ingstad, of Norway. Carbon dated artifacts from the site indicate an approximate date of AD 1000. It remains the only substantiated Norse settlement site ever discovered in North America.

Loki—god of discord and mischief. At Ragnarok, the twilight of the gods, he will lead forth the hosts of Hel.

Lysufjord—the second of the two known Norse settlements on Greenland was located on the southwest coast about 400 miles north of Eiriksfjord.

Markland—woodland, Labrador, Canada.

Mead—a fermented, alcoholic combination of honey and water favored by many Germanic tribes.

Njord—god of winds, navigation, and the sea. Father of Frey and Freya.

Nordsettir—northern hunting grounds of Greenland. The region along the northwest coast as far as 80° north latitude in waters free of pack ice during the Medieval Warm Period.

Odin—god of war, wisdom, and poetry. The Valkyries attend him in the Hall of Slain Warriors—Valhalla.

Otherworld—world after death.

Ragnarok—twilight of the gods. The final battle between the gods and their enemies that leads to the destruction of mankind.

Skyr, Skyrr—mildly fermented drink made from the curds of soured milk. A high protein, nutritious drink favored by Norse people.

Steerboard—large oar secured on the right aft side of the ship; a combination rudder and keel. Possibly the origin of the term starboard, or right side of a boat or ship.

Svealand—land of the Svear, one of the Germanic tribes that became modern day Sweden, the other main tribe being the Gotar.

Sweep—large, long oar, used to propel a ship in calm wind or close quarters. Usually plied from a standing position, the long sweeps were thrust out through holes spaced equidistant along a plank below the ship's rail.

Thing—the *h* is silent, thus literally *Ting*. An annual assembly that served as the governing body of Norse society, at which any Freemen could bring their concerns before the chieftain, or law speaker, for the rule of law. Although women could be heard at a *Thing*, they had no vote.

Thor—god of the sky and thunder. Thor may have been the favorite of all Norse gods. His hammer was a much-favored amulet worn by both men and women. As in any Germanic combination of *th*, the *h* is silent, thus literally *Tor*.

Thrall—slave or chattel of a chief or freeman. Not a Norse word, therefore the *h* is pronounced.

Trencher—a wooden serving platter of various sizes to fit the task at hand, usually with carrying handles at either end.

Underworld—realm below the surface of the earth in which the spirits of the dead reside.

Valhalla—Odin's Hall of the Slain in the Underworld where the Valkyries take the heroes killed in battle.

Valkyries—handmaidens of Odin, who select the heroes from the field of battle and transport them to Valhalla.

Vinland—an area somewhere in southeastern Canada or the northeastern U.S. Disagreement and conjecture surrounds both the meaning of the name and the location of the place.

Wadmal—tightly woven wool cloth used for clothing; also panels sewn together to make sails and tents. Virtually waterproof due to the tightness of the weave.

Yggdrasil—horse of Yggr, that is, Odin. A giant ash tree, the world-tree of Norse mythology. Odin impaled himself on a spear and hung from the world-tree for nine days to discover the secret of the runes. Believed to be supported by three main roots: one each in Asgard, the realm of the gods, Niflheim, the realm of the dead, and Jotenheim, the realm of giants in the earth. An eternal tree that will survive Ragnarok.

Sources:

Webster's New International Dictionary (G & C Merriman Co. Springfield, MA, 1948).

John Haygood, *Encyclopedia of the Vikings* (Thames and Hudson, Inc. New York, NY, 2000).

NATIVE TERMS

Algonquin, Algonquian—a reference to both the largest Indian language group in North America and any member tribe of that group, e.g.—Cree, Ojibwe, Chippewa, Potawatomi, Ottawa, etc. The range of Algonquin speaking people includes almost all of eastern Canada and much of the north central United States. They are the most numerous of all North American Indians.

Anishinabeg (pl.), Anishinabe—loosely translated as the 'original people or original human beings' or 'the people.' The pre-historical ancestors of the Algonquin speaking Ojibwe and Chippewa Indians. Bands of these native people occupied the lands around and to the north of Lake Superior. Today, they still refer to themselves by these names, often shortening them to 'Shinabeg or Shinabe.'

Beothuk—means "people" in their language. Pre-historical natives of Newfoundland and Labrador, Canada. Known also as the "red ocher people," for their practice of smearing red ocher over themselves and all their possessions.

Chippewa—members of the Algonquin speakers of Indians. The word Chippewa is considered synonymous with Ojibwa, i.e.—they are the same people. Usually referred to as Ojibwa in Canada and Chippewa in the US.

Haudeno—is the author's diminutive pseudonym of Haudenosaunee.

Haudenosaunee—can mean "the people" or "people of the longhouses". The pre-historical ancestors of the Iroquois Indians.

Kitchi-Gami—literally, 'big water,' the Anishinabeg word for Lake Superior.

Naskapi—pre-historical ancestors of the Cree. Also known as Inyu or Innu. Numerous bands occupied all the lands north of the St. Lawrence River throughout the province of Quebec, Canada from Hudson Bay to the Atlantic coast.

Ojibwa, Ojibwe—members of the Algonquin speakers of Indians. The word Ojibwa is considered synonymous with Chippewa, i.e.—they are the same people. Usually referred to as Ojibwa in Canada and Chippewa in the US.

Otchipwa—this Algonquin word means "to pucker" and is a reference to the distinctive puckered seams of the moccasins worn by the pre-historical ancestors of the Ojibwa and Chippewa Indian tribes. Both of these contemporary tribal names are probably derivatives of this word.

Thalmiut—a pseudonym derived from Ihalmiut, "people from beyond" or "people of the deer." Inuit native people of the Canadian Barrens who subsisted almost exclusively on the vast herds of barren ground caribou.

Tornit—pronounced *Dornit*. Also referred to as Tuniit (Tiniq-singular) Pre-historical people of the Dorset culture, a native people of Greenland and the Canadian Arctic islands. The Greenlanders encountered these people in the early years of both Greenland settlements before the arrival of the Inuit from the west sometime in the twelfth century.

Research Sources:

Wikipedia (Wikimedia Foundation, Inc. 2001).

Webster's New International Dictionary (G & C Merriman Co. Springfield, MA, 1948).

Johann Georg Kohl, *Kitschi-Gami,* (Chapman and Hall, London, UK, 1860). Reprint with new material, *Kitchi-Gami* (Minnesota Historical Society Press, St. Paul, MN, 1985).

* * *

Turn the page for a look at *Assimilation,* the next in the *Axe of Iron* series by J. A. Hunsinger

Assimilation
An Axe of Iron Novel

Near a Haudenosaunee Village, early winter

One hundred fifty leagues southeast of the Naskapi village of Sachem, two Naskapi warriors lay concealed in the thick brush near the top of a knoll overlooking a heavily forested river valley. They had traveled there by canoe at night to avoid detection. After three nights of travel they concealed their canoe during the midnight hours, well back from the river, and crept overland to their destination. They carefully checked their immediate area for security before se- lecting a spot in the thickest forest that offered concealment from all directions. Satisfied, they covered themselves with leaves and slept through the remaining hours of darkness.

A drizzly mist had cloaked the river valley for much of the night. The leaden skies promised more of the same. At first light a slight breeze rose out of the valley, stirring the damp air. The light of the rising sun filtering through the cloud cover elongated the shadows of each tree in the thick forest as the dark of night was chased west. A perception of weak warmth came with the sun.

A smell of smoke borne on the morning breeze awakened one of the sleeping warriors. He unfolded silently from the deep bed of leaves and crawled slowly forward to get a better

302

view of the village below. The other man joined him a moment later. In the increasing light of dawn they watched the sprawling village of their archenemies. The light of day began to bring definition to the shadows that cloaked the village. Familiar details remembered from previous raids, for both had been here before, began to sharpen.

"We must get closer, Manshipit," Atkaa whispered. "We will not be able to see him from here."

"It is too risky. If their sentries see us we are dead," Manshipit said, beckoning toward the two guards they had identified. "The boy's hair is the same color as Ingerd's hair and his skin is pale. He should be easy to see if he is in this village. We will wait here to see what happens."

His companion did not comment.

In the silence, Manshipit's mind wandered to the recent past, to the canoe journey back home from the village of Chisasi with the Northmen, Ingerd and Lothar. Sachem, the supreme chieftain of all the Naskapi bands had decreed that they be brought to visit Nipishish, their former prisoner and Ingerd's husband, after the Time of Falling Leaves. During the final day of the journey, the four men had talked over the capture of Ivar and what they could do to find out what happened to him. Ingerd and Lothar had been able to follow much of the conversation as the day wore on. Kejo felt that a war party of Haudeno warriors under the infamous war chief, Sakokaeah had probably been the ones to capture Ivar given that his was the closest Haudeno band to Sachem's village. It had been decided by mutual consent that Manshipit and Atkaa would trek overland to a lake where canoes were kept hidden and then journey south to scout the Haudenosaunee village for the presence of the boy, as Kejo had promised Ingerd. Kejo, Ingerd, Lothar, and Miknap would continue to the village of Sachem. The boy Lothar had made his mother understand what the men planned to do and Ingerd's effusive appreciation had made the four Naskapi warriors uncomfortable. They muttered among themselves good-naturedly taking her reaction as typical of what they understood about the Northmen, who seemed more prone to expressions of their feelings than the Naskapi, where stoicism was more the

304 J. A. HUNSINGER

norm. Manshipit smiled to himself over how complicated the story had become. *I was there for all of it and I cannot keep the details straight in my mind,* he thought, shaking his head at the twists of life.

His companion looked at him quizzically. Manshipit shook his head at his friend's questioning look.

They watched the village in silence for a time. Smoke began to rise from the longhouse smoke holes as overnight embers were stirred to life and the fires rekindled.

Both men were soaked to the skin and although they wore leggings and hip length pullovers, they were cold. Their pullovers became a shapeless, sodden mass as water penetrated the oily leather. In spite of that, their clothing afforded insulation from the creeping cold. The misery that came with being cold had little affect on them. Lethargy from inactivity accompanied their discomfort in differing degrees, causing them to doze off occasionally only to jerk awake a moment later as their innate situational awareness came to the fore, for their lives depended on it.

The upslope breeze carried the curling wisps of smoke toward their place of concealment. Soon, a whiff of cooking came to them as the Haudenosaunee village awakened and the people began their day's activities.

The smell of food borne on the heavy air made the two men salivate. They ignored their grumbling stomachs for a time, but the smell gradually overcame self-control. Manshipit rolled onto his back to gain access to the contents of the pouch at his belt. He tore a chunk of pemmican in two and passed a piece to his companion. Atkaa supplied two strips of jerky from his pouch. They chewed slowly, savoring the rich taste that flooded their mouths as the pemmican and tough jerky mixed with their saliva.

Below their vantage point there was little to observe. A trickle of people moved back and forth between the wigwams, but most had not ventured outside in the intermittent drizzle.

Midday came and went; the shadows lengthened as the day wore on. The men took turns napping. The village guards were changed. Later, two women carrying baskets walked from one of the wigwams and out the gate, turning up the slope. They followed a well-worn path in the general direction of the men's hiding place. The Haudeno women, one young and the other much older, walked slowly through the tall grass and low-growing bushes, obviously looking for something in the mast of the forest floor.

Fully alert now, the men remained still as the women passed out of sight under the brow of the hill. The only way they could have kept them in sight would be to stand and they could not do that. They made eye contact, but nothing was said as they waited for the women to reappear. A moment later the sound of voices and occasional laughter came to the men as the women topped the knoll and continued into the forest, eventually passing their place of concealment as they foraged on either side of the trail. The men had brief glimpses of them through the dense brush as they shifted their position on the ground.

Manshipit whispered urgently to his companion. "They will tell us if the boy is in the village."

Atkaa grunted in agreement. The two men rose from the ground, quickly secured their bows in quiver scabbards in preference to the belt axe that each wore, and stole silently after their oblivious quarry. They separated slightly, creeping rapidly forward in a crouch as each focused on one of the women.

Manshipit signed suddenly to Atkaa that the older of the two had a knife in her right hand as she stooped to cut something loose at her feet.

A single bob of Atkaa's chin indicated his understanding.

The women's low-voiced conversation served to cloak any slight sound coming from the approach and simultaneous attack of the Naskapi warriors.

The older of the two women, hearing or sensing the attack, wheeled on Atkaa at the moment before contact, snarling like a cornered animal as recognition dawned. Her knife hand swept forward in a vicious backhand slice; quick as a humming bird's wing she slashed at her enemy.

Atkaa tried to leap back; he almost made it. He avoided being disemboweled. She struck so quickly that her keen knifepoint opened the leather of his jumper like a grinning mouth and scribed a red line across his stomach. The knife entangled in the wet leather as he grabbed her wrist. At the same moment, the flat of his belt axe thudded into her forehead and she collapsed unconscious at his feet.

Manshipit had clubbed the young woman unconscious before she could even turn to face him. He grinned at Atkaa. The man stood over his target, examining his jumper and the shallow cut across his stomach.

"That was close. She almost got me," Atkaa said, looking down at his erstwhile attacker. Stooping he removed the knife clutched in her hand.

"It looks like she did get you," Manshipit said. He bent forward to poke a finger at the long cut. Atkaa pushed his hand away. Manshipit chuckled. "I think you will live." He poked the inert form at their feet with the toe of his moccasin. "She is something. If her arm or knife blade were a little longer, you would be trying to keep your guts from falling on the ground right now. How would you like to live with a woman like that?"

"I would not want to live with her." He stooped and picked her head up by the hair. "Her forehead is split open. I may have hit her too hard."

"No matter, we will kill them anyway."

"Of course we will." He looked up at his companion. "Now she needs to be alive. She cannot answer questions if she is dead," Atkaa said, dropping her head back on the ground.

"I do not think this one will tell us anything anyway," Manshipit said, looking down at her. "She is a tough woman." He looked around. "Find a pole to carry her. Dead or alive we cannot leave her to spread the alarm. I will tie the young one up before she awakens. We must get out of here before someone comes looking for these two."

Atkaa quickly returned with a freshly cut pole long enough to carry the woman between them. The two men busied themselves trussing her hands and feet securely. Manshipit pushed the pole between her trussed hands and feet.

Atkaa pulled the now conscious young woman to her feet. He gripped her chin in his hand. "Do not make a sound.

Do not try to escape or we will cut your throat. Do you understand?"

She turned frightened eyes on him and bobbed her head.

"Good, we go now." He tied a tether around her neck and looped the other end through his belt. "Follow right behind me," he said. He pointed to his companion. "He will be watching you." She nodded again. He stooped and picked up one end of the pole, while Manshipit picked up the other.

They moved off at a trot, with Atkaa in the lead and the girl following behind him. The unconscious woman hung from the pole, swinging back and forth as they made the best possible time overland toward the river and their hidden canoe.

Just before darkness, they came to the place where they had hidden the canoe. Dropping the unconscious prisoner on the ground at the river's edge they launched the canoe. Intent only on putting as much distance as possible between themselves and the Haudeno village, they quickly boarded with their prisoners and set off upriver, staying in midstream to avoid the rocks and snags along the shore.

"Paddle," Manshipit ordered the girl, handing her the extra paddle. She complied without comment. Visibility on the river was terrible, a matter of a few canoe lengths under overcast skies and the darkness of a moonless night. Atkaa rode in front, guiding the canoe by instinct and the sound of the river. The girl rode in the middle with her still unconscious companion, and Manshipit had the stern position. There was no conversation, the grueling pace saw to that, and they stopped for nothing. This stretch of river was deep and slow; there would be no portages to slow them down. Later that first night, they stopped at a mid-river island to take a short rest and question the girl. Atkaa tied her securely to a tree. He and Manshipit dumped the unconscious woman out of the canoe on the ground and then carried the canoe back in the brush a ways so it could not be seen from the river.

Manshipit crouched down to examine the other prisoner as best he could in the darkness. "She is barely breathing. You hit her too hard. I do not think she is going to awaken," he said.

"She is of no use to us, then. Pick her up, we will give her to the river," Atkaa said. Without further comment, they picked up the woman and threw her in the river.

Manshipit chuckled. "I wonder if she can swim?" he asked.

"Not with her hands and feet tied," Atkaa said, showing his white teeth. "They will never find her body. It will catch under a snag and the fish and other creatures of the water will eat the flesh."

The other prisoner had watched the men, her expression a mixture of disbelief and terror, as they threw her friend in the river and then turned toward her.

"Now it is your turn to tell us what we want to know," Atkaa said, untying her from the tree and jerking her to her feet. "We will ask you only once. If you do not answer truthfully you will join the other one in the river after we have finished with you." He nodded to Manshipit, who stood grinning at the girl.

She looked from one to the other, knowing these men would show her no mercy. The grinning one looked especially cruel. It was he who spoke.

Manshipit pulled her close to his face. "We came to your village to find a pale-skinned boy with hair the color of ripe corn. Have you seen such a one?" he asked, his sour breath assaulted her.

She nodded quickly.

The two men made eye contact, a look of satisfaction passed between them.

"Tell us about him," Manshipit said, releasing his grip on her shift.

She gathered herself; steeling her mind for the end she felt would follow. "A war party captured him. He is adopted into our band to replace the lost son of Odatshedeh."

"So, the boy is well?" Atkaa asked.

She nodded again.

"How is this boy called?" Manshipit asked.

"Ivar, he is called Ivar," she said.

The men again made eye contact at this final confirmation. They said nothing.

The girl watched the silent exchange. Glancing from man to man she averted her eyes, waiting for one of them to strike.

Manshipit chuckled again. "She waits to die," he said. "We will not kill you. A good slave is always welcome in our village. You have saved your life by answering our questions." He pulled her forward, untying her bonds and tether. "Do not try to escape, you would fail."

Atkaa laughed aloud at the look on the girl's face. "If you try to escape you will be caught. We will not kill you, then. Both ankle tendons will be cut and we will leave you for the wolves," he said, watching her closely. "We go now."

As the trio paddled away from the island the young prisoner fought to still her trembling body. She gripped the paddle tightly to suppress the terror that threatened to boil to the surface of her mind. With an effort of will she calmed the heart thudding within her breast. As calm settled over her, she grappled with thoughts of her dead friend, her family, her village, and her people. For the moment she felt alive, regardless of what the future had in store for her. She resolved to face captivity with her head held high, proud of what and who she was. Her people would expect no less of her.

* * *

Naskapi Village of Sachem

Nipishish, formerly the Northman, Gudbjartur Einarsson, had done his best to appear stoic and unconcerned, but he fooled nobody. They all knew what occupied his thoughts. He had tried to keep busy, to maintain some control over his raging emotions. Although Glooscap told him that he need not help the village women any longer, given his earned status of a warrior of the people, he had insisted that he wanted to help them finish the new wigwam and the harvest. The wigwam was long since finished, the families had moved into it, and the framework became firewood.

Some of his days were spent hunting and fishing with the men. The necessity for stealth ensured that hunting and fishing were endeavors that did not contribute much to his conversational abilities. Most of the men had little to say any-way. Not that they were unfriendly, he had been readily ac-cepted by every man after the battle with the Haudenosaunee raiding party; rather most were taciturn by nature.

Helping the women harvest the last of the squash and pump-kins from the scattered gardens and burning the accumulated debris to enrich the soil for the next year; however, had just the opposite effect. Their constant chatter provided him a level of expertise with the language that would not have been possible otherwise. He chuckled to himself at the thought. *Why, their gossip alone ensured that I had to gain facility with the hand signs and words of the Naskapi language in order to spend any time at all with them. Much of their gossip was at my expense.* He smiled, glancing up in time to catch Meshika's eye as she twisted a pumpkin loose from the tough vine. She returned the smile, dropping her eyes back to her work.

He had found that pulling the vines and cornstalks from the ground as he searched for pumpkins and squash hiding in the debris from the growing season, simplified this end of harvest work. The vines and stalks accumulated in piles while the produce went into the baskets scattered about. After a time the garden plots looked like a rampaging bear or a whirl-wind had done the harvest.

The women watched him in amazement as he tore through the garden. He smiled at their chatter, adding comments here and there.

Thoughts of Ingerd, his sons, and Halfdan returned to mind. Since Glooscap had told him about Kejo's journey to Halfdansfjord at Sachem's behest, he had thought of little else. Sachem had decreed that Ingerd and his sons could visit the village during the Time of Falling Leaves. That time was about over, and as was his daily habit concerning the weather, just this morning he had noted a surge of cold air from the north that carried the promise of an early winter. *If they do not arrive soon, they may be trapped somewhere by a snowstorm.* He straightened from his crouched position among the pumpkin and squash vines and rubbed his lower back as he looked out over the gardens and his busy companions.

"Nipishish," Meshika called softly.

He glanced at her. She responded with a lift of her chin back toward the village. Turning around he saw a smiling Ingerd and Lothar standing together with Kejo. His heart seemed to jump into his throat and a chill coursed through his body. He stood rooted for a heartbeat, thinking it all a dream, a hallucination, until Ingerd, unable to contain herself another moment, shrieked his name and ran toward him.

They came together about midway.

"Oh Gudbj, my love, my life," she blurted as she leaped into his arms. Her eyes brimmed, but the tears were belied by the radiant smile she beamed at him as her eyes searched his.

A low moan escaped the man who could be hard and violent, now overcome by a wave of emotion he seldom felt as he clasped her to his chest and drank in her smell. Their mouths hungrily explored. Breathless, he held her at arm's length, a mist seemed to dim his vision as he looked at her. "You were never out of my thoughts, Ingerd, even through the worst days after I was captured. Memories of you sustained me when I despaired. You are my love, woman," he said, kissing her again.

"It was the same for me, but I never gave up, nor did Halfdan. He swore to me that he thought the gods had chosen you for a special task for our people." She turned slightly and indicated Kejo with a lift of her chin. "When Kejo came with Chisasi and told us that Sachem's band had captured you, I felt as though I had been reborn. Much has happened since you and your men left Halfdansfjord."

He threw his head back and laughed happily. "Much has happened here, too. I cannot wait to tell you everything." He held out an arm to Lothar, who still stood beside Kejo. "Come here, son!"

www.ingramcontent.com/pod-product-compliance
Lightning Source LLC
Chambersburg PA
CBHW070541260626
47161CB00002B/473